Edisto Bullet

Book 10: The Edisto Island Mysteries

by

C. Hope Clark

Edisto Bridge Books

This is a work of fiction. Names, characters, places and incidents are either the products of the author's imagination or are used fictitiously. Any resemblance to actual persons (living or dead), events or locations is entirely coincidental.

EDISTO
BRIDGE

Edisto Bridge Books
140A Amicks Ferry Road, PMB 4
Chapin, SC 29036
Print ISBN: 978-1-968423-18-6

Visit Hope at chopeclark.com

Cover design: Debra Dixon
Interior design: Hank Smith
Photo/Art credits:
Beachscape (manipulated) © Romolo Tavani | Dreamstime.com

:Lbes:01:

Praise for Award-Winning Author C. Hope Clark

Hope Clark's books have been honored as winners of the:

EPIC Award, Silver Falchion Award, Imadjinn Award,

and the

Daphne du Maurier Award.

"Characters that linger in your mind long after the last page is turned."
—Karen White, *New York Times* Bestselling Author

"*Badge of Edisto* further establishes Clark's well-earned reputation as a master of the mystery genre."
—Jonathan Haupt, coeditor,
Our Prince of Scribes: Writers Remember Pat Conroy

"*This writer does not put a foot wrong.*"
—RK Shohami, *Amazon Reviewer*

"Mystery lovers on your list will be thrilled to receive C. Hope Clark's latest in The Edisto Island Mystery series."
—Betsy the Book Whisperer blog

The Novels of
C. Hope Clark

The Carolina Slade Mysteries

Lowcountry Bribe
Tidewater Murder
Palmetto Poison
Newberry Sin
Salkehatchie Secret
Lake Murray Money

The Edisto Island Mysteries

Murder on Edisto
Edisto Jinx
Echoes of Edisto
Edisto Stranger
Dying on Edisto
Edisto Tidings
Reunion on Edisto
Edisto Heat
Badge of Edisto
Edisto Bullet
Edge of Edisto
Edisto Storm
Hidden on Edisto

The Craven County Mysteries

Murdered in Craven
Burned in Craven
Craven County Line

Dedication

This story is dedicated to Nanu. We'll do all we can to get you that television part.

Chapter 1

CALLIE JERKED UP in bed, the thunderclap vibrating her bones. What sounded like fingernails ticking at the glass impatiently tapped faster. The rhythm crescendoed, the drops angry at not being let in. Faster, fatter, louder until rain pummeled the windows hard enough to deafen her pulse.

The storm held its breath . . . then released a crack of thunder that rolled and rolled into the Atlantic.

Jesus, that thunder had been close.

Beside her, Mark slept through the cacophony. She stopped herself from nudging him awake to take note of the storm, knowing he'd nod, roll over, shut his eyes, and go back to sleep.

She unclutched the covers as the rain steadied and became expected. Her breaths came easy now.

She turned over to see the time on her nightstand clock, only to remember she'd turned the clock face away before bed. Once she methodically took in her surroundings, the dark wasn't just dark, it was pitch. The power was out.

Easing to her feet, she lifted her phone. Two in the morning. She and Mark had taken Saturday off and enjoyed themselves on the beach while they could, aware this warm front would push in rain, wind, and disgruntled weather activity by midnight. And here it was right on time. In the kitchen, she groped her way to the sink.

Another thunderclap sounded, and a tremor crawled through the floor and the soles of her feet. As another wave of hard, demanding rain made itself known, she reached in the corner to take hold of a flashlight kept for times like this.

Peering out the front door, the flashlight off, she hunted for signs of power elsewhere. To her right, toward the west, streetlamps shined as fuzzy halos in the deluge but no house lights. Looking left, up Palmetto Street toward the Pavilion, nothing. Half the beach had lost power.

Fully awake now, she poured a glass of water and peered outside again, across her porch toward the sea across the street. Too much rain came down to measure the ocean activity on the other side, but the tide should be almost out. High tide during a cantankerous storm like this could do damage to the high-demand, top-dollar rentals built on the sand. As if to make her argument, a hard gust blew the rain against the porch and sent the hanging red swing a-rocking.

She retreated to the living room and curled up on one end of the navy, tufted sofa, the flashlight beside her like a firearm. Taking the afghan from the sofa's back, she wrapped up and replayed the outing she'd had with Mark, a day full of enough pleasant memories to take her through this storm and well past it.

They'd stolen an entire day, the first since they'd met. Usually some crisis or duty ever beckoned one or the other of them, her in law enforcement and him with the restaurant, but this was pre-season time, the first week in April before too many spring break people lost their minds and tourists filled the rentals. The sun was just warm enough, and they'd picnicked on the sound side atop the flat sand, tucked up against the sea oats and buffered from the energy and noise of waves. She'd even fallen asleep barefooted holding his hand, sunglasses on, with a belly full of chicken salad sandwiches, strawberries, and ginger ale.

He'd given her twenty minutes and awoken her with a curl-your-toes kiss, his sweet face blocking the rays. "Can't let you sleep away our time together, Sunshine." He kissed her again. Rearing up, he took a sweeping study of the beach in both directions then swooped in for affection that slipped hands under clothes and stole breaths, only to release those same breaths in huffs of enjoyment that carried them just short of a place they couldn't go in public.

She popped back to the present at new noise.

"Hey, where'd you go?" Mark felt his way out of the bedroom, reaching and touching furniture for bearing.

Callie flicked on the flashlight. "Right here. Thunder woke me, but you stayed dead to the world. I couldn't sleep so I slipped out here." She snuggled up tighter under the afghan, the wetness outside giving her a sense of chill.

He had his phone with him. She wished he hadn't. She liked the sense of cut-off-ness with no power, no lights, and only each other, but he still sat next to her, his body nudging hers from shoulders to knees. She tucked her legs, rested her head against him, and shut her eyes.

The siren in the distance snapped them open. She listened for where it might be.

Edisto Beach wasn't three square miles in area. With *Windswept* being halfway down the coastline, a half mile from the municipal complex housing the fire and police stations, she could guestimate within a close margin where an issue may be.

This one sounded like something on Wyndham. Tree down, car accident, no telling, but she wasn't jumping up until someone sounded a call.

Still she listened harder. No second siren let her settle deeper into the cushion. Before she knew it, Mark carried her to bed, sliding in beside her. The rain reconciled itself to a steadiness barely heard, and the world slowed back down again.

From a deep hole, she heard her phone. Then again. Slowly she climbed from a luscious sleep back into her life. Through squinted eyelids, sunlight greeted her through the curtains.

Groping, she found her phone. "Yes?" *Hell, nobody could hear that.* Clearing her throat, she gave it another go. "Yes?"

"Chief? Sorry to get you up, but we have a couple break-ins."

She sniffled to clear her sinuses, open her eyes, and make sense of things. "Thomas?"

"Yes, ma'am."

"Where? Do you need backup? And more importantly, do you need me?"

Thomas Gage had been on the force longer than she had, barely thirty years old. He lived back on the island, not in town, in a small ramshackle place where he fished and babied a forty-year-old boat, saving his money and working every hour of overtime Callie would give him. She trusted him more than any other uniform in her employ.

"We need Mark over here," he said.

Callie reached over and shook Mark then put the phone on speaker. "Go ahead," she said to Thomas. "He's listening."

"Sometime during or after the storm last night, someone broke into two venues in the strip mall," he said. "The Undercurrent and Mark's restaurant."

Mark kicked covers off. "We'll be right there. Don't let anyone in until I arrive." He already had his pants on, snatching a lightweight sweatshirt over his head.

"Will do. How long—?"

"Ten minutes," Callie said and hung up, grateful for the decent night's rest before the thrust back into work. She was also glad they'd showered last night.

In her patrol car, they rushed to Jungle Road, noting the deep puddles alongside the asphalt's edges and the palmetto fronds scattered across lawns and streets, a lot of buildings dark. The damage was minimal, however, and a far cry from the annual hurricane near-misses each year. Ordinarily she'd marvel at the gorgeous, sun-kissed, warming April morn, such a refreshing difference from the dark, maddening night before.

They parked in the lot beside El Marko's at the westernmost-end venue of the small strip mall of a half dozen small businesses. The cleansed air still held the scent of ozone, and with Mark leading, they took the stairs two at a time to the walkway that stretched across all of the mall's storefronts. The six-by-eight picture window with its red, green, and yellow hand-painted lettering and assorted floral and ethnic symbols of all things Mexico had only sharp toothy edges remaining of the glass which had been smashed to allow entrance.

Dressed in civilian clothes, but with enough forethought to don the badge, weapon, and hand radio, Callie became Edisto Beach Police Chief Callie Morgan. Without words, short of Mark's cursing under his breath, she waited at the still-locked front door of El Marko's, standing behind its proprietor, Mark Dupree as he unlocked to assess the damage.

He had eight inches in height on her, and in attempting to read his emotions, she realized his black Cajun hair was now lapping his collar. He'd grown accustomed to the laid-back air of Edisto, and she was growing accustomed to his steady presence and their new habits as a couple. For instance, he'd promised to rustle her up an egg-burrito breakfast this morning before she headed down the beach to her office for an informal check-in and before he prepped for a Sunday lunch crowd. She could almost taste the cilantro he'd taught her to appreciate on it.

"Aww, what the ever-loving-hell . . . ?" was all she had to hear before she knew there would be no burrito. She scooted around him, poised to see the damage for herself. Mark was retired SLED, South Carolina Law Enforcement Division, and he didn't shake easily.

Chairs were strewn haphazardly around the room, tables overturned. Wall decorations of crepe flowers, sombreros, and picado banners lay bent, mashed, and soiled across the tiled floor. Pieces of the hostess station trailed from the entryway to the kitchen—kicked and stomped, and kicked again to cover as much area as possible—splinters everywhere. Crumbled pieces of terra-cotta pots lay scattered along the wall where they'd been thrown.

Jaw clenched, Mark moved quickly to the bar to take measure of the items most open to theft: the liquor, a small safe, and a handgun.

"Good gracious," Callie uttered. Out of habit and a deep-rooted fear of fire crime, she sniffed for smoke, found none, and silently prayed, *Thank you, God.* Since the loss of her other home—to arson and currently still under construction—and the rash of fires last summer, her relief was legit. She couldn't take any more fire.

She turned aside and called to her officer, Thomas. "Where's Annie?"

But the blond female officer, barely six months on the force, piped up instead. "Here, ma'am!" She was scheduled for duty this morning when Thomas's shift was to end. He always worked late and she arrived early. They might not be an item yet, but they acted like a relationship might be on the horizon.

"We got this, Chief," Thomas said, and they stationed themselves outside to take pictures, hunt for the obviously out of place, and to cordon the area before having to manage the eventual crowd.

Callie loved Thomas. He was her favorite. Not just because they communicated without saying a word sometimes. He'd saved her life twice and come to her defense more times than she could count. After the loss of a younger officer a couple years ago, Thomas had stepped up, assumed his new role with a deeper passion and demonstrated a mature instinct for policing.

He'd had a major hand in her sobriety, too, catching her off the wagon one time too many in the early days. Through it all, they'd remained a team. She appreciated that as she watched him direct Annie toward the thickening crowd.

The officers gone, Callie turned, barely catching sight of Mark palming something off the bar and disappearing it into his pants pocket.

He didn't even check to see if she caught him, moving fluidly behind the bar.

"What was that?" she asked.

"What was what?" he said, then extracted a Sig P220 semi-automatic from its hiding place under the bar, out of a lined, wooden sleeve cubby he'd had custom created so it was not only difficult to spot under the top but remained protected from everyday bumping around. He laid it on the bar and, fingers resting on the firearm, he leaned stiff-armed against the counter as if he were poised for the culprit to just try and come back in.

"Well, glad they didn't take that," she said.

Few knew of the weapon's existence, but she still hated it being there. *Her* job dealt with trouble requiring a gun, not his, but he felt he could take one more obligation off her by handling his own trouble. A cop never quit being a cop, and she kept telling herself he was a decent shot.

She'd seen him admiringly stand behind that bar and take in his retirement dream a hundred times, arms stiff like this, without the weapon, of course, but with smiles in the creases of his eyes. He loved his life on Edisto. She loved him loving Edisto, and Edisto loved him.

He wasn't so smooth and charismatic this time, and he seemed to be avoiding eye contact. Worry creased his forehead, synced with a justifiable anger. "Safe hasn't been touched," he said.

"Two good things then. What was on the bar?" she repeated.

"I have no idea who did this," he stated hard and sound. "And I haven't had anyone stir up trouble in ages," he added, before she could ask him those questions, too.

He was hiding more than something in his pocket. *What aren't you saying?* Is what she should ask him, but *What are you hiding?* was more on point.

No reason asking him anything for a few more minutes, though, not in this mood. He had to adapt to this destruction, realize he had to stand down. Law enforcement didn't understand how to play the victim.

She'd asked twice what he tried to hide in his pocket, and he'd evaded her both times. Well, she'd give him this double pass, but she wasn't giving him a third.

That item might've been nothing more than a trinket, a quarter, or a key someone forgot to put in a pocket, but she wasn't leaving without an answer. The discussion might embarrass them both if she had to pull rank, but his refusal to answer a simple question spoke in bold no-uncertain terms that there were secrets to be had. And he wasn't keeping them on this beach . . . nor in her bedroom. That's not how this relationship worked.

Chapter 2

CALLIE CANVASSED the dining room with a hard and steady gaze. Mark likewise did so from behind the bar, studying the damage in hope of finding some sense of the why, maybe the who. The bright hues and shades of Mexico only served to accent the degree of damage. Mark, in his equally colorful Hawaiian shirt, scanned the loss yet again, his mind circling on a loop for answers he wasn't seeing.

"Anything you want to tell me?" she asked.

He said nothing.

Okay, then. "Try not to touch anything else," she said, hating to tell him the obvious, but people reacted differently when crime happened to them. In this moment, he wasn't a retired cop, he was a victim. His life had been violated.

"Let me check the kitchen, then I'll move out for your people," he said, quickly gone through the swinging door.

He needed space.

She waited four or five minutes, giving him his solitary moment to absorb this disaster. "Mark?" she finally called out, but he didn't respond.

Thomas came through the front door. "More help is here." Officer Ben Benoit, all of four months new, followed—the first person of color on the force. He was the uniform on duty today with Annie. "Can we get started inside?" Thomas said.

"You've got this," Callie said, deciding to find Mark instead of waiting. She found him seated on the threshold of the back door, head in his hand, phone to his ear.

Insurance agent? That would be Callie's guess.

Meet me out front when you are done, she mouthed.

He nodded.

Rather than traipse through the crime scene, she high-stepped over him out the door.

Mark might've lowered his voice with her near, she wasn't sure. She tried to believe she imagined it, but then he tilted his head away as well. "Not today," she thought she heard him say, then after he listened more, he responded, "Yes, ma'am, you should have."

Maybe he fell short on coverage? Had his agent failed to properly cover a routine loss like theft? Hopefully not. And why would he not want to take care of everything today?

Well, they could talk later. He needed to handle certain matters now.

El Marko's rented the west-end unit of the Jungle Road mall. Thomas met Callie halfway around the building, in the shadow of the light-hearted Mexican mural painted across the concrete block wall. "They busted through the glass to enter. Appears they exited the same way," he said. Both doors had remained locked.

Something she already knew, but Thomas always endeavored to be accurate and useful. This was pure vandalism because a Mexican restaurant would have little to steal. Question was whether it was random or intentional.

Mark had a cam on the front and another on the rear door. She reversed herself, Thomas following, and returned to the corner, Mark still seated on the stoop, and Callie examined the long line of stores. El Marko's rear cam appeared intact. Each of the others had a rear entrance, but the only other one with a cam was The Undercurrent, the other vandalized store. She found that ironic.

They returned to the front of the mall. She nodded toward the condo units on the other side of the fence, then to the other commercial properties in the surrounding area and the few residentials, even nodding to Wainwright Realty across and down on Jungle Road. In other words, start knocking on doors. She didn't have to explain.

But that storm . . . the thunder would've provided easy cover for the noise of a B&E. She could hardly hear herself think last night in bed.

"Already sent Annie knocking on doors, Chief," he said, proving his worth. "Ben is fielding calls and protecting the front. We'll interview whomever we find who saw or heard anything, but with the storm and the outage. . . ."

They headed up the walkway past the front of El Marko's.

"Ask everyone about cams, too," she said.

Instinctively, Thomas studied the ceiling in front of the long string of stores. Only two stores had cams—the two broken into. "How's Mark doing?"

Callie instinctively glanced back at the restaurant. "Rattled, angry, stunned, like you'd expect. Left him on the phone with someone, not in a good mood."

"Insurance," Thomas said. "Everybody hates 'em. They never pay like they promise."

Her first thought, too, but she wasn't sure that summed him up.

In the sixteen months she'd known him—him having moved to Edisto only four months before that—he'd been the smile in any situation, the even keel in a turbulent moment, and had proven to Edisto he could be a rock through almost any circumstance. He had bested the resident bully, councilman Brice LeGrand, and been her trusted backup on four cases when officers either weren't available or not up to the task. When she'd lost her way last year, stepping away from the badge then coming back, he'd patiently waited her out, making sure she was tended to, mentally and physically. Each moment, each incident, each evening around a plate of quesadillas had drawn them tighter.

No doubt in her mind Mark was in her back pocket. While it had taken her a while to accept a new relationship, he was worth the trouble, the doubts, and the mistakes she'd overcome, because he'd been patient in her figuring herself out. This was the first time he might need to lean on her.

And she'd be there. God knew she owed him.

"Here you go, Chief. Mr. Lassiter showed up."

Like at El Marko's, a six-by-eight window, the size of all the windows along the storefront walkway, had been bashed in at The Undercurrent. With what tool they could not say. Chunks and splinters of glass covered the display of bathing suits, tees, and flip-flops, each sporting an Edisto Beach design. Nothing missing in the window that Callie could tell, but a wet boot print, size of a large woman or small man, left a partial, twisted mark on a pile of pastel towels.

Mr. Lassiter was peering in, trying not to touch anything. Thomas tried the front door and it opened. Callie entered first.

Without lights on, the place seemed tired and older. Trinkets seemed cheaper. T-shirts drab. A few of the shelves showed their need of dusting. Amazing the lifting effect that neon lights gave to a store's atmosphere.

The owner followed Thomas, waiting in an open area up front as Callie walked through. He stood four inches taller than Callie, but that wasn't saying much since she wasn't much taller than five feet. He was dwarfed by Thomas and carried an average, fit build for a man sixty-five years old. His long-sleeve shirt buttoned up to the neck, his cuffs fastened at the wrist, his chinos cinched at his belly button with a leather belt polished to match his loafers. He didn't roll up his sleeves until the thermometer read eighty. His button-up became short sleeves at ninety-five, but always paired with the belt and shoes.

Rob Lassiter was one of the many anomalies on the beach, but he was liked by all. Cordial, honest, and community-spirited, his store logo appeared in every newspaper, newsletter, and publication on the island, and on an insane distribution of coupons passed out in rental packets.

Callie came back and shook his hand. "Sorry this happened, Rob. Can you follow me and say what's missing? Try not to touch anything."

He proceeded, sighing and shaking his head. "From what I can tell, it's kids. I've got artwork and such worth more than what they stole. They went for flashy jewelry, which meant cheap." He pointed at the counter around the cash register. It was nearly empty. "They believed because things were in a case they were worth more, but then, they might've just grabbed whatever was near the register. Seems they gave that poor machine a beating, too. Jewelry could've been an afterthought since they would've found the register empty. Nobody uses cash anymore." He rubbed a hand over his bare head. "My biggest expense is the window."

Callie thought about that window, deciding to ask other business owners in the strip mall for their indoor cam footage. A thief might've walked by or been caught in a reflection.

He nodded toward El Marko's. "They take anything? Harm anything?"

"Besides the window, surprisingly only the tables and chairs sustained damage," she said.

"Well, could've been worse. Still no power, though they tell me they'll have us up and running by the end of the day. Spring break means business, and we're coming out of the winter slump." He gave his place a quick sweep. "Guess we'll spend the day cleaning and boarding up."

"Maybe later today," she assured him. "Let us handle our end first, if you don't mind."

She understood the hills and valleys of beach commercialism. Sunny days meant business. Spring break catapulted people to the sand and surf after months of chill and damp. This would have been a decent take-in for Mark today, and if he had to wait a week to open back up, it would cost him. A month earlier would have been better.

"Want to see my security camera?" Rob said. "One would hope they're worth the cost."

"I'm all yours," she said. "Lead on."

At the slightest chance of catching the violator, Callie studied the footage over Rob's shoulder. The best they could see was a medium-height person who remained somewhat stooped, gender nonspecific, in a gray, baggy hooded sweatshirt with matching sweatpants two sizes too big, hiding body type. Standard uniform for breaking and entering. Of course, they didn't look up at the camera. Who looks up at the camera? The intruder apparently was aware and hid their face accordingly.

The cam near the cash register, however, caught what might be a young man, complexion medium dark, hair dark from a tress that strayed next to his left eye. Rob said the missing pieces weren't enough to even file a claim over.

Callie asked for a copy of the footage, thanked Rob in advance, and returned to El Marko's, leaving him to take inventory and make plans to clean up later. He said he had help coming.

Cutting Thomas loose, she strolled back, answering a half dozen questions from the nosy and the passersby. A few more asked when the power would come back on. In between those questions, she wondered why the young thief had chosen The Undercurrent. There were stores on either side of it. Each had a cash register of some sort. Not much value to speak of, regardless of which store you considered.

Salty Art, for instance, maintained a rather upscale image with collections of paintings and assorted art with three-figure price tags. A lower-scale place like The Undercurrent would do more cash transactions with its trinkets and such, but the affluent feel of the art store begged attention. Fancy Mermaid as well. All clothing, no souvenirs, with price tags thirty percent higher than stores on the mainland. Worth snatching and pawning, or selling off the street.

Who knew what drove idiots like this one. Why choose a restaurant and a cheap-end souvenir shop?

She'd have Thomas check the indoor cams of the others. The pizza place and candy store would be open on a Sunday. Salty Art and Fancy Mermaid would not. He'd have to ask them to come in, if they didn't show up on their own. Word would spread fast, and each owner would want to check out their venue regardless of what their hours were.

The April day was proving to be on the warm side instead of a fickle colder one, with the temp already bumping eighty, the sky cloudless, the sun glaring. Callie pulled out her sunglasses while making her way back to the restaurant. Through the open broken window, she couldn't see Mark, and she went around back to see if he was still there making necessary calls to insurance, employees, and someone to board up the window.

He almost ran into her at the corner.

"Hey, you," she said, studying him from behind her shades. He faced her, but it was as if he wasn't seeing her, so deep were his thoughts. "You okay?" she asked, seeing he wasn't in tune.

His inhale went down to a deep, deep place and stayed there a moment.

"Wow," she said, reaching up to rest a hand on his chest. "What's wrong? I mean, besides the obvious?" He was stronger than this.

When he didn't immediately respond, she added, "Insurance will cover this, won't it? I'm not seeing physical damage to the kitchen. Nothing stolen. Pretty superficial, if you think about it." The unsaid being he could still feed people in a day or two if the power came back on this afternoon like Rob said. All Mark needed was tables and chairs, and surely those would take no longer than a week to replace at the most.

"Or, hey," she continued, "you could take a week off until we set things back to right."

"Adjuster is coming this afternoon."

She paused. He told the person on the phone *Not today*. "That's great!" Way faster than she expected. "Coverage okay?"

"Seems so," he said. "The deductible is what I expected and had set aside."

Fine. A certain degree of gloominess was expected, but thus far, his issues fell on the positive side.

He squinted a little over her head. Callie turned to see what drew his focus.

This time *she* sighed from a deep place.

The problem with a beautiful day at the beach was that everyone came out to enjoy it. Add three Edisto Beach Police Department cars in one collective group, and people gave the scene a second gander. It didn't help that El Marko's was at an address where five other businesses were opening up for a normal day, or that most of these onlookers had no power to keep them at home.

"Around back," she muttered, taking Mark by the elbow like she would any other citizen needing her special attention, and he rolled with her.

"Callie! Hey, Mark! What happened?"

If that recognizable voice caught up with them, there was no escaping her. The crowd hovered in anticipation. They knew it, too. If Sophie Bianchi, flamboyant yoga mistress of Edisto Beach was interested in what happened, she'd find out. And then, she'd return and tell them.

Sophie trotted up, makeup in place, nails done, blue-and-teal-swirled yoga leggings accenting those glutes, a walking advertisement for her yoga class which had to have not long gotten out. No sweat on the woman. At least she wore a loose off-the-shoulder lacey piece atop her tank top to not draw attention to all her lean litheness. Her pixie hairdo did a little dance as she hustled over, making her all the more spirited, which caught the interest of even more people. Nobody overlooked Sophie.

"My energies had me expecting something this morning," she said. "What happened? The storm? Thank God my power didn't go out."

Callie escorted Mark back around to the rear of the building, which meant Sophie would follow in her sandals and tippy-toe-sort-of-walk.

Her voice dropped to a whisper. "Why are we hiding?"

"As a courtesy to Mark, maybe?" Callie scolded. "Someone vandalized El Marko's."

Sophie did a wide-mouthed inhale, exhaling on a long "Noooo!"

Sophie worked there as a hostess in the afternoons. How did she not see the window missing out front? "It's still early so we haven't much to go on yet," Callie said. "Try not to make it into more than it is, okay?"

Sophie peered around the corner. "Well, it's not exactly nothing. You're already drawing a crowd."

"I mean, don't blow it up. No embellishment."

Sophie winced at the accusation.

"Don't even try to say you don't spread the goings-on out here. Now, that's it. We've got work to do."

Reaching over, Sophie hugged Mark. "I'm so sorry, Cajun boy. Guess I don't come in to work this evening?"

"Actually," he said, "I could use you to clean up. Unless. . . ." He turned toward Callie. "Unless the crime scene will be cordoned off that long."

Callie shook her head. "I think we can let you have it back by, say, noon."

Going back and forth between the two, Sophie displayed confusion. "But I'm a hostess." She held up the backs of both hands, as if her nail polish proved her limitations.

"You can get your lacquered fingernails dirty for once," Callie said, pushing for a lighter moment. "This is Mark we're talking about. He's practically the beach's favorite son."

Which gave Sophie a chance to turn the light back on herself, her favorite pastime. "Honey, please. You haven't seen my latest, and I'm not so sure he's not a keeper."

Everyone was a keeper in their early days dating Sophie which she firmly led them to believe . . . until they weren't. She was always the one to cut the other loose.

"Who do you have hooked on the line now?" Mark asked.

Ordinarily this wasn't the time for social updates, but Callie enjoyed seeing Mark's gloom lift a bit. He was fond of Sophie and had barely missed being one of her targets when he first moved to the area.

Sophie had even dated Callie's retired friend and old boss Stan Waltham for about two months, then they'd parted ways. She'd warned Stan. She'd even warned Sophie she was being nothing but a badge bunny, testing what it was like to date a cop. Life was one excitement after another to Sophie, and if Edisto didn't provide the excitement for her, she managed to create it for everyone else.

She leaned in, whispering, as if she weren't one prone to shout things to the world. "He's my own personal buck, if you catch my drift."

Mark grinned. "They're all stags to you. Or stallions or foxes."

But Callie got the joke that Mark didn't. "You're dating my contractor? Are you serious? How long's this been going on?" How much of their antics had delayed rebuilding *Chelsea Morning* that was a couple weeks behind schedule? Sophie lived right next door and was supposed to be keeping an eye out on Callie's place since she'd been living in Mike Seabrook's old house *Windswept.* Guess she'd been keeping an eye out, all right.

Buck Newell held one strong reputation for his building talent, and another for his rustic charm.

Callie shouldn't be surprised. Both Sophie and Buck scouted for dates on much the same wavelength. They should've caught up with each other sooner than this.

"Love at second sight, girl," Sophie replied with a toss of his pixie.

"Second?" Mark asked.

Scrunching her nose, Sophie cocked a hip. "We hit it off about five years ago. Don't even remember why we parted ways." With them seeing each other daily, they must've caught fire again.

Sophie winked. "It started with me asking him how to change the backsplash in my kitchen. Now it's three times a week, sometimes four. He's been showing me step by step what he's doing in your house."

Step by step, hell. Callie flashed visuals of where Sophie and her buck had left their experiences around her house. "Hope you were liberal saging my place when you finished your *lessons.* With a little bleach to boot."

The sarcasm drew a smirk out of their friend, validating Callie's visions.

"We have work to do," Callie repeated.

"Fine. See y'all." Sophie twirled and headed back to the crowd, no doubt eager to fill in answers to all the questions she'd receive, regardless of whether she held the answers or not. She turned back for a final word. "Oh, we need to double date some time, don't you think? I mean now that the *buck* is out of the bag?"

Callie didn't even wave. Sophie left.

"She beats all," Mark said. With the little whirlwind gone, however, his smile left and they returned to reality.

"We still haven't talked about who might have done this," Callie said.

"Yes, we did. I told you—"

"That you had no idea, which is bunk. People don't trash a place and not take valuables and cash. Not unless it's personal." *Plus, you're dodgy. You're holding back.*

"Consider it random," he said.

"What does that mean?"

"It means I'm not totally sure."

"But you have an idea."

He stared down at her. "Can't prove a thing."

She wasn't accustomed to his getting in her way like this. This just wasn't his spirit. "If you do nothing . . . if we do nothing, they'll be back, if not to your place, to others. If they think we don't care, we become easy targets. Tell me who you think it might be, even if it's a list, and we'll iron this out. Don't leave me hanging."

She didn't want to hear a counter fluff of an explanation. "I can tell you have an idea. Don't bullshit me, Mark. My responsibility is to this beach, not just you. You do not have the luxury of just saying forget about it."

Her fists had found their way to her hips, and if she weren't eight inches shorter, she'd have leaned in and gotten in his space.

"What did you swipe off the bar and hide in your pocket?" she asked.

His brows quickly raised then lowered, pretending she hadn't taken him by surprise. "Excuse me?"

"Show me your pockets," she said.

Not angry but a far cry from his affable self, he reached a hand in his pants pocket.

This was a first. In their relationship they didn't make demands of each other. She didn't like doing it, and he wasn't happy at obliging. She waited, unhappy at this new territory of secrets.

He pulled out his hand, and she hesitated to hold out hers, hoping he had a simple explanation to go with whatever it was.

He unfolded his fingers to reveal a .41 caliber bullet.

Chapter 3

CALLIE TRIED TO analyze any sane reason for leaving an unspent bullet lying around. Not dropped on the floor, and not left over from a shooter who didn't police their brass, but deliberately left on a bar in plain sight.

Regardless of how and where it was found, nobody left one by accident. This was a token, a symbolic message.

"I have no idea why it was there," Mark repeated.

Bullshit. She put a napkin across her palm and reached out.

He dropped it on the napkin.

She didn't study it. Instead, she stood rigid, focusing on him and trying to read those eyes.

However, he met the challenge. He had too much law enforcement in him to blink first. She wasn't playing this game, though, and gave him her back to retrieve an evidence bag from Thomas.

Today would be long and awkward at best, frustrating even, and it wasn't like Callie could stray far from Mark. Any other place and situation, he would go to his work and she to hers, but today that happened to be the same address. Mark had a restaurant in disarray and a steady stream of people calling and stopping by with questions, condolences, and suggestions on how to bounce back. Callie had his crime scene to process.

She hadn't turned away for more than minutes when, in all the busyness, she remembered she hadn't had the chance to study his security footage; however, she bet he had while she was with Rob. Mark hadn't suggested it earlier nor come to her later, not even to assure her nothing was on it. One more reason to feel uneasy.

He's a victim, she reminded herself, trying to write all this off as the shock of vandalism, but easier said than done with the bullet in the mix . . . and his evasion of questions.

"Let's study your cams," she said the next time he crossed her path, five minutes later. "All four of them."

She was familiar with Mark's security. She'd checked it when the place opened, and if anyone had decent cameras, it was a retired SLED agent.

He didn't argue but acted as if he simply followed protocol. He'd locked up his personality and showed little desire to pursue a culprit.

"Sure," he said.

This seemed so weird, these two roles they played. "Are you okay?" she asked, laying her hand over his screen to capture his attention.

"Not happy, but, yeah, I'm okay."

He didn't sound like it, and she was hesitant to ask what he wasn't happy about.

She could see it, feel it, hear it in his tone. Hidden thoughts now served like a buffer between them, as if he needed distance from her so that he could pay more attention to something compartmentalized. Something she wasn't entitled to be a part of. Being excluded left an unexpected bruise.

In their coming to understand each other in those earlier months, they'd danced and dodged ad nauseum just like this. Both had desired the friendship, then the physical enjoyment, but delving into each other's past hadn't been on either agenda. Parking their past injuries seemed safer that scratching off the scab before either was fully tested.

She could blame herself for most of that behavior because he probably followed her lead. God knew she'd justified her behavior and avoided letting him too deeply into her past for many dark and complicated reasons. She'd been broken too many times. Living in the here and now seemed best for both.

She preferred things that way. *Right?* He seemed to as well. That commonality actually let them enjoy each other more. No baggage.

But then he'd hung around way longer than she expected him to, which had forced her to dig out of a deep pile of life guilt to get to where she could welcome him close.

She'd come a far distance from her old self—the woman who'd lost a husband and a beau to the downside of being a cop, both murdered by villains. But Mark was law enforcement, too, like all the men in her past, and Callie couldn't completely rid herself of that strong sense of déjà vu.

Mark seemed to get it, never asking about her history and never volunteering his. While he'd spoken briefly of his disability retirement from being shot in the leg, he hadn't filled in the details of by whom, why, nor how. She'd said just as little about the eight-inch ropey burn scar on her arm.

They were a match made in heaven in a twisted way.

Law enforcement bound them. They discussed where they were from, some about her mothers, the one who raised her and the one who bore her, mainly because he'd crossed paths with both a time or two. His died a decade ago. Callie couldn't say if he had a single living relative otherwise. But she'd thought they were slowly coming round to the deep work of a relationship. She'd taken him to Mike's grave. She'd said the words out loud that she was ready to move on.

He'd moved in with her the day she moved back into *Chelsea Morning*.

Hairs suddenly pricked on the back of her neck at this weird sense of having arrived at a crossroad.

"Callie."

The fact Mark used her name instead of *Sunshine* snapped her back to the present.

"Show me your cameras," she said. "I figure you've already gone through them, and I take it you didn't learn anything to help or you would've called me over."

His nanosecond of a squint said he didn't like being read. "I learned I need more cams, more upscale equipment, or better angles," he said. "I also should've been notified on my phone of movement inside. Maybe I didn't have the settings right."

"Or the storm screwed with it."

He held out his cell, open to the app. His outside footage wasn't much better than the shop owner's down the way. The trespasser kept their head down, dressed unremarkable . . . yet different.

"That's not the same person who broke into The Undercurrent," she said.

He appeared stymied. "Are you sure?"

"Without a doubt," she said. "Dark hoodie there. Light hoodie here. Dark hair on the other one. This one is smaller and—"

"—not dark haired," he finished.

"A team?" she asked.

"Then why only two stores?" he said.

"Indeed," she added. "A sloppy break-in on both parts, but effective enough. They got in."

"And got away," he said.

She tried to find more similarities. More differences. More understanding of the why. "But to what end? They stole junk, more or less, from the other store, and nothing from yours."

"Interrupted maybe?" he said. "Before they could breach the other stores?"

The inside cameras, one on either end of the seating area, showed the glass implode and the person come through with fervor and more than moderate breathing. They didn't appear too skilled at B&E, in her opinion.

Then as if they'd flipped a switch, they parted the sea of tables and chairs with swings, kicks, and wind-up throws of whatever they could get their hands on, like the clay pots. A lot of anger. Not a very strong person from the gracelessness of their movements, and the kicking and tossing of knickknacks and decorations. They pressed through the room then back through, then around the perimeter twice, pacing with nothing left to throw, yet aware enough to tighten the hoodie so the cover didn't slip loose. Those movements right there almost made them seem like . . . a girl. Too hard to say.

Then the person stopped. They took what seemed a deep collecting breath then strode behind the bar. Taking out the cash box, they quickly put it back, which seemed quite odd considering their willingness to demolish a plate-glass window. They appeared to miss where the firearm was, too, or else did nothing about it. Maybe too flustered to notice? Then they poured themself a sloppy double shot of something resembling vodka and rested the glass on the bar, in their grip . . . pondering? Admiring? Considering the next step? Resting in almost the same pose Mark had struck when he checked for his Sig.

Then the person turned toward the wall behind the bar, downed the drink in two gulps, spun, and threw the glass across the room. They wore thin gloves on their hands.

The other burglar didn't. Callie expected to find fingerprints in The Undercurrent after seeing the video. Not at El Marko's.

This break-in seemed way more personal than the other.

Thomas poked his head through the swinging door from the kitchen side. "They walked here, Chief. Had everyone check their cams . . . everyone who had one . . . and nobody has this person parking anywhere nearby. The cam at the causeway shows someone in sweats walking up Jungle Road. They might've parked off the beach and approached on foot."

Odd. "They walked here alone?" That sure made for a more difficult getaway.

Puzzled at the question, Thomas scratched the nape of his neck. "Um, yeah. Gray hoodie, stooped. No facial features. Slim build. I'm getting you a copy."

"What about the guy who robbed Undercurrent?" she asked.

"He seemed to come from the same direction. Nobody shows them together. I've seen the inside cams at Pizza Pirate and Salty Art, on the east end of the building. They show The Undercurrent guy walking past. They do not show the burglar for El Marko's."

So the two robbers didn't come together. "Check the last two stores," she said. They stood closer to El Marko's.

She turned to stare at Mark. "Thank you, Thomas." Sensing the challenge between his boss and her guy, Thomas backed out leaving Callie still staring at Mark. "What the hell is going on? Can you tell who did this?"

"No," he said. "Not familiar."

She didn't believe him. "Who *might* it be? Give it your best guess, or is that too much trouble?" She regretted that last part, but it wasn't as if he would be surprised at the asking.

"Someone angry about my past."

She waited, lips mashed.

Yet he still stood up to the challenge. "Callie, I cannot confirm who. I cannot absolutely identify that person," he said, shaking his cell.

"But they are upset at, or might be related to . . .? Come on, Mark."

"My SLED past," he repeated.

She caught her teeth trying to clench. "A specific case, maybe? Maybe with real people you can name? Good heavens, Mark, you'd think I was trying to accuse you."

He tensed. "I want you to forget about the break-in," he said. "I'll clean up quickly and be open tomorrow if I can beg some chairs and tables off people."

She had to run the words through her mind a second time to make sure she heard right. "Just forget this ever happened?"

"More trouble than it's worth."

"It's not just your establishment nor your choice. Report's already been filed. Investigation already started. Evidence supports there was a B&E and property was damaged." She shrugged at the wall, in the direction of the other stores. "What, I'm to investigate one and not the other? I don't need your permission to pursue this."

He clouded over. "Can't be solved without me."

She wasn't believing his attitude. "That's mighty presumptuous of you, sir, and disrespecting of me, don't you think?"

He didn't try to correct the misstep. "Not trying to disrespect you. Just trying to make everyone's life easier. Trust me."

Her phone rang. Sophie. Callie hit her standard message that said she was at work and unable to take the call.

"Mark . . . we've sidestepped each other's demons for a long time now. I closed the door with Seabrook and took you to the graveyard to do it, if you remember correctly."

He gave her a gentle nod of affirmation. In uniform, after being re-sworn in, she'd driven him, her new lover, to the cemetery, introduced him to her old lover in the ground, and vowed to all of them she was ready to move on. She and Mark both slept soundly that night, the tumbling song of a king tide assuring them they were on the upward swing of a new future.

On the cusp of that memory, she leaned into him. "Isn't it time I deserve the same from you?"

His regard for her turned from soft to pained, his distress diluting her irritation. Instead of yanking him to her office for a hardcore interview, she yearned to tuck his long hair behind an ear, hoping he'd take her hand and spill everything.

"No doubt you deserve better," he said, making no move toward her. "Which is why I say drop it."

She still didn't understand, and she didn't like the sound of how he said his peace. She liked less the way he turned and disappeared into the kitchen.

They would have to leave El Marko's and all these onlookers to hold any sort of in-depth conversation with substance.

Once she returned to the front of the building, people shot questions from behind the makeshift ribbon line Ben and Thomas had set up. Who did it? What was she doing about it? How long before she let Mark open back up? The worse one was how had this happened to her own boyfriend?

She gave them her best, well-worn, generic answers.

Soon Callie had to send Ben on another call at the marina, so she took up residence in the parking area, diverting vacationers who'd grown bored of the beach, while taking calls from assorted town council members and the mayor, none of whom wanted to breach the gaggle of gawkers.

Her phone rang. Sophie again. Callie let it go to voice mail, but after refusing the call, she caught Mark watching her from the back kitchen entrance, the look striking her as more melancholy than anything else. He turned at the call from the one of his cooks he'd convinced to stick around and help.

If he was purposely keeping his distance, she was more confused than before.

Maybe there were just too many people hanging around. Just because she wanted to have the conversation didn't make this the right place to have it.

She missed another call. This time Sophie left a voice mail, and Callie listened, if for no other reason than to fill in a moment or two while she gathered her wits and made sense of something that made no sense.

Sophie's message was short. "I will keep calling over and over until you answer or call me back."

Callie hit redial. "What is it, Sophie? You were needed at El Marko's to help straighten up. Mark wants to be open tomorrow."

"Wow, listen to you. One might think you two were married and you were running the restaurant."

Not the right conversation for the moment, for sure. "Sorry. Hard morning."

"Must be if you are apologizing."

Touché.

Sophie rolled on nonplussed. Little stopped the woman, and a friendly spat only made her double down and engage more. "Since the restaurant is messed up, I'm inviting you and Mark to my place for dinner at five. We can clean up tomorrow."

In almost three years, that was a first. "You don't cook, Soph. Veggie trays are about your limit."

"Oh, I'm not doing the cooking." She laughed. "Buck already has a menu planned and has gone to the grocery store for garlic bread."

Of all times. "Sophie."

"It's me being magnanimous since you've both been so good to me, and Mark's had such a bummer of a day. Let me do this . . . please."

Annie appeared, leaning over to speak low in her ear. "Got another call, Chief. Domestic on Osceola Street. Want me or Thomas to take it?"

"Send him," she said, phone against her chest. "You stay, please."

Annie gave a small salute and disappeared.

Sophie's muffled shout came from Callie's shirt, and she returned to the call. "We'll be there," Callie replied, for no other reason than to move on. Sophie was relentless.

"Might be others," her friend added.

Wouldn't be anyone they didn't already know, but she wasn't up for a party. "Please don't make this some gala, Soph. We're tired. I've got to go."

Mark had returned to behind the bar again, to his usual vantage, but this time she bet he was studying the room in order to mentally recreate the act of trespass and destruction.

A social night might be good for Mark. Might also undo some of the awkward distance between them. Light chatter might give him time to think about the day, think about friends and community, put his life into perspective, and, hopefully, realize Callie was there to help.

A gruff voice from behind brought her back around. "What's the conclusion, Detective? Can I come in?"

She spun. "Hey, Stan. Sure."

Always a welcome sight, her old Boston PD captain followed her to the back kitchen door and stepped in, not touching anything—he knew better. He was the one to put Mark onto Hawaiian shirts, though his barrel chest outshone Mark's, with Stan's patterns more gregarious. His close-cut military gray needed a trim, and Callie kept hoping he'd let it grow out. She'd love to see a ponytail, but that was never going to happen.

This burly friend still tested her, asking her to report on a case as if she still worked for him. She enjoyed the role-play, and he enjoyed being needed.

Stepping them away from the crowd, comfortable in their old routine, she relayed details, him reserving his questions until she'd covered what she found, what she knew, and what she'd deduced.

"Yep, it's personal," Stan said. "Are you letting things slide like Mark wants or proceeding without him?"

She gave him a wry scrunch of her nose, taking in a whiff of his cinnamon gum. "Hoping to proceed *with* his cooperation, thank you very much. Sophie invited us over for a dinner soirée to help him chill a bit. Once he relaxes, I think I can turn him. I hope."

He smiled and shook his head, and she understood he chuckled at Sophie, not about Mark. Callie had listened to a handful of coded mentions about Stan's breakup with Sophie, but she hadn't pried because he wasn't one to spill his feelings. He liked being the shoulder, not the individual crying on one. She liked that he and Sophie had parted on somewhat humorous terms. Sophie was disappointed he wasn't more of a partier. He'd tired of her insatiable hunger for evening trysts four to five times a week. Dinner and a movie wasn't her cup of tea unless sex took place in between.

"Wish you could find someone," Callie said to him.

His shrug wasn't natural. He liked to grip life, not be swayed by it. "Seems the dating pool is rather shallow out here. Women are either too transient, too young, too old, too scarred."

"A bit picky, are we?" Him she could joust with. His skin ran thick.

"Damn right," he said, with a snap to of his backbone. "I'm not hooking up with just anyone."

She gave a smiling humph. "Listen to you and the lingo, old man."

"Frost on the roof, but still a fire down below."

"Oh God, I didn't need to hear that." Then she had an idea. "Come to Sophie's with us." If Sophie could be impromptu, so could she. "Mark might like having a wing man. He's a bit down, as you can imagine."

"Sounds doable," he said, not even asking if he was an expected guest. That's how Edisto rolled.

"Just be aware there's a new boyfriend," she warned.

"There will always be a new boyfriend," he said. "Makes me want to go all the more."

Chapter 4

CRICKETS AND TREE frogs were beginning to make their choral appearances as the evenings warmed. Not many, but a few. Come June, they'd practically deafen you, which rattled many a visitor unaccustomed to how noisy nature could be.

Callie held back and let Mark knock on Sophie's door, trying not to let it appear she'd dragged him to the visit. "This will be good for you," she said, hoping she hadn't said it before.

"Still waiting for you to say you're dropping this investigation," he said, making it clear he wasn't so easily distracted. "I don't feel right going out on a date when my restaurant was just torn up."

"You did as much as you could. Power's on. Kitchen works. Place was pretty much put back together."

"So let me move on," he said. "Drop the case."

They'd talked in broken phrases about the subject all afternoon. She'd drop the case if she felt the situation purely random, but his reluctance to open up and desire to can the case had proven the break-in anything but. Then there was the fact there were two targets of vandalism, and the other store owner. Mr. Lassiter hadn't demanded justice, just comments about his insurance covering damages, but he hadn't told Callie not to pursue the case, either. That made it pretty hard to ignore the evidence she might get from investigating Mark's break-in when it might aid in Mr. Lassiter's. Admittedly, Mark hadn't much of a comeback on that last one.

Despite her investigative logic, his attitude hadn't changed much since morning. The B&E weighed on him, and he argued he wouldn't be much company going out to dinner, but Callie had convinced him that he would hurt Sophie's feelings, plus he had to put up a positive appearance for the community, for the sake of his business. That he couldn't argue with either.

Zeus Bianchi answered the door, and warm dinner aromas wafted out with him. "Yo, Callie," he said, squeezing her against a tee shirt advertising his charter fishing business before turning to Mark. "My man." Men got hugs from Zeus as well. "Come on in. Mom's perched on her bar stool, ogling her latest. Somebody had to show manners and let you guys in."

Sophie had born two children. Sprite, the daughter, was a sophomore at the College of Charleston with Callie's son Jeb. What had started as curious study of each other as neighbors' kids on Edisto morphed into a real-deal relationship, and Callie was more concerned about them connecting too hard and too fast than whom her son had chosen. She was a sweet girl, not nearly as other-worldly as her mother, and equally, if not more, beautiful.

The son, Sophie's eldest, held enough likenesses in genetics and behavior for anyone Edistonian to instantly make the correlation. His hair jet black, with a curly, soft body to it just like the women in his family—the longer the fluffier—wasn't quite an Afro but lush enough to bounce in the sea breezes around his head. His brand was to put a band around it atop his head or wrap a headband just above his hairline when he was out on the water managing his outfitter charter business, guiding fishermen to their sea bass and grouper, or catering to tourists wanting to snap a pic of a dolphin rolling six feet away. His tan was year-round, and he slept on his boat.

Zeus leaned over from his lanky, six-foot four height. "No booze here," he said, leading them toward where the voices were. "In your honor. Not a fan myself, honestly. There are better highs than that."

"Like life?" Callie said, fully aware he smoked.

"Like life," he repeated and winked. Tentacles crept from under the sleeves of his shirt, and she remembered how in depth the tattoo was across his back.

They rounded the corner. Sophie's legs knotted up under and around herself atop a stool, dressed in a paisley print legging. She was teasing the cook by sucking on a cherry at the end of a toothpick. Her iced fizzy water had at least a half dozen cherries in it.

The doorbell rang again.

"Don't worry. I'll get it," Zeus said, rolling eyes at his mom.

Sophie jumped off her seat but not to answer the door. "Mark . . . oh, Mark." She hugged him to her, gazing up at him from the tight quarters. The woman never passed an opportunity to share skin with a good-looking male, regardless of whom they belonged to. "How are you holding up?"

"Insurance covers it. Just superficial, easily replaceable items, so I was extremely lucky," he said. "We'll be up and running tomorrow with a little bit of a limp, tables and chairs loaned by the rec center. I'll let you order more decorations."

She lit up. "Just hand me the credit card, fella." She turned to Callie. "And how long is it going to take to find the burglar?"

Callie peeked at Mark, then caught herself. "It's early days, Soph."

"Uh oh, can't get past me. What's wrong?" Sophie said.

Zeus reappeared. "Guess who arrived, Mom? I never got to spend time with him when y'all were hooked up, but gotta love a man who breaks bread with his ex and her new boy toy."

Stan entered the room with somewhat of an entrance Callie had to admire. "Hey, Bug."

Sophie wasn't deterred in the least, however, and nowhere near embarrassed. She dipped her head and slinked all sultry-like to the man, shoulders swaying to each step. "Come here, Captain, and give me a hug."

They embraced. Embraced hard, Stan handling this reunion way better than Callie expected. They *had* actually parted as good friends.

Mark glanced from the duo to Callie and then into the kitchen where the boyfriend du jour stirred, tasted, and smelled the food in progress, and he moved to block Buck's line of sight.

Leathered skin from a lifetime of outdoor work and hair lapping his collarbone, Buck Newell wore khaki pants, flip-flops, and a tee with a poem of the ocean across its back. He juggled three pots on the stove and something in the oven that set Callie's stomach to rumbling. He seemed oblivious to his lady's romantic overtures to every man in the room but her son.

"Wonderful, wonderful," he said, opening the oven. He decided something wasn't done and closed it, adjusting the temperature down. He stood and kissed his fingertips. "Y'all will love this meal. You just wait. Sophie's already given her blessing, and she doesn't eat enough for a bird." He searched around Mark for his lady, chuckled lightly at her flirting with Stan, then wiped at a spill on the range top.

Callie squeezed in beside Mark at the kitchen entrance with a question that couldn't wait. "Why didn't you tell me you were dating my neighbor, Buck?"

Buck did a flirty little click in his cheek and winked. "Didn't think it pertinent, but thanks for living next door to her. I hadn't realized what I missed."

A world filled with frequent sex, for sure. This was Sophie, which made Buck an obviously happy man. "Then let me rephrase," Callie said. "Why didn't you tell me you were enjoying my friend's assets under my new roof? On my new floors. God knows on what other surfaces." Hopefully not on her new counters. That would be an ick factor hard to ignore.

Wiping hands with the dishcloth tucked in his waistband, making Callie wonder what the end of that rag might inadvertently touch, he straightened, as though building into an excuse. "Let me just say that that woman—"

"Don't make her worse, Buck," Zeus interrupted. "Damn, Mom, aren't you offering them something to drink? Put a throttle on your libido."

From her location wrapped around Stan's middle, the mother retorted, "Says the child who beds half the females on his charters." She let loose of Stan and slid back on her place at the bar. "You fix them drinks, sweetheart. And respect your elders." Toothpick returned to her fingers, she turned attention back to Buck, stabbed another cherry, stuck her chin out and made sucky noises slurping it in. "And hush. I'm getting good at this."

The toilet flushed in the half bath, and Callie seemed to be the only soul who noticed there was apparently another dinner guest. Sprite maybe, though Jeb might've mentioned if he or his girl would be on the beach. Usually with one came the other.

A woman exited in low-riding jeans, tight-fitting turtleneck, a turquoise and blond-leather rope belt around her hips and dangling earrings to match. Wearing a little more eyeliner than Callie preferred, swooping up at the outer corners, the guest's exotic mien gave not only Callie pause, but Mark as well. Stan's brows raised. Buck just chuckled all-knowing from the kitchen.

The guest glided, not walked, to Zeus and melted over his arm, melting the twenty-two-year-old boy in the process.

"Oh, for God's sake," Sophie started, but Zeus spoke over her.

"Y'all, this is Maya Lecroix." He oozed a slow smile over his friend, his gaze like butter when she cut him a sultry one in return.

She was old enough to be Callie's sister, and not necessarily a younger one.

"This was worth coming for," Mark said under his breath, and Stan echoed with one of his soft gravelly laughs.

Callie held out her hand. "Hello. I'm—"

"The police chief," Maya said. "And that gentleman is Stan. Strong aura."

Stan grinned as if he understood what she was talking about.

"But you," she said, releasing Zeus to greet Mark. She took one of his hands without hunting for it, her attention on his blue eyes. "You are why I came," she said. "Your past and present have met, and it's disturbing you." She clenched his hand between the both of hers and pulled it to her chest, drawing herself in and putting but inches between them.

She kept studying him, hard enough to have captured everyone's attention and drop the room into silence. Mark's eyes darted questioningly at Callie.

"I see a woman," Maya said.

Sophie laughed. "She's standing right there. Or could be me."

Zeus spun on her. "Mom." About the same time Callie uttered, "Soph, stop."

Sophie pivoted away.

Maya continued, as if uninterrupted. "She will hurt you if you don't console her. She cannot rest."

Extracting his hand from her grip, Mark tipped his head. "Well, nice to meet you, too." He removed himself from her reach and took his fizzy water with its lone cherry to the sofa. "Next!" he told the room, as if they were in line at the carnival for a Tarot reading.

Maya started to follow him, but Zeus draped a ropey arm over her shoulders. "She's a psychic, in case you hadn't noticed."

Facing Buck in the kitchen, Sophie spoke over her shoulder. "So she says."

"I have some skills, Sophie, as do you," Maya said in little more than a coo. "There's room for both of us in this world."

But Sophie's tight, coral-colored lips didn't agree.

"Goddess. . . ." warned Buck long and low from the sink opposite the bar from his lady. Apparently, Sophie had a new nickname to go along with the new beau.

Callie snaked around to make her way to occupy the seat beside Mark before Maya did, the psychic's attention still clinging tight to him.

Zeus seemed more worried about his mother's threatened ego than his girlfriend's fixation on Mark and went to talk to Sophie. Maya glided—why couldn't she walk like everyone else—to the recliner and eased to sit. "What are your plans?" she asked Mark.

"About what?" he asked.

Maya nodded at Callie. "Her."

That took Callie aback. Surely she wasn't the woman in her vision, or whatever the hell she meant. "Can you be more specific?"

"What I see isn't always linear or sharply defined. It comes in metaphors or blurs, innuendo or snapshots. If I had time with you, or a few times," she added quickly, "I could possibly assist you."

A few times doing what?

"Buck?" Callie called out. "When's that luscious dinner you bragged about going to be ready? I'm starved."

"Give me ten minutes, Chief," he hollered back.

Sophie leaped off her perch, sandals slapping on the wood floor quite unlike her usual lightweight stroll and went in the kitchen. "Give them some damn appetizers, Buck. Make her eat and shut up before we all get brainwashed."

Maya ignored her, leaning forward with emphasis. "You need to make some decisions, Mark. Let's talk."

The woman was relentless, and, God help her, Callie couldn't help but feel more partial to Sophie's feelings right now. Yes, Mark had to come to terms that Callie needed his cooperation about his past to complete this investigation of the present, but this wasn't the place to discuss it. In fact, this sort of attention might do more to keep Mark dug in and uncooperative.

Callie shifted to small talk. "How long have you been on Edisto?"

Maya didn't just regard Callie; she slid her neck around like a snake.

Now everyone watched her watching Callie.

"A month," Maya said.

"Oh, that's a while. Where are you staying? We—"

"On the boat with Zeus." Maya gave him her attention now. "I have simply fallen in love with the sea, thanks to him. He gives it such power in his words, his fishing, his movements on the vessel, ever in sync with the water. I understand why he is so successful."

She didn't use contractions, each word enunciated.

Yes, the boy did well with his enterprise, very well. Though he was more like Sophie than his sister was, Sophie said little of her son other than he wasn't college material and managed fine as a business owner. Maya would have everyone believe he was some godlike attraction.

Callie identified the son as so much like his mother that they clashed.

"Eat it while it's hot." Buck threw a plate of steaming artichoke dip and pita chips on the coffee table before them. He rushed back with small paper plates and napkins then left. "Don't fill up on that stuff, though," he said. "Dinner's on the way."

Sophie remained hidden in the kitchen.

Stan dug in. "Don't have to tell me twice. Come on, y'all. He worked hard for this."

The shift in atmosphere was welcomed by all. Even Maya ate, her hands daintily lifting what everyone else was dripping, catching with open mouths, and wiping away.

"Hmm," Mark said. "I might need this recipe for the restaurant."

Maya perked back up. "May I come to the restaurant and do a reading for you?"

"I, um, why . . . I'm. . . ." He looked to Callie to bail him out.

But Callie capitalized on the indecision. "Why not? Do it, Mark." The sideshow might make him talk more, reveal more, yay or nay what Maya said about what happened and why.

Maya's mouth went agape. "Why . . . thank you, Callie. Your support means so much to me." She gave a dip of her head and set down her plate to continue. "I've helped law enforcement before. Once in finding two little girls who went missing in the UK. Another time to assist with the whereabouts of a boy in Finland."

Stan was wary. "They paid you to fly to other countries?"

"No need." She smiled, like answering a child. "Between Zoom and the fact that clairvoyant powers have no geographic limitations, one doesn't have to be present."

"They find them dead or alive?" Stan asked, unconcerned with nuance.

"Unfortunately, they'd passed on," she replied.

"Because nobody in law enforcement calls upon a psychic until they've exhausted all other avenues," Callie said. So now Maya saw dead people. "Nobody's missing here, but if you can see who might've broken in, I'm game. Cameras failed us." She reminded herself she was doing this for Mark.

"I'll try, and I'd be honored."

Stan chomped away on the hors d'oeuvres. Mark remained silent. Sophie pouted in the kitchen at the side of her fellow, and Zeus had parked himself on the rug beside Maya's chair.

Callie, however, hoped none of this got out to the rest of her department.

"The contention between you actually might help," Maya added.

Everyone focused on Callie and Mark.

When they left tonight, Mark would preach all the way home how he hadn't wanted to come.

"Why'd you bring her here, son?" Sophie appeared, tired of the show. This would not go well.

"First, I like her, Mom. Second, she had ideas on the break-in and asked to share. Trust me, I wasn't keen on putting her on display like this. Not with your reaction to competition."

His mother's mouth dropped open. "Competition? I swear, Zeus, that was totally uncalled for. I see now I shouldn't have let you bring her." Blowing out, she mumbled under her breath, "Competition be damned."

Zeus clouded over, the first time Callie had ever seen the island ocean boy radiate anything but laissez-faire. "Maya just wanted to help."

"Hah, drum up business, you mean."

Mother and son faced off while everyone waited, while the seafood casserole, hushpuppies, and red rice got old and cold.

Buck reminded them of the waiting fare. "It's on the table, folks."

But Zeus wasn't done. "What were your readings on El Marko's, Sophie? Or were you too horny and distracted by Bob Villa over there to think straight, oh Mother Witch of mine?"

Buck jumped in. "Whoa, young man. That's not how you talk to your mother."

"Not your conversation, man."

Stan tried to take Sophie by the arm and steer her away, but she jerked loose. Mark inched back to sit on the arm of the sofa, separate from the fray.

But there was nothing chagrinned about Maya. She acted like she hadn't heard and pushed through to Callie. "There's death on the mind of the violator. Past or present, I'm not sure. I've seen it," she whispered, using the bruhaha to hide the message.

The absolute in her voice snared Callie, and she had to remind herself this woman operated on dreams, thoughts, and most likely reading people. "Maya, the break-in happened only this morning and you just met Mark. You might be jumping the gun."

"Time isn't linear. I can see the past and the future. There's no controlling what I see or when I see it, but the break-in is only the start. The air is thick with this, with more to come."

Mark showed bafflement, having been unable to hear.

"See you at the restaurant in the morning," Callie said to Maya, loud enough for Mark to hear this time. "Before the staff arrives."

"The table and chairs are being delivered in the morning," he said, seeking an out.

"We'll do it early. Suit you, Maya?"

The fortune teller smiled that powder-soft smile of hers and replied, "Eight would be fine."

Callie left a message for Marie that she'd be in late, reminding herself she'd agree to this as a distraction, to lighten up Mark. She might've made a mistake.

Chapter 5

THE FOOD HELPED diffuse the sparring of personalities to a certain degree, with the exception of Sophie. Throughout the meal, Zeus beamed like a new penny as his lady friend relayed stories of what she'd accomplished with her powers. Sophie, the polar opposite of her son tonight, exuded a fierce gloom as if she hoped it would creep across the table and smother the other woman. Whether because of Maya's so-called abilities or age difference from her son, Sophie wasn't liking this woman one bit, while the men—all four of them—hung on her every word. Maya could tell a good story, and her supposed links to law enforcement only served to lure the men closer.

The evening's mood lightened a little more at the sight of banana pudding Buck had whipped up from scratch. At nine thirty, however, Callie made excuses to leave. Work normally began at seven, and she routinely rose at six which would slip up on her fast, especially if she managed to talk much with Mark tonight. Tomorrow, however, meant meeting Maya at eight, but Sophie was making it super easy to leave, with none of the feigned effort a host makes asking guests not to leave so soon. She wanted everyone gone.

Callie took Mark home, having coaxed him into staying at *Windswept.* Even with the night breeze coming off the water in the lower fifties, a thick quilt provided all the warmth the two needed on the red porch swing as Callie attempted to draw Mark into talking about his problem.

Liking her caffeine in small doses this time of night, she had let Mark fix his black, stout cup first, and used his grounds to make her one less strong. She enjoyed the swinging and sipped on her coffee, letting him settle, giving him silence. Trouble was he was a cop, too. Like her, he could sit for a long time basking in the quiet while waiting for someone else to fill in the void.

"Are you saying SLED never tapped a psychic on a cold case?" She hunkered, her shorter legs under the cover while she let Mark do the rocking.

"Never to my knowledge," he said. "And if anyone did call one in,

I understand why word never got out. That's just embarrassing police work, if you ask me."

"She said she solved at least two cold cases."

"So she said." He set his cup down on a rattan table against the wall and typed on his phone. "Maya Lecroix. Teaches people how to be a psychic, is published in a few magazines, and claims she's solved crime, though nothing links to anyone with credentials."

"Show me her picture." Did she pose as sultry online as she did in person?

"Just shows heavy, made-up eyes in one pic, and she's standing in shadows in the other. Guess you have to cough up her fee to see the real deal." He put away the phone. "That's consoling, Callie. Can't believe I'm getting up an hour early to give this woman attention when I have enough to do otherwise."

Callie nudged him under the covers with a toe. "I was being polite. She might help remove that burr from under your saddle. Don't you need to be in early anyway? To straighten things?" A pinch pricked her toe, and she jerked, relishing his rediscovered sense of humor.

"Most of the cleanup is done, but I could do some prep work and hang up the older decorations from the storeroom. People will be coming by early, I imagine. The curious always do."

"Asking questions and wanting to see for themselves," she finished for him.

It was also Monday, when the tourists who checked in on Saturday and Sunday took to taking in the sights, which usually meant a busy day once they'd gotten their fair share of sun.

Mark hadn't told her to drop the case since before dinner. They'd made light conversation about Maya. He seemed more like his old self. She debated whether to return to the bullet, and his reluctance to talk straight with her about who the break-in culprit might be.

"Back at the restaurant, when I asked you—"

"Let's go inside," he said, stopping the swing.

The ocean had disappeared into the darkness across the street, the tide almost fully ebbed.

Cups in the sink, she let him lead her to the bedroom.

Not that she didn't recognize the diversion.

She'd been wrong earlier this morning. She just might land some of that pleasure she feared was gone, and the morning might bring normalcy back with the dawn.

And put him in a better mood to explain.

WITH ONLY SHEERS on the windows, Callie routinely woke with the dawn. The empty lot on the ocean front across the street allowed the eastern sunrise to come through unimpeded and warm. She liked rising with the sun which meant anywhere between six and seven, depending on the month, the cloud cover, and how spent she was from the previous day.

Not the early riser, Mark threw her pillow over his head. "Don't talk," he mumbled into it, fighting to hang onto sleep.

She showered then dressed for Monday duty. She called for Mark as she zipped up her pants. "Rise and shine. Come on. We weren't up that late."

As he sluggishly toyed with covers, then feigned difficulty finding his way to his feet, Callie appreciated his old standard behavior. While he showered, she visualized them in her new house once fully constructed, imagining the both of them there, full time. This house-hopping between *Windswept* and his place made things less structured, less formally coupled. When the postal carrier finally delivered mail to the same address on Jungle Road for both Callie Jean Morgan and Mark Landry Dupree, they'd have to ponder about whether to roll with the same flow or grab a marriage license.

He hadn't asked her to marry him, but he'd hinted. He'd said more than a few times he'd be there until she decided she got comfortable with him. He claimed to remain her natural shadow, her permanent cheerleader. Said every synonym for partner short of husband, which she suspected he was afraid to say for fear of chasing her away. God, she'd alienated him so many times getting over her issues of Seabrook, fire, the loss of lives, and the resignations of too many officers that she'd amassed enough guilt for ten people. It took almost losing everything and everyone for her to grow up, wake up, and see Mark for what he was. No wonder he hadn't asked yet.

It had been too much about her for too long. She'd thought they'd had time to delve into Mark's past at his pace. But they didn't. His past was here and now. She wished he'd open up and accept that this new phase of their relationship had to be about him.

The shower had run for a while. Surely he was almost done. Leaving her heavy utility belt off until time to leave, she threw together two egg sandwiches and brewed two cups of coffee. When he still hadn't come out, she sat at the dinette table and bit into breakfast. She hated cold eggs.

"Jesus Christ and all the angels," he said, coming out half dressed, towel in his hand, his hair almost dry. "Knew I smelled food. Unburnt food at that." He went for the coffee first.

"Sit. Eat," she said. "And I can cook sometimes." Admittedly, he was the craftsman in the kitchen, normally assuming the task.

The moment was wonderful. This was domestic. This should have been her focus last fall instead of sequestering herself and quitting.

He sat, and a hand soon crept up her leg on a mission, as if it wasn't going to stop.

"It's after seven," she said, but closed her eyes anyway as he continued. This was one of his games. What came next . . . *son of a bitch.*

"Ten minutes," he said low.

"We already showered," she tried to say, voice fading on the last word.

She accepted her eggs would grow cold, rose, and returned to the bedroom to give him his ten minutes.

"Twenty minutes to eight," he whispered in her ear afterward, as she'd almost dozed off.

Her eyes snatched open. The two of them hustled on clothes and grabbed the cold sandwiches. The restaurant had a microwave and fresher coffee.

"We can't get into a habit of this," she said, bouncing off him once as he reached for keys on the kitchen hook. "We'll be labelled for being late to everything, with people guessing why."

"Takes ninety days to create a habit, Sunshine," and he winked.

There was the nickname. "Takes seconds to create rumor."

She donned the belt and firearm. They'd meet the psychic, then she'd see if he needed help prepping ingredients Mark needed to kick off the lunch crowd. Then to the office.

Ten to eight. Mark opened the door and held it for her to go through. Whether he believed in Maya or not, he was an on-time guy.

Callie stopped cold at the threshold.

A .41 caliber bullet sat perfectly centered on a small sticky note on a porch plank four feet ahead, between them and the stairs. It stood on end, two inches in from either side. The position made a strong statement, because it took them both a few seconds to take in the object before making a move.

"Get me two plastic sandwich bags from the kitchen," she said, taking in the whole porch before rushing around the item to the railing in hope of seeing someone leave.

Mark didn't debate and did as told. Callie turned one bag inside out, inserted her hand to use it as a quasi-glove to take the cartridge in, right the bag, and seal it up. Only then could she lift the yellow sticky with the second bag, seal it up, then read the message. *His love isn't worth the trouble.*

She turned to him and held the bag of evidence only inches from his nose. "What's the story here, Mark? One lone robbery and even one bullet, and I gave you time to come to grips because I respect you. But *two* burglaries and *two* bullets? They're not going away. They're watching you, and therefore, watching me. You have no right to ignore this, much less ask me to. You might not care about someone threatening you, but have you stopped to think about those around you? People you're supposed to care about?" She shook the bag containing the little yellow sticky. "What the hell does this mean?"

He took the bag and read through the plastic. "I . . . I have no idea."

She didn't bother talking further, instead leaving the porch, studying the steps, the railing, the silted drive below. The person had apparently swished a palmetto frond across the ground ruining any foot tracks. Several fronds were scattered the along the road, left over from the storm. There was no sign of tire tracks other than Callie and Mark's.

Because this was her temporary place, *Windswept* had no security system on the outside, no motion sensor, no cams, just sensors on the windows and doors.

She phoned Thomas first and asked him to give this scene a once-over then canvass all the security cams within a block of them on Palmetto Boulevard. He'd taken point on yesterday's break-ins. She didn't expect much, but just the fact they might catch the same person in similar disguise would connect the two incidents. Not like the two bullets didn't already.

Then she called Sophie to get in touch with Zeus and ask him to call her. After almost three years on the beach, she didn't have his number.

"We've gotten detained with a crime," she said when he called back within minutes. She watched Thomas study the grounds below from her perch on the porch. Mark had parked himself on the red porch swing after having reheated his coffee and sandwich. He sat stiff, jaw tight, and thinking hard, back to the person at the restaurant yesterday.

"We'll have to reschedule," she told Zeus, not wanting to explain bullets to civilians. "Something police-related. Mark's helping me." That last part was spoken to keep Maya from seeking Mark alone.

"No prob," he said. "We'll catch you. She's itching to read for you guys."

Callie hung up and tried not to scan Mark. He'd overheard, so no need to repeat. He had placated her by accommodating this psychic business to start with, thinking that if he did her this favor, she'd back off, but both of them fully understood that wasn't happening now.

This situation had gotten bigger and more serious. *This* was personal. *This* wasn't random. *This*, whatever *this* was, wasn't going away.

And this calling card, this .41 bullet . . . was a specific message. Nobody used that caliber these days. With less recoil than a .44, the .41 was originally designed for old-timey police revolvers. The average shooter, however, couldn't handle it with accuracy. The caliber packed a lot of energy, and departments struggled with their officers qualifying with such big weapons, so they went to other protection. That was in the sixties. Since then, the ammo and the gun it fit, would easily become somewhat of a signature for anyone. Today's shooters used it for big game and gun collections more than anything else. It was a somewhat macho weapon.

The more Callie deliberated, the madder she got. The puzzle couldn't be that hard. She just had to figure out whose signature this was from Mark's history. And do it in spite of him.

She went to the swing and sat. "Show me the note that came with your bullet," she said, not giving him the benefit of the doubt.

"There wasn't one," he said.

"Says the man who tried to hide the bullet."

His voice rose a notch. "There was no note at the restaurant."

She wanted to believe Mark. "Who uses a .41 caliber weapon?" she demanded.

At first she read his silence as a conscious refusal to answer.

A fire rose within her. She'd never been so frustrated with him before. Then uncertainty snaked through her as she recognized the possibility this silence was generated by his difficulty dealing with the past coming to light. For some reason he dug in to keep from telling it. The truth wouldn't change anything between them. At least she felt that way.

How bad could it be?

The longer he delayed, the more something told her she wouldn't like this truth, but the highs and low of their relationship could not impede her job to protect Edisto. She had let personal get in the way before. Someone had gotten hurt. Someone had died.

She wasn't doing it again. "Who the hell do you know who carries a .41 caliber weapon, Mark?"

"Someone I used to work with," he said, avoiding her gaze. Almost no emotion in his words or in his stare which focused not on her but at the end of the porch.

She almost replied with a sarcastic *duh*, but instead waited him out.

"Javier Harred." He took a deep breath and finally turned to her. "He's a guy I worked alongside during my time with SLED. He shot me. I put him in jail."

Questions stacked like a traffic pileup in her head. She tried to take a moment to sort and ask the right ones in the right order. Oh hell, there was no order. There was only a big untold story that needed telling, but the most obvious was clear.

"Another SLED agent shot you?"

"Yes. He was undercover."

"You put him, a fellow SLED agent, in jail?" she asked.

He gave a slight frown. "You forgot the part about him shooting me and forcing me into early retirement?"

"No, I got that." She didn't lay a hand on his bum leg or reach over to touch him in any manner. This wasn't that sort of moment.

He'd given her a name, connected the name to his former employer, and confessed the fact someone had been sent to jail. That opened up the world to Callie. She could work with this. What wouldn't be in any sort of record, however, was the emotional and psychological undertones that probably mattered more than anything else. Nor would he have access to anything left out of the reports for embarrassment's sake.

"Want to come to my office?" she asked, thinking of privacy. The neutral territory might let them air things out easier.

"So now I'm a person of interest?"

Wait, what? "No, Mark. I'm just wanting to find a place to sit and talk. Where nobody might interrupt us."

His tone rose. "What's wrong with here?"

This time she did lay a hand on his leg. "Mark . . . where would you prefer to talk? I don't care."

"I've got to prep to open at eleven," he said.

"You have others who can do that for you. Call Wesley." She used that young man's name on purpose.

She'd almost arrested Wesley for being in possession of stolen property in El Marko's early days, on the very day he was interviewing with Mark for a job in the kitchen. Mark had stood up for him, and Callie had taken enough pause to realize the kid had no idea that his four-hundred-dollar sweater was hot and not his to keep. Wesley worshipped Mark, as did a good many people on the beach now. Mark had a level head, patience to spare, and a smile that could light up a room and quell any sort of misunderstanding.

He seemed so out of his element right now. Possibly thrown back into an element he'd escaped from,

Rising, she went to the railing. "Thomas, you about through?"

"Yeah, Chief. Nothing here, really. I mean, I'll talk to the neighbors, and see what's on their doorbells, but I'm not expecting much."

Few people out here did personal cams on their doorbells. The salty environment wasn't kind to such things.

"Thanks. We're going inside. Talk later."

He gave her a loose salute.

She led to the door, Mark following. She brewed two fresh cups of coffee and made herself comfortable on the living room sofa after a quick text to Marie she'd be late to the station. Mark followed.

The sun was bright and the April air warm with a slight tinge of coolness. People would be on the beach, and despite their blankets and light cover-ups, burning their house-bound winter skin too quickly. Callie could open the blinds and throw back curtains to let all that pleasant April in, but they were discussing a stalker. Nothing light about that topic. She left the windows covered.

Mark had barely touched the sofa when he started. "I offered to do this psychic thing to humor you," he said. "You'd be amazed at how many things I've done to humor you. For God's sake do this for me."

She set down her cup. "Mark," she started, using his name to better connect, like she would any upset victim. "I'm not clear. What exactly are you asking me to do?"

"Let this *be*," he said, emphasis on the last word.

"Mark." How could she word this? "It's time you told me about what happened to you, because it's followed you to Edisto Beach."

He didn't deny that.

Had her phrasing made him think of Maya like it had her? "Something or someone followed you. That makes it my worry, too."

He didn't deny that either. "I'll handle it."

"But you aren't, and you shouldn't. I don't need a vigilante on Edisto. This is twice he's trespassed onto your home turf. So far I'm assuming our individual is this Javier Harred. Why do you think it's him?"

"It's not him."

"But you said . . . and the bullet—"

"That bullet was his preferred caliber. He was an undercover agent I was handling, and he went rogue for reasons I never figured out. I knew him well, or so I thought. I knew his wife Melissa and daughter Lily."

This was a start. She wasn't ruling out this being Javier yet, though. "How long did he get?"

"Five years, which I can assume was because he cooperated to a certain degree."

Callie could do the math. Mark had been retired about that long. "So he got out recently."

He stared through her toward the covered window without answering.

This was a very good start. Mark had contained this for a long time. Problem was he wasn't sure what to do about it. His exasperation tugged at her heart, but more than that, it put her on guard. For his safety, for hers, for anyone they were close to. He didn't want her in harm's way, but she knew how bad the outcomes could be when vengeance entered a person's world. She couldn't let his uncertainty or his macho need to handle this create danger.

When she'd moved to Edisto, she'd seen crime that the naive, laid-back people of the island didn't see. She could even feel crime sometimes, or sense it in the people who brought it. Learning law enforcement in a city as large and complex as Boston had practically taught her to have eyes in the back of her head.

She was feeling something incredibly dark in all this, with Mark's reluctance validating her concern. Last year, when she couldn't tell what was good for her, Mark was there. Now he had lost *his* way, and she was going to have to steer this ship.

"Gotta get to the restaurant," he said.

"We're not done talking," she said in turn.

"We'll talk more this evening."

"While this guy, what, sunbathes? Goes fishing?"

He stood. "Nothing will happen in broad daylight in the middle of diners." Not waiting for her reply, he left the room. "I can walk," he said, grabbing El Marko's keys.

"No," she said, standing to following him to the door. "I'll take you."

She wasn't so convinced Javier wouldn't draw down amidst El Marko's diners. If he hated Mark for locking him up and costing him his career, he might feel he didn't have much else to lose.

Chapter 6

CALLIE DROPPED OFF Mark at the back door of the restaurant to avoid the steps to the front where his limp proved more evident. "I want to log this evidence in at the station. I'll be right back. Unless you want me to come in and make sure—"

"No, Callie, I got this." He exited the car, a *damn* uttered under his breath. "Take your time," he said, shutting the door and speaking over his back, the stiff body language saying so much. Still, she sat and waited as he went inside. He didn't look back.

She pulled out, in no rush to the station. He wasn't too keen on being guarded, and rather than rush she'd give him time to himself. Mark lived logically. Surely, he'd bring himself around.

Marie, the office administrator, and all-things-Edisto PD short of a uniformed officer, had her phone to her ear when Callie walked in, typing on her keyboard. Monday mornings often began a little busy. The weekend had died down, the tourists were freshly moved in, not into trouble yet, and not in each other's hair from being on vacation together too long. Questions came in, mostly. Can the kids drive the golfcarts and may they drive them after dark? Is booze allowed on the beach? What about the dog? That sort of thing.

Marie gave a quick wave and went back to her work.

Once Callie logged in the second bullet and stored it with the other in her evidence safe, she studied a couple things on her desk, more to give Mark extra time, then left. Marie was still on the phone. Callie would fill her in later. Still she felt irresponsible sitting behind her desk. She couldn't find a satisfying middle ground between the need to watch over Mark while not smothering him. She turned to what she could do—mentally organize what she knew.

Someone trailed Mark, an angry someone whom they both suspected. She was a little surprised all Javier had done was leave the cartridge on her porch and not damage *Windswept*, especially after the show he'd put on the night before, but Callie reminded herself he probably wasn't done. She could feel it. Made no sense for him to stop. This whole mess reeked of incompletion . . . and vengeance.

Technically Mark hadn't confirmed Javier as the only suspect on his list, which she deduced as Mark not wanting to accept Javier as the guy. The hoodied person's posture and stance were not those of a full-blown, investigatory male agent, but things happened in prison. Five years could totally change a man's health, appearance, personality, and manner of logic. Had Mark pondered that, too? Was he shocked or was this something he'd expected to eventually happen one day?

She drove her patrol car back to El Marko's, wanting it seen outside the restaurant. People were out and about now, some nosey, some hungry, some peeking in the door window to see what all had been damaged the day before. But she waited to leave the vehicle, wanting to place a call first to a fed she trusted.

The FBI agent had come to Edisto a couple years ago with his own issue, to hunt for the murderer of his retired partner. Callie's own son Jeb had found the body in Big Bay Creek while kayaking with Sprite.

Callie had been a wreck back then, having not long lost Seabrook, her friend, her lover, fellow officer. Knox was an active agent on a personal mission, off the books, to vindicate his friend. She'd hated him on sight. He'd labeled her an alcoholic, and she'd pretty much proven herself such at meals—hers more liquid than solid. With her not wanting the Feds running rampant on her beach, chasing a case that was hers, they had no choice but to work together, but their mindsets and brokenness had them colliding over the simplest of discussions. By the end, however, she solved his case, and he championed her to the town council, right before council chair Brice LeGrand had been about to throw her to the dogs and ask for her removal.

Such situations forged hard friendships, and Knox had shared his personal cell with her a long time ago. The clock on her dash read noon, safe enough maybe not to interrupt much more than lunch.

He answered, muddled, "Hello?"

Maybe she was wrong about the time, the day . . . and what sounded like a rather social night. "Knox? Did I wake you? Thought you'd be at work."

"Took the day off. Just not motivated to get out of bed yet."

With visions of a partner at his side, sprawled under the sheets, she made excuses to try later. "I'm sorry, guy. Don't let me interrupt anything. Want me to call back?"

"No, I'm alone," he said, as if he'd read her mind. "Fighting a cold.

I really could've gone in, but you get how people think you have Covid, the plague, and Ebola rolled into one. I'm all right. How are you?"

They shared niceties, him asking about Mark, and her asking about whomever his partner of the day might be. He swore he dated nobody in particular at present. He played stud a little harder than necessary, in her opinion, and a niggle told her his tastes might vary to more than the ladies, something the FBI had no need to know. The agency wasn't renowned for its open-mindedness.

"Need you to look up someone for me, if you don't mind," she said. "He was arrested in this state and pled to five years. Javier Harred, a SLED agent who went undercover. Not familiar with the whys and whats of the case he was on, but I am aware he shot his handler, a fellow agent. He should be getting out about now. Probably drugs, maybe weapons, which makes me wonder if DEA or ATF was involved. The Feds are in your arena. Just need you to see what's on those monstrous, intricate, uber-encrypted databases you people claim to have."

She heard movement and the shrugging and shifting of what must be bed linens, and before she could stop herself, she imagined him naked hunting for something to put on. Knox was easy on the eyes, he knew it, and he went to lengths to maintain himself. "Okay," he said, and she heard a chair being pulled out. "Repeat the name."

"Javier Harred. Case should've been five or six years ago."

"Urgency?"

"Of course, I'd like it ASAP, but no, there isn't an extreme urgency. At least not yet."

He took a second, assumably writing. "Okay. Now . . . why is this of interest to the police chief of Edisto Beach?"

"Mark was the one he shot."

The silence went on a few seconds. "Oh, wow, okay. I'll get right on this. Anything else?"

"All I know. . . ." After a silent argument with herself, remembering Mark wouldn't like her spreading his personal stuff, she caved to telling Knox. It didn't take her long to cover all that had happened and what little history she'd learned. The FBI agent would stay mum.

The whole time, from her place behind the steering wheel, she watched El Marko's door. A patrol car didn't hide well, and sooner or later Mark was bound to hunt for her. Or maybe not.

"I'll get back with you tomorrow sometime if that's okay," Knox said. "Hey, keep your head up and stay aware. Vendettas are nasty, Callie. I don't want to hear about you getting caught in the crossfire, you hear?

I get you want to protect Mark, but—"

"This is on my beach, Knox. I'm not the only one who could get hurt. This person has made themselves known twice. They're here for a reason."

She heard him take a breath, a pause long enough to second-guess what he wanted to say. "Why aren't you asking Mark to contact his SLED people since it was their case?"

Which made her second-guess what she ought to say, because that blurred the lines of personal and professional even more.

"Never mind," Knox said. "I read you."

"Yep." She was grateful not having to say to keep this on the down-low from Mark, as if uttering the words would matter more than actually going behind his back. She'd wait to see what intel she got before she dealt with the ramifications on that.

After a big thanks, she hung up then tried finding Javier Harred's driver's license in the system. There it was. Expired, but all she needed was the photo right now, and the birth date gave her an idea of his age, which was within months of hers.

Hispanic for sure. Ink-black hair, long and pulled back. Large, strik-ing eyes. From his carved jaw to particularly striking brows, he'd be con-sidered lean but handsome until one became aware of his past. That knowledge gave unintended nuance to the photo. She tried to imagine a smile and someone warm and likeable, legitimate and carrying a badge. But the smile of the photo felt disingenuous; she knew what actions lay behind that facade. However, if Mark had been close to him once upon a time, Javier must have been decent once upon a time. Otherwise, Mark wouldn't feel so pained about all this.

That was her assumption, anyway. Time would tell if she was off base.

She doubted the Blythewood address mentioned on the license was worth a damn, but if it was, it was a hundred fifty miles away, outside the state capital, nowhere close to Edisto. That meant this guy likely hid on the island. She sent the photo and notices to all her officers to be on the lookout for Javier then studied the photo one more time, etching it into her mind.

Mark would be wondering where she was by now. She got out of the car, but upon reaching the steps up to the mall landing, a resident waved driving by. She waved back. Someone honked coming from the other direction, and she smiled and raised a hand again.

A man called from behind her, but she stiffened at the sound of his voice. He quickly caught up with her, a resident. Town council chairman Brice LeGrand.

"Catch the guy?" he asked.

"Don't start," she said. Brice's favorite pastime was finding the dirt and shortcomings of anyone under the town's employment, other than himself. He had hoped he'd gotten rid of her six months ago, when she'd quit and he'd brought on his buddy from another county. That scheme had backfired on him, that chief resigned, and the town re-hired Callie with much fanfare after she'd seized hold of and overcome the crime wave Brice's uniforms had allowed to happen.

No, Brice wasn't happy at all that Callie rode at the top of people's lists these days, and he couldn't say or do much about it without it being thrown back at him.

Oh, damn, he was following her into the restaurant.

"Ought to be cameras," he said, hunting around outside. "Yeah. Easy enough to catch someone on camera."

She opened the door for herself, letting him have to catch it. "Wow, cameras, Brice. I'll have to check with Mark on that."

Inside, she ceased talking. They'd crossed into Mark's place of business, and she'd be the last to put controversy on display here.

The setting was a little more rustic in appearance, but the kitchen had already filled the air with its signature scents of cumin, cilantro, and cheese. The chairs were foldout and the tables the same, but the rec center had come through. Someone—Sophie most likely—had thrown centerpieces together of candles, fake flowers, and seashells with the usual bright-colored napkins spicing up the scheme. If one hadn't been familiar with the place before, they might not be aware of the changes and adjustments.

Mark's tiny private table next to the kitchen door had escaped the mayhem, situated against the wall in the back near the pots-and-pans noise, the least palatable position to a paying customer. The rest of the tables were fully populated. Residents mainly, God bless 'em. Edisto Beach had done itself proud showing up in support.

Automatically, Callie scanned for Javier now that she had a face. She'd be scanning the streets, the beach, and every venue on the island for him until this was over.

Someone called out, "Chief," and she smiled over at them. The room was abuzz with conversation and the sound of dinnerware. No sign of Mark, but two waitresses scurried. He always spent more time in the kitchen than he did on the floor.

"Your place is waiting for you," Sophie said, having zigzagged the new irregular layout to reach her. "Mark's in the back. He's down one person." She held out her arms. "Isn't this great?"

Callie gave her a light hug. "Sure is. You included, Soph. Don't you work evenings?"

"After Zeus sabotaged our dinner last night, I felt it was the least I could do," she said, her signature pout assuming its place before curling back up on the ends.

"I'm sure Mark appreciates it."

"I'm always appreciated," she said. "The usual?"

"The usual," Callie said, and went to make her way to the table.

Brice stepped up. "Table for two, please."

Sophie's little nose went up. "Out of luck, fella. We're full."

Callie wanted to examine over her shoulder and see Brice's expression, but instead pushed through as if she hadn't heard, the natives welcoming and querying her about the break-in, and she thanked each and every one of them for being so supportive. Took her forever to reach her seat.

By the time she did, she had a bean burrito with extra jalapenos, and a sampling of mini-quesadillas. A ginger ale to drink.

Suddenly famished, she hadn't swallowed the first bite before Stan arrived, waved across the room at her, walked around Brice, and waded to the private table.

Brice stormed out.

Stan ate half her quesadillas before the waitress took his order. "These damn things are like popcorn," he said, licking cheese off a finger. Then he smiled. "We got some good people on this beach."

She liked his use of *we*. Stan might be a born-and-raised Bostonian, but he'd sunk roots into Edisto. He tried not to lean in and be obvious, but the room was noisy, she was short, and his voice could boom if he wasn't careful. "Get anything out of him last night?"

"A name. Javier Harred," she said, letting him have the last snack on the plate. "Undercover agent who also was the one who shot Mark in the leg and earned him his early retirement. Supposed to be getting out of jail any time now. That's it."

"That's it?" he said, taking a quick glance at the kitchen for Mark. "You ought to be able to take that and run."

"Got the FBI already checking for me," she said. "Don't talk to

Mark about any of this, okay? I'm trying to give him time to come to me on his own. A lot of pieces are still missing." She lowered her voice more. "Someone left a bullet on *my* front porch this morning."

Stan's brows went up then quickly down as Mark pushed through the kitchen door. "Got more appetizers coming for you, Sunshine. Stan's order came through and I put two and two together." He pulled up a chair. Three was the max at the small table, four if their knees bumped. Callie waited for Mark to keep the conversation going, but he didn't. His ears were engrossed in the room's activity, his attention only halfway on Callie and Stan.

"So, what did you think about the psychic?" Stan asked. "Did y'all meet this morning?"

Mark shook his head, as if he'd tossed this silliness aside. "These people . . ." and he dwindled off. He was touched by the community's endorsement and chose to focus on that. Who could blame him? Stan's meal came to the table, and Mark did his usual scrutinizing of the plate before nodding for the waitress to set it down.

"Sophie said you were down a person," Callie said, after a thanks to the girl.

A quick furrow replaced his positivity. "Wesley."

Callie lowered her fork. "He's the last person I'd expect. Is he sick? Or his mother maybe?" She knew the family that lived a few miles north of the beach, back on the bigger island. He was probably one of the nicest young men his age on the island. Employees came and went in a seasonal beach environment, the on- and off-vacation periods making running a business a roller coaster ride. Mark had dug down and hired him full time, to keep him on the payroll so nobody else snared him away. Wesley had remained for sixteen months straight, thus far, making his absence all the stranger.

"He didn't call." Mark grinned at a familiar person who'd tipped him a nod.

"Want me to go check on him?" she asked.

"Not alone, I don't."

Stan cut her a glimpse. Who told a seasoned police chief it might be too dangerous for her to do a simple health-and-wellness check on a citizen? Much less say it like an order?

"Anything new I need to be aware of?" She'd check on Wesley if she wanted to. "I mean, besides Wesley being AWOL. This is not like him."

Mark's glance took a fast bounce off Stan.

"He knows," she confirmed. "All of it."

Mark's mouth flatlined, but then eased as he reminded himself who Stan was and had been, and in whom Callie had confided long before Mark was in her life. Of course Stan knew.

"I made some calls," Mark finally said.

Callie set her fork down this time, sliding her plate back. "I'm listening."

"Javier's release date from jail was two weeks ago," he said.

Callie wasn't surprised. "I grabbed his driver's license pic and notified my officers already," she said. "Who else would leave his Lone Ranger bullet as a calling card?"

Stan aimed the end of a half-eaten quesadilla at Mark. "A .41 caliber is mighty defining. Rather stupid announcing yourself like that."

A cook pushed the kitchen door open and poked his head through. "Hey, Boss?"

Mark held up a finger saying he'd be right there, and the young chef retreated. Mark pushed himself back from the table. "Not defining," he said.

Callie considered Stan then looked back to Mark. "Pardon?"

"Javier didn't do anything," he said, rising. "He was murdered four days before he was to get out." He pushed the chair back in and vanished into the kitchen.

Stunned, Callie watched him, then turned to Stan. *What the hell?*

Chapter 7

CALLIE STARTED TO get up and march into the kitchen, take Mark out the back door, and demand details. Leaving her with the simple statement Javier Harred had been murdered only confused matters. Then who planted the bullets? Who broke into El Marko's? Her mission was simple now . . . dig deeper into her Cajun boyfriend's head. And past.

Did Javier have family that might seek vengeance? A friend, maybe? Or who had he been undercover with . . . who sought retribution, and now pursued Mark? She just didn't know enough detail to even begin to answer the myriad of questions she had.

Like why would anyone pursue Mark this late in the game? They'd taken care of Javier, or she could assume. Were they, whoever they were, after Mark now?

Believing the culprit was Javier had made more sense than the mess she had now.

Stan placed a hand over hers. "Don't. Sit here, finish your lunch, and let's think this through." He returned to eating as if Mark hadn't said more than he was out of queso for the chips.

She shoved a bite of burrito in her mouth and chewed it as if it deserved an execution. "He's investigating on his own," she said behind the swallow. "That's my guess. He isn't telling us everything. All I get are dribbles. First a name. Then a murder." She chased the swallow with the ginger ale.

"He's scared," Stan said.

"Mark doesn't get scared. He's rational," she said, adding, "most of the time."

"He's scared because he has someone to be scared for," he clarified. "You're the badge on Edisto. This bullet-dropping person is bound to run across your path. Mark has history, and his training is foreshadowing what could happen. When the clue is a bullet, the answer is usually violence."

She leaned in, whispering through her teeth. "Don't you think I'd be safer if I knew what to expect?"

"Not if he can't tell what to expect." Stan shrugged. "He's off his game, Chicklet."

His fifteen-year-old nickname for her gave her a quick taste of solace—reminding her she wasn't alone even if she didn't have Mark as a sounding board right now, and she took a breath. He continued. "Let's say he doesn't want to tell you anything until he gets his feet under him. Give him a day, maybe two."

"You're saying to sit on my damn hands?" The words almost came out as a hiss. "Wouldn't Brice love that? The person is on my beach, Stan. He could be in this very room, watching, and we have zero idea who they are and what they look like."

Stan threw one of the appetizers on her plate and shoved it to her. "Brice is the least of your concerns, so forget about him. Right now cool your jets. Nothing says you can't do your thing while Mark does his."

"We'll be crossing each other's paths."

He shrugged again. "At which time he'll realize he needs to work with you, not against you. I taught you to read people better than this, Chicklet."

"Hey, y'all." Sophie squatted down, head at tabletop level. "What're y'all so serious about over here? I could feel your secret-agent vibes from across the room."

Sheepish at not having seen her friend slip up, Callie relied on the obvious. "We're talking about who might've broken in."

"Well," Sophie said, ogling around as if someone might be listening. "Want to double date with Buck and me? Give this a second try without my son and his psycho girl?"

As if Callie hadn't mentioned the break-in at all. Sophie seemed hotter to trot with this beau.

"And me?" Stan inserted with half a smile, welcoming the lightheartedness . . . and the change of subject.

Sophie released one of her infamous eye rolls, her bright-green contacts making the gesture even more flamboyant.

Callie wasn't in the mood for a double date, and Mark for sure wouldn't be in the mood for something so silly, especially after last night. The evening would involve Sophie's flirtations with Buck to show him off, then gossip about Maya would be casually introduced, then she'd talk about whoever else in town had acted other than how Sophie believed appropriate. Humorous on most days, but not this one.

Stan tapped her under the table, and Callie perked, wondering what she had missed.

"I want you to like him," Sophie said, as if she'd had to repeat it. Sophie was a silly goose, but she was a loyal friend.

"Listen, Soph. We're focused on this burglar, and Mark is going to work himself to the bone over the next few days with this crowd. Until we identify who broke in, let's give this a week or two, okay?"

There. *Was that people-slick enough, Stan?* She peeked at him and caught him grinning more, indicating he'd recognized the effort. Ever the boss, he was. She ever the mentee.

But, surprise, Sophie pouted nonetheless. "What about just you then since Mark is busy."

Sophie would never give up, and Callie guessed she could go solo. Mark might appreciate her leaving him out, saving him the trouble. "Okay, sure. When?"

"Tonight?"

She should've guessed. Sophie lived in the moment. "Fine. Time?"

"I get off hostessing here at six. See you at seven."

Sophie stood to leave, and Callie went back to the now-cool food on her plate until a bump set the silverware rattling. Sophie's tight behind had hit the table. "Soph, for God's sake."

Sophie spun, stooping back down again as if nobody could see her if she was low. "She's here."

Callie scanned the room, spotting Zeus's tall frame before seeing his date. "Maya?"

"Yes," Sophie said from behind her front teeth, hunched down.

"Stop this, Soph. She's just another person, and she's no threat to your spiritual calling. Plus, you live here. She doesn't. I don't see her trying to damage your reputation. Be nice. She might be your future daughter-in-law."

"Oh, dear heaven," Sophie said breathlessly. "I never fathomed that." She turned her back to where the couple waited. "I don't think I could handle being called mom by someone who was born when I was in kindergarten."

"You can handle anything, Soph. They're waiting to be seated, by the way. Isn't that your job. . . hostess?"

Sophie rose, ran a hand down her front to sort her beads and remove blouse wrinkles, then in the flip of a switch, she shined her smile and strutted across the restaurant. Picking up two menus, she waved her hand toward an empty table against the far wall, leading them, dropping the menus, and leaving without a word. Zeus smiled at Maya. Maya's smile shined back at him. They hadn't said the first thing to Sophie they were so entranced with each other.

Callie'd had enough of her lunch, having started and stopped too many times for it to be palatable anymore. She stacked her plate atop the empty appetizer saucer to make room for her drink and elbows to talk the case with Stan.

"I'm thinking of researching Javier's relatives," she said. "See just who and what we might be dealing with. Then from there, check obituaries. But if I start snooping at SLED, which I really want to do, it'll get back to Mark, which I'd like to avoid."

"For now, stop just short of the kind of snooping that creates red flags. Do the other research first," Stan said, stacking his clean plate atop the others. A waitress noted and swooped in to take them all, leaving him room for elbows as well. "I say give him a day or two."

In silence they watched the room, Callie aware that Stan was like her in thinking this anti-Mark person might be a body at one of the tables, eating a burrito like the average person, taking in Mark's work, his life, and with whom he interacted. Familiar with the locals, the two of them scrutinized every tourist, noting whether they seemed natural or nervous, and how many times they might regard the small private table near the kitchen.

This unknown person had already identified her in Mark's life, per the bullet on her porch. She was thankful it was her, and not anyone else. She was glad she sat with Stan and not an ignorant citizen, in case someone watched. She wasn't happy Sophie was so obvious, though.

"They wouldn't come here if they knew Mark," Stan said. "He'd spot them."

"No way Mark could spot all the man's relatives, friends, or acquaintances."

"Are we sitting here the rest of the day?" he asked. "If so, I need some coffee."

Callie called this working, but after Stan's nudge, it didn't feel very productive. "Want to come to the office with me?"

"Got nothing better to do," he said, polishing off his beer.

They waited around for Mark, but he didn't come out, probably taking up the slack minus Wesley, which made her rethink her plans. He lived about ten miles outside of town. "Did you walk here?" she asked.

"Yep."

"Then hop in my car. Let's go someplace else first."

Mark would understand their leaving. He was pretty wrapped up in himself anyway and might even be relieved they weren't keeping an eye on him.

They wove themselves through the diners, thanking Sophie on the way out. In her patrol car, Callie moved her computer and workstation around to make room for Stan. "Mind if we check on Wesley?"

"Nah. I'm just along for the ride. Just don't roll down the windows," he said. "This pollen crap you have down here is tearing up my sinuses."

"Carolina snow," she said, not as bothered by it as most. Cars were covered with it, but the closer you were to the waves, the less it invaded your nose and mouth, watering your eyes. The breezes off the Atlantic kept it pushed back. Out away from the water, the golden pollen glistened on everything it touched. "Beauty comes with a price."

They headed out, crossed Scott's Creek on the edge of town, and made their way onto the big island. This being Monday with some of the area schools on break, the weather particularly bright, dry, and seductively warm compared to a mere week or two ago, traffic knotted entering and leaving Edisto Beach. Some were leaving, having arrived early enough to have already earned their early-season sunburn, while others were just getting there, hoping three or four hours might provide their introductory tan.

"Hate tourists," he said.

Callie gave him a snorted laugh. "Says the man who was one before he moved here. Every one of these people wishes they could live here and be like you. It's how these houses turn over so fast and furious. People come here, fall in love with a lifestyle you are blessed to have full time, and start driving up and down the streets house-shopping. A few of them buy. Beach residences become too much work post-hurricane then become beach rentals. Before they realize it, their beach dream is costing them an arm and a leg, and up it goes for sale. Wainwright Realty has probably sold some of these houses ten times, making thirty to eighty thousand a pop."

Stan's head pivoted on his thick neck at a tiny SUV with a surfboard sticking out its rear window, almost as long as the car. "Crazy loons." He turned back around. "Maybe I need to date Janet Wainwright and get a piece of that action."

"I'd pay good money to see that." She chuckled to herself, then chuckled again at that image. Her six-foot burly, barrel-chested, crewcut, fifty-five-year-old buddy getting down with a sixty-five-year-old, retired Marine drill sergeant whose arsenal exceeded that of the entire Edisto Police Department. After a second, she worried Janet might take him up on any hint of an offer. He was the closest personality out here who could handle her.

Her humor ebbed. God, she could actually see them as a thing.

CALLIE TURNED DUE east onto Indigo Hill Road, where Wesley lived with his mother. His cousins and a couple aunts occupied similar small, fifty- to sixty-year-old siding houses a mile down. She found no sign of Wesley's old Toyota sedan with mismatched hubcaps, the weathered finish leaving doubt as to whether the original paint would be gray or blue. His car was often the family's community vehicle.

"This boy's a good one," Stan said, as Callie pulled in the dirt drive.

"His momma raised him well, for sure," she said, getting out of the car, wishing the kid would break free and venture into the real world. The island had limited income opportunity but strong magnetic pull on people's roots, so a smart, hard-working soul like Wesley had few options to make something of himself.

Wesley had worked hard during high school and after doing minimum-wage seasonal work when thirty hours a week was the best money a restaurant worker could get. Until Mark came along. Mark pushed him up to thirty-eight hours a week year round and five dollars more per hour than Wesley had gotten anywhere else, the result being a damn fine employee everyone wished they'd courted better sooner and a kid deeply loyal to Mark. Such unnatural behavior for him to skip work.

"Coming?" she asked.

"Nope. Don't want to taste any more pollen than I have to. We'd also resemble a posse."

She walked up, took the wooden steps, and rapped on the screen door. Screens were an absolute necessity with the Lowcountry's array of no-see-ums, mosquitoes, and assorted stinging, flying, biting bugs. This screen was like most others these spring days, coated in yellow, some of it puffing off with the vibration of her knock, but the spring beauty of the lavender George Tabor azaleas beside the steps made you overlook the pollen.

Ms. Josephine Pritchard came to the door in a lightweight housedress, mule slippers on her feet, a dishtowel in her hands. "Hey, Chief. Something wrong?"

"Hey, Ms. Pritchard. Nothing's wrong as far as I'm aware. Was hoping to catch up with Wesley. Is he in?"

The woman was Callie's age, on the slim side, a sweet expression ever present in the early creases around her eyes. She exuded a warmth everyone liked, explaining a lot about how gentlemanly Wesley was. His smile resembled hers.

"Chief, just call me Josephine, all right?" But she still seemed wary, because Josephine knew police didn't just visit your home on a whim. "He's gone to work." Her puzzlement showed in answering, because Callie's coupling with Mark had long become common knowledge on the island and the beach. In other words, she ought to know that already.

Callie believed her. "Did he take the car?"

The mother's sweetness dimmed. "Normally does. Why?"

Mothers and their children was a relationship Callie knew better than to antagonize. You didn't rattle mothers until necessary, and you didn't always rat out kids to their mothers, either. "El Marko's was vandalized early yesterday morning. Mark managed to get it open today, and the place is unexpectedly slammed with customers. Wesley didn't come in, and we couldn't get him to answer his phone. Just wanted to make sure nothing was wrong."

The mother's soft scowl crossed into a hard frown. "I didn't hear anything about that, but I'm assuming he left here for work." Clearly, she questioned why Wesley hadn't been open with her. Callie pondered the same thing.

Josephine looked past Callie at the patrol car. "You came with back-up to discuss this? What aren't you telling me?"

Callie released a slight laugh at Stan's prediction coming true. "Him? He's a friend. My old boss from years ago. You've heard of Stan, the Hawaiian-shirt man with the Boston accent. Used to be a cop, and sometimes I let him ride along to make him feel good about the old days."

Some of the wrinkles eased out of the woman's forehead. "Yes, I have." Her focus went back to Callie. "Still, should I be worried?"

"No, ma'am. Sounds like a misunderstanding. Can you call him for me?"

Josephine went inside and returned with an older-model Android phone to her ear, waiting for Wesley to pick up. "Went to voice mail," she said. "That boy knows better than to dodge my calls." She dialed again with the same result. This time she left a message only a mother could leave, a statement wrapped in scolding.

Callie didn't want to stir up family trouble. "Well, when he gets in, tell him to call Mark about his hours at work. I'm sure it's just a mistake."

"Will do," she replied. "And thanks for telling me my boy done skipped work."

Callie held up a palm. "No, listen. We love Wesley to pieces. He's a good guy. Don't be too hard on him."

Josephine gave her a smile, but Callie read that motherly expression. The one that said her child had some explaining to do. Even with Wesley being twenty-two, he was her child and living under her roof. Rules were rules.

Callie turned and took the three wooden steps down to the gravel walk. Something rolled under her foot on the second step, but she caught herself on the board railing, snaring a splinter in her hand.

"Whoa, watch yourself," Josephine called, opening the screen to check on her. "Sometimes my grands leave sticks and rocks and things around here. Are you all right?"

Instinctively, Callie searched at her feet for the offender that tripped her up. She was going to kick it off the step and out of anyone else's way, but Josephine stooped down and retrieved the item first. Callie's blood froze.

A .41 caliber bullet.

Callie waved at Stan.

He got out of the vehicle, standing beside the car with the door open. "What do you need?"

"Bring me an evidence bag," she said.

"Good Lord," said Josephine, frozen in place. "Take it, take it."

"Hold on. Hold on," Callie said, until Stan came up, holding the bag open for the mother to drop the bullet into.

Josephine did so, yanking her hand back like the bullet was a snake able to bite her back. "Nobody's been shooting around here. Not since deer season anyway, and even then not around our yards. That's not even a spent one, is it?"

"No, ma'am, it isn't. When's the last time you were out on these steps?"

The woman mashed her lips, narrowing her eyes to think, the hand that held the bullet up against her chest. "About nine this morning, maybe? Swept them off and weeded a little around the flowers. This time of year, I just like being around them."

Callie sealed it up. "When did Wesley leave?"

Josephine didn't have to think hard. "Ten or so. But he went out the kitchen door, Chief. He wouldn't have come this way."

The culprit would not have known Wesley favored the side door. Callie stood, unable to take her eyes off the cartridge, Josephine's attention glued to it as well. "And he drove off?"

"He took the keys, and the car isn't here, so how else did it get gone?" she said, getting short at so many questions about her son's comings and goings with none of them explaining why. "What's going on, Chief? Who loses bullets? Who loses them at my house?"

Then before Callie could answer, the mother put her own two and two together, and words stumbled out in defense. "My son doesn't have a gun. I don't have a gun. Nobody in this house has a gun. My nephews hunt," she said, pointing across the street and down. "But they haven't been here today. Or yesterday, for that matter. And it ain't hunting season."

"Any of them use a .41?" Callie asked. Not likely but she had to ask.

"I'm not versed in guns." Josephine wrung hands in her dishtowel, as if she had to keep her hands busy not to get upset. She spoke in clipped phrases. "The boys aren't home. They're at work. Our boys are taught to keep busy, stay out of trouble. Want me to ask them? A .41, you say?"

Callie could tell her not to, because if any of them did own that unique a weapon, it would quickly disappear, but to tell her to keep quiet would be a waste of breath. Once Callie left, Wesley's mother would be all over her family asking questions about guns and her son's activities of late. She'd talk to her sisters, and they'd be all over the rest of the family. The cat was out of the bag.

"Ma'am, somebody could've just lost their souvenir," Stan said. He reached into his own pocket and pulled out a keychain with a bullet casing dangling from it.

While Stan had Josephine's attention, Callie did a quick scout of the grounds around the steps, against the porch, under the azaleas.

"You aren't hunting for more of these, are you?" the mother asked, wary, almost scared.

"No, ma'am. Don't worry."

But Josephine held questions in her eyes. Callie tried to smile to give the woman peace. "Don't worry," Callie said. "Just tell Wesley that Mark needs him. You have a good rest of your day." She added, "These azaleas are just lovely. What do you put on 'em to make them so pretty?"

"Coffee grounds," she said. "Wesley and I have our coffee each morning then dump the grounds around the plants."

Callie smiled and nodded for Stan to head back to the car. "Thanks, Josephine. I'm going to start doing that when I plant new azaleas around my house."

"Not too much on new plants, Chief. You'll burn 'em."

Callie nodded. "Thanks. You have a good day."

She kept the smile on as they backed out of the drive and returned toward Highway 174.

"Is the kid missing?" Stan finally asked, waiting to get out of view of the Pritchard house before talking.

"Yeah," she said. "And I want to find him ASAP. I've got no authority out this way off the beach to start asking to see people's guns, but little chance somebody out here hunts with that caliber either."

She radioed Thomas, not wanting to put out an official notice about a missing young man just yet, and told him to be on the lookout for Wesley, and to tell the others as well. No description necessary. Everyone knew who he was.

"Surely they haven't graduated to kidnapping?" Stan said.

"Not making that leap yet," she said. "They could've just threatened him and scared him into hiding. He wouldn't have informed his mother to keep her ignorant of the danger, for her own well-being." She drove a little ways. "Maybe this was aimed at Mark, too. Who knows? We need to tell him, though." And ask if he'd heard from anyone. Anyone he might've *forgotten* to tell her about. She intended to hammer the heck out of the man until he painted details for her on everything crossing his mind.

"Agreed."

Callie'd seen no need to question Josephine about a note. If she'd not seen the bullet until then, she hadn't seen the note. However, Wesley might have, and he might've taken it with him. He might've been too scared to touch the bullet. He may have missed the bullet altogether.

The note might've told him to disappear. That's the story she'd lean on for now. She told herself it made the most sense. She prayed she was right.

Chapter 8

ON THE WAY back to the beach. Callie tried to mentally visualize the people who'd been at El Marko's when she was there. She could name over half of them as residents. The other half consisted of couples, families, and no singles. If the break-in artist was there, they'd come with a partner to avoid attention, but then there *were* two different vandals.

"Might be two working together," Stan said.

He never failed to read her mind. "Yep. Not a very tight timeline other than the break-in happened one night and the bullet at my house twenty-four hours or so later. The one at the Pritchard house happened between nine this morning and when we arrived, but the fact that Wesley missed work tells me before he left. . . ." She paused. "Bet he got a note."

Stan grunted in agreement. He'd been quite taken with the concept of a note from the outset, claiming it referenced premeditation, Escalation, and emotional attachment. So why hadn't Mark gotten a note with his bullet? He'd even suggested an endgame in mind that the note might refer to.

She agreed though they were still very much in the dark.

She and Stan thought in silence all the way to El Marko's, pulling into the drive, having to park two rows over due to the crowd. Callie didn't have one foot out of the door before Maya waved from the walkway in front of the restaurant.

She spoke something to Zeus, then headed toward them. "Callie," she hollered. "We've got to talk."

Callie spoke across the car hood to Stan. "They arrived to eat right before we left. For God's sake, have they been waiting for us?"

"For you, maybe."

They reached talking distance. "Kinda busy right now, Maya. Sorry we missed our meeting this morning, but some work issues demanded our attention. Not sure how long you'll be on Edisto, but we can reschedule."

The little lady didn't seem to hear. "After meeting y'all last night, I went home and did some remote viewing. I saw something, and you need to be cognizant of it."

Home. As if Zeus's boat were home. Sophie would have a conniption fit hearing that, but that wasn't what intrigued Callie. She turned her head, as if she hadn't heard right, but she was sure she had. *Remote viewing.* Viewing via what kind of camera? In person? Binoculars? "I'm listening."

Maya panned the area. "Can we talk somewhere else? Say, on the boat?"

"Is that where you did your remote viewing?"

"Yes."

"Then sure. We'll follow you. Where's he moored today?"

"The marina," Maya said. "Way down at the end, so we won't be interrupted."

Callie nodded and turned back to Stan. "Want to come along?"

"Sure," he said. "I rather enjoy being your sidekick, Chief." He got back into the car.

"I'm intrigued as to what she spotted from that slip at the marina. Help me read between the lines here, Boss. Not sure this lady could speak plain, straightforward English."

"Ain't that the damn truth," he said, clicking on his seat belt.

Callie texted Mark before she left the parking lot, informing him where she was headed and that she had already checked on Wesley. He wasn't at home, she said, and left it at that. The bullet had to be explained in person, in her opinion, requiring more explanation and deeper digging, both of which she'd rather do eye-to-eye. She hung up and took Stan to head the short three miles to the marina.

This troublemaker with an affinity for strange ammo remained on Edisto, still active. She was sure of it. Callie would be happy Easter-egg hunting for bullets all day long except she was afraid they led to some sort of scripted ending. She wished she wasn't going to Sophie's tonight, but Mark would be working late anyway.

She drove up Jungle Road, turned right on Lybrand, then followed Docksite Road to the marina. Zeus's Toyota Prius, bright cobalt blue and easily spotted amongst the white, black, and gray vehicles in the Big Bay Creek parking lot, had beaten them there. The couple waited at the Thirsty Fish Tiki Bar, a dock patio behind Pressley's, the current quiet mood so in contrast with the evenings when live music from the likes of Captain Phillip Albenesius or local Sam Plexico drew crowds to drink, dance, and hang alongside the water. Someone was already setting up speakers for later that evening.

Zeus's boat was moored almost at the end, a tenth-of-a-mile walk. The boat had been negotiated in Sophie's divorce, or at least the value of it. She had been married to an NFL player whom she ditched after he'd slept around with a female trainer. At least that's who she caught him with, the rumor mill indicating the trainer wasn't anywhere near the front of the line. Sophie made out well in the split, and like the mama bear she was, she'd nailed down additional funds for the kids.

Fifteen-year-old Sprite had wanted to go to college, so the father set aside an educational fund, gave her a car, and funded a solid bank account with room to spare for college incidentals, an amount which could buy the child a moderate house. Seventeen-year-old Zeus had been more the free spirit of his mother, in spite of their butting heads, with college nowhere in his future. Instead, he requested a boat to handle fishing charters for a living, that had to come with living quarters for a place to live. He was young enough to crave escaping his mother's oversight, but not old enough to fully grasp his dad's financial offer, and he sank all his eggs in one basket. Half a million dollars later, the kid had what he wanted, a Boston Whaler 380 Outrage, the dad warning the kid to watch what he wished for, because he was stuck with that and no more. Sophie hadn't argued, figuring the lesson would play out. At least he lived on the coast where the boat had a market if he needed to sell it when the novelty wore off.

The kid had proven them all wrong. Zeus Bianchi embraced the gift with underestimated savvy. Five years later he'd made a living out of Bianchi Charter as well as a home, and not asked for a cent more because he didn't need it. His schedule filled quickly, and he could operate fifty-two weeks a year if he didn't want his down time to be mellow and chill. He worked closer to forty-two, the rest being whatever he wanted it to be, and as the youngest member of the chamber of commerce, he had saved enough to be respected as a contributing member of the community. Regardless of how Bohemian he was, he had a mind for business.

Zeus led them down the planked walkway to *Heaven's Door*, thirty-eight feet of vessel with three Mercury outboards, a boat even wealthy folks waited until middle age to afford. Some tourists attributed the name as Christian and loved the connection. Others attributed the name as a hat tip to a slurry Bob Dylan song from the seventies. The Bob Dylan crowd was correct.

Familiars threw up a hello as he passed. "Hey, Zeus. Nice day for going out."

Others recognized Callie. "Chief, how's Mark?"

"Stan, my man, how many of those damn flower shirts have you got?"

The answers, smart retorts, and thanks took a few minutes, but that was okay. That was Edisto. Folks waved here, and people, the locals anyway, stopped to chat and be cordial. Some asked if El Marko's would be shut down any length of time. Others asked Zeus when he was opening back up for tourists, because visitors were asking.

"Probably next week," was his answer. He didn't like working a lukewarm market.

Sophie might be an oddball, but she'd raised bright kids.

Finally they made it down the marina walk, and Zeus helped everyone onto the boat, then went below and brought back up four bottles of fitness water. Stan frowned reading the label, then went along with the gesture, a sip, and then a pucker, deeming the drink not so bad.

The view of Big Bay Creek calmed Callie, and she settled back against the boat cushions. Gazing north then south, she counted six kayakers. Yep, tourists were arriving. In another month, this marina would be hopping with boats, kayaks, and wall-to-wall people itching to see, feel, and smell salt water, pretending they lived here. She and her officers would be busy with the minor infractions of drinkers, speeders, and squabblers. At least she hoped that's all they had to deal with. A Charleston beach had not long ago stopped speeders carrying handguns. Four teenagers were searched, one possessing a weapon having been used in a murder.

Edisto wanted no piece of that, but post-Covid, people who'd never heard of Edisto but were hungry for travel began flooding the area. Along with the sea of new people came an elevated level of crime. The department had six uniforms, and Callie wasn't far from asking for two more. Not that council would approve the request, but at the rate rentals had almost doubled since the pandemic, and raised rate of beach house property taxes, they should.

In the meantime, staffing shortage or not, she needed to stop whoever was infiltrating her beach with an axe to grind with Mark. He wouldn't be hiding thoughts from her if it wasn't dangerous, and coming to the boat to talk to Maya and Zeus felt rather negligent in that light. This visit had to be short.

Maya seated herself ninety degrees to Callie's left and leaned back on her cushion. "Is this lovely or what?" She shut her eyes and basked in the afternoon sun. Her respite with Zeus over the last few weeks had given her an attractive tan, making Callie wonder what sort of tan lines defined her at her age. With the hippie vibe of these two, there might not even be any.

"We don't have time to relax," Callie said, fighting the desire to lean back like Maya. She hadn't time to kick back with three bullets in evidence and their owner loose on the beach. "Explain to me about your remote viewing," she said. "How are you watching, who are you watching, and why the heck have you been doing it?"

Zeus laughed but didn't try to answer the questions, drinking his drink and turning to watch up the creek toward the open water where the dolphins were more likely to play.

Maya set her bottle in a cup holder and leaned forward, elbows to her knees. "Remote viewing. It's a clairvoyant's way of attempting to see the past or the future, sometimes the details of the present. It's an attempt to receive impressions remotely, thus, remote viewing. It's used for predictions. I've used it for solving cold cases and doing personal readings."

Well, damn. Not what Callie expected nor had time for. Stan's grunt to her left said he agreed. "We didn't come here for a reading, Maya." Callie set her water aside.

"Please." Maya laid a hand on Callie's knee. "Give me five minutes."

"Five minutes," she said, mentally agreeing to give Maya to the end of her own bottled water, then she and Stan had things to do and places to be. She'd hoped to return to the office and research Javier's family tree, for starters.

Maya continued. "After last night, I went by El Marko's for a few moments, then came back here afterwards. After grounding and readying myself, I tried to open up to the gestalts of Mark's world, specifically the present involving the break-in."

"Gestalts?" Callie asked, trying to avoid Stan for fear of seeing a comical expression. She'd heard even self-important spiritualists could have real information if you knew how to sort facts from guesses. She wasn't sold yet, but she'd promised five minutes.

Maya turned more serious. "The *thingness* of a viewing. Sometimes they form from an array of parts. Can be a person, place, thing, event. It can be coordinates like letters and numbers or as detailed as longitude and latitude. Not like searching the internet and getting a precise picture of what you seek, but more of a sense of it. You may not see the intricacies, but you sense the importance of the whole." She was into this and reached for Callie's hand before drawing back. "As much about the subtle as the defined."

Callie tried not to act lost . . . or unconvinced.

But Maya caught the feelings. "A clairvoyant needs experience to interpret what they see, Callie, and some people are more in tuned than others." Zeus grinned back at her, his thick curls dancing in the ocean breeze. "He's been a good student, and he's practicing to get better," she said. "He has a bit of a gift, which I attribute to his mother."

Callie started to ask if Sophie was aware of Zeus practicing visions, or whatever this was, with Maya. For someone else to be teaching her son a craft that Sophie owned down to her soul, didn't sound like something she would embrace. That had inevitable disaster written all over it, but it wasn't Callie's business, even if Zeus was practically dating his mother's likeness. She didn't want to think about that too hard.

"Had no idea you had such talent, Zeus," Callie said, remaining noncommittal, telling herself to not mention Sophie.

"Yeah," Zeus added, sliding his words like he always spoke. "The past, present, and future exist in the Matrix, the Collective Consciousness."

Now all Callie could think about was the actor Keanu Reeves.

Zeus continued, proud of his new ability. "The Matrix is shared with the subconscious mind via a funnel, then along a signal line. There's a continuum of subtleties there if you can prep yourself to get beyond the noise and ideas of your daily life."

"The viewing?" Callie said, controlling a sigh and taking note she only had a third of her drink left.

Zeus nodded. "If you can settle and sink into this state, you receive information. It can be on a continuum, or like a radio frequency."

"Son," Stan started, more willing to cut this short. "We've got to get back to Mark."

"Just a minute," Zeus said, and Stan sat stiffer at the young pup semi-correcting the big dog. "To appreciate what Maya's done," Zeus continued, "you have to understand the process. Otherwise it sounds like hocus-pocus."

"Well," Stan said, "you read my mind on that one."

Zeus's good-naturedness ebbed at the comeback.

"It's all right," Maya said, her smile soft and assuring. "Might be better if I describe what I saw."

"Good idea," Callie said, "but Stan is right. Let's wrap this up."

Maya nodded. "I made an ideogram. Briefly, an ideogram is pen on paper while in your state, where ideas, images, and so on travel through you. It can be a piece of something or can be symbolic. Can be a building in the distance versus where a body is actually positioned in a nearby park, or a sense of water versus land. The process makes you note energy, senses, color, landscape, lines, movement, the list is endless." She stopped there as if everyone had to grasp that much first.

Callie finished her drink. This had turned into Maya demonstrating her prowess to a captive audience instead of delivering facts. Maya had made an impression on them for sure, but not the one she probably wanted. "Maya, we have to go."

"She's solved cases for law enforcement," Zeus bragged.

As the website said. "Appreciate the drink and the visit, but—"

"Mark's in danger," Maya said.

Callie dropped her head, her patience thin. "We're aware."

"His partner is dead," she added. "While he didn't do it by his own hand, he started the momentum to cause his death."

Callie raised her head. How did she know Mark had a partner, much less that he was dead . . . even less that he was murdered?

Unless there'd been an obituary. Unless Maya had researched Mark at great length and put him together with his past, in which case, Callie was suspect of her.

"What's your interest in Mark?"

Maya hadn't expected that question. "Um, none. I just saw things revolving around him."

"Then get to the point, Maya. What exactly did you see?" There was a strong chance Maya was getting her intel from someplace more tangible than visions in the clouds, but the information might tell Callie as much or more about the seer than what she claimed to see. You kept your mind open at times like these. You let people talk as much as they wanted to.

You studied people, often times differently than they assumed you did.

Maya calmly said, "I see a man on a road, unable to walk."

"That could be a bum on the street," Stan said, having had enough.

But Maya ignored Stan, and focused on answering Callie, regarding her deeply as if she fought through to her mind.

"Who?" Callie asked. "Give me a name." That description could just as well be Mark, back when Javier shot him.

"I rarely get names," she said. "Dark hair?"

That could be either or both Javier and Mark, and no telling who else.

"I see a woman in the background."

"A woman was there when the man went down?"

"Not necessarily. She could be shaken, angry, related . . . an observer. She's affected by all of this."

"Affected by what, exactly?"

"The old and the new," Maya replied. "There is a past and there is a present, and there's a damn strong future."

No, not vague at all. "A wife? A daughter?" Callie asked.

"Unclear. Could be related by association or by blood, but I'm leaning blood. But the blood is confusing since so many people were shot."

She could have seen the case on the news way back when. Again, with the ambiguity.

"The man on the ground is surrounded by bullets."

"Casings or bullets?" Callie asked. The aftermath of a shooting, the bullets they were finding now, or something symbolic?

"I just see bullets. Not sure what a casing is."

"A spent bullet. One already shot."

"I couldn't tell that."

"Is the man dead?" Callie asked.

"Possibly. The energy around him is still."

Callie hadn't found out yet exactly how Javier was taken out. Mark hadn't said. The bullets could be from the five-year-old shooting or the ones being found over the last three days. They could be representative of Javier or Mark. Javier could've had a wife, a daughter, a mother, a girlfriend, a mistress, and so on. Possibly even a fellow agent.

Interpretation suddenly had a very broad meaning. Reading tea leaves and Tarot cards came with a certain talent in savvy interpretation. It's how clairvoyants made their money, by being convincing and coincidental.

Oh, God, look at me. I'm taking in this junk like it contained legitimate clues to something. Scratch this. "Thanks for the help," Callie said, and rose hunting a trash can.

Zeus took the bottle, then Stan's. "She was really bothered about this last night," he said. "Please don't brush her off."

But Maya's vision appeared little more than randomness cobbled together to sound like a crime scene. "Appreciate the hospitality, but we must be gone." Callie didn't want to tell the woman where she was close and where she wasn't, especially where she was abstruse as hell.

"Yep," Stan said, standing with a deep sigh as if he'd been waiting hours for this moment.

"Wait," Maya pled, with earnest concern. She reached for Callie's arm, pinching the sleeve. "Have y'all been finding fat bullets on Edisto?"

Callie slowly turned. Fat wasn't the term she'd use, but to someone unaffiliated with ammo and firearms, she could quasi-see how the word might fit. "Why?"

"They are connected to Mark. And they'll keep coming until—" She sighed. Clearly, she'd been disbelieved before and seemed unsure whether continuing her explanation mattered . . . unless she was delivering an overly dramatic pause.

Callie understood the feeling of being dismissed. She'd endured it on multiple occasions when she pursued a situation based on gut, or worse, when she chased a case everyone else considered over and done with or no longer held merit. Being underestimated and fighting for your truth could be a lonesome feeling.

"Until what, Maya?" The incomplete hook of a thought had snared Stan.

"Until somebody dies," she said. "I just kept feeling death."

Zeus pulled her to him. "Tell them when, sweetness. Tell them what you told me."

Maya snuggled up under Zeus's tall frame for assurance. "Within a week after the first bullet," she said, her front arm reaching around his middle. "There's a clock on this thing, y'all."

Callie stopped in her tracks. "Somebody dies within five days?"

"Maybe. Possibly. Something happens. And I see six bullets, not counting the one that winds up being shot."

"So, someone gets shot?"

By Friday, too.

"I believe so. At least shot at, but like I told you, I'm sensing death." She took Callie's hand. "You are in his circle. That puts you in danger as well."

Three bullets in two days already. Today was Monday.

The forecast—accurate or not, vague or not, suspicious or not— sent chills up Callie's spine, and Stan's glance at her wasn't too at ease either. But why was Maya sticking her nose in this at all?

Chapter 9

THROUGH HER remote viewing, Maya had established a timetable for the bullets and their ultimate destruction of someone on Edisto Beach. Callie and Stan stood stunned, unsure whether to toss her vision as bunk or believe it with a grain of salt. Regardless of the woo-woo aspect, Callie was afraid to dismiss it all. *What if she's right,* gnawed at her. She felt sheepish thinking that, her logic telling her Maya knew too much. But then again . . . *what if?*

Zeus made an urging hand gesture, pushing Maya to continue, to do more to aid her credibility. "Show them your drawing, Maya."

Eager at the suggestion, Maya skittered below deck. Stan sucked on his teeth once, as if speaking in code to Callie. He wasn't complex. He wanted to go. Maya quickly returned, a piece of white paper in hand, and she held it down on a small table anchored to the boat floor.

The eye easily homed in on a raw drawing of a person on the ground. Way in the background was a tiny figure of a woman per the skirt over her stick legs. Their heads had scribbles for dark hair. No real shape to them. Just not bald.

There were pockets of dots here and there. "What are those?" Callie asked.

"My pen on the paper. You hold the device with your non-dominant hand, waiting for the messages. While waiting, while trying to see, while readying yourself to feel, you keep making contact with the paper." She keenly waited for Callie to study the paper more, to ask more.

The bullets were obvious. All six of them encircled the man lying on the ground like a crime scene pose. A building with what appeared to be two stories—the top and bottom different in style—was positioned between the man and the woman. The woman was indeed way off. A straight line with the words *still, minimal energy* lay written to the left, as if it applied to the man.

Below the visuals were questions using the words: *verticals, horizontals, diagonals, topology, mass/density/space,* and *energetics.* Under *senses,* she'd written *black and red for colors, wind or waves for sound, warm for temperature,* and *salty for taste and smell.*

Mark's name was at the bottom.

"No other people? Where am I? Where's, say, Stan? He's Mark's closest friend other than me out here." Where was Javier?

"Don't let his name shock you. He's the easy reference. I need to do this a couple more tries, at which point more details may materialize. Maybe this dead man knew Mark."

"You said the person might not be dead," Callie said.

"True, true, I did."

Callie wanted to be so skeptical as to be a hundred percent dismissive, but she couldn't.

"How many bullets have you found?" Maya asked.

"I'd rather not say," Callie said.

Maya came over from Zeus and reached for Callie's hands, both of them. Callie allowed her to take them, halfway expecting an exchange of energy. What had started out as a patronization of Maya had morphed into a slight sense of concern.

"Be careful," the woman said, squeezing Callie's fingers. "I sense danger around you, too."

"She's the police chief," Stan said under his breath. "Bet your name is on the next sheet of paper," he tacked on.

Maya squeezed again and gently released Callie's hands. "Take care. You know where to find me."

"Much obliged," Callie said, and stepped up to leave the boat, but an urging made her turn back. "May I have the drawing? The ideogram?"

"She usually charges," Zeus said.

"Then never mind." Callie stepped out of the boat, disappointed at this whiff of commercialism that only muddied up anything Maya tried to present. The boy had sales in his nature but combining it with reading the future reeked of nothing but scam.

But Maya rushed over and handed out the paper. "Take it if it helps." She didn't apologize for Zeus, only wishing to please Callie.

Callie took the paper, rolled it up to avoid creases, nodded in appreciation, and left.

Maya and Zeus watched, her having returned to his embrace.

A tad on edge but clearly not wanting to show it, Stan threw his shoulders back as they made their way back up the wooden walkway, the tide high enough to be seen easily through the planks at their feet.

"Where's the *Twilight Zone* music when you need it? They're still watching us, aren't they?"

"Yep," she said, giving the couple a final wave. Callie enjoyed Stan's humor after all that dark talk. "You need to find that ring tone and cue it next time we have a psychic helping us solve crime."

"Hopefully never."

"She knew about the bullets," she said, lowering her voice as they approached the Tiki Bar again.

"Crime plus cops equals bullets," he said in a subdued growl, hushing as folks got within ear shot. "And that drawing was bullshit. A three-year-old could've done better."

"Don't think it was about winning a blue ribbon for artistic ability, Boss."

Callie wasn't eager to blow off the reading just yet. Maya might have feelings, or talent, or whatever you wanted to call it. Sophie did, and though she was the butt of a lot of jokes at her sensations and predictions, she'd been right more times than a few. If Sophie could hit the mark here and there, why not Maya?

But then the investigator in her queried how the psychic conveniently was visiting Edisto when this criminal behavior was going down and could describe things nobody else was aware of. Coincidence wasn't a word in Callie's vocabulary, which upped Maya almost to the level of person of interest.

Time to not only research Javier's history and family, but also Maya's, assuming that was even her name.

They returned to El Marko's to update Mark. Though not quite dinner time, it was close enough for the early diners. Stan held the door open for Callie, and they entered. A young girl manned the hostess station in lieu of Sophie, who, Callie remembered, must be home preparing for their evening social. She hoped Soph didn't skip work, especially with Mark already down a cook.

This late in the day, the aromas seemed more intense, as if more concentrated for the richer, bigger meal. "Want to be my date to dine at Sophie's?" Callie asked as she and Stan made their way to their private table. "If so, don't eat. We're just here to talk to Mark."

He smiled at the same waitress they'd had before. "Just grabbing something to drink," he said when the girl tried to take their order.

The waitress left. Mark would be out any moment. All the employees knew to inform him if Stan, Callie, or any member of the police department or town administration came in.

Mark appeared from the kitchen before Callie's ginger ale and Stan's beer made it to the table. "Find Wesley?"

Callie shook her head. "Was just about to ask if you'd heard from him." She motioned at the empty chair. "Sit a minute."

He did, and leaning in, she kissed him on the cheek, to make their coming in seem informal and social. Plus, she kinda liked kissing the man. He grinned and kissed her back. He wasn't holding a grudge. But then, she hadn't started asking him more questions, either.

"Do I need to leave?" Stan asked, signaling to the door with his cold mug.

"You're fine," she replied. Nobody around them seemed to be listening, so she started filling in Mark. "Wesley's mother says he left for work as usual, and she hasn't seen him since. She couldn't get him on her phone. She's supposed to call when he comes in."

"That doesn't sound good." Mark stared at Callie waiting for the other shoe to fall.

"We found another bullet on his doorstep. His mother hadn't seen it this morning, so we have a rough time frame of between nine and one-ish when it might have been left. At nine she swept the steps and we showed up around one."

Dropping his forehead in his hand, Mark rubbed, thinking . . . hiding his thoughts.

"My guess is that he read the note, was afraid of touching the bullet, and took off based on whatever the note said. I'm not seeing him kidnapped," she said, watching him hard. "That feels over the top."

"You first, me second, and Wesley third," he said, referencing the bullets. "Makes me wonder about that Maya woman's soothsaying." He laughed. Callie didn't. "What?" he said.

"We just left her," she said, and pulled out the ideogram, moving glasses to avoid condensation ruining the paper. "This . . . ideogram, supposedly is her mental visual of whatever this situation is we're dealing with." She tried to explain the body, the woman, the building, and the bullets on the ground without sounding ridiculous.

"You didn't mention the bullets?" he asked.

"No. It's an ongoing investigation."

He pointed to the body. "And again, this might be . . .?"

"A man with dark hair."

"And there are three more bullets to go before one is shot at somebody?"

"Yes," she said.

Mark sat back. "Don't trust her as far as I can throw her."

"She dances around this stuff too close to be totally ignored," Callie said. "I'm checking her out."

Stan stepped in. "Damn dingbat, if you ask me, fella." He took a big swallow of beer and set the mug back down. "Back to the real detective work. Don't discount this person or persons returning. They may not be done."

Callie craved more intel, more to go on, more to chase. "Mark, I need the secrets you're holding back, and I want them all. You owe me as police chief of this town and as your significant other. I've cut you slack to get the restaurant back up running and to let some of the shock wear off, but. . . ." She scouted the room of customers, with more coming in the door. "Not here," she said. "Sophie asked me to dinner, but it won't run late. Afterwards I intend to meet you home at *Windswept* to have a long talk."

"I don't want you involved, I said."

"I'm already involved."

She sighed so damn hard, narrowing her eyes at him and his roadblocks. "Are we still an item?" Then she threw something else at him, harder. "Were we building something . . . real? Or not?"

Stan didn't mention a word, got up, and headed to the men's room.

"Sure we are," Mark said low.

"Then I deserve better respect."

God, it pained her to say these things. And it pained her so much that he remained so entrenched in his past, denying its potential impact on his present.

The five-day timetable stuck in her head, even if the number was set by a psychic. Could be two. Might be ten. She hoped it meant nothing, but the seed had been planted.

"Let me put it this way," she said. "I'll be at *Windswept.* If you arrive after closing down here, you agree to talk candidly to me." She didn't add an *or else*, or what it meant if he didn't show because she didn't want to go there.

The hardness in his face told her that he heard her words as an ultimatum anyway.

"I care," she said, laying a hand on his forearm. "But I also owe Edisto citizens their safety. I can't afford for them to get caught up in whatever is chasing you."

That didn't sit any better with him.

He got up, pushed in the chair, took a pause to think about whether to say more, then didn't. He left.

Stan returned to Callie sitting alone. "Make any headway?"

"We shall see," she said, studying her ginger ale more than Stan, fighting not to be angry . . . unsure whether she had a right to. Mark might show up at home and spill his guts, with this talk having been the catalyst to open the faucet.

Or he might show up having dug in deeper.

Or he might not show up at all.

What now? She wasn't due at Sophie's until seven, and it was too late to get folks on the phone for questions about family histories. She sort of liked having Stan around her as a voice of reason before she rationalized too hard about Mark's obstructive behavior.

"We've got two hours before Sophie expects us," she said, brandishing a smile at a business owner across the room who'd just noticed her. If Mark's nemesis wanted Mark, her, Stan, or even Sophie, they damn sure knew where to find them easily enough.

She pushed back her chair. "Want to inspect how *Chelsea Morning* is coming along?"

"I need to shower before dinner."

"You don't smell too rank to me, and it's not hot enough to get sweated up. But if a cold shower puts you in the right frame of mind, we'll go by your place first, let you throw on some baby powder and change clothes. Makes no sense going to my house first since it's right next door to Soph. Come on."

Soon she sat in Stan's kitchen in his rented house on Pompano Street, drinking a Coke since soft drinks were about all he kept around.

Alone and bored, Callie rose and studied the living area, noting the packs of Big Red cinnamon gum on Stan's desk, the furniture and curtains smelling like the aftershave he'd worn since the day she'd met him as a rookie recruit. She knew him better than almost anyone other than her son. Maybe knew him better than her own mother.

In other words, Stan was her closest ally.

She smiled at his awards on the wall, remembering them on display in his Boston office, recalling which one hung where from her almost daily vantage from the seat she always took across from his desk. He'd trained her, mentored her, worshipped her when she assumed the occasional pedestal, blistered her when she erred, and picked her up when she fell from grace. He made her look inside herself and had no qualms about correction.

She clung to her nickname, Chicklet, able to read his mood from when and how he said it. In an honorable, maybe a bit of suck-up gesture in their early days, she'd brought him a small rectangular box of Chiclets, cinnamon flavor. Not his brand, she learned. He preferred Big Red, a bolder, older brand dating back to before her time on this earth.

But he'd loved the gesture, adding a K to the name, since she was a *chick*, he said, and had called her Chicklet ever since . . . well, when the audience was appropriate.

The shower turned off.

She wandered to the screen porch, not large by island standards, but big enough for three rockers, four if they almost touched and left no room to walk around. The tiny screen kept most of the mosquitoes out, and there was almost nil traffic since Pompano was an off street that dead-ended at the lagoon. His place also backed up against the lot where they'd found a dead body under poison ivy, after a dozer ran over it right before Christmas a year ago, back when she met Mark, quarreled with him, then decided he wasn't that bad of a person to have on Edisto Beach.

Another law enforcement officer finding his way to the beach and leaving the past on the other side of the William McKinley bridge, he'd kept his past to himself. Nothing out of the ordinary since that choice was almost a ritual of the residents, each with some past that didn't merit dredging up. Very few other than Stan, Sophie, and Mark understood Callie's past, and even Sophie hadn't heard it all.

Which explained her gut conflict about forcing his past from him. Mark would have preferred to be known only as retired SLED, half Cajun originally from Louisiana, and a man who limped sometimes from an old *war wound* as he liked to call it. He didn't want any other information added to the equation of how he'd arrived at this point in his life.

Again she studied the plank floor, like she had done coming into the place . . . hunting for a bullet. While she didn't tell Stan, she noticed him scouting the steps on their way up, too. Why not? The rhyme and reason for the bullets wasn't exactly obtuse. Mark's place, Mark's girl-friend's place, Mark's employee's place, why not Mark's best bud's place, unless the person hadn't made that connection quite yet. There was still time. Five days per Maya.

"Chicklet?"

"Coming." She scooted back inside.

He stood in the kitchen, arms wide. "Wanna smell me? All clean and fresh."

She laughed and scrunched her nose once. "I'll trust you on that."

"We going to your place for you to do the same?" he asked.

If she'd wanted to, they would have. He'd have waited like a gentleman, their platonic friendship carved in stone.

They'd crossed that line once. Well, almost. The slip had been in her first months on the island, when she was at her worst and drunk off her ass, and they'd stripped down to a hundred percent nude and slipped under her sheets, fully intending on taking things all the way to glory. An opportune phone call from his ex-wife interrupted them both physically and mentally. Stan, bless him, had been the proper person and nixed their intentions, calling them ill-timed and inappropriate.

She'd have done the deed without reservation that night . . . and would have regretted it to her bones the next morning. And Stan knew that.

The memories made her go up and hug his middle. Not to sniff him, but to say, "I love you, Stan Waltham. Thanks for being my best friend."

He squeezed her back, engulfing her five foot two-ness with his six-foot thick-chested stature. "You all right?" he asked, with one final scrunch.

"Yeah. Just a little unsettled about Mark and the bullets, but we'll figure this out. Like always. Just might need you a little more on this one."

His gravelly laugh, the old aftershave, and the fresh stick of Big Red inside his cheek did her heart good. She pulled back. "We've got just under an hour to walk through my house. I've still got to pick out a few colors, and I hate doing that crap. You want to do it?"

He laughed aloud that time. "Take a gander at this place and ask again."

The kitchen with its dated paneling and Walmart curtains, placemats that didn't match, and an assortment of Rubbermaid cannisters on the counter stained and faded, spoke for him.

But it seemed good because it belonged to Stan.

"Come on," she said. "*Pretend* you have taste and tell me what you think."

They drove the half mile to *Chelsea Morning*. With Daylight Savings Time taking effect the week prior, the sun still shone strong, the light peppering through surrounding trees onto the bare ground around construction. Workers had gone home.

Callie had to prep herself to come to her own home. The original had burned to the ground, killing the woman inside who set the blaze. Callie had taken a few months to decide whether or not to rebuild. The dead woman had been the second person to die there—the first one the son of a neighbor, murdered in front of her eyes.

But her mother and father had built *Chelsea Morning*, where they'd introduced her to Edisto from birth. People had experienced good times in that house. They'd argued and loved, fought and made up, discussed the world and shut doors to it. Those walls had seen birth and death, embraced adult affairs and childhood sea-shell collections. Ultimately, Callie had decided that walking away from *Chelsea Morning* was like walking away from her life, her son's life, and the lives of her family and friends. Good and bad, it was a major thread in the fabric of her being.

Chelsea Morning 2.0 just wasn't going to repeat her mother's style. Same floorplan, give or take, but fake PVC hardwood instead of real since sand scratched the real stuff. She added to the plans a tall, five-foot wooden wainscot around the hallway, living room and kitchen, with shelving at where it met the sheetrock for . . . well, she wasn't sure what for yet. Shells, artwork, knick-knacks, maybe one day the play-dough sculptures and crayon scribblings of grandchildren.

The outside steps numbered twenty like before, with a landing half-way up, and the wood, though treated, remained bare and raw because she hadn't decided on the color. She and Stan started up those stairs, but instead of eyeing the front porch, they watched their feet.

The steps were ten feet wide at the bottom, narrowing to eight by the second flight. "You take the left side," she said. "I'll take the right." She didn't have to say why.

Both hunted for another bullet.

Chapter 10

BY THE TOP STEP, Callie could let out her breath, satisfied at finding fresh lumber, decent workmanship, and no bullets. After taking a moment to experience the view which was now a foot higher than before—and two wider, she and Stan entered the house.

"Close to the same," Stan said, noting the same guest bedroom on the left, then the hallway that led to the living room on the right, the master further on the left, and stairs going up to one more bedroom and bath.

"Found the old plans," she said. "I kind of owed it to Mother to build the same footprint, but nothing else like before. I hate pastels."

"All I see is plywood and bare sheetrock in half the rooms," he said, wandering around the living room and into the kitchen. "Sure seems familiar, though. Surprised you didn't go totally different. You know, for a change of scenery." He meant removal of bad memories, but she understood what he meant.

"Guess I missed the old place," she said, not wanting to go into the philosophical discussion of choosing which memories to toss, which to preserve. That bar where Seabrook sat, for instance, where they shared mint-chocolate-chip ice cream. The bedroom she'd almost slept in with Stan. Jeb's bedroom which had been hers as a child. The side porch where Sophie spent so much time nursing Callie back to health after she'd almost succumbed to pneumonia. The back steps where she'd calmed Sprite late one night when she worried Jeb had set her aside for another. The side porch where she could wave at Papa Beach next door when she was a child. On and on.

The view of the marsh in the back, however, had been altered, giving her less of the neon oranges and golds of a summer sunset off the water. While beautiful to most, the vista too much resembled fire, her phobia, and she owed herself that much peace. Especially since fire had ruined the original structure.

"Well?" she asked when the air had gone too silent.

"Hmm," Stan said, studying walls. "Green?"

"What color green?"

"Um, like the jungle? Or maybe like algae."

Trying to envision algae on her walls, she busted out in laughter and rested a hand on a living-room stud. "Pond scum in this room, maybe?" Then she skittered over to the hallway. "Blue-green marsh algae here accented with a sage green on the wainscot. Like Sophie's sage?"

Stan chuckled. "The color before or after she burns it in here to ward off demons?"

By then she struggled between hee-haws getting the words out. "They make brown algae, you know."

"Put that in the bathroom."

The dam broke, and they both broke down in those deep rolls of hilarity one rarely experiences, and they cried enjoying the never-ending feel to the fun.

This man . . . she loved him to pieces.

Took them a good five minutes to reach the end of the algae dialogue. The laughter waned when they sat on the back steps, and it was then Callie inspected her architectural alterations to the view and determined the changes had been spot on. The glare off the water was hidden, with enough vista open through oaks and palmettos on the lot across Jungle Shores to give her a muted panorama that didn't scream flames.

"This is nice," she said, leaning back on her hands from her seat on the top step, the warmth of the day mingling with the spring chill of night, the breeze caressing and soft.

"Indeed," Stan echoed at her side.

They let silence drop around them, such that they could hear the birds settling in for the night and the nocturnal animals waking up to forage. The clicking of a raccoon could be heard from the shadows of the house across the road, and a squirrel chased another into the branches of her own live oak reaching seventy feet overhead, the only green thing that survived the fire.

"What time is it?" Stan asked.

Callie lifted her phone. "We have ten more minutes."

"Don't want to be early, huh?"

"Just want to enjoy this right here," she said.

Like teenagers, they reared back on elbows, feet stretched out two risers down for her, three for him.

"We're gonna have pollen all over our butts when we get up," she said.

"So much for my shower, huh?"

They relaxed a while more.

"Two minutes till seven," he said.

"Let's go." She stood and reached out a hand to assist him up, him cocking a brow at the audaciousness of her thinking she could pull his dead weight to its feet.

Returning through the house, locking up behind them, they hesitated at the front, again canvassing the stairs sprawling down before them.

"We're obsessing," she said.

"Maybe," he replied, speeding up and going on down in his clumpy way, her fast toe-tapping method beating him to the gravel drive.

"No bullets," she said.

"No bullets," he agreed.

Leaving the car in her drive, they merely walked the thirty yards from her steps to Sophie's. Buck's GMC truck was there. Sophie's powder-blue vintage Mercedes, a nineties make, parked beneath the house like the majority of the vehicles on the island, protected from weather.

Sophie busted out the front door, arms wide at the top of the two levels of stairs, a mirror design of Callie's. "Hey, y'all!" She came to the top step, waiting for her guests. Lowering hands to her hips, she scolded. "Stan, you old copper, you. How dare you crash my little dinner party." Then her smile spread. "Come on. Glad you came."

As she had at her own place, Callie watched for cartridges en route, feeling paranoid and foolish by the time she reached her hostess.

"Come on, come on." Sophie hurrying them inside to where she had waiting vegetable juice poured in heavy-based highball glasses, celery and carrot spears tall and garnishing. "Spotted y'all messing around the house next door and got these ready for you."

Callie took hers, admiring the colors. "These are pretty, Soph. Nice job." She turned her focus into the kitchen. "Hey, Buck. Stan has ideas on the indoor paint. Don't listen to him."

"Awww," Sophie said with a soft pout, hugging Stan. "No respect, huh?"

"None," he said, daring a taste of his drink, deeming it worthy. He knew as everyone else did, that having Callie at a party meant non-alcoholic, and as much as Callie had told them they could imbibe, she appreciated the loyalty of friends in keeping her on the wagon. Sophie had learned to get creative doing so.

"Any new ladies?" Sophie asked her ex-lover.

Callie stopped mid-sip. "Wow, how blunt."

Sophie shrugged. "Hey, I care. I can even line up some if he wants me to."

"Sounds like hookers," he said, plopping himself into the recliner with his refreshment.

"Not all of them," she said back, giving rise to laughter.

Buck stooped down at the bar opening. He was appearing rather natural in Sophie's kitchen. "Fifteen minutes, tops, people."

Leaning through the opening, Sophie made smacky noises and kissed him with embellishment. "I so love that you can cook."

Stan flashed humor at Callie. "Don't worry. I've had my taste of her. He can have her now."

Sophie turned sly and did a wave of herself from head to toe. "That's okay. Not everyone can go the distance with this."

There was nobody like Sophie Bianchi. If she ditched you, you left grateful for the time you had, understanding that the man following behind you would be in your shoes soon, feeling the same way.

"How's Mark doing?" Buck said from the kitchen.

"Quite well." Callie had to holler back, having assumed a place on the sofa. "Wall-to-wall diners. Everyone worried he needed help getting back on his feet, and, man oh man, did they come out. What've y'all been up to this afternoon? I'd like to think you tended my house more than my neighbor."

Sophie painted on a coy smile, throwing her nose up in the air with a wink in her eye.

"Can't I handle both?" came his reply from the kitchen.

Callie returned to her drink. "Sorry I asked."

In a snap, Sophie jerked out of that pose into one of wonder, both hands out, eyes wide sporting their lavender contact lenses. "Ooh." Sophie reached into one of the deep pockets of her tiered floral maxi skirt. "Look what I found today."

In slow motion Sophie opened her hand.

"Did one of y'all lose a bullet?" she asked. "Haven't ever seen y'all do that before, but there's always a first time."

Callie almost dropped her glass. In her hand, Sophie played with the item, turning it over and over, with Callie cringing at how much that .41 cartridge had already been handled. "Where did you find that?"

"On one of my front steps. Is it yours?"

Frustrated, Callie shook her head. "No, it's not mine. Cops don't go around losing their bullets. When did you find it?"

"About six thirty this afternoon. And I didn't find it. Buck did."

Which meant it had been handled by two people in addition to its owner. Callie went into the kitchen, pulled out a clean plastic sandwich bag, and had Sophie drop it in. Buck stopped cooking, concern in his features. "Did we do something wrong?"

Callie had no business getting upset with them. "No, no, of course not."

The odds of finding a print on this bullet were slim to none, in a world where finding usable prints on bullets was about five to ten percent anyway. And whoever was doing this probably knew better than to handle it so precisely as to leave a clean print. Josephine had picked up Wesley's bullet. Mark had handled his, too, sweeping it off the bar into his pocket. Still, she parked each in an evidence bag. Just in case.

Sophie continued stunned, as if she couldn't see the need for excitement. "What's the problem?"

Across the room, Callie looked to Stan, as if this wasn't to be believed. Stan gave the slightest of shrugs at Callie, unable to offer suggestion without saying more than these people had a need to know.

Unsure whether to enlighten her friend or not, Callie chose someplace in between fact and fiction. "This isn't the only one we've found," she said. "We're trying to figure out who is dropping them. You don't need kids picking them up." She didn't ask about a note, because Sophie would've already brought it up if there was one.

Buck's expression said he read through the bull, but as Callie hoped, he kept his mouth shut. Coming from years of working alone or working in houses where the owners didn't think the contractor was listening, he wasn't a big talker.

Sophie, however, sensed something more and wilted right before their eyes. "If it isn't yours, then who climbs these stairs and drops them on a porch? That's rather going out of the way, isn't it. And why *my* porch? That doesn't make sense, Callie. Don't bullets come with guns?"

"They usually do," Callie replied, unable to argue that logic. "One is no good without the other, for sure. Might be the postman. He hunts—"

"Quit patronizing me."

Sophie was no dummy and Callie had to quit treating her as such. But telling her that she was identified via her relationship with Mark at the restaurant would make her fear being stalked, which she probably was. And when Sophie was nervous, she talked to the world.

Time for a hit to left field. "Maya said she was concerned, too."

"You consulted Maya before you consulted me?"

Buck returned to his meal prep and added whistling. Stan got up and feigned interest out the back window.

Maya wasn't a fun topic of discussion but one probably easier to handle than the one about planted bullets. "She ran into us in the parking lot," Callie said. "She'd had a vision and wanted to explain it to us."

Sophie's manicured brows dipped to almost touching as she stared across the room and shouted, "You went behind my back, too, Stan?"

With his back to her, he just held up his hands, going for innocence.

She puffed out, then puffed again, like some sort of wild animal pondering which adversary to charge first. "Did she bash me?"

"Didn't even mention you," Callie said. The comment about Zeus taking after his mother in his hocus-pocus talents didn't count, in her opinion.

"Hmm. Not sure that's good or bad. What did she see?"

Callie wasn't sure how to talk clairvoyant stuff. "You mean, the vision?"

The eye rolling wasn't flattering. "Yes, the vision. What's she doing, predicting weather or guessing lottery numbers?"

Meow. "She was worried for Mark's safety, Soph. And I believe she was serious about what she thought she saw."

Only one eyebrow arched this time. "So what did she have to say?"

"First," and Callie pulled the rolled-up paper from her purse. "Is this familiar in any way?"

Sophie took the ideogram and studied it, hiding a mild double take when recognition set in. "It's scribbles, but that's normal. I assume she gave you her interpretation of it. I can't study this and duplicate what she told you, if that's what you're wanting." Sassy, but that was probably fair.

"Do you do *remote viewing*? That's what she called this." Callie'd never seen Sophie practice nor talk about it, but if she could do it, why not ask her to try it? Might even make Sophie feel needed, a tact Callie's learned ages ago went far in keeping her friend happy.

"I've studied remote viewing a bit," she said, staring holes in the paper, attempting to read between the scratchings. "It's not something I do very often, so I would be rusty at it." She looked up. "Is this what she does all the time?"

Poor Sophie. She really needed to talk to Maya. They had a lot more in common than Sophie cared to accept.

"Not sure about what you mean by *all the time*, but she claims to have done it for law enforcement before. She called me after doing this in relation to El Marko's break-in. She said Mark was in danger, and there would be more bullets showing up around here. I want y'all to be aware of your surroundings, okay? Note anyone suspicious. Anyone on people's porches who shouldn't be."

Buck wandered over and narrowed his eyes. "Do you have any sort of theory on the why? Is someone upset about something?"

That's what Callie would ask right off the bat, too. The why would dictate the who. "Mark's retired SLED. We're suspecting an old case. He isn't sure. I'm not sure." She wasn't about to say he wasn't saying. "I have the FBI doing some research for me. Mark's talking to his people. Let's let the people with the power do their thing before we get too upset. This might be no more than someone who found out where Mark is and wanted to be a nuisance. Chances are they'll get bored and move on. Mark's watching for familiar people."

Stan had returned to his chair, but remained quiet, waiting to be called on as needed.

"Will they come back for the bullet they lost?" Sophie asked.

Bless her little heart. Callie shot a brief glance at Stan, and he scratched his chin with a glimpse that said their friend was a unique individual, for sure. "No," she said. "I believe they've got enough others not to come searching for one they dropped, Soph."

She resembled a waif, uncertain how to find her way.

"So, what do you think of the drawing?" Callie asked.

"What are these?" Sophie referenced the specific seven dots.

"Maybe more of what you had in your hand." Callie waited, not wanting to feed any more information than she had to.

"Who is this?" Sophie asked about the man on the ground. "Is he dead?"

"Maya said there wasn't much energy around that man, but she couldn't tell if he was dead or just lying there. Injured perhaps. She was also unsure whether this scenario was in the past or the future."

"Or the present," Sophie murmured and ran her hand over the page, as if hoping to read the vibes.

Buck wasn't happy with the conversation and eased his arm around his honey. "You all right, Goddess?"

Sophie leaned in a little, but not much. She kept her focus on the paper, occasionally touching the ink with the slightest of touch. "There's an important woman figure, I see."

"Yep."

"The man is laying on a road or drive or something man-made."

"That's what she said."

Her friend looked up. "Mind if I borrow this?"

Why not? It wouldn't hurt to have the local psychic fact-check the guest psychic, and Sophie a part in the play.

But then Callie checked herself. If Maya wasn't Miss Innocent, if she was all too conveniently on the island, she could easily become a person of interest. "Can you take a picture of it to keep? I need to take the original with me."

"Yeah," she said, the lone word trailing. Sophie wasn't bashing Maya's abilities anymore. She was instead intrigued with the story on the page.

Callie remembered she needed to move the evening along. Mark could show up at *Windswept* as early as ten thirty. It was seven forty-five. She did the mental arithmetic of helping set the table, eating, talking over the food, clearing the table, talking in the living room, dropping Stan home, then making it to her place. All she had to do was let Sophie steer the conversation, nod at her opinions, wash dishes, and leave. Ten was a good goal.

Callie rose. "Let me help you, Buck."

What Callie had hoped would be a simple dinner filled with Sophie's gossip wound up ominous and foreboding. Ever since Sophie'd touched the ideogram, she'd faded from social conversation. For a short while she spoke of her worth as a seer and about how premonitions worked, and   while she didn't do remote viewing, she had dreams and sensed spirits. Other-worldly beings gravitated to her, she said, giving examples as if she cited her CV for a paranormal job.

She couldn't talk about anything but clairvoyance, but she wasn't rattling off in her normal chatterbox manner. She could only speak of visions. She couldn't stop touching the paper.

Sophie worried she was being replaced as the go-to soothsayer on Edisto. She wanted to be appreciated on the same ground as Maya.

"Aren't there different kinds of mediums?" Stan asked, which to Callie sounded like a decent question. It was also a nice move on his part to pull her out a little bit to show her stuff.

"All kinds," Sophie said. "The fake ones give us a bad image, though. Maya is channeling. She goes into a state and waits for energy to find her, and she notes it on paper like this. Later she'll answer a long list of questions, and if she's working with cops, as she claims, she gives them some kind of report."

Not critical. More informational. A more mature side to Sophie that came with a description of a soothsayer that didn't sound too ding-a-ling.

Stan winked at Callie. "How come we have our own island clairvoyant and don't use her?"

Sophie didn't think the question a joke and waited for the response. "I would, you know."

Thanks, Stan, and a flash of chagrin told Callie he noted the *faux pas.*

"I rely on Sophie here and there," she parsed together after a split-second grappling for explanation. "She's come in handy. Like at the Julia Legare mausoleum, remember that one? Sophie was practically sitting in a spirit's lap that day."

Stan hadn't moved to Edisto yet when that one happened.

"All of that started when a woman died from anaphylactic shock, opening a door to an annual serial killer. I learned a heck of a lot from Sophie through that case. She all but solved the crime."

Callie hoped that was sufficient, unable to draw upon any other cop slash Sophie spiritualisms off the top of her head.

Stan, bless him, kept trying to entertain. "Hey, Soph," he said, using Callie's handle for her instead of his pet name *Bug.*

"Were you *clairvoyanting* me when we were in the sack?"

Callie dropped her forehead in her hand.

The contractor laughed. "I might want an answer to that as well. There are some instances when I feel quite . . . other-worldly."

Stan guffawed, with Buck on his heel doing the same.

"No," Sophie said, not rolling with the wittiness of the conversation. "That's not funny."

The wet blanket fell over them as if it weighed a hundred pounds.

No jocularity, no smart-ass-iness, no cackling at the ridiculousness of the question.

Sophie was unwilling to accept flippancy about her craft, and the sudden gravity around the table draped an awkwardness that turned everyone's attention to their food.

"The grouper is good," Callie said, holding up a bite on her fork before shoving it in her mouth.

"You know your fish," Buck said.

"Kind of comes with living on an island."

"It's just fish to me," Stan added. "It has a shell on it, or you catch it on a hook. Just don't serve it to me raw."

Callie squeezed on more lemon. "Amen to that."

The table went silent again. At this rate, she'd be home way before Mark.

Stan tried again. "First time I've ever been on your boy's boat. Damn nice one."

Sophie scoffed at that, and Callie already ran the phrases through her head having heard them before. *His dad can afford it. His dad's an idiot for giving him such a big gift.* So on and so on, but Sophie wasn't herself tonight.

Callie tried again. "Love the pilaf, too, Buck."

"It's my go-to side dish. Seems fancy but takes nothing to fix."

"Well, it works."

Everyone's plates were almost empty, and with conversation exhausted, everyone messed with remnants, taking side glances at Sophie. The ideogram sat next to her plate, and she'd hardly taken her eyes off it.

Soph wasn't discounting the ideogram. She wasn't discounting Maya. She was trying to read the paper.

She wasn't feeding off the people in the room at all. If anyone knew anything about Sophie, it was she loved people, learning about them, interacting with them, leading the conversation. This quiet side of her said one thing, and that was she wanted people out of her house so she could be alone. There was nothing introverted about Sophie, but tonight she was withdrawn.

While Callie itched to meet Mark, if Sophie started speaking in tongues or spouting premonitions about bullets and killers, he'd have to wait. But Sophie wasn't being her metaphysical, out-of-this-world self. Callie didn't get it, but she didn't have the energy to try and understand Sophie's mood. Better to stick to bullets and notes and cam footage and get back to old-fashioned police work.

Chapter 11

"IS THERE DESSERT?" Callie asked the subdued table of four. Subdued wasn't the standard at a Sophie dinner party, but there they were, four people unsure about the course of etiquette when the bubbly yoga queen of Edisto Beach was lost within herself.

Sophie was too engrossed in Maya's ideogram, and Buck and Stan had maxed out their one-liners. Callie had even tried bringing up discussion about hers and Sophie's children, but Sophie wasn't biting.

"Oh yeah, dessert." Buck got up and returned with lemon meringue pie and little saucers. He cut slices and served plates, and Stan smacked and um'ed and ah'ed over a taste off his finger. Apparently, Buck had made the pie, too. He set a piece before Sophie, then reached up and ran his hand over her hair.

Tonight Callie had come to see the man as more than the island contractor. He was a decent guy. Not because he could cook, ever a plus on anyone's talent list, but because he watched over Sophie so tenderly. Maybe he wasn't one of her fly-by-night beaus after all. Time would tell.

"There's a lot of badness infused in this," Sophie said, interrupting the silence, holding up the drawing by a corner.

They all stopped in place, waiting.

"Mark's troubled, Callie," Sophie continued. "And this woman—" she tapped the paper with a coral-painted nail. "She's troubled. And she's underestimated."

Was this Sophie doing a remote viewing off someone else's remote viewing? If that was a thing. Or had her powers exceeded Maya's . . . again if that was a thing.

The distress in those contact lenses, the creases in her forehead spoke concern, even distress. Callie'd seen Sophie upset, but always in the aftermath of something, not in advance like this.

Callie gently laid down her fork. "What should Mark do?"

"I'm not sure," she said. "Be watchful of himself and everyone around him. Study people."

She sounded like Callie in the zillion times she'd warned Sophie,

Jeb, and the people in her world. Always be aware of your surroundings.

"Trouble's coming to Edisto, Callie. It's festered and festered and come to a head. Mark's not talking to you because he's not rightly sure of what's happening, but he's positive it's coming because of him. The air crackles with it. I felt something odd the other night, but it's more intense now that Maya's connected."

This was not the Sophie whom Callie knew. The lady who acted playful about old dead aunts turning off lights and Edisto spirits making anniversary appearances wasn't seated at this table. This was someone different.

"This . . ." and she made a circle with her hand over the paper, ". . . means it'll get to him even if it means coming through you. . . ." She turned to Stan. "And you. And anyone else in the way. Mark may consider leaving, which he's thinking about, by the way. I sense a need to escape. But the danger will follow, and he has no answer for that. There are secrets to protect in all of this, and there's a reckoning about to happen."

Buck gazed at his lady as if he'd never seen her before.

"Whose secrets?" Callie asked.

"Not sure. Might belong to more than one person."

"What kind of reckoning?"

Shaking her head, the movement traveled into Sophie's shoulders until she was almost shaking all over.

God help her, Callie was believing her.

"Oh, honey." Buck leaped up to Sophie's side of the table, got down on a knee and tried to pull her to him, but she wasn't having any of it.

"Stop!" She drew her forearms up over her ears, eyes clinched shut.

The three of them halted any movement. They waited, Buck still on his knee.

Finally, she lowered her arms. "I cannot see what's going to happen, Callie, but something is brewing like a Category Five, and it feels like storm clouds creeping in on the night."

Anyone who lived on an island understood that metaphor. "Maya said within a week," Callie added, throwing more on the table. "Six days from the first bullet. A total of six bullets plus one that might be shot. Do you see anything like this?"

"No. Kind of wish you hadn't told me either. Now it's in my consciousness."

"Sage the house when we're gone," Callie said, using the go-to Soph used to cleanse whatever they'd talked about.

"It's not something that can be saged," she said.

Sophie passed the picture back to Callie. "I don't want this in my house anymore. Don't even want a picture of it on my phone."

Honoring the request, Callie quickly hid it out of sight in her purse wedged in the sofa's corner cushion. Since she was already up, and everyone's appetite appeared sated, she gathered plates and dinnerware.

"Here, let me help," Stan said, rising to do the same.

With Sophie not too social, her own worrisome storm etched around her mouth, Buck cleared an armful of dishes to speed up the clearing.

"Let us," Callie said to him at the sink. "Go deal with Sophie."

"Wait," he said, feeling in his pocket. His hand came out holding a yellow sticky with the words *Chill or be still forever.*

She should've known. Callie retrieved another plastic bag from Sophie's kitchen drawer and held it open for Buck to drop in the note. She sealed it tight and slipped it into her pocket. "Don't tell her."

"Wanted your opinion about that before I would," he said, making more noises in the sink to cloak their words from Sophie. "What do the words mean?"

"No idea yet."

"Were there other notes or was she just the lucky one?"

"At least one other. Keep quiet about that, too. Safer for us all. Please tell me you get that," Callie said, plain and flat.

Buck nodded and left. Stan slid into his place. "What the hell was that about?"

Turning on the water first for background noise, Callie mumbled, "Another bullet, another note."

"Jesus Christ and all the angels," he uttered. "But I was talking about that idiot paper in there, and her reaction about it."

"You've never seen Sophie touch base with the other side any time in your brief love affair?"

He grabbed a towel and started drying. "Not at all. Just a lot of flirting, laughing, and . . . the other stuff. Lots of the other stuff."

"Maybe you lucked up then. Nothing urgent going on during your dating period. I've seen her *see* things three or four times. I've seen coincidences twice that. Am I a believer? Depends on what you mean by believing and believing in what. Let's just say that odd things happen more around Sophie than other people." She handed him a wet glass. "Tonight was just damn weird."

"Make you think Maya's the real deal?" he grumbled back.

"No clue," she said, allowing the forks and spoons to make more noise than she had to. However, she leaned toward yes. Maya was real to some degree or Sophie wouldn't have fed off of the paper so much. Callie could read Sophie's nonsense, and this was not one of those times.

Stan took a gander through the bar opening, noting Buck and Sophie on the back porch. "Well, that paper creeps me out now."

"Ditto."

They finished the dishes, put away the leftovers, and straightened the table. Stan waited for Callie to dictate their next move. It was nine fifteen.

Callie led them to the porch where night had dropped. "Hey, anyone want something to drink?"

The couple sat in the dark, no porch light, as much to avoid bugs as to be alone.

Nobody took Callie up on the offer, and she quickly got what she wanted from Buck . . . a nod saying he and his lady wanted to be alone.

"Well, I'm thinking we'll be off. I need to—"

Sophie leaped up and gripped Callie by an arm. "Talk to Mark. You can fix this, right?"

"I have no idea what *this* is," Callie replied. "The bullets, needless to say, have me worried."

"Someone gave me one of them," she reminded, as if she had to.

"Yes, they did, and you gave it to me. So now it's not your problem." Maybe Sophie would believe in the danger being passed over to Callie. Pointless telling Sophie to watch her comings and goings, because Callie already knew she'd obsess over every person, place, or thing. She was observant enough as it was. Whether she judged them good or evil was another issue altogether.

"But they put it here because of me."

Callie took Sophie by both forearms. "Or they assumed Mark and I were coming over to your place and put it there for us. You just found it first."

Sophie looked skeptical. "Why not put one at your house?"

Callie might as well say it. "They did, Soph. I got one, too. While Mark was there. And he got one at the restaurant."

A hint of tension melted from Sophie's shoulders. "So it *is* about Mark."

"Without a doubt, hon. You can sleep easier. You were just a means to a message. Nobody's coming in your house."

"Damn straight," Buck said. "I'm spending the night, and I carry."

Most contractors packed a firearm. Toting a piece came with the territory of meeting strangers and disreputable subcontractors and being alone on a secluded property for hours at a time.

The night was a bust socially, but if one considered it in any other terms, the evening was a sign of things to come . . . assuming you halfway believed in psychics. Callie wasn't discounting the *hocus-pocus,* as Stan liked to call it now. Two psychics were in sync forecasting nastiness on the horizon. Like Mark, Callie had never used a psychic in her law enforcement history. She never fathomed the need. Never deemed it credible. Taking it seriously held potential to do irreparable damage to an investigative career.

But she was on Edisto now, at the top of its law enforcement food chain. Big fish in a small pond. They still had voodoo in pockets of communities around there, and that population respected Sophie. Callie had never asked Sophie for her view before, but she was glad she had this evening.

Sophie's credibility almost gave the *hocus-pocus* credence.

More than ever now, Mark best be showing up at *Windswept* to explain himself. Otherwise she was banging on his door in the middle of the night. Wherever he landed, she'd make sure he spilled by dawn.

First Callie had to drop off Stan at his place. It wasn't even ten. She didn't rush. She rather preferred this time of night.

The streets were desolate. It was a new moon night, or close enough to it, plus the sky was dark with enough cloud cover to block the stars. She drove with her window down, the waft of moisture warning her of the potential of rain.

A calm before the storm. Not only the calm on the cusp of tourist season and its influx of people, but also of whatever this was with Mark. Frankly, she'd hold tourist season over his head as a need for him to educate her fully, before his past, his present, and innocent beachcombers collided.

She pulled into Stan's drive. "Thanks for the date," he said, getting out and bending over to say goodbye. "Can't remember when I've had a better time." A wink tried to lighten the moment.

"It was a rather entertaining evening, wasn't it?" She allowed herself that tad of sarcasm on a social event that left everyone expectant and edgy.

No rain yet, and she hoped they didn't get any. They'd had enough of late, more than the normal spring. Stan's place was two blocks off the water, three rows of beach houses in between, but that didn't stop some of the breeze. It was late enough for the bugs to have gone to bed, so they rested there a moment since Mark wouldn't be off work. Not yet. Stan finally sat back down in his car seat and closed his door to shut off the interior light.

Once a cop, always a cop. No need to draw attention to themselves.

"Don't let those two women get in your head," he said. "Sophie might be woo-woo material, but that doesn't mean she can make the stock market crash, you know what I mean?"

"I'm only thinking about what I'm aware of. Bullets, notes, a break-in, and Mark's old partner being dead. That's more than enough tangibles to occupy my worries."

"Go over these notes with me again. What'd they say? All on yellow sticky papers?"

"First of all, Mark didn't get one," she said. "The first was mine on the porch. *His love isn't worth the trouble.*" Hers scared her. Were they calling her out or warning her that time was of the essence?

"That could mean any of several things."

She just sighed. "I believe Wesley took his or it blew away, so we have no clue. Then there's Sophie's reading *Chill or be still.*"

"Stay out of it or die," he said. "Sophie's message is over the top, in my opinion, and unnecessary. She can't impact anything."

"Someone could just be messing with whomever Mark knows. They just see a connection to Mark. And when you consider Wesley, they made the connection to all of us through El Marko's, following people home as they identified his friends."

Wesley. She hadn't called about him, but his mother hadn't called her either, which was a good sign. There had been no sign of struggle at the home. Note to self to call in the morning. To do so now would only upset her.

Staring past the drive and into the jungle of woods behind Stan's place, Callie inhaled more of the night air, letting its softness soothe her nerves. She used to be a morning person in Boston, but Edisto had reversed that. Here people went inside by nightfall, and restaurants didn't stay open much past nine. The soothing slowness of nothing needing attention and nature reclaiming its dominance did wonders for her some nights.

But it was also a time when thoughts amplified, the unsolved grew sharper edges, and what-ifs tumbled too fast to keep grip of. It's when she used to skip dinner, grab a drink, and check her security system cams before roaming the streets nursing her wounds.

Mark and Stan had a lot to do with turning some of that around. Thomas as well. Now evenings included Mark, meals he made her eat, and a temporary residence at *Windswept* in sight of the ocean while *Chelsea Morning* was under construction. No cams to watch. No booze. No demons to chase.

Suddenly she wished she had those cams. Demons were peeking around corners.

"He's my best friend out here, Chicklet. We'll set him straight."

She patted her old friend on the arm. "They're wandering our beach," she said. "Our island."

"Yeah. Studying us."

She was comforted in his use of the word *us*. "I'll talk to Mark," she said. "Then I'll start my research. Then talk to Knox at the FBI, though I don't expect much from him yet."

"And SLED? You have every right to talk to them," he said.

She understood that, but she was giving Mark the chance to do that first.

"Callie," Stan said, going to her real name, meaning business.

"I'll get him to talk tonight," she said. "And if I sense any holding back, I'll contact SLED myself."

He seemed satisfied and sat back, taking in the night like she was, both of them trying to make sense of random details. Clues in the form of .41 caliber bullets strewn around the beach, were most likely connected to Javier but not him exactly since he was dead.

"Well," Stan said, opening the door again. "Let me get to bed. Call if you need me." He got out and leaned back in. "Good luck tonight."

She nodded in thanks, watched him take the steps to his door and disappear inside. Slowly she left the gravel drive, took Atlantic Street south, then instead of heading home to *Windswept*, she went the other direction and found Mark's place on Mary Street, his car in the drive.

He lived close enough to walk to work, which he often did, not just to remain in shape, he said, but to keep his limpy leg as toned as possible. This morning she'd driven him to El Marko's, so he was on foot. No lights on, so he wasn't home yet. She backed out and went to the restaurant. Those lights were still on as the staff closed down inside.

She parked, went dark, and waited. No need going in, interrupting, and pushing the man when she'd asked him earlier to make up his own mind.

Instead she did a search on her phone for Javier Harred.

Unexpected. She wasn't sure if the name was on the mundane level of John Smith, but the results showed a fairly famous movie director, a Texan who sang at county fairs, and a soccer player who retired fifteen years ago. She added SLED and South Carolina to the search.

There he was.

Harred's takedown happened after she'd left Boston, his plea accepted sometime between the bottles of vodka she enjoyed while staying at her parents' place in Middleton after her husband was murdered and she'd lost her job. A twinge grabbed her chest at the memory of her father being alive then. She'd not been the least bit interested in anything law enforcement at the time. No wonder she wasn't familiar with the case.

There'd been a significant dustup in the state's news about how a SLED agent went down for being dirty; however, the press wasn't well-versed in the details. He'd been turned and labeled as rogue, having been taken out one night in a warehouse parking lot by his fellow agents. There was no mention of Mark. The only SLED names were the chief, the head of narcotics and vice, and the informational affairs person. Rightfully so.

Then not much else was written about the matter. A flash in the pan then silence.

Lights went out in the restaurant. From her vantage in the parking lot, she watched the side of the building, far enough back to see if people came out of the back or the front. They exited the front. With the picture window boarded and jerry-rigged secure, Mark had a repair to take care of tomorrow. Instinctively she watched for Wesley, hoping he had just shown up late for work and nobody had told her, but only two of the regular girls left. Mark followed and locked up.

He headed down the wooden stairs from the walkway in front of the small strip mall where he'd either see Callie and catch a ride or walk home. He gave the slightest pause at seeing Callie waiting in the dark, tucked away from the street lamps. Not like a retired SLED agent to miss a patrol car, regardless of the shadows.

He came over, walking a little tired, normal for work that kept you on your feet most of the day, and got in on the passenger side.

"My house?" she asked, as if nothing hinged on his choice.

"Sure," he said, buckling his belt.

He'd been at *Windswept* enough to have backup clothes for impromptu overnighters, extra toiletries stocked in her bathroom, and his coffee cup and favorite grind ready to go in the kitchen. Since they'd been friends, their relationship had been more about him tending to her, and her trying not to worry him, but they'd made a hundred-and-eighty-degree flip of late, and this change was new for both of them.

At the house, he did his usual with his keys, emptying his pockets, and tossing his food-smelling clothes in the hamper before showering. Often she waited in the bed for him to slip under the covers all clean and soap smelling, but this time she put on coffee, slid into sweats and a tee, and set up on the sofa, the room lit only by a lone lamp on the end table. Didn't take him long to show up, fill his mug, and settle in beside her.

"How was Sophie's dinner?" he asked.

"Buck broiled grouper and cooked rice pilaf. Lemon meringue pie."

Mark's cup halted inches before his lips. "Sounds like he can seriously cook."

"Sure can," she said.

He did a mouth-shrug thing and finished taking his sip. Then he leaned back, head on the sofa's back cushion, cup resting on his thigh, and gave a long, end-of-the-day sigh. "Busy day."

He dragged. Maybe more than normal.

"A good thing," she said, melting into her cushion as well. "At least you were open. Who's tending to that window?"

"Waiting for a call back on that," he said. "The town is already asking."

"As in Brice?"

"As in Brice."

They both propped bare feet on the coffee table and sank into personal reflection. She wanted him to speak up first. If he didn't after five minutes, she was taking the reins.

Chapter 12

"A LOT DIDN'T make the papers about Javier," Mark said after they shared a few moments of watching the night sky through the living-room window.

Callie waited. He had delayed these details for two days, and she wasn't ruining his presentation with her impatience. He'd be stupid not to think she hadn't already searched for details on Javier and what happened five years ago, yet she saw no need to jump in with what she knew. His past. His pace. She stayed silent.

"I appreciate your patience," he said.

To that, she smiled. "God knows you've been patient enough with me."

And he smiled, too.

Time passed. Not enough wind outside to make sound. No traffic. No sirens. The surf most likely out from the sense of vacuumed silence.

He exhaled long and hard and removed his feet from the table. "Seems I owe you a story."

"I'd love to hear a story," she said, staying where she was, telling herself to be the most polite, least judgmental audience she could be.

"Six years ago, Javier Harred and I were agents with SLED."

Almost sounded like *once upon a time*.

"We had a cadre of cartel types in the state digging a foothold in the drug business. Fentanyl was gaining ground. He went undercover. I was his handler. He went in as himself, offering to sell protection to the cartel by informing them of our movements and investigations . . . and purportedly misleading us when they had a shipment coming in, or a decent-sized buy going down."

"A crooked-cop cover."

He nodded yes. "He was half Mexican, spoke fluent Spanish, and charismatic as hell. I was chosen as his handler because of how close we were. We'd been friends for eight years, with me going over to his house or out with him at least once every couple weeks if not more. I could read him. I knew his tells."

The betrayal must have been intense.

"I knew Melissa, his wife, and Lily, his twelve-year-old daughter. Melissa's birthday is March 2. Lily's is September 12. His mother came around on occasion, her name Amalia. He lived in Blythewood, outside Columbia, about five miles from me."

He stopped to let that part of the story take hold. She could see how personal this was for him. More than a co-worker, Javier sounded like family.

She could relate. Just look at her and Stan.

"He was convincing. The cartel took him in after a full year of setup. When we learned of meetings and potential buys, he would tell them. They'd reschedule, move the location, or change the date. He earned their trust and proved his worth to them, and we played along."

Seemed too easy to her. Javier had to have been damn good at convincing people of things. It was hard to play double agent like that, difficult to remain true. Only a strongly talented individual could appear pure to both sides.

"The cartel threw you a bone or two? To keep SLED from becoming suspicious of him? I mean, he couldn't always be right. He couldn't unravel each and every planned meet, could he? Wouldn't that seem too convenient . . . for either side?"

"There was some give-and-take involved. They sacrificed some people, and I'm sure some dates were purely staged to balance the reality. He was good, Callie. Very good." Mark took a moment to take a last taste of his cooled coffee and put the cup aside on the table. "Too good."

She tucked a leg under her, needing to shift.

Mark waited until she stilled. "Of course, the situation couldn't be long-term. We told Javier we needed the information to start working the other way now, with him playing his role. We let them get bigger and bolder so that we were taking down more than nickel-dime stuff. The first time we didn't sync he said we miscommunicated. We showed up and nobody was there. I gave him that one since he danced a fine line. A dangerous one. The second time we wore egg on our face I confronted him, and I confronted him hard. He had an excuse about his cartel people harboring last-minute doubt and pulling the plug. But my friend or not, misunderstandings or not, I couldn't afford a third miss, so I changed tactics."

"Sure," she said, though she'd never dealt with undercover. She knew guys and gals who had, but she never had a case involving that level of dynamics. Wasn't her thing. It took a certain type of person to handle that degree of mental compartmentalization. She preferred the traditional good versus evil, identifying who was whom, which side was which. That was hard enough on any given day, but delving undercover could insanely muddy the waters until serious mistakes got made, getting people hurt.

Mark continued. "Finally, I chose to only speak to my immediate supervisor. Orson DeLuca. Twenty-year veteran and decorated enough times to be respected. And I told him of my concerns about Javier and how we needed to amend how we handled the next time Javier told me about a scheduled buy. I told Orson and Orson alone." He cleared his throat. "I told him we were it and it had to be just the two of us. He was reluctant, but he had no other suggestion. At least this way we'd sense whether to trust Javier. If this turned out to be his third strike, Orson said he'd pull him from undercover work and decide what action might be needed for his career future. A pivotal night for us all."

Mark nodded a couple of times as if to wind up again. "Javier was on leave from SLED the day of the so-called meet, our first concern, so I shadowed him, rather than act on the raid of the purported shipment." He turned to stare at her. "Not that I had hard-core proof of anything. Not yet. They could've been on to him or testing him." He inhaled then spoke a little faster. "Him being on leave . . . I just had to be sure. Javier didn't broker the deals, mind you. He didn't broker anything. He just provided protection and intel. He turned in the money they paid him, Callie. He was just making sure SLED was busy elsewhere, and not where the cartel was. A shell game."

Like water finding a steeper slope, his words came faster, and his increase in the energy of telling the story made her muscles tighten. He wasn't fond of replaying this story, and his discomfort was becoming hers.

"He went to where the real shipment was taking place, not to where he said it was. Later we learned it was a larger-than-normal purchase. Later. . . ." He hesitated to relive the betrayal. "Later, in talking with Javier, he said he just wanted to be there. He sensed he was on the cusp of truly being trusted and was proving his worth and offering them his support. He was playing the role, he said, and that night he had to choose whether to be more SLED or more cartel. He couldn't afford for SLED to interfere, he said, and he chose to be more useful for the cartel than for us. He'd thought he could clear it up and ask for forgiveness later when he explained his choice. He just didn't realize we considered this his third strike."

Callie was trying to understand. "You're saying . . . you want to believe he wasn't all bad, then."

"No, I really don't think he was," he said, his voice fatigued. "I suspected he feared for his family."

She wanted to hug him when she heard the hurt in his reply, but she couldn't. They weren't done here. She was only beginning to understand how bottling up this memory and these feelings, these mixed-up feelings, took a toll on him. He wasn't sure if his friend was friend or foe or someone who got so hung up in the middle he screwed up both jobs. She sensed a lot of regret and pain.

She did reach over and lay a hand on his chest. "Let me get you another cup of coffee." He needed a break.

"We'll be up all night if we keep drinking caffeine," he said, but her read of his body language told her he could use it.

She got up. "We'll just be up all night, then," she said. "Mine's cold anyway."

Taking her time, she hunted for something in the pantry to snack on, and finding nothing worthwhile, she toyed with pulling out her hidden gin bottle, but that was the wrong alcohol to pair with coffee. Plus, he'd refuse. And he'd be upset she still had a bottle in the house. She could say she hadn't touched it since Lumen Townsend had died back in October, but nobody trusted when an alcoholic kept a bottle and vowed it was never touched.

So coffee it was. She soon handed him a steaming second cup and resumed her place beside him, close enough to touch but far enough to give him breathing room to talk and not feel crowded.

"Halfway through the buy," he said, "I was spotted."

Callie gave him a puzzled glance. "How?"

"Orson sent suited-up guys to follow me. Said it was for my own protection. Said with us worried about Javier already, he sent guys to the site where the buy was supposed to happen, to confirm it fake. Then he'd radioed the guys following me. They didn't have intel, Callie. Nothing about this was very structured. Too much of it was off-the-cuff behavior. A complete clusterfuck."

"Wow, sounds like it," she said, having as many doubts about Orson as she did about Javier. Orson had altered the game plan without informing Mark. Had he lost trust with Mark, too? There was always that chance with Mark having been so close to Javier. "Then what?"

"One of their guys got froggy and shot at us, and it went to hell from there. Two of theirs were killed, the rest escaped. No drugs were confiscated."

Callie waited for the rest, because there definitely was more. She had no idea how late it was and didn't want to derail Mark by checking. They were sharing the story that had altered Mark to the bone, literally and figuratively, and it deserved all the time it took to tell it.

Mark bit his lip, then took in a breath, as if in the final stretch. "We shot at them, but not him. He shot at us, and while I like to tell myself he wasn't aiming at us, I can't deny one huge, goddamn fucking piece of reality that tells me otherwise."

She could guess. "Your leg."

"A .41 magnum slug in my leg, to be precise. His signature weapon for undercover. Something flashy but not too much so, he used to say. In the end, the authorities didn't crucify him for shooting me, though. My leg should have had his name all over it, but he said that in the scuffle he lost his firearm and the cartel exec grabbed it up. Someone who'd always said he admired the gun."

Bullshit.

How Mark could have one iota of sympathy for Javier was beyond her. To shoot at anyone other than the cartel was Javier's choice. No way to ask forgiveness on that one, if you asked her. "You're lucky you didn't die."

"You're right. He could have killed me, Callie. He was a crack shot, except for that night, except for the shot he missed while aiming at me. I like to think on purpose. That was five years ago."

Callie's pulse had amped up, and she wasn't hiding it. "Pisses me off. That whole night sounds incredibly insane, Mark."

"That's because it was," he said. "I don't have to describe how disappointed I was with everyone involved. Myself included."

Many stupid, ignorant civilians have yelled *why didn't you just shoot him in the leg?* when some perverted miscreant was shot by law enforcement dead center and dropped cold. Yeah, an officer shot to kill, but most folks failed to understand that a bullet to the leg could kill you, too.

He kept talking, as if he read her thoughts. "Bullet nicked my femoral artery and a bone. They got all the fragments, both bullet and bone, they say, but the muscle healed back with serious scar tissue. The nerve damage is there but minimal, and X-rays still show a chip out of my femur."

Only then did Callie realize she'd covered her mouth with one hand. He'd been so close to not being here. She lowered her hand, putting it back on her cup. "What happened to Javier?" Not that she didn't care about Mark's wound, but something about hearing how it happened unnerved her. She'd rather hear about Javier right now.

"One of the two guys killed was a junior-level cartel lieutenant in South Carolina. Javier testified that all dealings he'd had were with him and only him."

"Who wasn't around to testify," she said.

He nodded softly. "Javier confessed to misleading and lying to SLED, i.e. me, on that shipment alone."

"What about the other times?"

"He said that those times the deals fell through, and he had no idea why. He wasn't high enough on the ladder to ask, much less be told. The prosecutor couldn't prove otherwise and cut his losses, took a check in the win column, and went home early with a plea agreement for five years."

"Javier should've gotten a helluva lot more," she said, admittedly angered at the man getting less than he deserved.

"You're familiar with sentencing guidelines. He had no criminal history, he accepted responsibility of what they could prove, and he cooperated."

"Of w*hat they could prove*," she echoed. "And he cooperated? That's bullshit."

"I know and you know how all this works. We have to prove every-thing. They have to prove nothing."

"He was law enforcement. Held to a higher standard."

He sadly nodded. "Yes, he was."

Okay, Callie got it. She wasn't happy about it, but she got it. How-ever, there was a big thing she didn't get. She studied Mark, weighing all that she had heard. He studied her back, waiting for her to ask her question.

"So why wait five years and kill him four days before he gets out?" she said. "He didn't have to be inside or outside to cut some sort of deal or tell some big reveal. The cartel could've gotten to him the whole time he was inside. They would've taken him out within weeks of when he entered if he was a threat. Feels to me like something changed recently."

"That's what I can't wrap my head around, Callie. That part makes no sense."

He pulled her to him, ready to be consoled. She set her cup on the table and obliged. Together they tucked and wrapped each other into a tightness they both needed. He'd finally divulged his past, and it had worn on him. She'd gotten what she'd hoped for, and it had worn on her, too.

However, she wasn't anywhere near satisfied with what she'd learned, and to be honest, had been left even more curious and disturbed. This case should be as dead as Javier. Maybe others still breathed who disagreed with what Mark had done. People in the cartel. People within SLED.

Unless it was more about what Mark hadn't done. If they were supposed to be like family, then Mark hadn't been family to Javier in that moment. After all, he'd taken the side of SLED and let Javier fall from grace, his career forgotten, his awards and retirement stripped.

Now, more than ever, she wanted to learn about the people in Javier's life. Because at the end of those five years, his wasn't the only life permanently changed or someone wouldn't be out here dropping clues that aimed at Mark.

She had no solid proof yet, but she didn't believe in coincidence. She had Javier's caliber. Javier's handler. Javier's death. And a targeted constellation of Mark's new family. What happened five years ago had to be at the center of this mess.

Chapter 13

CALLIE SLOWLY WOKE, the sun through her curtains and across her bed telling her she was late. Mark sprawled unaffected beside her. She grabbed her phone for the time. *Shit.* She hadn't set her alarm. It was a quarter past seven, fifteen minutes past the time she was due at the station.

She tried to pour herself out from under tangled covers unnoticed since Mark needed his sleep after last night. They hadn't fallen into bed until four, Mark having replayed his story several times, each rendition with a new depth.

Bottom line, he hadn't wanted to create an accusation on something so nebulous as a bullet's caliber and possibly traumatize Javier's family making them relive everything, especially after Javier being murdered. But sitting with her in the quiet, once he'd poured out his feelings, he'd realized he should've trusted her discretion from the outset, along with her compassion . . . and her instincts.

He apologized a half dozen times.

And she loved him more each time.

Callie called Marie. She preferred calling to texting Marie. Sometimes she had things to say you didn't want in writing, about people who didn't like to hear they'd been talked about. Not that Marie hadn't heard it all. Marie had dirt on the dirt of the people who were actual experts on the dirt of Edisto Island.

"I'm late," she said, when Marie picked up. "Jumping in the shower now. Anything I need to handle on my way in, or is it a green light to come straight to the office?"

"I've got a man wanting to see you. I told him you'd be in any second."

The water was finally warm. She threw a towel over the door. "Crap, then I won't wash my hair. Anything else?"

"Our own beloved Brice LeGrand pulled a speeder over about fifteen minutes ago. They weren't happy. Called from their car and said they'd be in this morning."

Son of a—

"What the hell was Brice even doing up that time of morning?"

"Fishing maybe? Who wants to even know what Brice does and why he does it?"

"True that." Callie stuck her leg in the shower. Hot enough. Some mornings it took too long for the hot water to travel all the way up from the water heater downstairs, and that's when she did one of her polar bear jumps in and out of the shower. "Well, be there in a jiffy then."

"Ten-four, Chief."

Callie hung up. Telling Marie this wasn't a radio was a waste of breath. She hung up with a *ten-four* on anything. Sometimes even texts.

In and out and done. Took her longer to put on the uniform and its assorted accoutrement than to shower, but in fifteen Callie'd kissed a comatose Mark and run out the door. Marie had coffee, and Callie hoped there was still a peanut-butter protein bar in her desk drawer.

Still, she took a hard second glance for another bullet on the porch. Thank God the planks were bare.

This morning the officers were Annie Greer and Arne Webb. At first the department had used their first names on the radio and texting, but Annie and Arne soon proved cumbersome, so, Arne had become Webb.

She radioed Annie first. "Check-in?"

"All good, Chief. Nobody fully awake yet."

"Remember to keep an eye out for Wesley," Callie said. "If you see him, tell him to contact me or Mark. If you see his car, the same."

She hadn't told her officers about the bullets. Not yet. What was she supposed to say? She thinks someone is threatening Mark's circle of friends? And what if she did find whoever did it. What could she hold them on? Littering? She did tell her officers to cease hunting for Javier, though. No longer an issue, was all she said.

Sick of being in the dark, she swore once she took care of the immediate tasks this morning, she'd be all over researching Javier's family.

"I'll be at the office the better part of the morning, I expect," Callie said.

"Are things all right, Chief?" Annie asked. The new lady cop wasn't keen enough yet to read Callie but Thomas was, and the two were tight.

"Still a little disturbed about the break-in," Callie replied. "Would love to close that out."

"I can relate."

Callie signed out.

She relayed much of the same to Webb. Today was expected to be light. The weekend had been full of day-trippers, and the week-long tourists, a fairly thin group from the activity around town yesterday, weren't geared up quite yet, so this being Tuesday, she could hope for the mundane.

Might make the odd person stand out more, she hoped. Or enable her to spot a person who may have repeated crossing hers or Mark's path. While the hoodies stuck in her head, the burglars wouldn't be front and center. Not in broad daylight. Sophie, no doubt, would be keeping her eyes open, as would Mark and Stan. Hopefully Zeus as well, though his focus these days seemed to be stuck on Maya. Stan would totally be on guard.

She reached the station on Murray Street in no time, being not even a mile from *Windswept*, even after having crept down Palmetto scouting the houses and making a police presence known.

She hadn't had time to think deeply about the Mark and Javier story this morning, and she prayed whoever was on her beach would get over their frustration, see the danger in pursuing this further, and either leave or chill on the vacant sand with everyone else. No trouble. No more bullets.

Just leave.

Pulling into her designated parking spot, Callie immediately eyed Brice hanging outside the door. No one could miss the barrel-bellied, half-bald man who in no way was dressed for fishing as Marie had suggested.

She wanted to drag-ass and take her time making her way by him, just to spite him, but a citizen waited inside, someone Brice probably took note of, not wanting to stand in line and be second to anyone in order to be heard.

"Brice," she said from about twenty feet away. Nobody else was outside.

"Chief," he replied. One could draw a chart of his facial expressions and understand his frame of mind. A Brice set of cartoon emojis. This current one demanded a reckoning for something he interpreted as completely wrong and out of order. He'd aimed it at her many a time, like a parent staring down the child as they came in from the fight outside in the neighbor's yard.

Callie'd bet a week's pay that it had something to do with his need to play traffic cop.

Best she talk to him on the stoop and save the inside person from enduring the pomposity of the town government's poorest representative. Callie hated to be introduced to a visitor with Brice anywhere nearby.

"Where are your officers?" he demanded.

"My *two* officers," she said, emphasis on the two, "are rolling, trolling, and overseeing the safety of both the citizens and the guests of the Town of Edisto Beach."

"Not on Docksite Road. I had to wave a man down running almost fifty in a thirty-five, which should be twenty-five, if you ask me. Not a blue light in sight."

"The blue lights were probably pulling someone on Palmetto," she said. "Or Jungle, or Myrtle. And how can you even tell how fast they were going?"

"I can tell. Plus, I clocked him in my vehicle."

She tried terribly hard not to grin. "By exceeding the speed limit yourself?"

"I have the authority to—"

"No, you don't."

He shifted his polo, though it hadn't been out of place. "Docksite Road has more people this time of year with Wyndham right there. I waved the car over into the Wyndham turn and gave the driver the riot act."

Oh good heavens. "Well, that's a tourist that will never come back to visit us, Brice. I hope they don't blow your as—, um, your name up on social media as the anti-Christ of Edisto hospitality. Did he take your picture?"

His cheeks reddened, taking his tone deeper than his permanent sun-and-bourbon ruddiness. He wasn't embarrassed though. This was temper. Brice loved his temper. Now a tourist knew what the residents already knew about Brice. Not that Brice cared. Nor did he care the visitor might not return, despite the fact Brice was part of the council in charge of protecting tourism. All Brice cared about was living there, being in charge, and not being accountable. Nobody could touch his Edisto credentials, him being fifth-generation Edisto. Repeatedly voted into office, the powers that did so took care of him and he took care of them They were mostly a generation of islanders angry that Edisto had grown four times its size in their lifetime. One day in the not-too-distant future, enough outsiders would move in and vote him out, something he'd never see coming nor accept readily when the time came.

"So, did you give him a ticket?" she asked.

"I do not have the ability to give him a ticket," he retorted.

"Thank goodness for that. Now, did you get his name in case he comes in to file a complaint?"

He snorted, two steps up from a normal person's scoff. "He wouldn't give me his driver's license."

"Smart man." Like so many times in the past, she tired of Brice's overbearance. "I should be stunned you asked for it, Brice, but I'm not. Your gall has no end."

He reached up to point at her chest then thought twice about it. He'd done that before and rued the decision when she reversed his finger's direction until it pointed back at him. "Your people aren't doing their jobs," he said.

She smiled. Brice couldn't have set up the conversation any better. "A pure sign of a need for two more officers," she said. "I'll have my proposal ready for the next council meeting, and, bless your heart, Brice, I'm using this example as part of the justification. We cannot have our town councilmembers doing double-duty as speed cops."

She gestured at him with an air-scooping gesture to let her by and went inside. Brice, like the dunce he was, followed, ever in need of the last word. A gentleman sat on the sofa against the wall, with the patience of a Biblical Job defining his demeanor.

She turned to Brice, asking under her breath. "Is this your speeder?"

"No."

Thank goodness for small miracles. "Well, let me tend to him, please. If you're still here when we're through, we can talk." Then on second thought she added, "Your speeder called Marie already and said he'd be in sometime soon this morning, so feel free to hang. We can compare your story to his."

Marie, head down, peered up over some readers, fought a grin, and went back to her computer duties.

"Now." Callie walked over to the waiting gentleman. "What can I do for you? I hope you're enjoying your stay on Edisto Beach."

The man rose, manners intact, but he couldn't take his attention off Brice. "May we talk alone?"

"Absolutely," she said, leading him to the swinging door that took people behind the counter, through to the only private room in the station . . . her office.

She took measure of him en route. Nothing extraordinary stood out. Two inches shy of six feet and middle-aged with ample gray waves of hair that exceeded his collar. Not overweight but not fit, either. He carried the scent of cigars, a peppery flavor, not fruity.

While one couldn't always read affluence in a tourist's clothes, she noted the Target-store-brand tag sticking up on his shirt, the khakis definitely not from a place on Charleston's King Street, though the deck shoes were three-hundred-dollar Mephistos. A man who'd had to make do with his wardrobe last minute? Or a man whose shoes commanded his wardrobe dollar? Where he stayed on Edisto might give her a better indication.

"Have a seat," she said, signaling to the lone chair in front of her desk while she assumed hers behind it. "I'm Police Chief Callie Morgan. And you are . . .?"

"Leo Maddox," he said. He didn't say from where, however, which is what most people did. For right now she wouldn't ask.

"Welcome, Mr. Maddox. How can I help?"

He looked around as if second-guessing his choice to come in. Most people did at this stage, feeling like tricks could be played on people who trusted police too much.

Callie had left her certificates and personal accolades off the walls when she returned from her . . . sabbatical. People didn't care how you got where you were in this business. They only cared about being taken care of now.

"I'm staying out here for a few weeks."

Most people did weekends or one week. More meant a story or a pocket full of money. And he said *I*, as in solo. Even more unusual. These sorts usually hid out from a stressful situation or ran away from work or family. Mental health-seeking.

"Where are you staying?" she asked, using the common question almost everyone asked everyone else out here.

"The Retreat?" he said, in a question, as if to say, *have you heard of it?*

Per the tight shoulders, his nerves were still telling him to reconsider coming in.

She smiled bigger, for him. "That's a nice place," she said, trying to meet the man in the middle. "The pool's remarkable."

He nodded a few too many times.

"So," she said. "What's got you disturbed? We're fairly low-key on Edisto and like to keep it that way, so any infraction that has you concerned is our concern."

"Well, first, I don't want anyone to hear I'm here, all right? I mean, no statement or anything."

Hiding, as she'd guessed. He had her interest.

"Might depend on what you saw, or did, or think you saw or did, but whatever it is, we'll do our best to keep your presence on the down-low," she said. "It's not like we broadcast you coming to the beach, much less visiting my office. We're not here to make your life harder. We're a tourist town, Mr. Maddox. We want people to continue to come here."

His pause told her he was about to launch his story, so she waited, the smile stuck on hard.

"Okay," he conceded. "This is about Saturday night. Well, Sunday morning, like around three thirty?"

The night of the break-in. Okay, he really had her attention, especially considering where he rented. The Retreat were condominiums over-looking the parking lot behind the strip mall, to include El Marko's.

"Listen," he said, "before I say anything, nobody realizes I'm here. Not my wife, not her brother, not her boss, and nobody's attorney. I'm hiding out."

"Before we get too far into promises, Mr. Maddox, have you done anything illegal?" She leaned in a smidge. "Are you wanted?" She'd check before he left, for sure.

"No, no. I left my wife, she wants me back, and her brother wants to beat the crap out of me for causing his sister emotional pain and embar-rassment. Her boss is my boss, too, a lady at that, and she took my wife's side since my wife works in the inner office while I'm in the field." His life just came avalanching out. "I'm just waiting for the dust to settle." He sniffed. Something had caught his attention.

Callie had caught the scent of Marie's fresh pot of coffee, too. She'd offer the man a cup, but she didn't want him to settle in for an hour to opine about his fractured marriage.

Poor guy sounded distraught and lonely. . . unless he was a schmuck. Didn't sound like Edisto's problem, though. He was doing what you were supposed to do out here, cross the big bridge and leave your other persona back on the mainland. More had done it than not on Edisto Beach. It's how many people had repatriated there.

"I hear you loud and clear," she said. "Now, it was Sunday morning about three thirty a.m., and . . ."

". . . and I couldn't sleep, so I got up and poured a bourbon and water."

At three in the morning? She kept that to herself.

"I heard some banging in the distance but didn't really care. Sat down on the sofa and went to turn on cable news when the lights went out. The banging stopped. Wasn't until I finished my drink, during those rolling balls of thunder, that I wondered who would be in the rain making that kind of racket. Slow thinking, but my head has been filled with so much else these days, so I don't think clearly. Anyway, I decided to pour another drink and sit on the balcony and watch the rain. Ink black out there, you know? I couldn't see a thing."

Callie waited. She always preferred to let the tale play out before asking for details.

"I started to light up a cigar with that second drink, but the bottom fell out. That wind was blowing like hell. Thank God I was on the side of the building I was on, away from the beach."

The first time Callie'd heard anyone glad not to be facing the ocean.

"Still there was overhang, the wind not coming at me, so I stood there, just watching the weather. The salt air smelled so good, so I pulled up a chair to just sit there. Besides, I craved that cigar. They don't allow smoking inside."

"You never saw who was banging?" she asked, wishing to return to the main plot.

He shook his head. "No, but I'd reached the nub of my cigar, my drink down to melted ice, when someone comes out of that long building. The one with the pizza place and souvenir shops? And the Mexican place."

"Yeah?" she said, trying not to act overly intrigued. "Go on."

He wasn't as rattled now, but he had noticed Callie showing interest. He leaned forward. "All dark clothing. A hoodie, which can never mean anything good. Standing there all alone, like they forgot which way to go. But then. . . ." He stretched out that last bit as if waiting for her to plead him to continue.

Callie slightly turned her head, to show she waited.

"But then a car came rolling up, barely stopped enough for the person to hop in. Then took off."

This was something. "Make and model of the car?" she asked, pen in hand.

His expression dimmed at that being the first question the police had, as if Callie could do better. Not an unexpected reaction; most witnesses wanted to talk emotion, first impressions, and interpretations, not facts.

"The car was dark," he said. "They hugged the edge of the fence between The Retreat and the parking lot, so the angle was all wrong for me to see much, plus it was damn pitch. No lights by then, so I got little more than movement. The car was a dark, mid-sized, four-door sedan, though. Dated, but not more than ten years. Not black, but maybe gray or brown or even a gunmetal silver. Trust me, I've asked myself what color over and over, and that's all I could come up with. Everything is black and white in the middle of the night."

Not bad for his saying he couldn't tell much.

"Did you take any pictures?" she asked. Phones were permanent extensions of people's arms, especially tourists. She still bet Brice's speeder had taken a picture of him.

"No. Left the phone in the bedroom."

She sighed, then followed up with an understanding smile, as if she would do the same.

"Who doesn't carry their phone, right? But listen, I've been staying off of it while I'm down here, keeping the thing shut off. So nobody can trace me."

Callie started to tell him that he'd be smarter to disable the location tracking on his phone altogether, but she didn't. Instead she got them back on topic. "Get the tag?" she asked. She could hope.

He shook his head, forehead scrunched saying no way that was even plausible.

Callie was losing her enthusiasm about this witness, but he had come in. He had seen something. At least the timeline was corroborative to the time of the break-in, his details not bad. "Which way did they leave?"

"They did a tight turnaround and left from where they came in. Then they turned right on the road that runs in front of those stores."

"Heading to the entrance to the town, right?"

"Right."

"See the driver . . . by any chance?"

"Nope. Sorry."

Maddox's report wasn't much, but it wasn't nothing. There was no telling if the driver was the second burglar who'd invaded The Undercurrent or a third person waiting for just the El Marko vandal. Or even if this was the El Marko's vandal. Maddox didn't see anything other than a hoodie—two hoodies had been seen that night.

Callie could check the town's cam at the causeway installed for reasons just like this—in order to catch tags. They'd thought the burglar just walked into town. Now they could look for a car. As soon as she finished with Maddox, she'd have Marie check the footage again, say, between midnight and four. Marie had already done a quick look-see, to take note of who came and went that night during a respectable window for the break-in, but the power had been out, everything dark as ink. There weren't but a half dozen tags that time of morning anyway. At least she could show the vehicles to Maddox before he left.

And she could ask Mark to take another look at his back cam, but she wasn't holding her breath his caught anything.

But first she made Maddox repeat his story for a recording, which took strong coaxing but she finally tapped into his sense of good.

"What made you come in now?" she asked, once he'd signed his statement, leaving off the qualifier in her head—*because you're supposed to be in hiding*. "Which we are very grateful for," she added, emphasis on the *very*.

"Well," he said, "got to thinking if someone witnessed a robbery at my place I'd hope they'd say something. I like that restaurant. Owner seems to be a nice guy. But I went to bed about five, before it got light, tired from mulling over whether to call you people in the middle of the night. Slept in late, but when I got up the cops were there, and I wasn't about to walk into the middle of that. Guess I just wanted things to calm down first. Less attention. So, here I am."

He waited for confirmation whether he'd done well or messed up, so Callie gave him his proverbial pat on the head. "Totally understandable. There's a getaway car. That really helps." At least she hoped it would.

His mouth lines softened.

After more assurances nobody in the department would call his wife, Callie left him with Marie to study cars, but everything was shadows and maybes. About four possibilities, they decided. He left a half hour later, not wasting any time, not paying any attention to the new man who'd appeared in the last five minutes. Marie noticed and said he should have a seat. No sign of Brice.

Callie bet good money the guest was the egregious speeder Brice had confronted at the crack of dawn. "Be with you in just a moment, sir." Callie went over to Marie's desk, whom she'd barely greeted yet.

Often underestimated because her efficiency had made everyone's job easier for two decades, Marie had run the scene behind the scene since she'd graduated high school. She didn't mind being the person prioritizing the office chaos, the individual who didn't have to be the face of Edisto PD but remained pretty darn powerful. Every officer was more dispensable than Marie, to include Callie.

"Things got started early today, huh?" Callie put her back to the guy in the lobby. "God, I need some of your coffee. And you need to be brought up to speed on the weekend, and about El Marko's. . . ." She stopped.

As habit, she'd spoken while glancing over to whatever Marie was working on.

She hadn't expected to see what she saw. "What the hell is that?"

Accustomed to the occasionally salty word usage, Marie picked up the .41 bullet and twisted it around, studying it as if it might have writing on one side. "Found it when I unlocked the door this morning."

Chapter 14

"SET IT DOWN, Marie."

The sudden seriousness sobered the station's office manager, and she did as she was told and gently placed the bullet on a clean notepad. She awaited further instruction. They both analyzed the bullet as if it had the potential to explode.

"Did you find it inside or out?" Callie asked, again thinking about prints, and how this bullet would probably show little more than pieces of Marie's.

"Found it on the doorstep. Outside. I almost stepped on it unlocking the door, thinking how funny it was to be right there in my path. What are the odds if it were . . . dropped. . . ." and she stopped, a realization coming over her. "It wasn't dropped, was it?"

"You ever heard of an officer dropping a bullet, Marie?"

"No. What's going on, Chief?"

Damned if Callie knew, but once she got rid of Brice's speeder, she might try for prints on these bullets despite the odds. This culprit was flaunting themselves, and after three days, didn't appear to be leaving. That meant purpose. That meant Maya was closer to being right than wrong. This was bullet number five, for God's sake.

"Was it standing on end or on its side?" she asked.

"On its side."

"Was there a note?"

"With the bullet?"

"Yes. Under it, most likely."

Marie gave her a cocked regard at the *most likely* remark. "Um, no, but I didn't look for one." Marie pushed back from her desk, grabbed an evidence bag from her drawer just in case, and headed to the door. Callie followed, pausing to add, "Be right with you, sir," to the man in the lobby. He scowled.

Marie eased the door open, gingerly. Then she eased herself out, stepping wide to go further out, so she could stand where she'd stood when unlocking the station for the day. Callie remained in the entryway.

"There." Marie pointed to the right of the door, peeking out from beneath the live oak leaves that had collected from the hundred-year-old tree in the front. But she didn't go to pick it up. Instead, she backed away for Callie to do so, handing her the evidence bag.

The leaves stayed somewhat damp in that bed, especially this time of year, before the summer heat cooked everything. The note was square and yellow like the others. The ink was blue like the others. The writing was block lettering, again, like the others, and while it had absorbed some of the moisture making the writing spread, the message was clear and legible.

Infinite possibilities.

Marie let out a hint of a moan. Not distressed, because that wasn't Marie. "Should I be worried I was the one who found the bullet?"

Thinking hard about what her day needed to consist of now, Callie didn't hear Marie at first.

"Chief? Should I be worried?"

Laying a hand on Marie's shoulder, Callie sought to soothe the woman, because she wasn't sure what to say. The question about being worried was solid, though, with no immediate right answer. Callie could assume the bullet was meant for herself, but she'd already received one at home. Was this one for Marie, Thomas, Annie, Webb, and any other Edisto PD person?

The message made her lean toward the last. *Infinite possibilities.* How astute was this adversary? Or how ignorant?

This whole charade of notes was a setup, because Callie could feel it in her core, but a setup for what? No one had been threatened directly, and to interpret the messages as promises of physical danger, one had to stretch the imagination.

His love isn't worth the trouble.

Chill and be still.

Infinite possibilities.

They could be little more than memes about living life, found so often on social media, yoga bracelets, and T-shirts. Except these memes came with bullets.

Bullets of a caliber that had only one connection on Edisto Beach— a connection to a five-year-old nasty past of a man nobody fully knew . . . Mark. He was liked, loved, respected, and appreciated, but who really *knew* him? She would know him most, best, and deepest, but her education of him appeared to be limited. She'd learned much of who he used to be last night, but not everything. He spoke a lot, but had he said it all?

Suddenly that bothered her.

Stan, maybe? He'd befriended Mark first, and they were brothers in blue. Stan had even hinted at Mark having a painful time leaving SLED, feeling his life so unfairly altered, but Stan had told her Mark's history was his story to tell, not Stan's.

"Callie?" Not *Chief.* Marie had patiently waited for guidance.

"Check the complex cams," she said, which was a given. Marie loved watching who came and went around the station, giving them a once-over every morning when she found time between early visitors, urgent phone calls, and impromptu drop-ins from town staff.

Callie's thoughts had pinged at lightning speed in an attempt to answer Marie's question. *Should I be worried?* and resulted in nothing concrete.

"And keep aware of your surroundings until we get a better grip on things, Marie," she finally said. "And I'll be working here today."

Marie was a grounded individual, and nobody had to talk to her twice to be understood. She even shrugged. "Will do. You'll tell the others?"

She hadn't told all her officers, but Callie would now. She'd contact each, off the air. She'd go over the details with them, letting them ask their questions and offer input, but she only did so because to not do so seemed wrong. What was she to tell them anyway? Watch for more bullets and notes? Scrutinize people in hoodies? Well, they were already loosely doing that, like those same hoodies would traipse around the beach in sweats. The department could expand their search of private cams and security systems, asking people if they'd seen anyone wearing a hoodie on their cams over the last three days, but seriously, was that efficient use of her officers' time?

This was still a wait-and-see. In spite of more clues to some endgame nobody understood, they could do little more than wait and see what the individual, or individuals, had in mind.

One bullet remained in Maya's prediction of six bullets then one shot. Seven bullets within as many days. However, that was assuming all the bullets had been found and reported. Callie didn't want to learn later that they'd missed one. The only safe assumption was that someone might be ever ready to shoot the seventh.

And here she was . . . leaning on Maya's vision again. She hated that, but was she supposed to ignore the psychic altogether? Especially since Sophie had almost validated the woman's powers. Especially since bullets kept showing up.

She had to delve into Maya's history. She'd call Knox earlier than she'd planned and add a query about Maya. She'd owe him after this.

Callie watched the glass door to the station slowly shut. Marie had reentered the building and returned to her desk, and as always believed that Callie would inform her as needed.

Marie trusted Callie. Trouble was whether Callie was capable of earning that trust this time. She had little more than hunches and theory to work with, and that was a far cry from enough.

She returned inside.

Callie always gave Marie an overview of pending cases, and in a few of them, a more intense detailed briefing if it might need her to get personally involved with evidence, people coming into the station, or running interference for officers when their business wasn't for others to learn. Also, Marie knew these people, their histories, and could bring a different perspective than the officers in the field. She was already scrutinizing the front cam.

"Be aware of people around you in all your comings and goings," Callie said again. "Until we get a handle on this, we don't see where this case is headed, nor what these bullets are saying. One at El Marko's, one at *Windswept*, one at Wesley's, then Sophie's, and now this one." She wasn't about to explain Maya and Sophie to her.

"This one could mean all police, don't you think?" Marie asked.

"That's my read." Callie glanced at the waiting customer and smiled. "Let me take care of him, Marie, then you can ask me anything else. In the meantime, call Wesley?" She opened her phone and wrote down the number on a sticky note in case Marie didn't have it. "Don't call his momma, though. Let me do that."

Marie took both evidence bags, for the bullet and the note, and started logging them in. Callie painted on a welcome, spun, and greeted the speeder, his features more clouded from the wait.

Back in her office again with the new guest, she did her best to console a citizen who was totally in the right about being pulled over by a man who couldn't show identification nor had the right to be checking people for speeding. The title *town council chairman* didn't mean beans to a family from Ohio hurrying to grab breakfast they would have to eat in the car, on the way to the airport to catch a flight. A breakfast they ate in the rental instead because no way they'd catch the flight. They luckily grabbed another flight that was to leave that night but not without some expense due to missed connections and assorted other arrangements.

Brice had outdone himself this time.

Callie listened to the complaint. Then she listened again. This man wanted vengeance, and he wanted an answer on the spot as to what penalty would befall this crazed town employee.

"I manage five-hundred employees," the man ranted. "Each and every one of them understands their job description. The mail clerk doesn't pretend to write computer code. The salesperson doesn't hire and fire staff. I don't care if the man is a long-term elected official, which he repeated over and over again, that doesn't make him the police." He took in a breath and let it out slowly. "Unless you're so short-staffed out here that people are allowed to write speeding tickets."

"No, sir, I assure you we do not delegate police work to civilians. This gentleman had only the best interest of Edisto in mind, and he might have just gotten a bit overzealous in his protection—"

"He's an arrogant, pompous, elitist who hates the very tourism that pays for his employ."

Callie wasn't about to disagree . . . or agree. "Who is protective of his constituents and their property," she tacked on.

"I want him dealt with," he said. "And I want his name, his address, and how to present this to your town government."

If the man did much digging, he'd find Brice's name on the website, but the council had shied away from their photographs being posted a long time ago, just because of situations like this when visitors developed a taste for blood. A lot of that fear had come from Brice's tactics being construed as that of the entire council.

Callie danced around, using every tactic she had in her playbook short of giving Brice's personal information away. She did, however, say she'd speak to the mayor and the council.

"There's reimbursement needed," the man demanded.

"I'll tell them," she said, stopping short of saying she'd see what reimbursement was to be had. She wouldn't have had to say that much if Brice hadn't given himself away by touting his government position to the man.

"Reimbursement," he repeated. "Good. I was hoping we'd reach this part." He laid a piece of notebook paper before her. Bulleted and underlined, Callie had no problem deciphering the list which included the cost of changing flights . . . then the cost *of* the flight, the rental property cost, the rental car, and the extra meals involved . . . for six.

"Such compensation will dictate whether or not we return to Edisto in the future," he said. "Also, whether or not my family mentions this disaster across social media. About how Southern hospitality is dead. How Edisto doesn't respect visitors." He cleared his throat. "Three of my four children are teens, the fourth twenty-one, each ambitious to get home to friends and social demands, and after this detainment, they are chomping to engage in a smear campaign, depending on what dear old Dad comes back with from meeting the chief of police."

A bit over the top, in her opinion, not that any sort of agreement was going to stop the online disparagement. She hoped the town actually did something for him and his family, but that list of expenses wasn't going to happen. That would be a hellacious precedent to set.

But if Brice could be shamed into paying it himself. . . . She held up the paper. "I promise to pass this on to the *powers that be*, and someone will no doubt be in touch."

The man wanted more, and he wanted it before he left rather than hold his breath for weeks down the road, but there was no more to debate. Besides, he had another plane to catch.

Callie followed him to the lobby and watched him leave, listening to him rant on his phone before the glass door to the station had fully shut.

"Well, that's thirty minutes I'll never get back," she said to Marie, glad the man wanted to leave as early as he did. "Brice is an idiot, you know that?"

Marie continued typing and didn't echo the sentiment, ever playing the neutral middle-person, but Callie caught the grin.

"Of course you do," she said. Enough of that. "Did you get in touch with Wesley?"

"No answer, Chief."

"Leave a message?"

"Sure did. Said I was calling on your behalf, checking to see if he was okay."

Good enough. With no more visitors in the station, she had a list of ideas to pursue.

Standing beside Marie's desk, she made a call, leaving a similar message for Josephine to that Marie had left for Wesley.

"Here's who left the bullet," Marie said, matter of fact, turning her screen so Callie could see better.

If she weren't so earnest about all this, Callie would laugh. Marie was methodically taking everything in stride.

But the picture was taken at dawn, when everything was shades of gray, particularly being shaded beneath the massive live oak out front. A person in a hoodie visited the entryway; someone who knew how and where not to look up.

Only this one resembled the burglar in The Undercurrent more than the one in El Marko's. Bigger. Was this the second burglar from The Undercurrent?

What next, call the FBI? See if Knox found out anything? But they'd just talked yesterday, and lunch wasn't an hour away.

She hated to think she was corroborating what Mark said, but she guessed she was. But Knox also might find things Mark would not know about, too. Yeah, she'd hang her hat on that.

"Marie," she said, coming to a conclusion. She went to the coffee pot in the corner and poured a cup, amazed she was functioning this well and this long on a few hours' sleep and no caffeine. "I'll be in my office, making calls and researching a few things. Not anyone else's business as to what I am working on, okay? This El Marko's case is my priority, so unless a murder or something equally egregious pops up, I'm occupied." She headed toward her office to get busy.

"What about Brice?" Marie asked.

"Applies to him, too."

"What about the mayor?"

"Him as well."

"Neither will like it."

"They can leave a message like everyone else." Callie paused once more. "Brice is on thin ice. Even he ought to know better. The mayor is professional enough to leave a message." Then she hid herself away.

Her tongue was thick from talking herself dry this morning. Three visitors before coffee, for God's sake, but, glory be, the wait made the first sip of caffeine taste better than any top-shelf gin. She found the protein bar in her top right drawer, and after two bites and a half dozen sips to wash it down, she could feel the ingredients racing to jumpstart her brain.

The rush told her to call Mark first.

He picked up on the third ring, kitchen noises in the background. "Missed you this morning. Barely remember you leaving."

She humphed. "I'm fairly sure you don't remember anything. Is today's activity like yesterday or have the locals done their civic duty and left you to the tourist gods?"

"I just opened the front door. No lines. Nobody seated yet, so I hope we're not feast or famine here."

Sounds of chopping and low-key conversations carried in the background. "Listen, I need to update you on something," she said. Then she heard someone call his name. She waited for Mark to handle whatever issue had arisen so he could return full attention to her.

He came back. "I've got to go and take this call. Let me call you back."

"Okay, but before you—" But he'd hung up.

She knew better than to wait for him. Managing a restaurant could mean one brush fire after another, so she popped up a search engine on her screen and typed the obvious, delving into this mess. *Javier Harred.*

She scrolled past what she already knew of his conviction and clicked deeper into the search. Javier had been a good guy, or at least a good average guy. His name wasn't in anything untoward prior to the case, and she ultimately found where he'd been awarded for his work in a puzzling murder in Spartanburg. He'd coached soccer for two seasons when his daughter was young per a small mention in *The Voice*, the local Blythewood paper. Otherwise, nothing. No social media, but anonymity was not uncommon for an agent with any department, whether local, state, or federal.

The daughter's name was Lily. Yes, that's what Mark had said, along with Javier's daughter's birthday being September 12. The soccer piece was about a team of eight-year-olds, and it was dated five years before the cartel case went sideways. That would make Lily eighteen today.

Callie started a list for Javier's family, friends, and acquaintances, beginning with Lily. Eighteen was old enough to hold a serious grudge and be mature enough to act on it. Just ask law enforcement about the ages of people who brought guns into schools.

Callie printed off most of the case articles to start a folder and to have something handy to discuss with Mark. She even copied the soccer piece before running a separate search on Lily.

At first blush, Lily came off on Instagram and TikTok as your stereotypical teenage girl with selfies, partying with friends, and the occasional smooch on the cheek, then the lips, of a certain boy who'd been around almost a year from the sizzle on the screen. Her mother must have worked hard to keep her daughter normal and not bitter. Had to be difficult.

But then the boyfriend's presence disappeared, roughly a year ago, with ample comments to confirm he was no longer her significant other.

Memes about disappointment took over every post. What teenager didn't milk drama for attention?

I'm tired of getting my hopes up and being disappointed. That one was in a black box with white lettering. Stark.

It hurts when you realize you were never really as important to someone as they pretended you were. Sans serif font, blocky, and, again, a stark graphic.

Six more appeared along the line of these.

I hate it when your mind is telling you to stop loving someone, but your heart won't let go.

I feel like I'm waiting for something that isn't going to happen.

The poor child had it bad over this guy. At first comments felt for her, agreed with her, then told her there were others out there who were more her style, but she almost acted as if she didn't want the camaraderie. The support died down to nothing.

Then Callie read a couple of posts that made her blood run a little bit cold. Several down, she found more that made it run colder.

I fucking let you in and you completely destroyed me.

I miss me. The old me. The happy me. The bright me. The laughing me. The gone me.

Lily had snapped from angry to . . . giving up.

Jesus. That was eight weeks ago and before the dad died. If Callie had been the girl's mother, she would've been frantic trying to find professional guidance. The girl wasn't getting over the guy. She'd fallen into a deep, dark chasm, and no telling what shape she was in after Javier's murder.

Again with the black and white. *I wish I could hurt you the way you hurt me.*

Then she repeated the same words, only adding, *Maybe I'll hurt me instead.*

Chapter 15

CALLIE TRIED NOT to reread Lily's social media posts, to experience for a second time the negative almost tangible vibe coming off the computer screen, but she was part of Javier's story, which made her part of Mark's, which made her part of Callie's. Lily's followers hadn't been terribly active in defusing her quest for martyrdom before, and not enough dared to ask if she was okay. Some asked her to post lighter notions, but when she didn't reply, they didn't either.

Surely Lily had been watching. It's what the hurting did; they measured who cared. She probably counted the responses, hurting at the dwindling lack of interaction. The last one was only a week after her last post.

How did I ever give someone the power to fuck me up this bad?

That was the last one. Two months ago.

The depth of this darkness made Callie fear the worst.

A horribly creepy finality sensation made her do an obituary search in South Carolina. She found nothing.

She went back and studied the profile information on all three social media sites. All basically blank. Very uncommon for a teenager. Callie scrolled back through the pictures. No mention of place. No symbols to judge from. No names of restaurants. No open list of followers as if she'd scrubbed her life clean of them, or made them private. Using a couple of databases devoted to law enforcement, she could not find much more about Lily Harred other than an address in Blythewood—though not the one on Javier's driver's license—and a cell phone. Callie was unsure whether she'd graduated early last June or was supposed to this June . . . in two more months.

Callie hoped the girl bothered to graduate and reach a meaningful milestone . . . a positive one versus all the negative ones. She was so young and so in pain, without even a sibling to confide in. Social media made her seem so dark.

Unfortunately, this girl's past made her so likely to be someone who'd seek retaliation for how life treated her.

Was she independent? Homeless? Dead under some Jane Doe name?

Callie backed out. Enough. Time to hunt for the mother.

Melissa's social media, however, was non-existent. As an agent's wife, she might have been leery of putting her family's presence out there. As a crucified agent's wife, she could've become reclusive. These days people condemned others for the pure joy of it, from what they ate to the color of their house, and with her family having been in the newspaper, Melissa Harred could've circled her wagons and removed herself from as much attention as possible.

Callie could imagine the scrutinization she'd experienced during that investigation, throughout the reporting coverage, then afterward with her husband in jail. One day a law enforcement patriot, the next a criminal who'd turned on his own, and shot his friend and partner. Might explain why Lily was so careful about not posting specifics in terms of people, places, and social activities. They'd learned to dodge the public eye.

Their lives had dried up and disappeared.

Callie sat back in her chair, a wash of foreboding over her. She threw away the wrapper from her protein bar and downed her last swallow of coffee. Then suspecting the worst yet again, she combed the state's death records.

This time she hit the target.

Melissa Banks Harred, birthday March 2, had died from an overdose one year and one month ago.

This family had totally fallen apart.

Tales of depression and disastrous endings were far from uncommon in Callie's professional world, often the basis for many crimes, major and minor. Her own history had similar versions of spiraling, out-of-control feelings where the only way out was to find a way to forget. Her poison of choice had been gin . . . *still was* gin. An alcoholic never fully escaped the danger of relapse.

But she'd had family, friends, a financial safety net, and a place to land. She'd lost so much in her life, but compared to others with less to lose, she remained wealthy. Many got stripped of all hope.

She pulled back up a tab on Lily and studied the driver's license picture. Age sixteen at the time. Young, light brown hair, her father's tanned complexion and her mother's blue eyes.

All youth was beautiful, but few appreciated it until it was gone.

Youth is wasted on the young, was the old cliché her mother had used. Her grandmother had said the same while forever chasing it into her sixties.

Lily had much of the sweet sixteen look but not the innocence. There was a slight hardened edge there. Understandable with your father in prison, your financial future in question with the family's breadwinner broken, and your mother dabbling in pills. What used to be eight-year-old soccer games with palpitations of boys, parties, driving lessons, even a prom, had become darkness and bad reputation.

With a stabbing in her heart, Callie drew yet another parallel, too close for comfort. Jeb's driver's license had been granted during a bad time in their lives, too, with Callie unemployed, having run home to South Carolina in hope that her parents could help her raise her son, freshly alone without her murdered husband. She'd returned to the bottle like never before, having decided law enforcement was the root of all evil and something she never wanted to experience again.

Her parents had supported them. So who had supported Lily when her mother died? Callie did a search for the driver's license address and came up with someone else named Harred. Amalia. Mark mentioned an Amalia. A grandmother maybe?

She wasn't sure how long she'd fixated on that poor girl's photo, but when she came around, she leaned on her desk, hand over her mouth and nose. Throat tight, she dropped her hand, stunned at how little difference there was between Lily and her own son, and how that blink of a difference sent one to college, the other to God knew where.

How delicately life balanced between the haves and the have-nots. How precarious and fine a line existed between the survivors and the lost.

She pulled up the cam footage from Mark's. Sweats, formless clothing, no hair color. This person could be anyone, but Callie studied the violator from a different perspective now. They moved as if young. They moved as if unaccustomed to ravaging property. They moved . . . as if angry at the world.

Delving into every angle of every listing available to her, Callie hunted for a more current footprint of Lily. Javier's Blythewood address showed title records of the house being sold at a distressed sale by the bank, two years after Javier went to jail.

She identified the high school for that area, but found no record of Lily having graduated.

After the house sold, Lily and Melissa might've wound up at Amalia's address. Then the mother died. Then when Lily found a boy, when she'd dared accept there might be a light at the end of a tunnel, he left her. The why and how didn't matter. Nothing mattered other than he was no longer there . . . like others in her life.

Then someone killed her daddy.

There were hard-luck stories then there was insufferable misery, and as a tear trickled down her cheek, Callie reached for a tissue from the box on the front corner of her desk, the box reserved for distraught visitors. She wondered if Mark knew about Lily's situation. Something deep inside told her he did. Her gut told her he might be protecting a kid from ruining her life even more.

God, please don't let this be the person leaving bullets around Edisto.

Please don't let Edisto PD be the last nail in this girl's coffin.

Based on very little internet and life footprint, Callie guessed Lily lived somewhat off the grid now. If she didn't go to school, didn't work, and didn't pay the rent . . . didn't update her driver's license or pay taxes, then finding her could be difficult. If she existed under another identity, even more so. Establishing a new identity was doable even for a kid if you knew the right underground parties to assist you in pulling it off.

Callie sat back, unsure what the hell else to do about Lily . . . except send her driver's license picture to her officers and tell them, if spotted, to pick her up.

Her cell rang. Mark. What seemed fifteen minutes had apparently been almost an hour.

"I've just been sitting here waiting the whole time," she answered, trying to lighten her own mood. "About fell asleep at my desk."

"Yes, I'm sure you did. Sorry, but we had a rush come through. We're down another staff, too."

"Who didn't come in this time?"

"Stella."

Another regular. Another reliable. Wesley's cousin. "She call in?"

"No. Just didn't show. Can't get her on the phone. I started to send someone to her house but couldn't afford to spare the help. People continue to hear about the break-in and want to support us, and while I'm touched, we can barely breathe here. I frankly forgot amidst the stampede to call you back. Sorry."

Wesley and Stella would've talked.

"Stella lives near Wesley," she said.

"Yes, cousins, I think."

"Same road." Callie had a bad feeling.

"Wesley introduced us," Mark continued, not having caught Callie's concern. "Strong work ethic runs in the family, because both of them are damn good." He stopped. She could almost hear him thinking. "Shit."

"Yeah." She asked him the question that begged asking. "Any more bullets?"

"No, but I doubt he'd come here," he said.

No, *they* wouldn't. They'd want their clue to be noticed and not lost in the fray. Callie wasn't so quick to label the El Marko's culprit a *he*. Not after her research and learning about the dark mindset of Lily. Her father had died on the eve of being released, only three weeks ago, and if he and his daughter were close, that would unravel her, especially a child already depressed.

"Give me a second," Mark said. The phone sounded muted. Maybe he sought privacy. The kitchen wasn't big at all, and when you put four or five people to work there, it got downright claustrophobic.

"I'm here." He spoke more natural, less performed, and the background was quiet short of the occasional car going by. "Went out to the parking lot. They're working on repairing the front window atop of the lunch crowd, which means way too many ears. There's a tiny lull at the moment. Listen, I just heard from Wesley's mother."

Callie'd left word for the woman to call *her* back, not Mark, but contact was contact, and appreciated all the same. "Is Wesley all right? Hope she can account for Stella, too."

"He left town," Mark said, keeping his tone low. "He came back just long enough to grab Stella. He tried to take his mother, but she refused to leave."

When Callie visited Josephine, notes weren't an issue. Today, Wesley was the only one without one. "Did you ask her about whether he got a note with that bullet? Did she address any of that at all? Did she say where he was?"

If he wasn't too terribly far, say a hundred miles or less, Callie'd jump in her patrol car, catch up to him, and collect that note. Interview him. Interview Stella. Now Callie had a few pieces to go on, or at least get started with.

"Josephine has the note," he said.

"Brief me."

Someone hollered from the restaurant because Mark told them he'd be there in five minutes. Then a car horn sounded, then some idiot raced his engine.

"You there?" she asked when he waited too long.

"Just trying to find a few seconds to get a word in edgewise. Anyway, the gist of the story is this. Wesley went to leave for work a little after ten, like always. He left out the kitchen door and came around the house to his car. Said he was almost seated behind the wheel when he noted a yellow paper on the front step. Thinking it was for his mother, and not wanting it to blow away, he got out and retrieved it."

"Did he see—?"

"The bullet? Yes, he did. Said it scared him to death. He tapped it with his toe to move it aside, too unnerved to pick it up. Especially after reading the note. His was different from the others, Callie."

She still hadn't told him about the one at the station that Marie found, and she wasn't sure any of them had anything in common, to tell the truth.

"It said, *Taco or bullet*," he said.

"Hmm." The message was a little different. It held a clearer threat the others fell just short of. "He thought if he went to El Marko's he might experience that bullet," she said. "Don't blame the guy."

"He left without telling a soul so he could think about what to do," Mark said. "Then after he found a place, he called his mom, slipped back on the island, picked up Stella, and disappeared again. He was worried since she was family working in the same restaurant. His mother refused to come with him. Said she wasn't running from trouble and could keep a better eye and ear out by staying put. Sounds like a cool lady."

Callie tried to let that note sink in and gel. Now she envisioned Lily as the burglar and the threat, and she wasn't too eager to explain why to Mark over the phone. Not with him about to be called back into the kitchen.

"Tell me all the notes," he said. "I need to write these down. I have yours. Don't recall Sophie's. And I didn't get one."

"There's a new one," she said.

"What?"

"Just let me tell them to you, and this is in the order we think they were expected to be found, okay? To see if you can find any rationale or pattern."

"Be right there," he hollered to someone distant. "Make it quick," he said, back to her. "Go."

"This is in the order received. Mine said, *His love isn't worth the trouble.* Wesley's would be next, *Taco or bullet.* Sophie's read, *Chill or be still.*"

"Hmmm," he said, almost as if trying to convince himself they weren't that bad.

She found them quite threatening. "They are ultimatums, Mark. This or that. Wesley's and Sophie's could be read as keep your nose out of things or find yourself dead. Mine says to stay clear of you."

"Yes," he said, "but they're still ambiguous in the eyes of the court."

"They're premeditated warnings before someone drops a body."

"This is a concern, Callie, but not Armageddon. One step at a time. We can't overreact."

Why wasn't Mark feeling the urgency she did? "The situation is threatening enough for me to worry about what might happen if we don't figure this out. I don't want to regret having done nothing. I do not need someone's injury or death over my head, your head, Marie's, Sophie's, and Wesley's heads because we chose to wait and see. That is not an option, Mark."

The silence told her he pondered what had changed since that morning. "What's wrong? Wait, you said Marie? She was the new one?"

"Yes, there's another. Not so sure it's hers specifically." She gave him the abridged version of Marie's discovery that morning. "It read, *Infinite possibilities*."

"What the hell is *that* supposed to mean?"

Exactly.

"We think it means anyone with the Edisto PD is fair game," Callie said. "The station's cam shows someone different than the person we caught breaking into your place. More resembles the one who broke into The Undercurrent."

"Hmmm."

"Yeah. Listen, we need to talk."

"No joke, Sherlock. But it has to be after work. I can't shut down the place, and that's what I'd be doing if I left. We're two people down and Sophie not on the clock yet."

He had to be aware of Lily, but over the phone wasn't the place to discuss her. The fact that he might already know niggled her.

"Were you close to Lily?" she asked.

"Until things went bust. I'm mighty sure she hates me now. Why?"

"Did you keep up with Melissa?"

"Do I know she died? Yes. I sent flowers. The florist told me they were refused."

She and Mark had been in their early stages of a relationship a year ago. Funny how he never said anything about Melissa, or Javier, for that matter. "Do you have any idea what happened to Lily afterwards? Where she wound up living?" She heard Mark taking steps, assuming he was being beckoned back inside.

"No. Have to assume the grandmother."

Next research rabbit hole once she hung up. "What's her name again?"

"Amalia Harred. His mother. What's going on?"

"Says the guy running back to the job. We'll catch up later. I'll pick you up tonight. Don't walk the streets alone, understand?"

He didn't laugh, but she could hear the humor in his words. "I believe I can walk two blocks—"

"Don't do it, I said. And keep one eye open for Lily. I'll text you her picture."

"What? No, Callie. I'm not seeing that girl as—"

"Shut up, Mark, and just listen! What little I've learned about this girl tells me she might not be in a good place. And the more I study the cam footage, the more I see a young person full of fury. Do as I say so you're one less problem I have to be concerned about. Please?" She was forceful at the end.

She felt frayed, like a thick woven rope from the marina, strong enough for the time being but loosening and unraveling at the end. "Now do you see why I wanted you to talk to me?" she tacked on. "You know more than you're telling."

He lowered his voice, the way he always did trying to calm her. "Nothing concrete, Callie."

"I'll take anything right now. What's it going to take for you to work with me on this, Mark. A bullet? And I don't mean on somebody's front porch."

"Callie. . . ."

"Go back to work, Mark."

She hung up.

Chapter 16

ELBOWS ON HER desk, Callie stared at the old driftwood-framed print hanging on the wall opposite her desk, the only break on that window-less wall in the small ten-by-ten office. The door was closed, the air still holding the faint smell of paint from when her temporary predecessor had changed the color from ecru to light blue.

Admittedly, the blue matched the picture better. The thirty-year-old print showed *The Sarah Jane* shrimp boat docked at Edisto Seafood, as good a representation of the beach town as any symbol she could think of, and she was grateful the photo hadn't disappeared in the short turnover of personnel. Few tourists realized the vessel was what she was, a vestige of times past and how life used to be before tourism. Mention *The Sarah Jane* in a roomful of people and one could readily make out the natives from the nods and soft reminiscent looks.

The old versus the new never ceased out here. Seemed no matter how hard Edisto Beach and its adjacent island tried to protect itself from commercialism, the more urgently developers and outsiders tried to force it upon them. Everyone who discovered Edisto imagined they could improve on it, build one more house, make one slight improvement, forgetting that they came there because it was so unique and set in its ways. A daily tug-of-war that some days seemed noble . . . others a fight against the inevitable.

And with all came more crime.

Yeah, the phone call cast her into turmoil, and the day's events wedged her between being defensive or offensive. She owned her share of patience, a virtue she prided herself on and begrudgingly credited to parents who'd sat around the dinner table late into the evenings discussing long-tail tactics to beat some adversary.

But there was such a thing as too much patience for too long, enabling whatever force you were up against to gain a strong foothold and grip an upper hand.

She wanted to sit at El Marko's on her laptop to watch Mark but she was more needed at the station watching Marie. Mark might've poo-

pooed her concern for his safety, but he wasn't an idiot. He'd keep his eyes open.

Callie'd written the grandmother's name on the notepad containing scribbles about Lily and Melissa. *Amalia Harred. You're next.* Callie logged back in and went to work.

There were results for Amelia Harreds and Amalias with a wide assortment of other surnames, but no Amalia Harred. No real surprise since like Melissa and Lily, she'd probably been painted with the same damning brush of disgrace.

After some digging, in cross-referencing the address on the driver's license with years past via databases that people in the real world would have a fit about if they knew, she located enough breadcrumbs to tag what was probably the grandmother's current identity. *Amalia Coates.*

Why hadn't she changed her first name as well and disappeared deeper? Some unconscious need to still be that former person? Or some stupid oversight? Sentimentality?

The woman hadn't changed her phone number, though, thus, the connection between the names. Still, no other address since Blythewood. Not much of a disguise.

Amalia was possibly the getaway driver, assuming Lily was involved. Callie'd briefly considered the boyfriend reentering the girl's life. The concept wasn't too far-fetched if the social media was staged, or the boy did play the hero and return. Or Lily ran to the boy once her father was murdered, and he took her back.

But when the list of what-ifs went on and on, Callie's rationale fell only a smidge short of fabrication. There wasn't one shred of evidence Lily had been on this beach.

Throwing back in her chair, she fussed at herself. She was thinking like Maya, using *might-bes* and thin interpretations rather than leaning into proven facts. She had to be careful she didn't create a story for the crimes instead of investigating what the real story was.

But the legitimate truth was someone familiar with Javier's weapon back in the day was leaving .41 cartridges as calling cards at the feet of particular Edisto people important to Mark. Crediting those actions to some person connected to Javier just made good sense.

Marie appeared in the doorway. "Think I found the car on the Scott's Creek camera."

Callie hopped up to follow. *Please, give me some kind of break.*

But thanks to the power being out, the car showed as little more than a dark shadow, the tag impossible to read, assuming there was one at all, because one couldn't tell. A small, dark domestic sedan, a General Motors product most likely, with at least a decade plus change under its hood in age, drove across the causeway with its lights out. In the rain.

People had drowned in that causeway at high tide.

Odds were they weren't staying on the beach. She wouldn't if she were them.

Callie grabbed the best still of the car, along with the DL photo of Amalia, and notified her on-duty officers to come in for a briefing.

Maybe thirty minutes later, Thomas made an appearance in jeans, with Annie and Webb in tow, still dressed for duty. Russell and Ben would be caught up to speed next shift. Raysor was on assignment with the county, so nix him. She needed more people, but damned if Brice would let that happen.

With nobody in the office, except during a quick moment when someone darted in to drop off some lost car keys, Callie filled in the details while the three officers lounged on the lobby sofa and desk chairs and listened.

"Mind if I have a list of what those notes said?" Thomas asked after she'd covered most of it.

Webb gave him a puzzled glance. "Why? What good are they to us? This isn't a treasure hunt."

That instance defined the difference between the two men. Thomas functioned like a detective. Webb was happy in his role as a beat cop in a beach town. Her department would make use of both.

"Just curious, is all," Thomas said, taking the paper Marie handed him off the printer. She'd printed off enough copies for all, whether they wanted them or not. "*Infinite possibilities*, huh?"

He'd lasered in on the note found at the station. "I don't think this is about you, Marie. First, all this centers around Mark. Every single note somehow connects to Mark The one at the bar wasn't meant for you to find, I don't think. That one was a hundred percent Mark. And the word *Taco* on Wesley's? Pure El Marko's. And yours." He paused at that one. "It talks relationship . . . to Mark. Chief. These are all directed at Mark."

She couldn't contain a small grin.

"But you knew that," he said. "Listen, this is about you, too, because you're everywhere he is, and anyone who knows Mark's allies, surely knows how close you are to him."

She waited for him to explain more, but Annie spoke up. "They've watched Mark to get a lay of the land," she said. "They didn't just arrive."

Webb turned the debate back on her. "But don't you think Mark would've spotted the girl in the restaurant, Annie? Our man takes note of his diners." He waggled a brow. "I mean, I was in civies when he spotted me and a date and brought us those mini-queso-whatever things."

"But that's what I'm saying," she said. "Mark pays attention. Let's say he hasn't seen Lily in five or six years. I still think he'd have recognized her. It's all in the eyes." She batted hers for effect.

Callie let them take jabs and compare notes, taking their assumptions, deductions, and wild-ass guesses into account. To her, the contrast between a thirteen-year-old adolescent and an eighteen-year-old girl, especially one who might've been ravaged by stress, death, and disappointment, could mean baby fat versus skin and bones. As much as eight or ten inches in height. Hair style, length, and color experimentation. Especially with a teenage girl.

Like she did, everyone assumed this was Lily performing this show.

They had nobody else to blame.

"The grandmother," Webb began. "That's another story. She'd be the same. He should spot her too."

Annie laughed. Thomas watched her admiringly, enjoying his new lady friend jousting with their co-worker.

"So once a grandma figure, always a grandma figure? Same hair with the same hairnet, same floral dress, same Red Velvet lipstick she wore when she got married?"

Web's eyes narrowed. "My grandma didn't change much," he said, in justification.

"Your grandma wasn't running from the police," came her answer. "And some women step up their game as they age. It's why they have gyms, makeup, protein shakes, and hairdressers."

Enough of the competition. "Okay, you have the descriptions, you guys. You have the notes. We can't expect these people to waltz into El Marko's and wave, but we can be on the lookout for them everywhere else they might be in order to watch Mark's comings and goings." Then she added, "And mine, too, because I agree with Thomas that I'm probably on their radar as well. I wouldn't put it past anyone to get at Mark through his acquaintances, which not only means me but also Stan."

Thomas squinted. "He hasn't gotten a note, though."

"He still might. But more El Marko's workers might start staying home. Mark's lucky Sophie's still coming in."

"Luck?" Webb said under his breath. "That woman's a ding-a-ling."

Thomas's voice turned scolding. "The chief's friend, buddy. And neighbor."

Webb quickly threw back, "Nothing personal, Chief."

Annie rolled her eyes, ending the effort in Thomas's direction. *Can you believe him?* She shrugged off the antics and straightened. "This person may disappear altogether, too, but in the meantime we're to pay extra attention to El Marko's. Can we assume you will be escorting him . . . home?" The dragged-out ending said she shouldn't have asked.

Callie couldn't care less who knew she was sleeping with Mark. This was a small town. They were key players. "I'm staying here with Marie and will make sure she gets home. Then, yes, I'm headed to the restaurant to camp out. You be my eyes and ears on the streets and in the parking lots. We have no idea what these two look like these days, so just give everyone an extra second or two of scrutiny."

They nodded. While Thomas wasn't on duty, Callie could see him trolling the streets on his own. The guy lived to be police. "Can't pay you overtime, Thomas."

"Didn't ask for it, Chief." He paused then raised a finger. "A thought, though. You fingerprinted the bullets?"

"You ever searched for a print on a bullet handled by several peo- ple?" she asked, almost in justification for not having done so.

None of them had. They got the point.

"Y'all be careful out there," she said, wrapping up. "Y'all update Russell and Ben when they come on, okay?"

They went to leave. Thomas turned. "Where's Raysor?"

The Colleton County deputy was on quasi-permanent loan to Edisto Beach, and had been for the five chiefs before Callie, but he'd been absent for a week.

"Sheriff said he needed him more in Walterboro."

"We could sure use him, don't you think?"

Callie held up her hands in mock surrender. "We can use more of him seven days a week, if you ask me, but we take what we can get. Still I plan on asking for a couple more entry positions at the next town council meeting. If y'all can come up with some colorful incident examples of how two more officers would've made the difference, feed them my way."

Thomas elbowed Annie, whatever that meant. Hopefully, he had ideas coming. He's where most ideas came from, and he could be more than colorful.

Her phone vibrated. Knox. She hadn't expected to hear from the FBI quite yet. Hopefully that meant something. She waved her officers off and headed back toward her office. "Hey, what you got?"

"Got a minute?"

"Always. Surprised you called so soon." She closed the door.

It was as if he waited to hear the click before continuing. "Anything escalated on this situation?"

She had to recollect how many notes and bullets he'd been made aware of. Just two. She brought him up to speed. She shared her assumptions, guesses, and two-plus-two summations. Then she shared about Maya.

"I'll assume she's a person of interest, not a . . . collaborator?"

"You assume correct," she replied.

"Thank God. I've met your yoga friend. Just don't need all that fairy dust infecting you."

Callie could take that the wrong way, but she couldn't spare the time.

"Javier died four days before release," he said.

"Yes, I'm aware."

"Figured you would be by now."

She wished he'd talk faster, but this was Knox. He was friendly, and he liked telling a tale.

"So, I got to thinking. I went to the prison system. There you've got a treasure trove of material. Visitor's logs, phone recordings, friends, enemies. I wanted to see what happened in the month before he died. He'd be making arrangements, informing family, that sort of thing."

Smart. "Of course, they record phone conversations," she said. "You wouldn't need a warrant. But how'd you get them to accommodate you so fast?"

"I know a guy, and it helps being Bureau."

"Bet you use that like your last name. Agent Knox FBI. No first name."

"It's Agent, like you said." He chuckled, smug. "Perk of the job, Chief, perk of the job. Anyway, Javier made several calls. Mostly to his mother." Knox rattled off the number. The same one Callie had dug up, but calling his mother only made sense. She was likely his lone outside anchor.

He rummaged through some papers from the rustle. "Took me a couple extra steps to find out where he was being kept, because he was max security. He'd been in McCormick."

There were six maximum security facilities in the SC Department of Corrections system. Two in Columbia with Kirkland housing the state's death row, and four in the small, outlying towns of Pelzer, Ridgeville, Bishopville, and this one, McCormick.

"Huh," she said. Javier had lived in the same facility they'd locked up murderer Alex Murdaugh, a Colleton County trial that captured the attention of millions around the world for weeks and spawned podcasts and documentaries that made a handful of people famous. Walterboro still hadn't gotten over all that hoopla, and she bet that's why Deputy Raysor wasn't on Edisto Beach these days.

Callie hadn't realized, hadn't really cared which facility housed Javier. He was dead by the time she knew he existed. She was more concerned about the people he'd talked to. She assumed he spoke with his daughter as well, via the grandmother's number. Who else would he be calling?

"The other numbers, Knox?"

He read off another and waited. "Called that one twice. I'm talking about the month before he died, to give you a reference."

"Who is that?" she asked.

"SLED," he said. "The trunk line into SLED. From there it's difficult to tag whose desk. Nobody mentioned anyone's name on the recording though the discussion was definitely noteworthy."

Callie wasn't exactly floored at Javier calling his former employer. He was about to re-enter the real world. He might be asking for favors, introductions, recommendations, even as slim as the odds were of receiving them. Even an endorsement for a fifteen-dollar-an-hour mechanic's slot at the local garage was better than nothing. "What made it noteworthy?"

"He asked for money."

"Well, that's still not too terribly over the top, Knox. I mean, his whole social circle had been law enforcement, so I imagine he was desperate. Someone might've still been sympathetic."

"He said he wanted to meet, talk about old times. It smelled cryptic, Callie. They realize they're being recorded."

In his place, she would've been tiptoeing on eggshells, too. "Can we get a copy of the recordings?"

"I'll see what I can do. There are steps, and I sort of side-stepped a couple of them to get this much. Give me a couple days."

"Okay. I appreciate all you've done. This helps. Not sure how much, but you wouldn't believe how little I've had to go on. They've avoided detection well, except where they wanted to be seen, and even then they were impossible to identify."

She held back on the warning from Maya, that six bullets would be deposited then the seventh discharged. He wouldn't believe in giving the premonition credence, and she wasn't up to being chastised for deeming it worthy of repeating. "You mentioned another number," she said.

"Yeah, another was called twice." He read the number.

Callie's heart skipped. "Are you sure?"

"Of course, but not surprised," he said. "It's okay."

No, it wasn't okay. The number belonged to Mark. And he hadn't said a thing back then, nor anything since, even last evening when he'd supposedly spilled his heart to her on the sofa in *Windswept*.

Chapter 17

CRESTFALLEN WAS the word that came to mind, and she tried to banish it, feeling it overly dramatic and in the vein of a schoolgirl whose dreams had been dashed by a Prince Charming who'd turned out to be anything but. In other words, she was trying hard not to feel like a fool.

Mark had tried not to tell her. He'd even said he wanted to handle things himself. How could she feel justified in being deceived when he'd fought so hard to keep her arm's length from his past?

Screw the rationalization. Damn right she felt deceived.

"What else?" she asked, realizing Knox waited on the other end of a phone she'd almost forgotten she held in her hand. He was probably waiting for her to give voice to her anger, but that wasn't going to happen right now. Later, maybe. "Who visited Javier during that time?"

"Only his mother."

Why was she relieved at that?

"Y'all need to talk," he said into the silence. "This is a big burden for Mark, Callie. Find out why first before you jump to conclusions."

"Have you seen me readily jump to conclusions?"

"No, I haven't, but . . . ," he hesitated, ". . . you have jumped into a bottle."

A fire rose from her gut, up her neck and into her head, her ears ringing. Then she reminded herself that he'd eaten Chinese across the table from her while she dined on a three-martini lunch. He might have known her during the roughest of times, but he wasn't her keeper.

And neither was Mark.

But Knox had come across with information, as always, and he didn't warrant an emotional rebound from her just because he found information she didn't want to hear. Loyal, reliable, and a friend who committed himself to the meaning of the word, Knox continued to repay her for helping him solve his dead partner's murder, which as fate would have it, happened on Edisto Beach. "I appreciate what you've done, Knox. This is enlightening. What would I do without you?"

"You would've eventually done what I did." He stopped short of saying, *You or Mark*. She was grateful to him for that. "Feel like I kicked you in the gut, though."

"That's on me," she said. "I see the reasoning."

"Well, whether you're lying to me or not, go easy on the guy. He'll come around. Listen, gotta get to a meeting. Let me hear how things turn out, okay? And don't let it be on the Charleston evening news."

"Gotcha. Thanks again, Knox."

She hung up and dropped the phone on the desk. For several long minutes she rested chin in one hand, the other tapping fingers on the notepad that listed all the phone calls, all her cryptic note messages, and all the forensic history of Amalia, Melissa, and Lily. Her head was as messy as the assorted notes, arrows, asterisks, and circled words on the paper.

Did she understand the true Mark? Then like a wet smack between the eyes, she fathomed that Mark had indeed left his life on the other side of the bridge, and while Callie and every other native on Edisto Beach talked about appreciating that choice, she had not grasped how literally Mark had embraced the tradition.

Was it her right to make his past a condition of their future?

She turned her phone over. It was almost four. Marie went home at five, at which time Callie expected to go to El Marko's to continue her vigil, only this time over Mark. Regardless of her feelings about his secrets, she still needed to go.

But she didn't have to go alone.

She called Stan. Nine times out of ten he'd be dining there anyway.

"Care to meet me for dinner at five thirty?" she asked.

"Does a chocolate donut have jimmies?" he replied, talking about the sprinkles that were a Boston tradition.

She fought it a second but had to bust out laughing, breaking the melancholy. That was Stan. That's what he did, at least when he wasn't chastising, which he could equally do with ease while maintaining your sense of dignity.

"I haven't thought of Boston donuts in ages," she said. "Frankly, haven't thought of donuts in forever, period. I'll see you there?"

"Sure. We eatin' or are we . . . eatin'?"

"The latter," she said. "Need to pick your brain. My gyroscope is wobbly."

He hesitated. "Come again?"

"Getting too lost in my own brain."

"Ah," he said. "See you then. Mark eating with us?"

"I hope not," she said. "At least not for a little while. We need to discuss him most of all."

His tone softened. "I hear you, Chicklet. See you then."

Hanging up, she took a second to ponder what to do with her next hour. Marie hadn't needed her. She turned to her keyboard and typed in Maya Lecroix, hoping the name wasn't an alias.

Maya Lecroix was her real name, her birthday January 1. Her address was way inland, near Asheville, North Carolina, which explained why the sea and the boat were so exciting for her. For grins and giggles, Callie drilled down on Google Earth to visualize the residence, which turned out to be . . . a cabin. A small, quaint structure with a covered front porch and Adirondack chairs in the front. No yard, just trees and leaves and woods.

The image of a psychic, alone with herself high up in the North Carolina mountains full of Appalachian folk magic and witchcraft, rang almost cliché, but cliché was usually based in reality. Maybe that's where Maya did her best thinking, forecasting, dream weaving, or soothsaying. Maybe that's where Maya hid out.

Callie returned to Maya's website and spent time trying to pick it apart. Her testimonials were either first name and last initial or generalized like *career police detective* or *law enforcement official*. The minimal identification read like an infomercial. *Better than I expected!* By Amy T. or *She predicted things I never told her, and I'm not an easy mark.* By John G.

The website didn't lead people to her address, though, and she appeared to sell her services and perform primarily online.

Callie did assorted searches for Maya's name with the words *cold case, prediction*, and *case solved.* Then she added Finland and Britain into the mix since Maya had mentioned cases in those countries specifically, but nothing came up. So she changed from Maya's name to the word *psychic.* A Finland case actually appeared.

They had hunted for an eight-year-old boy for three months before reaching a dead-end. Callie guessed the press in Finland weren't the rabid animals they were in the States, because Maya's name never came up. She didn't have to be there, she'd said on the boat, and the story might've not been dramatic enough for journalists to warrant the man hours to dig up anything on the psychic. After all, they found the boy's remains, and the police department would want the credit.

He'd been hidden in a barrel, wrapped in plastic, and left in a shed thirty miles from a very small, what some might call culturally traditional, town of Kokemäki, Finland. The father had blamed Romani transients for kidnapping the boy, and he'd been a person of interest but nothing could be proven. Callie went so far as to Google Romani and sensed they were considered a sort of nomadic people, like gypsies.

However, she did find a newspaper piece in the small town's weekly paper. They'd interviewed Maya. Had to be Maya, though they gave her anonymity. Once under a trance, or in the mindset, whatever, the unnamed psychic claimed she experienced pressure on her chest, couldn't move, couldn't stand. Said she went claustrophobic and had even sensed a final breath. She predicted what he'd been wearing down to his black socks with white stripes around the tops. He'd been strangled, his rib cage crushed in the process as someone's knee pressed down.

Callie hated the press, even this tiny one, for posting details like that. No, she could just stop at the concept of hating the press . . . period. Reporting like this did nobody any good. Just say the boy was murdered not long after he was kidnapped, and now he'd been found. And they could not determine who killed him.

There was no proof the police department had used Maya, or that Maya did what she professed, but the details sounded damn incredible. But if Callie could find information like this, might Maya have as well? Easy enough to pretend the psychic had been her.

Also, what brought her here? Why Edisto?

For a second Callie considered calling the Kokemäki police department, but a quick check on time differences put it about midnight there.

Maya was a borderline person of interest, but Callie couldn't see the connection. Not unless Amalia or Lily or someone who knew Javier had hired her. Callie felt more like she wasted time pursuing that avenue. She wouldn't remove her from the investigation quite yet, but she wasn't on the front line of people to pursue. The worst thing Maya could be doing was showing off for and taking advantage of Zeus. Zeus seemed to be taking equal advantage.

Callie shut down the computer, but when she opened her door, Marie was speaking to a tourist, Midwestern from the accent.

"The sand drop-off is almost twelve feet tall," the thirty-something woman complained. The tides of late, especially after a King Tide, had eroded the beach causing mini-cliffs. Kids usually loved them. "Who is responsible for raking the beach? We don't need our children falling off those sand hills, and how are the turtles supposed to crawl up and lay eggs? There has to be a regulation or law. For goodness's sake, you're stricter with golf carts than you are with the safety of the waterline. Who's in charge?"

"Ma'am," Marie said, just as cool as a cucumber salad. "Mother Nature dictates the beach. Tides, weather, storms, and time of year. The last time we had beach rakers was maybe six or seven years ago, and between hurricanes and the budget, we had to let them go. They just couldn't keep up."

"But it's so difficult to stroll the beach."

Callie smirked at the whine.

Marie remained ever so serious yet empathetic, offering a slight smile. "Yes, ma'am, but on the bright side, the steeper the slope the higher the odds for finding treasure. Edingsville pottery pieces, mastodon vertebrae, and shark's teeth the size of a child's hand have been found after the most eroding tides. Trust me, feel privileged this happened during your stay."

The woman's facial expression morphed to one of puzzlement, then slid into a smile to match Marie's. "Well, the kids might be pretty jazzed about that aspect."

"Most are," Marie said. "Have fun and lots of luck."

"Um, ok. Thanks. Sorry to bother you," the woman said, backing up, then turning to leave. "Wait, one more thing. Can we keep the artifacts we find? They don't belong to the state or anything?"

"All yours," Marie said. "No problem at all. Enjoy."

The woman left, and Marie followed her, turning the lock behind her.

"We had a beach-raking team?" Callie asked.

Marie began her routine of straightening up, clearing up, ready to go home. "You've got to be quick on your feet around here sometimes. So many of these people have no idea what the beach is about."

"Well, we aren't exactly like the other beaches," Callie said. "A far cry from the commercialism of Hilton Head and Myrtle. Nature is mighty shocking to city slickers." She helped with a couple of final duties. "Let me see you to your car," she said as Marie lifted her purse from a drawer. "I'll follow you across the causeway, unless you want me to follow you home."

Marie straightened. "I need that much protection?"

"I'm leaving, too, Marie. It's not like I'm posting uniforms at your door."

Marie hadn't moved.

Maybe that hadn't been the right thing to say. "Let's just go home," she said, like today was normal.

"You've waited in your office all afternoon. You don't do that. Is this about protecting me?"

"Not totally. I had things to do. But if you sense anything wrong, just call us, okay? I expect nothing though. Like Thomas said earlier, this is about Mark."

"And the people around him," Marie reminded.

"Nothing's happened," Callie said, then feeling as if she wasn't helping, she decided to offer a solution. "You can stay at my place if you like. I've got extra bedrooms."

For a second Callie expected Marie would accept, even wondered if there were towels in the extra bath.

"No," Marie finally said. "That would keep me closer to Mark, if you get my drift, and I'm not about to tell you to keep Mark away."

"Oh, good heavens, Marie. Mark is a big boy and can sleep in his own house."

But Marie shook her head and collected her purse. "Nope. I'd be happier at home. Besides, where are you going now?"

"El Marko's."

"To do what?"

Callie started to say to keep an eye on Mark and stopped. She got Marie's point. Callie wanted to protect Mark. Bringing Marie to *Windswept* would expose Marie more to potential danger because of the proximity to Mark, but if Mark stayed away—alone at his place—that put him in more danger.

"What about Thomas?" Callie offered.

But Marie had made up her mind. "I have a gun at home, an alarm on my house, and a neighbor with two pit bulls. I'm on speed dial to you, and I am quite comfortable with 911. I'd probably identify who answered by their first name. Come on, let's just go."

Callie loved this woman who didn't let people get terribly close. Nobody went to her house socially, and she didn't often appear at parties and shindigs elsewhere. Marie was Marie. While she knew everyone, and everyone recognized and appreciated her, nobody expected her to kick back at Coots with friends or lay out on the beach. She might appear at the Wednesday craft market on her lunch hour, and she made her appearances at the parades and fairs, but nobody could name a man or woman anyone would consider Marie's bestie. Something about that made Callie sad. After this crap was over, the Edisto PD needed to do something about that.

Made Callie want to protect her even more.

Ten minutes later, Marie was on her way home, and Callie halfway to El Marko's. She made it in by five twenty-five to find Stan already perched at the tucked-away VIP table against the kitchen door. Before she made it across the room, Sophie came flying in the front door, pausing up close to Callie long enough to say, "I'm late. Oh my God, but if you knew the reason why!" Then she cackled all the way to the kitchen, the door hardly making a full swing before she was back out, her mouth pouted and sour, a plate of mini-quesadillas in hand.

"What's wrong?" Callie asked, not even having sat.

"Here," she said, slinging the plate on the table before Stan. "I might have to play waitress, Mark said." Blowing out like a spoiled ten-year-old, she shook her pixie. "He hasn't been able to replace Stella and Wesley."

"Sorry, Soph. He appreciates you a lot."

"He damn better," she said, reaching the hostess station and morphing into Miss Universe in smile and attempted stature when a couple came through the door.

Mark was accustomed to playing waiter when he was down one person, but he couldn't be everything to both the kitchen and the dining room with a person down in each. Sophie could get over herself. The dining room wasn't packed, but it was two-thirds full with more showing.

Callie sat, the plate of snacks smelling heavenly after only a day of protein bar and coffee.

"In uniform and everything," Stan said, a compliment.

"On purpose today." She lifted a hot tortilla—blowing on the cheese—and dared a bite, pretending she wasn't scanning the room.

"Who are we watching for?" he said, noting her effort.

She chewed tentatively, slightly burning the roof of her mouth, sucking in air to cool the spot. "Javier Harred's daughter or mother." She pulled up her phone and slid it across the table to him so he could see their driver's licenses.

"And his wife?" he asked.

"Died a couple years after he went in. Pills."

"Damn. And he just died. Sucks for the child." Funny he hadn't eaten a bite yet. "And we're hunting these two ladies why?"

"I'm not so sure they're not on this beach," she said. "The daughter's messed up. The mother, let's call her the grandmother, maintained contact with Javier in prison. I lucked up calling Knox." She chewed the last bite of the snack and wiped hands on her napkin, swallowing so she could speak. "Turns out Javier spoke to three people his last two months in prison. Someone at SLED, his mother, and Mark."

Stiffening in his chair, Stan wasn't as much stunned as he was braced for the other shoe to drop.

"Yeah," she said, understanding her old boss's body language. "How much more are we going to learn that he hasn't told us. And why?"

Chapter 18

THE NOISE LEVEL of the restaurant went up a touch; plus, Sophie had increased the volume of the background music. Both of those suited Callie fine.

She relayed the night Mark was shot, then the information she'd dug up on Lily, Melissa, and Amalia. "He told me his backstory four or five times, Stan, with no mention of the women or phone calls with Javier."

"But he told you the main story," he said. "He's trying the glass is half full, Chicklet."

She shook her second mini-quesadilla at him. "He's picking and choosing what to tell me when the whole truth is the only way I can help."

"We haven't confirmed these ladies are here, have we?" Then he popped an entire snack in his mouth, cheeks puffed out.

Sophie showed. "Guess I'm your damn waitress. What do you want?"

Stan chuckled from behind the last snack in his hand, and Callie openly laughed, happy for a reprieve from their former discussion.

"Our usual," Callie said.

"Well, I have no idea what that is," she said, pen and pad in hand, totally exuding her opinion that this type of work was beneath her.

"Burrito with extra jalapenos," Callie said.

"Surprise me," said Stan.

His response merited an accusatory, air-stabbing jab of Sophie's pen. "I'm working my ass off here, so I'm not in the mood. Just tell me something."

But Stan wasn't done. "Don't you even remember my favorites? Have we been separated that long . . . Bug?"

The growl fit nowhere in the normal smooth, sassy ways of the yoga queen. "Stan. . . ."

"Make it easy on yourself," he said. "Just give me the platter."

Almost bending the pen writing on her pad, she reached for menus that weren't there. "Argh!" she growled again and disappeared into the kitchen.

Sophie wasn't gifted at taking orders, and the room was filling. "Makes me want to ask if I can wait tables," Callie said.

"Let them manage. Eat. Bet you haven't today, or not enough to feed one of those seagulls out there on the beach."

"Those gulls eat a ton of food, kind sir. About a quarter of their weight daily. And they eat anything." Then she added, "Tuck this in your memory file, too. They drink salt water. The other birds out there don't."

"You're changing the subject. What did you eat?"

"A protein bar."

She received *the look*.

Bless him, he'd gotten her out of her own way. He had a knack for that.

Through the meal, the room filled, got noisier, and the two of them could speak in peace in the middle of two dozen people. She'd brought in her file she'd gathered in her office, full of facts, addresses, Facebook comments, newspaper clippings, and so on.

Mark had come in and out, speaking once, at which time Callie had explained she was there to watch over him. He scoffed, then sensed maybe he shouldn't have, apologized, and went back to work.

Dinner over, file dissected, and story told to the fullness of Callie's knowledge, she sat back. "Well, what's your take on all this, Stan?"

But before he could answer, a new voice traveled across the room, joking with diners. The natives knew who he was without turning. The locals stared and wondered who the hell had such few manners.

"Son of a bitch." Callie tried not to show interest, but she could hear his steps.

"He's coming," Stan muttered.

"Make us disappear," she whispered.

"They took those powers away when I retired," he quipped, and Callie almost spit trying not to giggle.

Brice reached their table, pulled out the third chair, and sat as if he'd been invited.

"Did I forget an engagement?" Callie asked. "My apologies, but my calendar said my dinner appointment was with Stan this evening. Did I get my days mixed?"

Brice twitched one cheek, and Callie couldn't tell if he was being snide, nervous, or simply odd. "I came for an update," he said. "Did you get the man's name and address? Tell me you wrote him a ticket. If not, we're mailing him one."

Stan hadn't been updated as to Brice's latest speeding-ticket hobby, and he didn't ask. Brice never failed to expose his abilities, inabilities, and screwups. Nothing secretive about the man because he just couldn't help himself.

Callie tried to make this quick. "I have his name and address, but only to give to the mayor first, the council second. He deserves an apology, Brice. Your stop caused him to miss his flight, and he had a family of six. Don't be surprised if he doesn't want compensation."

"He's out of his fucking mind! What's his name?"

Callie was no idiot. "Sorry, but you will be the last person I give it to. As we discussed earlier, you and the council have no right to issue tickets. Stop doing it, Brice. This is, what, the second this week . . . the fourth in as many weeks?"

"Fifth," he said, and slapped fifty bucks on the table. "Caught a kid speeding up Myrtle a little while ago, told him I was in charge of the town, and that he deserved a ticket. He begged me not to give him one, handed me this, and said add it to the town coffers as his appreciation for what we do. So, here you go."

"Good heavens," Stan grumbled.

"What?" Brice said to him. "You got a problem with me stopping crime and helping the budget at the same time?"

Callie didn't want to touch the money, and she had no doubt that Brice would turn it in, but this was not legal. "Brice . . . you cannot keep doing this! That's impersonating an officer."

"I don't say I'm a cop. I don't have lights."

Stan shook his head, and Callie turned to him as if this moment was too stupid to believe.

"It's called the reasonable person test," and she had to stop herself from calling Brice an idiot. "It's what a typical person, with ordinary prudence, would believe and act on in certain circumstances."

Brice's puzzlement made her almost want to slap him, but that wouldn't help him understand any better. Those marbles in his head were limited, no matter how much you shook them up.

"The kid," she said, trying to dumb this explanation down, "was pulled over, right?"

"Yes. I waved at him to stop."

"You identified yourself as an official of the town, right?"

"Yes."

"You told him he deserved a ticket. Am I right again?"

He was getting bothered. "It's not rocket science, Chief."

"We at least agree on that," she said. "But the kid felt you had the power to write him a ticket, so he gave you payment, called it a donation to the town, and expected to get out of a ticket. How close am I?"

"Pretty damn spot on I'd say considering you weren't there," he said.

"Brice," she started slowly, hoping the lesser pace would assist in the message sinking in. "You gave him the impression you had the power, and since only cops can write tickets, he assumed you were some sort of cop. Maybe off duty, but you presented yourself in such a way that he believed it."

Brice shrugged. "His problem. Now he watches his speeding, and we have fifty bucks to put toward something useful. Here." He pushed the bill over to her.

She went palms up. "I'm not touching that. You handle it."

"But it's payment in lieu of a ticket."

"No, it's a donation to the town, you said. Your problem to deal with."

He snatched the money, his knuckles thumping the table in the process. His frown etched deep, Stan sobered from grinning, ready to react if Brice were so inclined to be stupid enough to act on his temper. He'd done so before.

Brice's voice dropped low. "We should have never brought you back as chief, Morgan."

"You should never have put your college buddy in my place. He brought hard-core crime to this island, Brice, the likes this place has never seen. We were damn lucky to get ahead of that mess."

That temporary chief had come with two officers in tow and connections to a human-trafficking ring. The chief retired, one officer killed, and the third turned into a pretty decent officer that Callie held onto . . . Annie.

And Brice lost a hell of a lot of credibility. Word on the street was he would not be reelected in the fall.

"Any problems here?" Mark had appeared out of nowhere. He was not a Brice fan, and he'd dealt with the man handily several times inside the walls of El Marko and would love to deal with him outside that parameter, but Callie had assured Mark that that territory was hers.

Brice exhaled with a taste of drama. "Just wonderful. The gang's all here." He had to crane up at Mark, who made no effort to stoop and lessen the distance.

"Are you ordering?" Mark asked.

"I'm supposed to meet Walker here for dinner, thank you very much. I will be dining with him when he arrives."

"He's right over there." Mark tilted his head toward the front, where a white-haired gentleman about seventy waited alone at a table. When everyone stared over at Walker, he waved.

"That's my cue." Leaning on the table for assistance, Brice stood.

Callie didn't remind him not to pull another car. She'd made herself clear, and to embarrass Brice in front of Mark wouldn't do anyone any good. "See you, Brice."

After his standard stare of revulsion, he crossed the room to dine with his cohort from the council.

"I didn't want an issue," Mark said. "Y'all need anything?"

"No, we're good," Callie said. "And you're busy."

He didn't say another word in parting, just spun and left. Callie turned to Stan, her brows raised. "What do you make of that?"

"Brice, or Mark, or Mark dealing with Brice, or—"

"Stop it, Stan. Brice is a no-brainer, because . . . he has no brain."

Stan chuckled, liking that one.

"But Mark isn't being congenial. He's guarded. He's still pissed I'm even delving into this."

"Listen, Chicklet. I'm telling you that he thinks he's protecting you."

Callie rolled her eyes and moved on. "What if Lily was in trouble? Legal or criminal trouble. Javier called Mark, wanting him to do something about it?" she asked. She'd thought of so many scenarios this afternoon.

"But Javier was about to get out," he replied. "He'd be available to take care of his own daughter. Makes even more sense with him talking to his mother, the grandmother, who was tending the girl. They'd be talking the problem and coming up with solutions. Mark wasn't SLED. He wasn't law enforcement of any kind, so what kind of pull would he even have?"

Stan playing devil's advocate again.

"Okay, smart man," she said, mind working hard to best her old adversary. "What about Javier calling SLED?"

His smugness melted. "That feels like a man desperate for connections, to me. He's about to be released and has no idea what to do with himself."

Her thoughts as well.

They did this back and forth for two hours. Then three, going on four as they replayed old history of cases that might have likenesses and similarities. They went through four drinks each, and Stan couldn't help but order another appetizer that Callie let him devour alone. They could do this all night.

Mark quit checking on them, not particularly happy with what Callie was doing judging from his clipped words and purposeful walking to appear and quickly be gone. Not that he cared about her talking with Stan. More that he wondered what she'd dug up, because he knew her well enough to suspect she'd found something more. Because, one, he wasn't telling her everything, and, two, she didn't walk away from criminal behavior on her beloved Edisto Beach.

Callie hoped he couldn't stop thinking about her presence there, wondering what she'd found out, and questioning what to expect when he got off work.

"Are you seriously waiting here till Mark gets off?" Stan asked, after the latest time Mark walked by. People had started clearing. Few came in past eight, and it was a quarter to nine. The staff wasn't running around frantic anymore. The air felt . . . tired. Like she did. She hadn't gotten a good night's sleep, and sitting here practically on stakeout only made her feel that weariness way down in her bones.

"Yes sir, I'm sitting right here until I can take him home."

"Well, I'm bowing out, if you don't mind." Stan rose from his chair and stretched, releasing a groan. "Not that I go to bed with the chickens, but your guy's about to have more time on his hands with the diners gone, and he just may take a moment to come see you. Not so sure I want to be in the middle of his querying, your querying, and both of you digging in about the other's stance. Just don't take it personal, okay? He's more about caring for you than not respecting you. Somehow all that is jumbled up together, and I'd hate to see you two butt heads over something that is neither of your fault."

Ever the middleman. She wished Stan would stick around, but she couldn't blame him, either. She got up and hugged him before he left.

Then she sat back down to nobody.

One table of four finished up their meal. Sophie had been told to pack up and go home at nine, and Callie thinking of Sophie made her then think of Zeus and Maya. They'd been awful quiet for Maya being so earnest about danger. Callie still didn't trust the woman, but nothing condemned her as doing anything more than taking advantage of a young man's hormones and his boat. The jury was still out on her forecasting talents. She was somebody to keep an eye on.

Funny how Sophie hadn't said a word about either of them tonight. Hadn't even asked how the investigation, if you could call it that, was going. That was unlike her. She usually peppered Callie with questions during a case, and she should be particularly demanding answers with one of the bullets having shown on her porch. Maybe Sophie was taking her note seriously. *Chill or be still.*

The last couple had paid and now they gathered purses and set napkins on their plates to leave. The lone waitress hung at the door.

Callie went into the kitchen. Mark was closing down and wiping down.

"Let your girl out front and this lucky fella go home," she said. "I'll stick around and help you close."

The young man at the sink lit up at the possibility.

Mark waved a dishtowel at him. "Sure, go on. It's been quite the day, and you've been incredible, Gary. Go on since you're coming in for Wesley again tomorrow. Tell Bella out front she can go as well."

The worker finished up the dishes before him, dried his hands, and saluted Mark. "Thanks so much, Mr. Dupree. I'll talk to my friend to see if he wants some hours since we're short-handed."

"I'd be much obliged," Mark said, his smile genuine but weary.

Callie'd seen enough of the routine to pick up where the boy left off and donned an apron to cover her uniform.

"Let me double-check she locked the front door," Mark said. "Be back in a sec."

Tying the apron, she launched into and finished the dishes, deliberating whether she and Mark would talk better here or at *Windswept*. He might be more comfortable here, but she didn't want him to get flustered enough to have the choice to retire to his house versus hers.

She moved to the fryer and started cleaning, the heavy, leftover odors not nearly as appealing as the ones this grease and griddle created and delivered to hungry diners. Then she remembered how often Mark's clothes reeked of cayenne, chili powder, grease, and fajitas when he came home. Yep, this uniform was dry-cleaners bound.

She heard Mark talking and stopped. Surely his two helpers had gone. Who would he be talking to? She then worried Brice had backtracked to cause trouble, and Mark was convincing him to leave.

In case it was Brice, or in case their burglar decided to return for a bigger reward, she slid the apron off and eased to the door. With a slight push, quite familiar with how much movement would cause the top hinge's squeak, she gave herself a two-inch opening.

Yep, he was talking to someone. Not adversarial, but still he stood stiff and uncertain. She had to maneuver the door another inch to see who bothered him so.

He stood in the middle of the dining room, his angle of attention indicating the person was positioned near the entryway. Sounded like a woman, and not one Callie knew.

Not wanting to feel like a chump when whoever turned out to be a visitor just checking about reservations, she played it safe and allowed another silent inch with the door.

Tan skinned, black-and-white hair bordering on gray. *Holy Jesus.* Callie almost yelped in surprise at the sight of Amalia Harred, or Coates, or whatever the hell her name was, standing in El Marko's.

Chapter 19

CALLIE WASN'T walking into the dining room. If Amalia Harred had appeared to speak with Mark, she expected privacy, the reason for the late entrance. The uniform alone would scare her away. Instead, Callie texted Mark. *I will stay in the kitchen.*

She hoped he found that a good thing. She hoped he didn't mind her listening in, because she damn sure was. With so much animosity and history and only God knew what else between them, that might be a while. She hunched down to the floor for a more comfortable position and set her phone to record, setting on high. The two in the dining room danced around each other with introductions and finding the right words, so she figured she hadn't missed much.

"I'm so so sorry to hear about Javier," Mark said. "His passing hurt me terribly, Amalia. He'd been my friend for too long for it not to."

"He didn't deserve—" but she stopped herself, self-correcting per se. She seemed to have a bigger purpose than to just fuss at Mark for things that could not be undone.

"No, he didn't," Mark finished for her. "Please come sit down. I'd like us to visit. We're closed to diners so we shouldn't be disturbed." He pulled out a chair at the table nearest to him, and luckily closer to Callie.

Callie never failed to admire his style in dealing with people on the edge. She'd seen him handle drunks, couples at each other's throats, and armed men . . . twice. He had a way with people. He had a way with her. Which explained why he'd been a handler for someone undercover. But with his last case labeled an epic failure between no drug recovery, an agent gone bad, and people shot on both sides, he'd ended his career on as sour a note as one could. Then that negativity had continued domino-ing to Melissa, then Javier, then Lily. Amalia had to be an in-your-face reminder to him about how horribly wrong can go wrong. And likewise him to her.

Mark pulled out the chair for Amalia, trying not to appear stiff. She dropped her purse to the floor before tucking a plain shift of a dress under her to sit. Her gray hair with streaks of dark would have hung mid-shoulder-blade range, but she'd slicked it down, held in a banded pony-tail. She wore functional makeup, covering age rather than adding beauty.

Mark cleared his throat. They almost acted like strangers. Or maybe people who'd broken up and were trying to reach back across the chasm to settle the divorce.

"How have you been doing?" he asked. "Wait, first, can I get you something? A snack? Something to drink?"

"Nothing to eat. Maybe a soft drink?"

He disappeared behind the bar, where Callie couldn't see, but she heard him going into the refrigerator beneath where he kept a stash of drinks. She heard the pop and fizz, ice into a glass, and the gurgle. He reappeared, setting the glass on a coaster, treating her as a full-fledged guest with the respect for someone a generation older. "There you go," he said.

"Thanks so much." She took a big deep sip. She'd been thirsty. Thirsty enough for Callie to wonder why. Nerves? Sitting outside too long without anything to drink? Saving her money?

Oh crap, her car might be in the parking lot. Callie yearned to slip outside and see if there was a dark, four-door sedan resembling the description Maddox told her, or the shadowy car Marie located crossing the creek with its lights off.

But her patrol car was out there as well, four rows out from the building. She'd arrived when El Marko's was busy, at the time cursing the fact she couldn't park near the entrance so the police presence would better protect Mark. Now she was glad the car was where it was, appearing empty and little more than a deterrent for the speeders. A good thing the car's presence hadn't stopped Amalia from coming in.

Callie almost texted Stan, then Thomas or Annie. One of them could collect the details of the vehicle. While she could slip out the back door, Callie didn't want to miss Mark's conversation. No, she'd run out and check when the woman left.

"What can I do for you?" Mark said.

"Not sure what you mean," Amalia replied.

He held his hands out to the side, indicating where they were. "You came here, after hours. Something's not right or you wouldn't have. You needed to see me. Why?"

She finished the drink, and Mark patiently waited, the ice cubes loud in the empty dining room, then she pushed the glass and coaster away.

Clasping fingers, she rested both hands on the tablecloth in preparation for the interview.

"I've been here for three days," she said.

"Where are you staying?" he asked, falling back on that same routine question everyone asked everyone on Edisto.

Pointing over her shoulder, toward the front of the town at Highway 174, Amalia replied, "Back up that way. Found a tiny Air B&B we could afford." Shaking her head, she tacked on, "Couldn't afford anything in this town. Only the wealthy can afford this place. Only needed one bedroom for me and Lily."

She'd brought her granddaughter. On paper Callie would have written Lily's name with double underlines. She wasn't surprised.

"Hope you're enjoying yourself," Mark said, no doubt hiding his urgent need to ask a dozen different questions.

Amalia's tired eyes appeared weary of the pretense. "Yes, I came to talk to you, Mark. I also came in the hope that I could appease Lily, but I've almost given up on that even being a possibility."

"We have spoken on the phone, Amalia. Before and after . . . Javier. You could've called again. You didn't have to spend money you don't have to come see me in person. Who are you renting from?"

"A place called Wainwright Realty?"

He started to reach across toward her and changed his mind. His expression held pity and pain at a plight he knew way more about than he'd told Callie.

"I can talk to Wainwright" he said. "You two can just stay at my house. I have a friend I can stay with for however long you need to be here."

The woman's expression didn't slip into one of gratefulness, instead taking on that of someone not wanting to be bought, bribed, or whatever Mark's offer meant. To Callie he was genuine. To Amalia . . . well, she'd just lost her son who'd gone to jail mainly because of the man seated across from her while she attempted to manage a granddaughter who hated his guts. She might have once trusted Mark, but that was five years ago. Now she wasn't so sure. Yet here she was, needing something, and neither one sure how to approach each other, the subject, or simple conversation.

"Lily would never stay in your house," she said with a slight edge.

He tried again. "She'd never have to see me."

"She blames you for her father's death, for God's sake, Mark. Just your things around would trigger her."

Mark dropped his head, his shoulders sagging. "I had not given up on him, Amalia."

Amalia didn't appear convinced.

"Let me reword that. I was trying to help him. Please tell Lily that. Javier made mistakes. He admitted as much, and I believe he admitted the same to you. He went undercover and had to choose one side or the other one time too many. Bad choices placed him in prison. Not me, and not SLED. I suspect he explained that to Lily as well, but before we get too deep in the right and wrong of things, how is Lily? She's the center of all this. You've hinted, but, please, tell me how she's holding up?"

The woman sniffed at what might have been the slightest sign of tears. "She wanted to see you for herself. I tried to talk her out of coming, but she was insistent. We arrived as I said, and she immediately wanted to drive around, so we did. We found your restaurant. I tried to get her to come in and eat, to see you feeding people for a living instead of being an agent. I figured she'd soften about you, but she refused, suddenly unable to come face-to-face. I hoped this trip might actually be good for her. You knew Javier in his good days, and you used to bring Lily birthday presents. While she's fussing about never wanting to see you again . . . and fussing is a mild word, she needs to. She needs to hear you talk about her daddy."

Mark remained sad but patient, wanting Amalia to deliver all she came to say.

"She only got angrier," Amalia said. "She'd take the car and come sit and watch for you, wanting to see you from a distance to understand how you lived, how you dared to continue with your life after what happened to her mother, then her father. I rode with her twice, until she had another one of her horrible fits the other night and took off on foot without me in the storm."

He stared down for a long moment before responding. "I don't know what to say." He reached over and, this time, laid his hands over one of hers. "My apologies, Amalia. I should have asked earlier . . . how are you holding up? First Melissa, then Javier . . . now Lily's anger. God, this is so much on your shoulders."

"I'll be fine," she said far too quickly, and the stiffness of her lip said she was doing the best she could to not appear damaged. "I am all Lily's got, and I understand why she is like she is."

But did she? Was she familiar with Lily's social media? The grandmother's inability to keep a rein on the girl had just made Lily a suspect in the El Marko break-in. Was she just picking up the pieces of damage Lily left in her wake, or did she truly have a grasp of her granddaughter's mental instability? Had she seen how far Lily had strayed, assuming she was the culprit who'd busted up El Marko's?

And here was Mark, believing every word. Master interviewers had to learn early on to overcome personal bias in what to believe of the soul across from them in order to stick to an objective assessment of behavior. He had to be careful. No doubt he wanted to believe Amalia Harred, which could lead to his seeking reasons to justify that belief, up to and including blaming himself for any insensitivity.

Mark sympathetically fixated on Amalia, showing he was truly listening. That or hunting for reasons to be on her side. Ordinarily he was good at listening. Callie knew that all too well. He didn't believe in filling the air with words. He believed in hearing you, absorbing not only your words but the pain that went with them. That silence told his person that he respected only the real them, not their façade. The challenge was not to fall into their feelings such that you could not remain objective, especially with someone you owed.

This was Javier's mother, for God's sake. Would she be honest? Would she not be vindictive? Would he be able to tell?

From the slight quiver in her chin, Amalia was not as strong and together as she struggled to present.

Then tears ran down the woman's dark complexion, reflected by the ceiling-fan light directly over their heads. "Javier had a plan to come home and be everything to Lily. The only thing that tore him up more than Melissa dying was Lily coming apart. Lily was all he could talk about those last days. He counted the hours before he could get home to tend to her."

She sniffled, and Mark rose and brought back napkins from the bar. "Thank you," she said, and took time to compose herself. Callie could see this was tearing Mark up.

"Orson DeLuca came to the funeral and gave his condolences," she said, with one last wipe to her nose. "Even still working with SLED, he came."

"Good of him," Mark said.

Callie wouldn't have had a clue who Orson DeLuca was except for last night's chat with Mark. Orson was Mark's and Javier's former boss, and apparently still active as a supervisory agent.

"Yes, it was very good of him," Amalia said, better composed. "But you didn't come. What does that say about you?"

Mark wilted in his chair. "Amalia," he said, then nothing for several long seconds. "When Melissa died, when y'all's anger intensified, I decided it best not to disturb you. Too much undue strain on you both."

"On you, you mean." Amalia stared him down as the tables turned.

"I just couldn't think of what to say," he said, trying not to argue, grabbing for the right words. "Then when Javier passed . . . I . . . I thought. . . ."

"You didn't think," she scolded, emboldened by his discomfort.

But her comment, instead, brought him alive. "Oh, there you're wrong. I can't *not* think about the case, Javier's choices, and what hand I had in him taking a wrong turn. I was his handler, for God's sake, Amalia. A day doesn't pass I don't agonize over how we both could have handled things differently." His voice choked, and now it was his turn to fight to keep it together.

Callie had tears dripping off her chin.

He sucked in a shaky breath. "I wrote Javier and told him I was here for him. I offered to help him get back on his feet. He called, and we finally talked. Neither he nor I had any idea what kind of help I could even offer, but we agreed to meet up once he got out." He choked on those last few words. Callie almost did the same and desperately fought to swallow any noise.

"An ex-coworker told me Javier died," he said, more stable now. "I . . . I had no idea what to do. I was just devastated, Amalia. Please say you understand."

She took his hands, this time, squeezing them. "I wouldn't be here otherwise. Javier would not want us to remain estranged."

He smiled a melancholy smile, and Amalia reflected his in kind. Callie sat on the kitchen floor, watching, listening, her own hands over her mouth at the matronly caregiving this woman could give after losing a child.

Emotion filled the room, cutting clean through Callie, as she was sure did the same for Mark.

She hated herself for doubting Mark so much. For not understanding how devastating this whole ordeal had been for him for so long, culminating in this family's train wreck when Javier died.

Callie hadn't seen his pain, at least not this level of pain. What did that say about her?

But this wasn't about her. This was about Mark. This was about

Amalia. And this was possibly about a teenage girl so outraged at how life had treated her that she was willing to hurt Mark by hurting those around him.

Question was how far she was willing to go in that effort.

"Did Lily break into the restaurant?" he asked.

The question snared Callie, the timing such that Mark could have been reading her mind. She made the slightest shift to ease out a kink in her leg. Amalia didn't immediately reply.

"Was she the one who broke in?" he repeated.

"I believe so," she replied after a deep sigh.

"You don't know?"

"The night of the storm," she started, trying to sort her words. "Lily got angry and left on foot, not wanting to leave me without a car. I didn't take note until she'd been gone about fifteen minutes. Lightning shook the ground, and lights flickered. I worried hearing how close the storm was with her walking in all that, so I jumped in my car and went looking for her. I didn't see her on the road and wound up traveling to the beach and up and down the streets, then back around the town buildings. It was the middle of the night, she knew nobody else, and I learned later she hid up under someone's porch until some of the storm passed. She was a child who trusted nobody and didn't bother to try and call anyone, to include me."

He waited until he had to ask. "And?"

"The lights went out while I was hunting for her. I watched half the beach go dark, right in front of me as I went to cross the water again."

She spoke with maybe more tears. Callie couldn't tell.

"After about the fifth pass of this place, I found her in the parking lot. Crying, rain-drenched, totally lost. That poor baby had lost her mind. I drove up, told her to get in, and sped off. I didn't ask and didn't want to know what she'd done. Would I be surprised? No."

The grandmother believed Lily did it, or did something, because why else return to their rental across Scott's Creek with her headlights off? The woman acted on instinct, protecting her own, or rather her son's own since he wasn't around to do it. An even bigger obligation.

But who was the other vandal at The Undercurrent? Not the getaway driver. The odds of two burglars in the same strip mall on the same night, totally impromptu because no way they would predict the lights would go out, was so incredible. Either Amalia wasn't telling the full story or wasn't aware of it. Sounded like Lily was marching to her own drummer these days, and the grandmother wasn't able to keep up.

"She never confessed?" he asked.

"No."

She wouldn't admit it anyway.

"Is she . . . okay?" he asked after a moment or two of silence.

"No, Mark. She's never okay," came the answer. "Not anymore."

That left him speechless.

"There's something else you may not realize," Amalia continued.

"I'm all ears," he said.

Callie ensured her recording still functioned, trying not to make a sound.

"Javier confessed something to me," she said. "A week before he was to be released, he asked me to come in and talk to him."

Callie could see that. He hadn't wanted any revelations recorded on the phone for the prison administration to hear.

Amalia lowered her voice, as she likely did during her visits. "Javier said he didn't act alone with the cartel."

Forehead creasing, Mark spoke with more firmness. "Who did he mean, Amalia?"

"He didn't tell you?"

"Maybe he did, but I need to hear what you know first."

Callie's gaze froze on him. *Oh, good heavens, Mark. You're not even surprised.*

Chapter 20

"JAVIER TOLD YOU what he told me," Amalia said to Mark over the small table in El Marko's, her comment flat and disenchanted, hanging in the air for answer in an empty room accustomed to several dozen diners.

"And what would that be?" he asked.

They hovered in the age-old stand-off of *show me yours before I show you mine.* What caught Callie most was that he wasn't shocked at Amalia's news that someone within SLED may have been as dirty as Javier.

Unexpectedly, Callie prayed Mark wasn't the one, then kicked herself. The cop in her had bested the girlfriend for a split second, and she wasn't proud of the slip. No doubt Mark was solid. Or rather, she shouldn't have a doubt. But there had been a whole other piece of Mark he'd held back, and some of that unknown scared her.

"Javier said it was Orson DeLuca," Amalia said. "That's how Orson knew to show up that night, he said."

Callie was stunned. Royally stunned. Mark had been managing an undercover agent, sandwiched between the rogue agent and a dirty boss? How had he not seen that?

She studied his reaction so damn hard, praying he reared back and yelled, "What the hell?" *Be surprised, dammit. Be shocked!*

But he wasn't thrown by the news. Not the first flick of a brow. No double blink as he digested a message that should be unbelievable.

Hey, but agents and detectives possessed an array of expressions, right? Callie did. Surely, he did.

Better yet, let Amalia be erroneous in her belief. Javier could've told his mother that story in order to give her peace.

From the story Mark told Callie last night, Mark had told only Orson about his plan to follow Javier to what he expected to be the genuine cartel meeting while SLED sent agents to Javier's decoy drop. The goal was to prove Javier wrong, not start a gunfight. However, the goal was for Mark to report back, not for Orson to send armed agents on his tail.

Orson's autonomous change from the plan had cost lives and Mark's career.

Why had he sent agents to start with if he was in bed with the cartel?

To cover his ass? To make Mark appear lame? To kill certain people?

Nobody had blamed Orson for anything.

Orson couldn't be Mark's favorite person by any means of measure because that shift had resulted in Javier's cartel contact killed and Mark shot. Javier went down for it all. If Orson was involved, why hadn't he gone down with Javier? Rather than go to jail, wouldn't Javier have hollered *deal* and ratted on the boss?

So many pieces falling into place yet creating more questions. How convenient was it for Javier to get caught, Mark to get shot, and Javier's cartel boss silenced, leaving Orson the only player still in place?

Her mind straying with a zillion what-ifs and whys, Callie forced herself back to being attentive to the conversation. Stiff, she stretched her shoulder blades back, holding her breath when they popped. Readjusting, her hand slid on something stuck to the floor.

What exactly might Mark be slipping into . . . or slipping *back* into?

Amalia bent in. "I have Javier's documentation on Orson's involvement. Orson told him he'd work with the solicitor's office to cut Javier a deal if he kept his mouth shut. Otherwise, he'd work against Javier, and get him put away for decades. Orson also threatened the family to ensure he took the deal. Javier had no choice."

Whoa. The ridiculously small sentence of five years made more sense now. Orson pulled strings and used cold-hearted bullying to save his own hide.

Callie's head leaned against the door tighter, trying to hear better. Her weight-bearing hand slipped. Her forehead hit the doorjamb.

Amalia perked. "What was that?"

"Icemaker," Mark said, covering.

Gingerly, Callie resumed a better position, ensuring the phone still recorded.

"Amalia, think about this." Mark looked doubtful, unconvinced. "Why kill Javier? Why wait and kill him years later? He held up his end of the deal by going down alone and hiding Orson's involvement. Something happened, Amalia. While he wasn't everybody's pal in prison, he watched his back and stayed out of trouble. What changed?"

He'd asked the question that begged the asking.

Amalia scrunched her hands into fists then released them along with a huge exhale of frustration. "If we open this door, there's no closing it," she said. "But this is where I need you."

"I can't even tell where the door is," he said.

She breathed out hard again. "I have to protect Lily. She doesn't know."

"Know what? And I'd never compromise you two."

Amalia did a nod to herself, agreeing to proceed. "Like I said, Javier said Orson was involved back then, and probably still is, but he had no proof. He kept quiet, as promised, for almost five years. But as time approached, he contacted Orson several times with the same reminder: Orson got money while Javier got jail. He demanded Orson do right by him financially. We lost Melissa. The house. Javier lost his retirement, had to let his insurance go, and spent almost every dime he had for attorneys and taking care of us. Lily can work little more than fast-food places. I live on Social Security, for God's sake, and Javier's money ran out. Lily needs help, Mark. She needs to get straightened out without learning about Orson. I won't have her living her life with a vendetta." She took a deep breath. "That is left for me to do."

Mark stared her down. "What are you asking?"

"First, don't let Lily get in trouble for your restaurant," she said, studying the front window again. "Then maybe you can finish what Javier started. Maybe you can back Orson in a corner and make him pay. For Lily."

Like that wasn't much to lay at Mark's feet. Callie wiggled toes gone numb.

Lily. No wonder Mark demanded the break-in case be closed. Callie could go ahead and charge the girl with several things, but without Mark, her job was uphill. All he had to say was she was a family friend and stand by her in her mental time of need. No prosecutor would take that case.

"Lily, I can do," he said. "I've already refused to press charges. The other I'm not so sure, Amalia."

"I am sorry if Lily cost you much damage," Amalia said, watching her hands as they smoothed out the tablecloth.

"That's what insurance is for," he said. "And yes, to confirm what you asked earlier, I spoke with Javier on the phone while he was still inside, but I never got to meet with him to collect details. I suspected Orson colored outside the lines back then, but I had zero leverage, and when they retired me after my injury, I lost access to anything to make a case. Not sure there is anything we can do now."

"I told you I have Javier's proof."

He took a long breath in, holding, then out. "I thought you might. I missed the funeral because I didn't want to show on Orson's radar in case Javier had information, which I suspected from the urgency in which he wanted to meet. I thought you might eventually come to me."

Callie had mixed feelings about Mark holding so much back from her, but, as Stan promoted, Mark was protecting her. He also had zero clue what to do about something he had no proof about. What he did know was that as a sworn law enforcement officer, she was held to standards, and the less she was aware, the less obligation she'd have to arrest Lily, report Orson, and have people question Mark for his possible involvement. If Mark got sucked into something unexpected that brought in other law enforcement, she'd be questioned damn hard.

The bigger picture became more clear. This was Mark being a hundred percent Mark: the caregiver, the protector, and the just. This was also Mark being the pragmatic intelligent soul Callie already appreciated. He'd harbored history about Javier and suspicions about Orson with no real outlet, and he wasn't stupid. Javier's family had been totally vulnerable those years with him in jail. This hadn't been his fight to have, not with Javier and his family in the balance.

Callie had no idea what to do with this information. Breaking into El Marko's seemed miniscule in light of all this past coming to light. Mark surely kicked himself for allowing her to listen in, unhappy at what she'd learned.

Amalia sat back in her chair. "That's it. If Orson doesn't pay the money, I turn in the documentation Javier gave me. I can't not do it. However, I was hoping you'd convince Orson for me so that didn't have to happen. You're most familiar with him. You're stronger."

Callie could sense the heaviness of this burden on Mark. Was he to tell Amalia no and leave this old woman to go up against a man who'd already proven he put little value on human life? After all, who did everyone think killed Javier? The guy who did the shanking was rarely the person who wanted the shanking done. Javier had contacted Orson right before he was killed.

Mark studied her, not happy with where they'd wound up. "Money is one thing, Amalia. Revenge is another. Which is it?"

"If he gives me the first, we don't worry about the second," she said. "I have Javier's records. That has to count for something."

They quieted. Amalia waited. He wrangled with his thoughts. "What kind of proof?"

Amalia lifted her purse to her lap and reached in, sliding what appeared to be a lone photograph across the table.

He didn't touch it. Callie would have hesitated, too. Best Mark have plausible deniability having never laid eyes on whatever this measure of proof was. He could help Amalia by simply saying times were hard, and maybe Orson would be willing to take up the slack. They didn't exactly have to mention the specifics.

"What is this?" he said.

"It's Orson, Javier, and a cartel boss at a soccer game . . . in Mexico City." She ran her finger over an object. "See the sign?"

He leaned in closer, then he picked it up. "Not sure this—"

"He will know," she said.

The message was clear. The torch was being passed.

"I'll talk to Orson," he finally said. "You stay out of it."

Amalia reached for her purse. "I have Javier's notes, more photos, and a flash drive right here. You'll need them."

No. Callie rose, ready to enter the room. Regardless of the proof, Orson could still pin some of this history on Mark. Nobody would care who killed Javier, a convicted felon. Backing Orson in a corner could easily rebound on Mark.

Amalia was right in one regard, though. Being familiar with Orson made Mark the best person to reason with Orson rather than blackmail him with documents. She didn't want him anywhere near those records. For now.

"You keep the records," he said. "They're safer in your hands. This one photo is sufficient. Don't tell me what the rest is. Don't tell me where you keep it."

Thank God. Callie could see Orson coming after Mark for that information the second he learned about it.

"One last thing," Amalia said, setting down her purse. "Lily knows nothing of this documentation. Please keep it that way. She's too upset to not spout off to the wrong people. If she became aware of Orson, no telling what she'd do."

Smart move.

The slight woman held out arms, and Mark went into them, hugging while at the same time consummating the deal.

What had Mark gotten himself into?

Amalia turned, a little sluggish on her feet, and headed to the door,

Mark behind her. When diners filled the place, nobody heard the squeaky hinge on that front door, but in the quiet, Callie stood, stumbling once at the stiffness in her legs, and waited for the squeak before she scooted out the back door.

Outside, the parking lot held a haunted deadness, the ocean a block over whispering the soft lull of low tide. Callie waited, eyesight adjusting, then came around from the back toward the parking lot, feigning she'd been doing a security sweep of the mall. Mark and Amalia spoke to each other, the lack of contrast noises from the day allowing their voices to carry. Social niceties, mainly. Their conversation kept either from seeing her move in.

Mark should have expected her to come up on him, making her grasp just how dedicated he was to this woman and their shared past. He should've been cognizant of her and hadn't been, yet here he was wanting to take on this business of dealing with a potential criminal alone. A criminal with a lot of history to hide.

The two were almost to the sedan, coincidentally the car resembling both descriptions Callie already had for the getaway car. She trotted up, not hiding her approach, but hurriedly, not wanting Amalia to disappear before they had a chance to meet.

Seeing the young blond girl behind the steering wheel almost brought her to a stop.

Nervously, Amalia reached for the door, uncomfortable at the sign of a cop. Lily flashed wide eyes and fumbled for the ignition.

"Wait," Callie said, laying a hand on Amalia's door before she had a chance to get in.

Lily's resemblance to the driver's license picture was there. Callie wouldn't have recognized her except she'd studied her so much earlier in the day. That and she was with Amalia.

However, the smiling teenager on the license did not match this tightly wound, way-too-thin girl who had to weigh thirty pounds less, and that was considering the earlier version didn't have weight to lose. The shoulder-length, sun-streaked tresses of the former fifteen-year-old had faded over the three years to a muddy brown, limp and hanging eight or more inches longer.

The poor girl exuded stress, and Callie's heart tightened at someone so young so out of focus. Made her think of her son Jeb and the close calls Callie'd had at her own life being taken. He'd missed a year of college to babysit her when they'd lost his father, proving the better adult, but what if she had died in any one of a dozen situations. Would he have deteriorated like this?

No wonder he hated law enforcement.

Mark studied Callie, surely wondering why she'd made an appearance now and what the game plan was. "Y'all," he said. "This is Callie, my girlfriend."

After a flash of betrayal, Amalia pushed past Callie and into the sedan.

"Wait," Callie said, stopping the door from slamming shut. "You're Amalia, right?"

Unable to close her door, Amalia leaned toward Lily, purse tucked up against her.

Lily yanked on the purse, her movements jerky, matching the sharper angles of her elbows and wrists, in her effort to pull her grandmother closer. "Come on. Let's go, Grandma. It's a setup."

A stranger, a girlfriend, or a cop, Callie had a split-second choice to decide which to be. "Hold it right there," she said, choosing and regretting the need to fall back on police tactics, but they were ready to flee, and Mark hadn't asked all the right questions. The command was needed to gain control.

"Lily," she said, then strode around to the driver's side to not have to yell over the grandmother. "You broke the window at El Marko's and went inside. You are the one who left the bullet on the bar. A .41 caliber, which was what your father used for his undercover weapon. A weapon, I sincerely hope, you do not have in this vehicle."

She studied both of the occupants for tell-tale reactions. "Are either of you armed?"

"I don't have to answer that," the girl spouted back.

"Either you answer or I search the car, which I may do anyway if I sense a threat."

"Lily," Mark said in a soothing tone, after a disapproving glance at Callie. "Answer her."

"No," she said with a hard pout. "I don't have a gun in the car or on me or in my grandmother's purse, or, or, anywhere."

Her anger was up front and center at being caught and cornered.

"Amalia?" Callie asked.

The older woman shook her head, then added, "No."

Callie didn't like interrogating someone in a dark parking lot with spotty streetlights, amidst shadows and the disadvantage of not being able to read body language or facial tells. "Again, Lily, you left the bullet in Mark's restaurant. Am I correct?"

"Yes. Doesn't mean anything."

"Alone, no. You're correct. But what about the bullets at my place, at a resident's home, at the home of Mark's employee, and at the police station? There were multiple bullets."

Lily blinked, then again, faster, pleading at her grandmother for advice. "I only had one bullet," she said. "It's one I carried around with me to remind me of Daddy. I gave it up wanting Mark to see it and recognize exactly who was watching him and remembering what he did." She stared down Mark standing in front of the vehicle now.

"There were others," Callie said.

"Why would I go to those other places? How would I even know where those other places were?" She turned to her grandmother for help, and Callie briefly considered the grandmother for the deeds. Not that Callie could a hundred percent rule her out, but the notes on the bullets more resembled the tone and one-liners from Lily's social media.

Lily patted on Amalia's upper arm. "What is she talking about, Grandma?"

The girl's mood had flipped in a snap, switching from the angry adult to a pouty teenager to a child needing her grandmother's unconditional support.

Amalia wasn't taking her attention off the uniform, however, not even in answering her granddaughter. "I don't know, honey. Be honest is the best I can say. They think you did it." She spoke sternly to her granddaughter, sharing the disgust of the situation, glaring at Callie with a couple of glowers toward Mark.

Lily stared at Callie's hands on the door, giving Callie a sense that if she let go, she would mash her gas pedal and be gone.

"Let's discuss the restaurant," Callie said, hoping to open more dialogue here, while she had them both. "On second thought, we could take this to the station where everyone would be more comfortable and away from prying eyes."

"I'm calling a lawyer if you do that," Amalia said.

That was no kind of threat. Callie liked dealing with a lawyer. They operated on a more practical plane than their emotional clients, and she'd often collected important information from an attorney nudging his client to cooperate, explaining that to do so would make everyone's life easier.

"We don't need the station, Chief Morgan," Mark said over the roof of the vehicle, not recognizing what Callie attempted to do, which was to get them to talk here and now.

Unexpectedly, Lily bowed up at him, not Callie. "You do *not* get to speak for me, Mark Dupree. Daddy trusted you, and you threw him to the dogs. You are *not* my keeper. A lot of good you did while he was inside jail."

"Lily—" warned Amalia.

"Un hunh, no, Grandma. You do *not* tell me to listen to that man." Lily jabbed a finger over her steering wheel toward Mark. "I told you not to come here, Grandma. He cannot be trusted."

"We have no one else, baby," Amalia said.

"We need no one else," Lily yelled. "We are each other's anchor. Isn't that what you said? Yet here we are talking to this traitor . . . for God knows why!" Her spit flew out the door, just missing Callie, the pout so caustic and semi-permanent that she had trouble seeing this girl as ever being sweet and innocent.

Callie hadn't handled this correctly. Neither had Mark, making promises he had no business making. Lily was lying, dodging, diverting in a fit of anger she couldn't put the lid on. No telling what the girl would say just to get a rise out of those present, finally having an audience for the seething resentment she'd built higher and steeper with each loss in her life.

No wonder Amalia was so desperate to do something, anything, for Lily.

"The notes," Callie said with less cop-speak, trying to bring everyone back around. "Why the notes, Lily?"

"What notes?" Lily shouted. "First bullets then notes. You're totally inept as a cop, you know that?" She crossed her arms, the first time she'd removed both hands from the wheel.

Callie held her calm. "The notes that came with each of four bullets. The ones that said, *His love isn't worth the trouble? Taco or bullet? Chill or be still? Infinite possibilities?*" She'd tapped the end of each finger reciting each note.

A deep voice cut through the dark. "You can add *Limited Edition* to that list, Chief."

Heads turned toward the words. Stan had slipped up, holding out two plastic bags. As he came into the streetlight, the players could tell one held something small and heavy. The other a yellow sticky note. Callie took the note first, to read the message. Sure enough. The words *Limited Edition* were written in blocky letters, just like the others. She touched the bag around the bullet. Another .41 caliber.

"Arrived sometime in the last hour," Stan said.

Maybe Lily hadn't been waiting in the car for her grandmother to talk to Mark. Maybe she'd had other business to tend to while her grandmother was busy.

Chapter 21

CALLIE TOOK THE two pieces of evidence, spun, and showed them to Lily. "Look familiar?"

"No!" Lily's anger redirected at Stan, a shaky finger aiming. "Is he one of your *friends*? Is he helping to pin this on us?"

Reared back in a quasi-comical reaction, Stan made a *what do we have here* face.

"See? He is, isn't he?" Lily continued. "Your partner in crime."

Stan marveled at the girl's audacity. "She's . . . something."

Callie continued holding out the bags. "Lily, did you place either or both of these at that man's house?"

"Jesus, what don't you understand, lady?"

"Lily," warned Amalia again, but she clearly had no control over the girl. Probably hadn't for quite some time.

"I don't understand what you mean about notes," Lily said. "I didn't do any damn notes! I admit I bashed out the window to get in. I was furious he got to continue his life while my daddy lost his, when they were doing the *same fuckin' job*." She screamed by the end.

Mark gave Callie a pleading look. He didn't want Callie out here involved. But his safety, and the safety of those around him, however, were her responsibility. This little girl had already demonstrated violence.

Callie asked the question as if it didn't sound utterly stupid. "The bar bullet was yours, but not this one?"

Lily shook her head.

"What about the other four?"

Lily just gave her a scowl.

"There are six bullets," Callie clarified to all present. "And five threatening notes to go with them, counting this one."

Lily shook her head from behind the steering wheel. "Don't know what you're talking about."

Six bullets. Isn't that what Maya predicted? Callie couldn't put her out of her mind. Back when there were only two, Maya predicted six. Worse, there would be a seventh, she'd said, only it would be shot, not discretely set with a note to serve as a threat. The discovery of the unspent rounds and the final shot were supposed to take place within six days of the first round found at El Marko's.

Within six days, not necessarily on the sixth day. The six might have been partnered with the six bullets, or a misreading by Maya. Psychic readings weren't the driving force of any stage of this investigation, but Callie could not deny the occurrences that happened after Maya predicted them.

Fact was, however, that the latest bullet, supposedly the last unspent bullet, was delivered to Stan during the time Lily was supposedly outside alone, waiting in her car. Supposedly. And Mark's cam wouldn't record her that far away from the restaurant.

Callie asked for their driver's licenses. Lily's was suspended, as Callie had seen earlier in her research. Amalia's was current, and they still lived in Blythewood, a hundred fifty miles away. Callie palmed Lily's license.

"I still think we need to come to my office," she said. "We need to account for your time and whereabouts for the last few days."

"I was with my grandmother," Lily said.

"Not during the break-in," Callie replied. "And you can't account for tonight." She had to admit, however, that the cam at the station showed someone who didn't fit her build.

"Callie," Mark said, "not now."

"Then when? She's not exactly reliable," she said, stare on the girl. Lily had already given the sense she'd lie even when the truth would sound better. Spiteful. Resentful. Someone totally unwilling to cooperate regardless of how it played in her favor. Trusted no one, so she became someone nobody else could trust.

"I want to talk to you first," Mark said. "I'll vouch for them. I knew they were on the island all along ."

Callie tried not to appear stunned, tried to tell herself she wasn't surprised. Inch by inch she was learning what Mark knew. She was tired of being surprised. Not by Amalia and Lily, but by Mark.

She pointed at Lily. "You, step out and trade places with your grandmother. This license is no good and you are not to get behind a wheel until you make arrangements to get it reissued."

Lily said nothing, exited the vehicle and went around the car, holding the passenger door for her grandmother to get out and trade places. If Callie read auras like Sophie claimed to do, this child would read hot red to her, but Sophie claimed that a good color. Black was the worst. Appropriate that their meeting took place in the darkness of a sliver moon.

"Where are you staying?" Callie asked.

Lily couldn't give the address, probably wouldn't have given an accurate one anyway. Amalia named a small place off Oyster Factory Drive, a place Wainwright Realty managed, usually limited to college students and those far from the economic level of renting the beach.

"Don't leave the area," Callie warned. "We'll talk to you tomorrow."

"We can't afford to stick around as long as you like," Lily said, sarcasm not having dissipated in the least.

"Then I can haul you in right now."

Again, Lily turned child-like, this time turning to Mark. "Don't let her do this. I broke the window. I left the bullet on the bar. But that's all I did!" Tears started. "I didn't do any of this other stuff." Silent tears turned to sobs of a little girl.

Callie honestly didn't know who or what to believe. Now was the time to get her alone and turn her half lies into the whole truth.

"They'll stay. I promise," Mark said. "I'll cover the cost." Then to the grandmother, "And you're welcome to eat free in the restaurant."

"What if other renters need the place?" Amalia added, seeking an out. "We're due to leave in two days."

"I'll handle Wainwright Realty," Mark said.

Oh for Christ's sake. This was three against one with Stan abstaining, standing off to the side watching the show.

She'd call Janet in the morning and make sure Amalia wasn't pushed out. She'd done too many favors for Janet Wainwright and her nephew for the real estate broker to give too much push back. Besides, this wasn't one of her high-rate rentals.

"Or, Amalia, you can have my house," Mark threw in.

"Mark, they're fine where they are," Callie said.

She backed away from the old, dark-gray sedan, broadcasting they were free to go. Mark and Stan did the same. Amalia eased out of the parking lot with subtle restraint as if just issued a ticket with the issuing officer observing from behind.

"Damned if that young lady isn't a spitfire," Stan said, the three of them watching until the taillights disappeared up Jungle Road toward the causeway.

"What the hell, Mark?" Callie turned on him. "We could've made them account and been done with things . . . or had a guilty party sewed up."

"I'm not treating them like criminals, Callie."

"That was sort of my call to make, don't you think?"

"I have some responsibility here!"

The loud reply echoed in the night.

"Not sure you do," she said, fighting to be the calming effect. "You were just there when it happened."

"I should've predicted Javier. Should have stopped him. Could have kept him straight and unearthed who else in SLED might've been involved. Instead I get shot, removed from the investigation, and booted out."

Mark stood silent, hand rubbing his forehead, then down his temple. If he didn't have a headache from all this, he was made of steel.

Even if Amalia and Lily remained on the island, Callie expected another shoe to fall somehow, and she fought with herself over that shoe being Mark's.

"Let's go inside," Callie said, waving toward the restaurant. She'd prefer her place, but that was several blocks away. They were here now, and she wanted to pick Mark's brain on what he'd promised Amalia and hear the details of Stan's bullet discovery while concepts and experiences were fresh.

It was almost twelve.

Without conversation, Mark led the walk back to El Marko's. Stan gestured for Callie to lead on, but instead she fell in step with him. She gave an obvious glance at Mark and sighed, then gave a mild shake of her head. Stan put an arm around her and hugged.

Callie wasn't happy the latest bullet had been his to find, but she couldn't pass up the gratitude that he was here, now, her backup brain in talking to Mark about what the hell they were doing next.

Out of habit, Mark cleaned up the table he'd sat at with Amalia then went behind the bar to put on coffee. He brought back glasses of water to tide them over until their cups were ready, and they assumed seats at the same table. This seemed too big a situation to take to the mini VIP table against the kitchen door.

Callie opened the conversation after a taste of her coffee. The night was long already, but it would drag longer. "Someone else is in play here or Lily is lying through her teeth."

"Wait," Stan said, not having taken a sip, Callie's remark taking him aback. Between his surprise and the void of the room, his cup made a loud thud on the table. "You think that girl was telling the truth? I may not be totally up to speed, but in the diluted version I've heard, she sure seems good for all this."

Callie wanted Mark to say it. She wanted him out of his head and out in the open with what he was thinking and how he intended to keep his promise to Amalia. His promise to get Lily off the hook of breaking in to El Marko's was small potatoes compared to Amalia's other request.

But Mark wasn't talking, thinking too hard, maybe debating with himself. Stan darted a look at him, then back at Callie, uncertain whether to keep rambling or give the room silence until Mark figured *the story was his to tell,* as Stan was so noted for saying.

Callie tired of waiting. "Stan. It seems that Mark's old SLED boss, the guy who supervised the operation to take down an arm of a South Carolina drug cartel, might be even dirtier than Javier. At least as dirty."

Stan's expression turned sober and serious. The three were law enforcement entrenched, two retired and one active. Nobody said *dirty cop* lightly and without truth. "Proof?" was all he said, because maybes or gut feelings weren't acceptable.

"Seems Amalia has *proof,*" Mark said with a dip of head to acknowledge, "that Javier put aside as insurance for a future day. I believe her. I can see him doing that."

The other two waited, recognizing that Mark had more to say, his appearance guilty-looking, for some reason.

"I should have done more," he said, talking into his cup wrapped in both hands. "Back then, I should have spoken up."

But he had no proof then. He only had instincts, and attorney generals didn't prosecute SLED higher-ups on feelings and intuition. He knew that. He just had to work things through.

"They wouldn't let me anywhere near Javier when things went down," he continued. "I was angry at him. So angry. I suspected Orson by the end, and as much as I didn't want to believe it, Javier had been turned. He'd misled us too many times, had too many excuses as to why intel he gave us proved unreliable or downright misleading. And once he went down for it, getting anything on Orson was pretty much impossible. At least that's what I told myself."

"We get it. That's rough, man." Stan sat still, being the shoulder to lean on, the second option to seek if needed.

"So I need to do this now," Mark concluded. "For Javier. For his family. For all I know, Orson coaxed Javier into turning."

Mark sought atonement, and he'd grasp at any chance to achieve it. He'd leap at *this* chance, fearing there'd be no other, because right now he wasn't his normal, level-headed self. This was Mark operating on feelings and devotion, and while she'd embrace those qualities in dealing with their relationship, this situation was not where he needed to exercise them. Orson clearly held the upper hand, and if threatened, he had the power and malice to destroy those coming after him.

That's how the bad-guy world worked. Callie understood Mark's concern, however. Why wouldn't Orson also kill anyone else who took up that same torch calling him a turncoat? Like Javier's mother? Nobody would listen to an agent-turned-criminal's bereaved mother, but once Orson realized there was proof. . . .

They'd be in real danger, and they weren't prepared in the least to face what would be coming at them. Javier and Orson might be criminals, but the mother and daughter were not. They'd been left out in the cold, thrown out like the trash for nothing they did. And if Mark didn't step in between them and Orson, they'd go after him until he shut them up . . . one way or another.

"I need to call him," Mark said. "In the morning. No doubt he's on the island."

He said what Callie already surmised. After Amalia's contact, Orson had followed her to Edisto. To what end wasn't clear, though the obvious was he suspected Amalia sought out Mark. Everyone knew Mark had retired to the beach to open a restaurant. He'd had the occasional SLED employee drop in to test out the menu several times.

And if Orson followed them by car, he'd also been following them locally as well. At first it seemed like a long shot his following Lily to El Marko's that dark and stormy night, but if Amalia stayed home, why not? What at first sounded far-fetched now held potential. Once there, he saw Lily leave her souvenir bullet for Mark and came up with the idea to escalate things, everything falling on Lily's head.

A prosecutor would argue that she stayed angry and forged a plan to display her anger, with more bullets and messages to go with them. Notes for people in Mark's world, telling them to steer clear of going down with him, piling on suspicion about Lily. There would've been no need to leave Mark a note. The bullet was good enough because he'd understand. The flavor of the notes resembled Lily's social media. She was angry enough.

Who would anybody believe anyway? This deranged child or a decorated SLED captain?

Orson could have capitalized on the opportunity and manipulated

Mark's world by targeting his friends. To keep him off balance in addition to framing Lily and setting up the manic, irrational girl such that she was arrested, nobody believing her. Why would she confess to the one bullet and not the others? Teenagers were just irrational. A psych eval report could validate her propensity for the actions.

Then there was the obvious . . . he wanted to scare Mark into hushing Amalia. Mark had been the reasonable one with SLED. The honest one. Maybe Orson expected him to be the one who'd make Amalia stop her pursuit of Orson, to recognize what he had five years ago—they all ought to leave the dust settled. Maybe he hoped Mark would even financially assist them himself. Honestly, Callie almost preferred that choice. She'd pitch in if it meant removing Mark from Orson's attention.

Amalia had been smart hiding the proof from Lily. She'd have broadcasted that to the world, and maybe gotten themselves killed. Right now Orson seemed willing to settle for scare tactics.

"Why not call Orson now?" Callie asked, eager to bring this damn thing to a close. "He's close, and if you believe Lily didn't leave the bullet on Stan's doorstep, then he's very much awake." Plus, she and Stan were already there as backup.

"I want to call SLED first. To see if he's on leave."

"Building a case," Callie said.

Stan nodded.

"I heard the entire conversation," Callie said, holding up her phone.

Mark stared long at the phone. "Wish you hadn't recorded that," he said.

"No," she said, putting the phone away, then crossing arms atop the tablecloth. "You wish I hadn't heard so you could take off on your own. Well, that's not happening, sweetheart. You running solo could go south any of a dozen ways, like jail time." Emotions roiled inside her. "The worst case would be you meeting Orson and never coming back, Mark Dupree. He's a killer, unless the three of us are just stupid."

Her tone had risen well above a proper level, her heart rate thumping. *Goddammit*, this was Seabrook all over again. She forced a hard breath, but her pulse continued to rise as memories poured in.

Mark wasn't reading between the lines, but Stan was. Callie could tell. He'd known Michael Seabrook. He'd witnessed Callie so terribly sick with pneumonia, desperately trying to accompany Seabrook to meet his enemy, the man who killed Seabrook's wife. Seabrook's obsessive behavior and disappointment at the police had cost him his position as a medical doctor, pushing him to become a cop to solve his wife's crime.

In theory, fanatical, but in the day-to-day goings-on on Edisto, he became a favored son. Who couldn't love that combination of justice seeker and caregiver? God knew Callie had. And he'd fallen in love with her.

But when the time came, when Seabrook had researched, investigated, and set up a meet, the enemy accepting and eager to do so, Callie hadn't been able to function and be there. Pushing herself to her feet with a crazy fever, her lungs filling with fluid, scared to death what Seabrook had gotten himself into, she'd managed to drag herself to the scene to back him up. Only she arrived too late. Seabrook was alive, but barely, and he died in her arms. She killed the bastard who killed Seabrook but had almost died herself in the process. Took her weeks to physically recover. Took her months to think straight.

"Chicklet," Stan said, bringing her back around. "He's not Seabrook."

"He's a damn close parallel to him, though," she said, jabbing the tabletop loudly with a stiff finger, her neck and jaw so tight they cramped. Jerking around to Mark, she stabbed that finger at him. "You do not have the latitude to tackle this arrogant degenerate alone, you hear me? Not on my beach. You are too close to this case to fly alone. That's how people make mistakes, you idiot." She choked on her words and the tears in her throat and coughed. "That's how people fucking die," she pushed out in a wet, raspy voice.

Mark spoke, almost in a whisper. "Callie."

A hard turn of her head and a shaking fist told him to hush. Embarrassed at her display, she shoved her chair back and left for the kitchen, then unable to stand the four walls, made her way out the back door. She had to hear the ocean. She needed to hear, smell, and feel her Edisto.

Outside, she snatched wipes at her cheeks with a sleeve, still wearing her winter uniform, partly due to the fluctuating temperature and partially to hide the eight-inch burn scar on her forearm, a forever reminder of losing her husband. Arms wrapped across her chest as she stood southeast, toward the breezes that swooped in from the Atlantic a block over.

After Seabrook died, she had let guilt consume her, relentlessly, except when she was so miserably sick she forgot to. Then she'd drunk herself into so many stupors, blaming herself for her choices, his choices, and her shortfall in stopping him from following through on his. She was way more seasoned than he, plus he'd been too personally compromised to think sharp.

Two years ago.

But she wasn't sick this time. She was healthy, wiser, and a damn sight more determined. If something happened to Mark, however, she'd be done. History could not repeat itself.

Even if it meant losing him as a lover, she'd damn sure get in his way, or at least be there as backup. She wasn't letting him out of her sight.

The door creaked behind her.

"Chicklet."

Stan, not Mark. She wasn't sure if she should be relieved or disappointed.

Arms came up from behind then around her. Anyone unfamiliar with the two would mistake them for a couple decades married, the big burly guy comforting his wife.

"Stan, I can't go through that again. You saw what I saw. You see what I see. You spot the similarities."

"I do. Mark may be familiar of Seabrook, but he can't quite relate so don't blast the poor guy. He has enough on him already. He hasn't lost a spouse like you. You've lost John, Seabrook, and your father. You blame yourself since they were murdered by people after you, like any of that was your fault, Chicklet."

Stan was well aware of her demons. This one, however, seemed to explosively rear up from nowhere tonight. Despite the fact they'd been pursuing this case since Sunday, she hadn't felt the commonality to those crippling memories until just now.

Until Amalia asked Mark to confront Orson and make her financial demand, Callie hadn't considered this as any more than a teenage girl out of control. Sure, Mark could feel remorse over Javier and the subsequent avalanche of devastation, but Javier caused that. Fate dictated the rest. Mark had nothing to do with the man's choices, and, frankly, had already paid a price for operating on the right side of the law.

Such a harsh stance for her to take, but sometimes you took such stances to stay alive. Otherwise evil had a way of pulling you down.

But Lily and Amalia hadn't asked for any of this either. Mark was their last chance for a solution to the poverty they headed into. God knew they'd never escape the pain of their loss. Loss like she'd endured, too.

Dammit, she did not want to think of them. She didn't want to understand why Mark yearned to leap back into the business that was Orson and whatever nastiness he represented.

Stan squeezed her tight. "I told him to give you a minute, promising him an explanation. Whether it comes from me or you doesn't matter, unless it matters to you."

He turned her around, and she had to tilt her head back to see him. A breeze was picking up, and her hair pushed forward. With fingertips she fought it, tucking it twice behind her ears and failing.

"He has to do this," Stan said.

"I've seen how this works."

"Again, he isn't Seabrook. I wasn't as familiar with Seabrook as you, on the level you were, but I liked the man. Everybody liked the man. Now everybody likes Mark. You have great taste in men, Chicklet." He winked. "Including me."

She tried to smile for his sake.

"Let him slay his demons," he said.

She tore her gaze off him and rubbed her face. "Not alone."

He pushed the hair away this time. "I suspect you'll be there. I'll be there unless you tell me otherwise."

This time she hugged him. No words. Just a feeling that someone understood the depth of depression, sadness, and regret she'd carried on her shoulders for the last five years. Five years that felt like twenty.

"May I tell you something? Don't laugh," she said, stepping back.

He shrugged with his eyebrows, meaning he had no reason to.

Stan had been with her on Zeus's boat. While sarcastically skeptical, he'd heard Maya's forecasting, and she'd gotten some things right. Other items had yet to come to pass. Those are what worried her. "Maya's predictions . . . I can't get them out of my head."

"How do you mean?"

"Six bullets, Stan. Yours is the sixth. Remember what she said?"

He nodded. "That the seventh bullet would be shot, different from the other six."

"Yes. There was a man's body in her drawing, likely dead, and a woman in the background. I'd always assumed she was Amalia or Lily, mourning over Javier, but. . . ."

"What if the fallen man is someone contemporary, not in the past."

"Yes," she said. Then she gave an anguished growl and scrubbed her palms down from her forehead to her chin. "Why is this shit bothering me? It's mumbo jumbo, as you would say."

"Because this is you taking in all you can to solve a case, even if it flies in from left field with no rhyme or reason," he said. "I trained you. I ought to know."

"But that's it," she said, taking in a long breath before giving it a hard release. "Maya speaks in rhymes with a sprinkling of reason. And most of all, Sophie believes her."

Stan gave her a slight frown.

"Don't scowl at me like that. You dated Sophie. You've seen her visions. You don't have to understand her, but you damn sure have to admit she's forecasted a lot of things you and I cannot explain."

"True that," he said. "Reluctantly," he added.

"Maya said by day six the last bullet would be discharged. We're not quite at the sixth day, but she'd said *by the sixth day*. With your bullet, Stan, we've reached that window of opportunity."

Chapter 22

BACK INSIDE EL MARKO'S, their table sat empty with Mark tidying up since Amalia had interrupted his earlier closing activities. They found him at the bar, straightening beneath the counter.

Everyone needed a drink. This was such a situation. But everyone needed their wits a thousand percent about them, plus, she wasn't ruining sobriety over this mess. That and she didn't want to go home tonight without having a keen grasp of what Mark would be doing, what he thought about doing, and what she thought he might try to do without her.

She wasn't making this mistake again.

"I'm calling SLED tomorrow, asking for Orson," Mark said, checking the coffee pot behind him. "First thing," he added.

Callie hiked herself up on a stool, removing the height disadvantage. Stan leaned on the bar, beside her.

"While y'all were outside, I've been thinking."

Callie waited for what conclusion Mark had come to. She hadn't exactly listened up to now. She'd decided the best way to decide how to work with him was to learn which way he was headed and plan how to keep up.

Mark wiped off the bar top as if he hadn't already done it a few times. "Then I call Orson's cell. Unless he's changed his phone, I still have it." He snuck a glance up at Callie, her chin resting atop her hand listening. "I'm not trying to pull anything."

"I'm not questioning you, Mark. I'm just not letting you do this alone, regardless of what your plan is," she replied.

"I'm not Seabrook."

"Oh, shut up, Mark," she said, no longer patient. "You don't get to play that card. I'm involved, and there's no debate. Just tell me, or us, if you're so inclined to involve Stan, what we're doing, because it's evident you aren't just sending Amalia and Lily home."

Mark winced a little. "If I decide you—"

"What's the damn plan?" she said. "Or we'll be here all night."

For some reason, Mark looked to Stan, but before he could say anything Stan interrupted.

"She isn't budging, my man. Be happy you have her. You've seen things, but she's seen more than any ten agents."

"I'm not questioning what she's capable of—"

"The plan, Cajun Man," Callie said.

"I'm calling Orson and scheduling a meet," he said with an irritated rush. "And I'm asking him to pay for the package of proof Amalia is holding."

"So, blackmail," Callie said.

He frowned. "I don't exactly see it as that."

Stan pointed toward the coffee pot, sign language for *pour me a cup*. "Oh, it's blackmail, all right."

"Not unless it's reported," Mark said, as if he didn't know better. "More so, I'm not sure Orson wants to open that can of worms."

Callie sneered at the wishful logic. "Regardless of what you call this, he'll want to meet, curious about the proof. I would. Also, when he shows up, he'll think himself shrewd enough to confiscate the proof and not cough up a dime." She studied Mark. "Try to tell me I'm wrong."

His expression changed into a mixture of surrender to the facts. "Oh, you're right."

"Which makes this dangerous," she said. "My worry all along. He'll try something."

Squinting, Mark dragged out a long *hmmm*. "He's not that brave. He saw little action in his career, and nothing dynamic at that. His decorations are managerial."

"Which can make him unpredictable," she said. "Okay, then. Enough what-iffing and trying to label everything properly. How are we doing this? And note, the pronoun is *we*, not *you*."

After another half hour of guesstimating how the meet would go, everyone concluded to park the discussion until after Mark spoke with Orson. The man might say no. The man might even agree but not show. The best they could agree on was that instinct would drive what happened.

They dropped off Stan, with Mark coming home to *Windswept* with Callie. At two in the morning, the tide had begun making its way back in. They dropped off keys in the kitchen, set weapons in the nightstand, and dropped clothes on the floor, each item a reminder of how tired they were. When she dropped her shirt, a whiff of grease reminded Callie why Mark showered when he came home. They managed a joint shower, mechanical and minimal, then dropped into the bed naked, hair still damp.

Sheet and light quilt over them, Callie stared at the ceiling, exhausted but not sleepy. Like on the eve of a surgery, she needed to sleep but couldn't shut down. Mark slid up against her, not terribly amorous but welcoming of a lazy cuddle.

Two years ago, in this same bed, she'd slept with Seabrook for the first and last time. Long and slow, fast and electric, they had consummated a love held at arm's length for a year, finally embracing what the whole island already whispered about . . . that they were meant to be together. The night turned into the eve of his murder.

"You're not tired?" Mark said muffled into the pillow, shifting closer.

"Drained," she said.

"Maybe not too tired?" he queried, slowly feeling across her belly under the sheet.

She told herself no, she wouldn't, but she couldn't tell him that. Sex the night before. . . . God, how was this not fate teasing her, or warning her, or goading her? Deciding whether or not to accept Mark seemed a crossroad for some damn stupid reason, and she was afraid to choose him. Then she was afraid not to, because . . . because . . . declining him would mean she read him as Seabrook all over again.

A tear rolled out and down to her ear.

"I love you," he whispered, following the words with a soft kiss on her lobe while his fingers traveled her body. "I've never loved anyone like you, Callie."

Another tear trailed the other. "I can't lose—" she started, but she couldn't finish.

"Shh, I know," he said, kissing her again. "I'm not going anywhere. Promise."

But the choice might not be his.

She wiped away the trail of moisture.

The man wouldn't leave her by choice. Seabrook hadn't either.

She reached below the covers and maneuvered his wandering hand, no longer interested in being just petted. When he found her, she closed her eyes and fell back into his world, caving to the here and now by giving herself to him. Regardless about tomorrow, she found it only fair that she focus on him tonight. Just the now. . . .

Besides, she would be there this time. Dammit, if this Orson son of a bitch flashed the least sign of a threat, she'd blow his damn head off.

No, not now. Don't think about that now. In a flowing rhythm, she took herself back to the carnal present, fighting to cast aside the what-ifs that had no answer.

Maya's drawing flashed back. The man on the ground . . . what if he was Mark?

No, no, what if he was Orson. And what if the woman was her, killing Orson as he tried to kill Mark.

A surge of adrenaline coursed through her, and she disguised it as arousal, moving faster, urging him to do the same. She killed people. Criminals. Orson fell in that category, and she willed herself to admit she'd do it again.

Yes, she would. Without a damn half second of doubt, she'd blow his fucking head off.

She flipped over and straddled Mark, guiding him, the synchronicity instant, long, and powerful. Panting, small grunts in between, she leaned over, kissing him for all she was worth, for all he was worth.

She lost track of time. They repeated the lovemaking. Edisto time was marked by the tide, and the murmur of the surf told her at least an hour had passed, maybe two.

They settled, exhausted, Mark's breaths finding a deep peace. Lying on her back, the moisture on her neck no longer tears, Callie sank into the mattress, willing her body to seek sleep. She'd given Mark all she had to give.

She lost consciousness amidst tangled covers and Mark's arms. She told herself not to dream of Seabrook . . . and she didn't.

FOUR HOURS LATER, Callie awoke, reached for her phone, and relaxed back into place in bed, wanting Mark to sleep. Orson was on the island. That simple fact meant she'd stay glued to Mark, and the more rested they were the better they'd cope with the man, regardless of what level of coping that meant.

Callie texted Marie a message that something came up late last night that she had to tend to, then lay back down, replaying the night. The dreaminess of her après-sex fatigue coaxed her into another hour's sleep.

This time Mark woke her. "What about work?"

"Taken care of."

"Good. How about a real shower this time?"

No argument there.

After, she dressed first, in civvies. She wasn't sure why, but she felt more capable not being so obviously law enforcement. And as he dressed, she put the coffee on and fried up four eggs and toasted them each an English muffin.

They ate the entire breakfast, talking about anything but what was most on their mind. The day's purpose had been defined, but the starting gun for this race was theirs to fire. It wasn't until they'd eaten and washed dishes did Mark mention their mission.

"You record while I talk," he said, leading her back to the clean kitchen table, tossing a notepad and pen atop a placemat.

She messaged Thomas that she was busy this morning, and Stan that they were making the calls. To both, she said she'd be in touch. Then she muted her phone.

The call to SLED was not surprising. Mark identified himself on the voice mail, asking for Orson to return his call. Then he called the reception desk to double-check if he was in. He was informed Orson was on leave for a week. When Mark struck up conversation with the woman he'd known from years past, he was also told something about Orson visiting the Asheville, North Carolina mountains. So, Orson was supposed to have gone in the complete opposite direction of Edisto per his office in Columbia.

They took notes. Callie logged the calls and their results on the notepad, her phone recordings as backup.

Mark scrolled through his phone, finding the old cell for his boss.

Orson DeLuca answered on the second ring. "Mark. Figured that was you when El Marko's popped up on caller ID. How've you been, fella? How's restaurant life? Missed you at Javier's funeral."

Natural. Maybe spoken a bit too fast, and good that he gave himself away about the funeral. Interesting, he'd changed the caller ID in his phone to the restaurant.

"Sorry I missed it," Mark said, skipping the update on his well-being. "I didn't want to put the family through any more stress than they've already weathered. Makes me wonder why you went."

Orson's voice wasn't extraordinary in any capacity, about as average as a middle-aged man's voice could be. Not too deep, almost no accent, Callie guessing the origin Greenville or Spartanburg, someplace upstate.

"Just doing my civic duty," the senior agent said. "Javier might have strayed, but he used to be a decent agent. His family was hurting, regardless, and telling them I had many good memories of him was supposed to help. It's a crying damn shame people get remembered for their worst decision."

No. this man believed more in himself than how badly his presence would make Amalia feel. Callie could tell.

Mark's jaw tightened. "Tried your office, not that I expected to find you there."

Callie listened hard, pen on paper, her phone recorder running, watching Mark for reactions. She attempted to insert herself in Orson's head. He'd be wondering if Mark really did call the office, if he spoke with anyone, and if they told him where he'd said he was. Mark didn't elaborate. He didn't ask him how the mountains were.

He did say, "Regardless, I was hoping you'd answer your phone. Figured you were already here on Edisto, and I'd like to invite you to lunch at the restaurant. My treat."

Callie could sense Orson mentally rerunning the conversation, wondering when he'd given away the fact he might be on the island. He surely suspected Amalia had been in touch with Mark.

But he ignored Mark's reference to Edisto. "I'm on leave with nothing to do, so this is timely. It would be incredible to catch up. I'd enjoy seeing this El Marko's the agents keep talking about, too. Give me three hours, just in case, to give me time to wrap up what I'm in the middle of. You'll be shocked how many have retired. You've heard how law enforcement's been taking it on the chin of late in the press. They're never right in the eyes of this federal administration. Yes, it'll be great catching up."

Mark laughed at the not-so-subtle pretense. "That's good, Orson. Regardless, look forward to seeing you."

Just as Callie would assume to be recorded if she were a suspect, Orson kept the tone and subject matter mundane. He never confirmed where he was. He was uncertain if Mark called SLED. He was simply meeting an old colleague for a meal at the beach, never once asking why Mark called.

"See you then," Mark said. "Drive safe."

Callie made sure the call ended then signed off on the recording. She'd scribbled little on the pad with the call being so short, the conversation speaking for itself.

"He's baited," Mark said. "He doesn't understand the call."

"I'm not so sure," Callie said, tapping the pen on the paper, then abruptly catching herself. This pen tapping was what Maya did while forecasting, keeping the energy of the predictions coming. If Callie thought it would work, she'd tap the end of her pen to a nub.

"We learned from Knox that Javier had phone conversations with SLED, that we can assume was Orson. In coded phrasing he said they needed to meet once he was out. Something was mentioned about *a collection* that Orson would be eager to see. I haven't heard it word for word, but we can if we need to. Basically, they connected, with Javier hinting he had proof hidden away. Common sense tells us that Orson went to the funeral to get a feel for if there was any."

"Amalia would be the only person with that proof," he said.

"Or you," Callie added. "You said you and Javier were close before. Cookouts and parties and such. Who's to say Javier didn't trust you in lieu of burdening or endangering his mother? I bet Orson was saddened to not see you there." She shrugged on one side. "Just trying to think like the bad guy. Stan said I wasn't so bad at that once upon a time."

Mark admiringly studied her. "You're right. He studied Amalia at the funeral and now he's feeling me out this afternoon. I hate having him in a room of diners, though. All this sounded right before I said it, but now I'm not too sure."

"Close the place for a few hours." Her phone read eleven, the time El Marko's opened its doors.

"I could do that. Three hours means around two p.m. Meeting him two to four ought to be sufficient."

Right before his shower, Mark had called Sophie, begging her to open the restaurant for him right after her yoga class. She'd asked a half dozen questions before gasping, then oohing at it surely being something to do with the bullets. She asked if there were more bullets, but he dodged the question, then she promised to fill in only if he updated her later.

That was the Sophie whom Callie understood best. Way more entertaining than the quiet, introverted worrier from dinner the other night. Closing the place for a few hours, however, would ignite more of her curiosity, but Mark could handle her.

"You'd have to keep some staff, though," she said. "Someone has to cook and serve and take the calls from people asking when you're opening back up. You okay with that?"

He sat back. "I'll tell them it's someone from my secret-agent days, and they need to be invisible."

Callie was leery. "Like that won't light up Sophie."

"I'll let her go home."

"That works. If she listens."

A knock sounded at the door. Callie identified Stan from his distorted size on the other side of the custom lead-glass window, the sailboat in the middle dissecting his chest.

"Was worried when I hadn't heard from you," he said. "You weren't at work, and Mark wasn't at the restaurant. Am I welcome or have I been banned from the treehouse?"

She pulled him inside. "Just called Orson," she said. "He'll be here around two."

"Here?" he asked.

"The restaurant."

The frown prompted Mark to fill in the blanks. "I'm closing the place between lunch and dinner, just for him."

"You sure he'll show?"

Mark gave an *oh yeah* expression. "I believe he's too self-possessed to bypass the opportunity to learn what I know. He checked out Amalia at the funeral, followed her to Edisto, and is willing to meet with me. He thinks he's connecting dots."

"And he knows you know what he's doing," Callie said.

Stan took a cup of coffee from Callie. "You sure you want to do this, Mark? Blackmail is blackmail, and he's in a job that makes him darn astute as to how to use and abuse your involvement, man. You could get in serious trouble here." He tipped his head at Callie. "She could get in trouble as well."

Mark didn't immediately answer.

Callie noticed he'd gone from raring to go to introspective. "We can easily nip this in the bud. The worst that can happen. . . ."

"Is that he does something to Amalia and Lily because he's aware there's proof that might take him down. They'd go home. He'd have someone break into their home to search for it, or corner one of them, hold the other hostage, cause an accident nobody can explain. Once Javier told him he had proof, the switch was tripped. I'm not sure this is going away until someone is hurt. The feasible option I see is asking him to make an exchange and have him feel he paid for it. We can pray that's where it stops."

But Callie didn't see this situation as that simple. Specific people with specific knowledge that threatened Orson still walked this earth, and that had to irritate him, making him a wild card. If Amalia and the proof was right, he'd gotten away with years of stockpiling extracurricular income from unscrupulous people who wouldn't listen if he said he didn't want to work with them anymore. Like joining a gang, once you're in, there's no way out . . . well, there was one way, but that was out of Mark's hands.

"Nothing you're doing is a fix," Callie said.

"I know," Mark said.

"It's more like kicking the can down the road," she said.

"I know that, too."

"And once you approach him to pay for Javier's evidence, you get sucked in across the line. There will always be the possibility of a future recurrence, and the risk of you being accused of blackmail."

"I won't threaten him," he said. "I'll simply offer the man a chance to buy some documents. Sales transactions aren't blackmail."

Like last night, Stan watched the two, nursing his coffee.

"Why are you doing this, Mark?" she asked, her concerns from the night still haunting her this morning. She had to say it. "Doing this to yourself is doing this to us."

"I'm trying to keep it from hanging over both our heads indefinitely," he said, "while trying to cut Amalia and Lily free. In the long run, it *is* for us."

"Keep your enemies closer, Chicklet," Stan said.

She got it. She didn't like it, but she got it. If he did nothing, bad things could happen. If he did something, bad things could happen. But which bad thing could he live with best? Mark's point was to get through it and come out on the other side better in some way.

There really wasn't much of a solution here. Not without Orson dropping dead. God forbid another body dropped on Edisto, though. There'd been more than enough under Callie's oversight, as Brice was ever fond of reminding her.

"Let's get going," she said.

"Yep." Mark stood, collecting coffee cups, a habit from running an eatery. "Barely enough time to explain to staff—"

"And throw up a couple wires," she said. "I'll grab two from the station. You can't wear one. He'll suspect. With the room empty, he'll check."

"What about me?" Stan said.

Callie ran an arm around his middle. "We can't be present for this one, Boss. But we can damn sure listen. You and me."

She just hoped they could hide close enough for decent reception. She wasn't comfortable enough with this man she'd never laid eyes on, and she prayed Mark was on his toes. If indeed, as they suspected, Orson had gifted those bullets and notes, then he'd identified each of them.

She couldn't pretend to be anyone but herself, which meant she couldn't be in the room. She'd only make things worse.

Like with Seabrook, she wouldn't be there after all.

Chapter 23

THE ALREADY overworked staff welcomed the time off, and at the last minute, Mark let them all leave, unwilling to put any of them at risk. Wary, Sophie accepted the thanks for opening up without questioning the afternoon closure, especially when Callie showed up in civilian clothes with Mark instead of going to the station in uniform. Typical Sophie would expect an answer as compensation for being the good girl.

One hour before Orson's expected arrival, Mark trued up the dining room, cleaning and putting a sign on the door, while Callie hid a portable cam and mic in the kitchen, just in case. She'd already tucked a mic under the bar. Anything else in the dining area and Orson might notice.

Stan sat outside in Mark's vehicle, slack in his seat, windows down, a half breeze coming through. Mark's car would be expected, unremarkable. They couldn't deploy either the patrol car or her personal car since it could have been noted by Orson previously.

The mic was one-way, and Callie had Stan on the phone to double-check he could hear. "What if he doesn't show?" Stan said, after confirming he'd caught her test message.

"Mark claims he's too self-possessed to bypass the opportunity. He's convinced Mark's aware of everything. He's on a fishing expedition, Stan. I'll be surprised if he doesn't show."

One thirty. A half hour before Orson's scheduled arrival, Callie went back to the dining room. Mark tampered with the table, the bar, watching out the window twice while she was there. He'd just sent the fourth customer on their way, frustrated at the restaurant being closed to a private party.

His driven expression showed how deep in his head he was, and his lack of seeing Callie come up only proved it.

"I'm going," she said. "He doesn't need to see us, so we're taking a walk. Might hang out on Wainwright Realty's porch before we return to your car." The real estate agency was across the street and down a piece of a block, the porch a great vantage of which cars came and went in the parking lot. They'd sit there and listen if they could, but she expected the range to be too far. Neither would this work at the SeaCow, Stan's preference, plus they served too many people at present, especially with Mark's place being closed.

She held arms out. He made himself smile, which was her goal. His hug was average, but that was fine. She needed it more than he did, and she followed the hug with a kiss and a final smile. "Not sure how we want this to turn out, but we'll make the most of whatever happens, okay?"

"Okay," he said. "I'm sorry."

"For what?" she asked out of courtesy, but knowing full well what for.

"For bringing this to your beach. For keeping secrets. For risking your job with whatever you want to call this. Blackmail—"

"Sales transaction."

"I really don't deserve you."

He didn't deserve *her*? He'd picked up more shattered pieces of her than anyone could count. Always there. Ever the caregiver and the patient ear. If he hadn't been there for her when . . . during. . . .

"Oh, kind sir, it's me that doesn't deserve you." She kissed him. "Good luck," she said, and left before they forgot what they were there for, before too much personal got in the way of the task.

Outside she gave a small wave without drawing too much attention but playing the role well enough for Orson if he was watching. She headed up Jungle Road. She didn't wait for Stan. He was already there.

Wainwright was famous for in her decoration of the realty. Red geraniums only. The yellow lantana about to pop along the walk would accent them. The broker slash retired Marine believed in flaunting the colors of her beloved Corps.

A receptionist came outside. "Anything I can get you folks . . . oh, Chief."

"Mind if rest a spell on your porch?" Callie said.

The receptionist, ordered to maintain a vigil for her employer, wasn't sure what to do. People shopped for real estate indoors, getting their information, signing their papers, and then eagerly leaving to scout their dream home on the beach. Nobody tarried on the porch. The porch was for show.

"I'm watching for speeders," Callie said. "Some repeat offenders who won't spot me up here. That okay?"

"Um, yes, ma'am. May I bring you some water? A coke?"

"No thanks," Callie said. "We're good. Janet here?"

"No, ma'am. She's showing houses this afternoon."

Thank, God. They didn't need the retired drill sergeant demanding explanation. She could be as nosy as Sophie, only on a whole other planet.

Stan nudged her, his focus across the street.

"We won't be long," Callie said. "Thanks for checking on us."

The phone rang inside, and the receptionist ran back to her desk. She had orders from her employer to answer before the third ring or there'd be consequences. Janet went through two to three receptionists a year in spite of the fact she paid well.

Stan had been watching the cars entering the strip-mall parking lot, taking measure of which might be Orson. A man was exiting a white Saab at the restaurant's end. He climbed the walkway stairs and tried El Marko's front door. Mark answered, but the man didn't enter. He left.

"False alarm. Another person not happy with him being closed," Stan said. "Hope this doesn't hurt his business too much."

"Most of these people will be gone Saturday," Callie said. "The fresh batch of tourists will have no idea."

Two fifteen. "You don't think Orson played us, do you?" Stan said.

"Your guess is as good as mine, Boss. We're relying on Mark's judgment here."

Another car with a lone male. Another false alarm.

Callie wasn't feeling right about this. Not this long after the meet time. "Let's go back," she said.

"He'll see us."

"Who says he's arriving at the front door?" she said, mad at herself for not thinking of that possibility sooner.

Both shot up from their chairs and took the steps down quickly. But instead of coming straight at El Marko's, they headed to the east end of the mall, rounded the end around Pizza Pirate, and came up the backside of the building, its concrete block painted white, its metal doors giving rear access to each commercial venue.

Callie reached the back of the Candy Crab, next door to Mark's, and caught voices in her ear bud. Two men.

"I take it I'm getting a private party?" the voice asked. Callie had to assume it was Orson's since it wasn't Mark's. It could be the voice she heard on the phone.

"Of course," Mark said. "Come on through to the dining room. Table's already set."

"Go, go," she whispered to Stan, pointing to Mark's car. They'd stay where they were except they'd already drawn attention from a delivery guy about a hundred feet distant, and a family parking lengthwise with their car and trailer, probably destined for the state park campground.

In an effort to appear unassuming, they strolled to Mark's car, got in, lowered the visors, and scooted down in their seats.

Callie put the conversation on speaker, unable to see via the established cams in the dining room.

"The cams were fried in the storm," Mark said, likely at some remark about security they'd missed in positioning themselves. "Not sure you've heard, but someone broke in and trashed the place. That's why you see these borrowed tables and chairs. The community was pretty nice about helping us out with that."

"You cook the food?" Orson asked.

"As needed. I hire cook staff, but someone has to train them."

"Never took you for a cook."

"Never had you over back in the day. Javier always turned the grill over to me, and between his Mexican and my Cajun background, we whipped up some damn fine meals."

A couple of extra seconds passed. "Not bad, not bad. What are these?"

"Quesadilla appetizers," Mark said.

Callie knew those well. His go-to snack alongside some *pico de gallo* or white queso, probably both in this instance.

"Hmm, nice."

A small piece of time passed as Orson probably took bites of his appetizer, likewise giving himself time to decide what to say next. She expected more remarks about food, the weather, how time had raced by for them both.

"What about back there?" he asked instead.

Back there.

Stan had already glanced over at her at the question. Back there could only mean one of two places: the bar or the kitchen.

Orson must have gestured. "The kitchen?" Mark said.

"Yeah. In my coming through, I noted enough room for us to eat . . . and talk. It feels like an echo out here in the open."

Mark tired of the forced congeniality. "Seriously?"

"Seriously," Orson replied, and the clink of dinnerware and glasses indicated how *serious* he was about moving the conversation. "As a former agent, you understand that gut feeling, right?"

He didn't believe the cams weren't functional. Thank goodness for

Callie's gut feeling that there needed to be a video and mic in the kitchen, something Mark needed to consider in the future. At least the visual since audio required one person in the conversation being aware of the recording.

"Stupid bastard," Stan uttered.

"Smart bastard, you mean, but we're smarter," Callie corrected, with a mental pat on her back at wiring the kitchen.

"From crime fighter to beach restauranteur," Orson said, hushing Stan. "This spot over here works." Thumps and bumps sounded as Mark probably moved the small VIP table into the cramped kitchen.

Callie flipped into the app, and after some adjustments, a view of the kitchen appeared. The men stood awkwardly in the meager walkway, just barely out of reach of the swing of the kitchen door, measuring around themselves to make sure they could still sit and talk.

"Just so you feel better, Orson, give me a once-over." Mark unbuttoned his Hawaiian shirt, the more muted brown one with less personality but leaving Mark in character. "Nothing to see," Mark continued and remained standing. "Go ahead, pat me down. Because before we sit, I'm damn sure patting you down."

Orson laughed. "Fair enough."

He gave Mark the standard pat-down, finding nothing because there was nothing to find. Mark did the same only more thorough, awkward with them wedged between the metal workstation and the wall.

"Oh, damn," Callie uttered, as a car pulled in, the driver getting out. Stan followed her attention to Maya, walking up the steps to the restaurant.

"Hopefully she can read," Stan said, referencing the sign Mark posted.

But they heard knocking anyway across the mic, Orson twisting around as if he could see through the wall and that far.

"Ignore them," Mark said. "Otherwise, we'll have people interrupting us for the next two hours."

But the knocking continued. Mark and Orson continued talking about who had retired since Mark had. The knocking stopped.

"Shit," Stan said, as Maya came down the stairs and around the building, an urgency in her trot as she headed to the back. Wasn't long before they heard knocking again.

Damn this woman. "What is her problem?" Callie said.

"Callie? You in there?"

"Who's Callie?" Orson said, as if he didn't know.

"A friend," Mark said, playing along. "People are used to this place being open and finding my friends here."

"I've already been to the police station and her house on Palmetto. Nobody's seen her," Maya shouted.

"Oh, Holy Mother of God," Stan grumbled.

"Maybe you should answer," Orson said. "Sounds urgent. After all, your lady friend is a cop." The resolution wasn't good enough, nor the angle correct enough to see whether he smiled at the game.

"No," Mark replied. "You don't get it. We'd never get this woman out of here."

Stan motioned. "Go retrieve her!"

"No." Callie waited, watching. "She's bound to say something stupid, like, *Oh, there she is. Hello, Callie.*"

On edge, everyone waited. The men inside. Callie and Stan outside.

Finally, Maya gave up and reappeared in the parking lot, halting in her steps, probably pondering how to get inside some other way. At least she'd left the back door. Callie opened her car door and gave a whistle. Maya stiffened, hunting the beckon. Callie motioned her over. Maya broke into a legit run.

"Where have you been?" she said before she even got close. "Where's Mark? I'd like to talk to him."

"We're working. He's working," Callie said. "What is the emergency?"

Maya started to speak between breaths and caught herself. "Emergency?"

"You're panting," Callie said. "Is it an emergency?"

"It's important."

"Life threatening?"

"Not sure. Like the ideogram tried to explain—"

"Christ," Stan grumbled.

"Maya, I'm busy. Insanely busy. If there's not a body involved, call me in a couple hours." She gave Maya her card.

But Maya wouldn't accept the dismissal. "No, listen. My nerves have buzzed for the last two days. Have you found the six bullets?"

"Can't talk about that, Maya."

"Have you found the six bullets!" she asked, louder.

Callie grit her teeth. "Cannot say, Maya. Go. We'll talk later."

Maya backed away, calculating. "Something's about to happen."

"What?" Callie asked before wishing she hadn't.

"I'm not sure."

Now she really wished she hadn't. "Maya, I can't talk. Go."

Maya forced out an exasperated breath. "Then at least be careful. I'm scared. I can't sleep." She kept backing up, as if she hoped Callie would sense enough urgency to call her back, but Callie got back into the car. Only then did Maya walk away.

"How about another beer?" Mark offered across the speaker, reeling Callie back into the task at hand.

She slipped back in. "Did I miss anything?"

He scrunched his mouth in a sign that nothing important was said. Callie watched Maya until she entered her car and drove west, in the direction of the marina, taking the road way too fast. If she wasn't careful, Brice would stop her since he lived along the route she'd have to take. Might be a good thing. They'd keep each other occupied.

"Another beer sounds good," Orson said. "Dos Equis this time, if you don't mind."

At least the man had good taste in beer. She might not be able to appreciate one anymore, but she could remember.

After the first swig from a glass Callie assumed was chilled, Orson released an audible sigh of satisfaction. Mark served beer in a chilled glass whenever possible. Callie's mouth watered.

"So," Orson said after the second swallow, "I'm pretty sure you don't care how your old boss is doing. What's exactly on your mind?"

"I've been contacted by Javier's mother," Mark replied, getting down to business.

"How's she doing?"

But Mark skipped the subtleties. "She claims to have some materials that Javier compiled during his undercover operation. Material he kept for himself and didn't turn over to the authorities."

"That so?" came the reply.

"Not that I've seen any of it, but Amalia thought you might have a personal interest in the documents. Disturbing documents from what she tells me."

Stan gave a thumbs-up, glad for their getting to the meat of the matter. Callie appreciated Mark's restraint in spelling out the particulars.

"Well," Orson said, drawing out the word, "she seemed rather disturbed about something at the funeral."

"It was a funeral, Orson. It would be odder if she wasn't."

"I sensed more than that, Mark." The tone turned edgy, no longer affable. "I told her how much I still admired Javier, that his whole being was not defined by his one misstep. She'd lost her son, and she needed to hear positive memories. She didn't seem too grateful."

"So you said on the phone. I call bullshit," Mark said. "You didn't show to console Amalia. You'd already spoken to Javier. He mentioned he had information. You needed to sniff out whether she had it."

Callie could read Mark's body language as tense, but not Orson's. He was still sizing up where he stood. A cool man considering Mark had indirectly accused him of having Javier killed.

"I wasn't at the funeral long enough to do anything but pay my respects," he said. "She ordered me to leave, said I wasn't welcome. As I left, she told me that Javier would have his say and he would be heard. Interpret that as you wish."

Mark spread his hands on the table. "What do you expect? She's of the belief that you had Javier killed before he could use this information against you."

Orson didn't even rear back. Very controlled. "I didn't kill him."

This might be her first exposure to Orson, but her deduction was Mark had understated the size of this man's ego. An odd symmetry smacked her suddenly—Mark sat with his old boss, and here she sat with hers. She thanked the heavens she'd won the lottery in that draw.

"Jail is hell. No telling who killed Javier. Most likely his old cartel people," Orson said.

"You mean *your* old cartel people," Mark corrected.

Orson didn't immediately reply, impressing Callie that he hadn't denied the accusation.

"Ms. Harred is an old despondent woman," Orson said. "I assume she passed the torch to you or she wouldn't have come to Edisto. I recall five years ago that she hated you about as much as she hated me. We were the three main players with SLED and only her baby went to jail. Now you tell me she has these old journals or what have you, that she might just throw up on social media to crucify me because her boy got slighted."

"He was killed, not embarrassed." Mark didn't bite. "I have no idea what she has or what she plans to do with . . . old journals and what have you."

"My turn to claim bullshit, Mark. I am curious, though. Why fabricate something so unmistakably false, and why me? Why not, say, you?"

"Maybe because you're guilty and I'm not? Because Javier has proof of you and there is no proof on me? Honestly, I'm just hearing about this, and was shocked as much as you. It's more than a journal, though.

There was mention of a flash drive and pictures. Don't underestimate this mother's wrath."

Orson sat still, not so willing to disclaim this time.

"She did tell me, however, that I should mention a photograph of a soccer stadium."

Orson did a mild shrug. "And that's supposed to mean something?"

"A photograph of you, Javier, and someone Mexican."

The old boss just laughed. "That sounds so ominous, Mark. Very condemning." But he no longer sounded as confident, his laugh unconvincing. "Set where?"

Mark slid the photograph out of his breast pocket and onto the table. "She didn't say."

"*She didn't say,*" Orson mimed, analyzing the photo but not touching it. He seemed to study it longer than an unaffiliated person would.

He fondled his beer glass on the table, turning it around, the remaining third of it getting warm. "What is it she wants?" he asked, trying to keep his focus on the glass.

"Financial support for Javier's daughter."

Silence filled the room, long enough that Callie checked the app to see if they'd lost audio somehow.

"Is this blackmail, Mark?"

Mark shook his head. "I'm not threatening you with anything, Orson, so, no? Besides, that's such a harsh term. Think of it as more of a business negotiation. It's simply a request for you to provide some level of monetary assistance to the daughter of a murdered SLED agent whom you supervised. A humanitarian request is more like it, Orson. The girl has nothing. She's hurting after so much loss. I thought you might be moved to help."

Orson's chuckle was sour. "I'm sure. . . ." He hesitated and started again. "I'm sure the poor old lady and the daughter have had a rough time of it. If there's anything I can do to help, I'd certainly love to consider doing it. Is there like a GoFundMe page?"

Mark's shoulders rose as he gave a long *ummmm* to lead into his reply. "They were thinking like some kind of lump-sum assistance. Discreet yet substantial enough."

"What does that mean?"

"What would you give to someone who was financially broke and mentally broken?"

Callie could tell Mark avoided putting a dollar figure on it.

"Are you contributing?" Orson asked, probably wanting to avoid the same thing.

Again, Mark acted unsure about anything. "You see, my SLED pension isn't that great since I retired early. And most of my money is tied up in what you see here. I even rent my house, and you'd laugh seeing its floorplan and decor. I'm just not very liquid these days."

Callie appreciated the legal tightrope Mark walked. He was doing a fine job of keeping the pressure more on Orson.

"Did Ms. Harred happen to mention what her current debt load and obligations were?" Orson asked.

"Yeah, she said if she ever won the lottery, that would solve all her problems."

Orson chuckled. "I guess so."

"Do whatever you can do. They're destitute, man. Might be worth her exchanging your assistance for the documentation she spoke of. They want to move on."

Remaining back in his chair, Orson reached straight-armed for his glass, then finished the beer. "One would think that kind of money would warrant a full-fledge meal from you instead of these snacks."

But Mark wasn't fazed. "I'd be happy to whip up whatever's on the menu. Care to see one?"

Setting the glass down, Orson wiped his mouth. "Nah, not exactly hungry anymore. Money talk steals my appetite for some reason."

"I can fix you something to go." Mark played right along.

Instead, Orson stood. "I'll be in touch tomorrow. Gotta think on this, not to mention the time it takes to put hands on funds. Need to talk to my banker."

A chill raced through Callie. This is where they had to trust Orson was dirty. He could leave and report what had just happened to authorities, embellishing as he wished, then come back with guys with state badges and cuffs to take away all three of them—Mark, her, and Stan.

But if he was tainted as they assumed, afraid of being found out, he might just show up with cash and call it quits.

Worst-case scenario . . . he regrouped, rallied, and came back with something more devious in mind.

"Understood," Mark said, standing and going toward the dining room. "When are you coming back?"

"I'll get with you on that. Sorry, but I think I'll exit the back," he said, reaching out to shake hands.

Mark met his grip. "I'll be waiting. And please, don't bother Amalia."

"How do I know this money isn't for you?"

"Because I don't want the money, nor what it stands for."

Orson gave him a greasy grin. "Thought it was a business transaction."

"Still don't want the money. Be careful driving back. Let me walk you out."

Callie and Stan slumped further in the car. Orson left out the back, and Mark watched him drive away before returning inside to be near the mic. "He's gone, y'all."

Callie still gave Orson another five minutes, in case he doubled back. Then they entered El Marko's.

"Did you hear?" Mark asked.

"Yep, and saw," Callie said. "He came to size you up and left with a mighty sharp picture. The lottery?"

"Listen, if the man has been with the cartel for all these years, he's amassed a sizeable bank account. You heard him say he didn't kill Javier."

"Sure we did," Stan said, chuckling. "What would you expect him to say?"

"What if he didn't?"

"Is he still with the cartel?" Callie asked.

Mark's mouth flattened. "Logic would say so. Once in that circle you don't just check out."

"I read him saying he didn't kill Javier to mean he didn't physically twist the knife in his gut, but he still rubs elbows with those who do that sort of thing. He still could've ordered it."

"I'm not so convinced," Mark said.

"Regardless, can't prove it if he did. This meet, however, was to size you up," Callie said.

"He's deciding what hand to play next," Mark said, his neck tense. "And it's not something you should necessarily expect. He's under the gun now. If he's gainfully employed by the cartel, then he has to factor that into the equation. Orson is nervous. Javier dying should've been the end of any sort of threat, but suddenly that threat's taken on new life. He's even more dangerous after our meet."

He was thinking too hard and fast. They wouldn't solve Javier's murder standing here in the cramped kitchen. She moved them into the dining room, and they helped themselves to the ginger ales behind the bar.

"What now?"

She was stunned he'd asked and not just thought ahead on his own. He was indeed nervous.

"We wait," she said. "You put the ball in his court, so we wait and see."

He could do this. Law enforcement was accustomed to being patient. Rushing a case, pushing the bad guy to follow through only led to mistakes, which led to unexpected confrontation, which led to bullets in bodies instead of on front porches. And if he slowed down and took a second, he'd come to that conclusion on his own, so she didn't say it.

They put the table and chairs back in place and decided to leave the mic and cam in the kitchen, just in case. Though she was calmer than he was, Callie could not shake the chills creeping over her bones, a foreboding that Orson showed simply to size things up for his next appearance. Probably for the same reason Mark was antsy.

The great unknown as to whether there was proof, whether his career was in jeopardy, whether his cartel affiliates would find out Javier's threats were alive and well and in play, might shift him into self-preservation mode. He didn't need the cartel to learn of any of this. Not the first peep. Not the first hint of a word.

Once they ran out of straightening-up tasks, they sat, each thinking what-ifs and maybes, finishing their drinks . The limbo feel wasn't easy to manage after such an adrenaline-filled meeting, and waiting for the bad guy to make the next move wasn't comfortable, but necessary.

She didn't want to talk about Maya to Mark. Didn't want him to imagine her relying the least bit on spiritualism. The less said, the more they sat and waited, the more she convinced herself that Maya had come to Edisto, gotten bored, and hunted up information on the people in Zeus's world. To fit in, maybe? To garner new fans? Who the hell knew. Right now, who the hell cared.

Mark stared at a saltshaker, spinning it in his fingers. Stan looked at her, then Mark, then back at her.

Mark had gone silent, and like Stan, Callie knew Mark well enough to suspect he was making plans in his head instead of with his team.

"Talk to me," she said. "No walls. No half-truths. Otherwise, I'll ride your back like a damn tick."

"The point is I don't like seeing you in this. It's not your battle."

"Then you shouldn't have brought the fight to Edisto."

His mouth flattened again. "He'll escalate. No way around it now."

"I agree. So contact Amalia and tell her to be careful and keep Lily close. We'll take care of each other, but there's nothing we can do at the moment until he makes his move."

"Callie. . . ." He looked so disturbed. He reached across the table and touched her jawline.

She lifted her hand to touch his. "I'm not going anywhere. I'm also not letting you step into danger without backup. Quit thinking so hard. Call Amalia, then let's reopen the restaurant. We all need something to do."

With a soft nod, he put phone to his ear and strode toward the front door to remove the sign. Three thirty. Hopefully not too many people even noticed the restaurant closed for the last hour and a half.

"He's keyed up," Stan said under his breath.

"Which makes for mistakes, Stan," she said, eyes glued to Mark's back.

Mark stopped in his tracks two steps shy of the entrance, his tone raised in a clipped and interrupted effort to soothe the woman on the other end of his phone. "Stay there. I'll call you back. We'll handle this, Amalia. Just don't do a thing without calling me first."

Stan stopped straightening chairs. Callie held a fresh linen half spread over the table where Mark and Orson had been. "What?" she said, as Mark disconnected.

"He left here and went straight to where they are staying. He took Lily," he said. "Left a yellow sticky note telling Amalia he'd be in touch, along with a phone number that isn't his."

"Burner," Callie said. "Yeah, he's scared."

Seemed Orson was just as keyed up as Mark. Look who'd made the first mistake. Trouble was, they hadn't seen this option coming, meaning Callie had no idea what to do. Neither did Mark.

Orson had the upper hand.

Chapter 24

"ORSON PANICKED," Stan said.

"Over what the proof could be," Callie agreed.

"Because the cartel would have his head if they knew such proof existed," Mark said, bringing the subject around.

Orson couldn't have been much of a boss panicking like this. God, kidnapping? That move almost never came out well. "He's betting on us not saying anything," she said. "He gets the documentation and we get Lily back. The cartel doesn't learn about the documentation which keeps both Orson and Amalia safe. He wants all this to stay among us, here on the island."

"Stupid bastard." Mark sat at the nearest table. "He didn't have to do this. Nobody needs the cartel finding out or we're all dead."

She turned to Mark. "He doesn't want to pay."

"May not have the money," Stan added.

The air conditioner kicked in, a surprise. Like this ill-conceived plan, the day had heated up enough to need cooling.

"Nobody wants to give up money," she said, "but whether he has it or not, he's needing that proof. You never said give the money to Amalia and she'll give you the proof. He's not so sure he'll get all of it if he just pays for an even swap. There's the chance of more information or copies of any or all of it."

"Who says Amalia gives him all of it when he hands over Lily?" Stan said. "Do we trust her?"

Mark's comment came out dull and monotone. "Who says he's handing over Lily?"

"Pardon my French, lady and gentleman," Stan continued, "but this is a clusterfuck. We never should have met with him."

Callie tossed the linen cloth in a puddle on a table. "Amalia would've done it herself, Stan. He'd have killed them with a mere word to the cartel. That's all it would've taken. This way, he's too afraid to involve the cartel."

"Not much of a win," the old boss grumbled.

"Better than the cartel disappearing Amalia or Lily," she said.

She better understood Mark now. His heart went out to the family of his old friend, and he could not refuse assistance without wearing a mantle of guilt the rest of his life. Lily was already damaged, and whatever Callie had learned about her, she was sure Mark was familiar with more. He was trying to save their lives. And yes, the cartel would've killed them.

"Too many people know too much now," she said. "Is he such a mental misfit that he would kill us?"

"He can't think very far ahead right now. He's panicked."

But Callie wasn't happy with that answer, so she repeated, "Does he have it in him to kill five people, Mark?"

"Nothing in his SLED profile says he would," was all he could say. "But we share a common goal. We both want money and preserved evidence. What does that say about us as well?"

Callie walked over and pulled out a chair facing him. "Yeah, Cajun Boy, but your goal was to save two women. His was to save his ass."

"Which makes me the weaker party."

She rubbed his knee, loving a man so willing to come to the assistance of others. While she loved his tending to her all these months, she could see he cared for people as a whole. And for righteousness. He was a good, good man. "So," she said, ending the rub with a pat. "Are we calling him?"

"One condition," he said.

Stan leaned on the bar. He'd helped himself to the dregs of the coffee in the pot. He wasn't a man of many words, and he'd learned long ago not to interject himself when Callie negotiated with someone. He never corrected her in front of others, waiting until they were alone to remind her of how and when she'd erred or ruled the day.

Her awareness of that allowed her to simply focus on Mark. "I love you for what you are doing. Truly I do. But you will not get yourself shot, stabbed. . . ." She swallowed a thickness in her throat at that last one, a stabbing representing the beginning of the end when Seabrook died. She just didn't finish.

Mark's expression softened. He took her hand and kissed it. Seabrook would kiss the top of her head, their height difference accommodating. Mark, however, wanted to see her, lean into her when he kissed a hand. The magic never failed to penetrate her to her core, straight through to her heart.

He turned her hand over and kissed the palm, moisture collecting in her eyes.

She did him such an injustice. He was all in with whomever he made promises to, or those who needed his attention whether they wanted it or not. His devotion to humankind held such a subtleness that people loved him unconditionally with rare exceptions, and those exceptions usually meant he was taking up for those he passionately loved.

Why else would Amalia come to him, the man who'd helped lock up her son? Because she understood why he did it, and how much he regretted doing so. In other words, he could be trusted because his regret was genuine.

When people asked him for help, he fought his utter best to provide it.

"I've got to think on this a minute," he said, kissing her yet again and standing. He went back into the kitchen, his home away from home, and Callie remained in place, sensing him clearing his head and coming to some conclusion.

"That's a good man there," Stan said.

Callie wiped away a stray tear. "Sometimes too good. He'll try again to handle this without me."

"Maybe," he said.

"We should fight as a team, Stan."

"He doesn't see this as your fight, Chicklet. He's grappling with locking you in some sort of box for safekeeping versus including you out of respect."

"I'm supposed to just let him walk into danger?"

"Not my decision to make, Callie. Not my decision."

She wasn't letting this be Mark's decision alone. Whatever plan he came up with, she'd mold one in kind. Orson held the stronger hand because Amalia and Lily were Mark's Achilles' heel. Exploiting a weakness always raised one's odds. In his mind, all he had to do was set up a more clandestine meeting, bring Lily, demand the proof, maybe even flash a little money . . . then shoot them all.

The best-case scenario was his turning over Lily, taking the documentation, and leaving. Amalia wouldn't stand for that very long.

Callie struggled seeing a clean out through any of this.

"Does Orson have family?" she asked Stan, still watching the kitchen door for Mark's return.

"Don't believe Mark said anything about a family, why?"

"Just wondering."

She just wanted to set up her own chess board, so that if firearms became a factor, she wouldn't think twice about taking the man down.

Funny, she never expected she'd ever lose her badge by being the security for a blackmail scheme. She always imagined more the town tiring of her taking one step too many in protecting their honor, safety, and livelihood. She'd tried being the laid-back police chief satisfied with a placated life of writing tickets for tourist violators until the occasional hurricane raised their threat level for a week or two. By all appearances, she handled the life well. Internally, however, she craved more. And she'd gotten more, only most of the natives and just about every tourist had no concept of the lives lost, lines crossed, and sanity challenged that had occurred in the process.

Still, she loved Edisto. Now that Mark was such an intrinsic part of this beach, she loved it even more.

He was taking too long.

As she walked by Stan toward the kitchen, he turned toward the bar's counter, releasing a low, *umm umm umm* as she passed.

Checking at the sink then around the prep table toward the fridge, she tried to be surprised that Mark was gone.

She didn't go to Stan and ask why. She didn't run out the door to call Mark's name. She didn't even get mad.

A text came across her phone.

I love you, Callie Jean Morgan. I cannot afford to lose you. Selfish, maybe. I do not want you there, but I do want you involved. Just let me work this out. I'll be in touch.

So much for her calm. She stormed back into the dining room. "This is bullshit, Stan." She showed him the text.

He only ran brawny palms over his face.

"How stupid is this?" she yelled.

"Very."

"Fix it. Please."

His eyes widened. "Why me?"

"You're his best friend, dammit. Maybe he'll listen to you, because he sure as hell isn't listening to me."

"It's not about listening," he said. "It's about love."

"He'll be in touch," she muttered. How was she to stand by and wait? How was she to coordinate backup?

Seabrook had done this very same shit and died.

She snatched a saltshaker from one of the tables and almost sent it flying across the room, Stan watching from his stool. A key sounded in the front-door lock, and Sophie walked in. What the hell was she doing here?

"What?" Sophie asked, pushing the door back shut—noticing but ignoring the posted "closed" sign.

Callie couldn't tell Sophie the details. She couldn't tell her why she was mad. She could, however, ask her to take over the restaurant and re-open it at five as was the plan. Workers would be back by then.

"Where's Mark?" Sophie asked.

"No idea," Callie said, wondering what to do next.

Sophie arched a carefully carved eyebrow. "Then don't tell me. Maya came to see me, though." She laid a hand on her ample chest. "Me! Asked me for advice."

Callie ordinarily would've cracked a joke about Maya sucking up to her new mother-in-law, but right now she gave little shit about jokes. Instead, she worried how she was going to keep Mark alive. Did he even consider she might want to keep Orson off the beach?

"Tonight is creeping Maya out," Sophie said. "She tried to warn you, but you blew her off."

"No, I was working, and she was about to scuttle what we were doing."

Sophie cocked a hip, then released it. "I see you're in a snit. Anyway, I came to tell you that she's frantic about this evening. Wasn't sure why, but said something was going to rock this island. At first I read her being melodramatic, but the poor girl was shivering. You should have listened to her. I could feel the negative energy through her when we touched."

"And what was I to do, Soph? Let her ruin what we were doing while she prattled on about maybes and what-ifs and things that go bump in the night?"

That was mean. True but mean.

Sophie ran up to her and clinched her long, tanned, bejeweled fingers around Callie's sleeves. "I feel it, too. I keep feeling Seabrook."

Oh, for God's sake.

Callie shook loose. "Stan? I can't deal with this." She turned and left the building.

Mark's car was gone. Stan had walked there. She lived ten blocks down, and as embarrassing as a chief might seem without wheels, she walked up Mary Street to Palmetto and headed to *Windswept.*

Before long, Annie pulled up. "Need a lift, Chief?"

Did she? She'd made it three blocks, and her kettle still boiled.

"Just ironing out a problem, Annie. I'm good," she concluded.

Annie didn't question. Thomas would have. She almost wished Thomas had been in Annie's place. Then she didn't. She'd feel more prone to reveal the situation, and that might've only added him to the list with targets on their backs.

With the beach on her left, she couldn't help but scan between houses, watching for problems, listening for distress, like she did in her cruises up and down the town. With the walk barely two miles and her mind churning as tortuous as the tide coming in, time passed quicker than expected.

Mark's car was parked in the drive. He waited in the red porch swing. "Hey, you," he said, like a normal greeting. As if there was nothing wrong in the world.

The surprise didn't rob her totally of her words, but it limited the selection. "Hey, you, too. What the hell, Mark?"

"Told you. Had to think."

"Ever imagine I might be of assistance? I'm beginning to feel neglected."

He patted the red swing, and she planted herself next to him. He wasn't quite his congenial self, a cloak of worry in his posture.

"I shouldn't have listened to Amalia," he said.

"Maybe," she replied. "But that wouldn't be you."

He would normally pull her next to him, sharing the sway, watching the water on the other side of the road.

"Where?" she asked, not needing to form a complete sentence to get to what he'd been thinking about.

"An empty house on Palmetto," he said.

"You found an owner who would let you—"

"Empty, I said, but we won't meet inside. Beneath it. Lights out. There's not much moon tonight, two nights from a new moon, if you listen to Sophie. She never fails to remind me to burn a black candle and make good wishes for specific people."

That she did.

"Which house?"

He hesitated. She gave him a reproaching stare that preached not to leave her out of this.

"Four hundred block," he said. *The Great Escape.*"

She grimaced. "How appropriate."

At almost six in the evening during the summer, the road would be teeming with people coming in off the beach, packing up their cars to return to the mainland or dragging sandy towels and boogie boards back to their rentals. But with this being April, the road was practically bare. She was grateful for that. It would be even more vacant as night fell.

Callie was familiar with the house, a rather large one, almost three thousand square feet with side stairs coming up from the left and the right to a main set at a landing which took you the rest of the way to the porch. Ample coverage. More room to hide under, more shadows to camouflage, and with nobody in it, no lights. Too close to the Pavilion for her taste, four blocks, but Orson might not agree to something further down, closer to the sound and dangerously distant from the lone Highway 174 exit that came in close to the grocery.

Mark had left the restaurant barely forty-five minutes ago. "How'd you pick that place?" She twisted for a better view of him. "Why not on the island? Why not in the jungle?"

"He's a city boy, Callie. He needs asphalt and a strong sense of escape. He's already scouted the area, remember? He's been here, at Sophie's, Stan's, no doubt casing the area with a Wainwright map."

"When?"

"Ten."

Ten what? A.m.? P.m.? Tomorrow?

"Tonight," he clarified.

"What?" She leaped up. That gave her under four hours to grab officers and bring them up to speed . . . then she caught herself. Tonight was off book.

She plopped back onto the swing, the two chains shivering with the jolt. "We're not pulling in your officers," he said, firm and almost hard, at least hard for him. "The meet will be discreet. I just want to get Lily and be done with this."

Agreed. Her officers didn't need to be dragged into this.

"The money?" she asked, reminding him the swap involved a shake-down.

"If he has it, which I sincerely doubt, then fine. If he doesn't . . . I'll just collect Lily in whatever way I can."

He sounded resigned. The trouble was whether Orson was willing to let bygones be bygones, especially with this whole cadre of people think-ing he was on the take now. Any one of them could talk, which meant higher odds of the cartel becoming aware.

"You spoke to him, I take it?" she asked. When had he, she thought, in his car on the way here? It was a short conversation, wherever he'd had it.

"Yes. He demanded Amalia bring the proof, not me, and he said he better not see you, Stan, or any other police."

She could understand not being present, but surely she could tuck out of sight.

"No," he said. "I don't want you hiding nearby either. Something could happen to you. I can't risk that. I need to be focused without my attentions divided."

"How are you going to explain how you talked me out of this since I'm very much involved? I patrol the streets. My people patrol the streets, and we can see in the dark, Cajun Boy. We're used to degenerates pulling stunts under empty houses. Night patrol will be watching. What's your story going to be?"

"Not sure about that yet."

"Well, I am." Finally she could help. "Tell him we only patrol one car at night. At the appropriate time, the officer will get a call from you about a fender bender in front of the marina, at the opposite end of the beach. Not enough to require backup, but enough to dominate his time snooping around such that you guys won't be discovered. When the time is right, actually make the call. But I'll be the car on duty, and I'll come up here instead and park myself a block over."

"Where?" he said, scouting the road for the most opportune drive.

"Never you mind. If I told you, you'd look there, and we can't be having you give things away now, can we?"

He didn't respond. Instead they swung. No what-if-this-happens or what-if-that-happens. There was no predicting this event. They had a place and time. Four people would be present. Mark, Amalia, Lily, and Orson.

Callie'd take Stan with her, keeping her people out of the muck of this mess. If things went sideways, at least Thomas and company would come out of this clean.

Besides, Thomas would rip her up with a tongue lashing, but he had to realize this was for his own good, just like Mark not telling her everything was supposedly for hers.

Truth was, this was good for nobody.

Truth was, she wasn't going to be parked a block down.

Chapter 25

TEN MINUTES UNTIL meet time, and Mark waited behind the tall front wooden steps leading to the sweeping broad porch of *The Great Escape*. Large houses like this one weren't rented in the lighter seasons, costing six to eight thousand a week during the hot months when families threw money in a pot to afford beach frontage for fifteen to twenty people. Nobody would be watching this address closely except for the occasional drive-by glance by a uniform, no different than with all the empty rentals on Edisto Beach.

Callie wore her uniform, and not wanting to be seen by Orson leaving, but in case he was watching, she'd be leaving supposedly going on patrol. She left a half hour before Mark did and drove in her cruiser to Stan's place. He came down from his screen porch, dressed dark, reminding her of their days in Boston.

No mics, Mark had said. Orson might check. Time was too limited and the situation too dire to risk being sloppy with it anyway.

"What's the plan?" Stan asked when he opened the passenger door.

"First, you come over here and get in the driver's seat," she replied, opening her own door.

Mark didn't want her involved in the meet. She loved him for the protection of her reputation and her career, and for the most part she listened to him, but she chose to adapt, too.

Stan changed places with her, and when they reached Harrelson Street, she exited the car and slipped between two houses of older vintage that almost rode the ground, and crossed back over Palmetto. As Sophie had said, the night was on the darker side, what little moon there was remaining behind strips of clouds forecasting a front expected to bring rain the next day around noon.

Deceiving Mark sat wrong with her, but she did this for him, for his safety. Even if this meet went sideways and he got stuck with a blackmail charge, she wasn't allowing him to be killed in the process.

The contradiction wasn't lost on her. The very reason Mark didn't want her involved was the exact reason she was. She skirted across

Palmetto three houses down, not visible from where Mark waited in the shadows of *The Great Escape*, and she traversed beneath houses, between pillars, and around storage rooms, golf carts, and a couple of cars.

The air hung thick, briny. Not quite up to summer levels, but salty enough, a scent she'd come to cherish. No rain, thank goodness, and no high tide, another plus.

Finally, she made her way into the enclosed wooden shower on the ground level of the rental next door to *The Great Escape*, the shower designed to wash off the feet of beachcombers before they tracked sand inside. She stepped up on the wooden seat and, after some trial and error, found a good slit between slats to watch.

There was Mark, beneath the stairs next door, in plain view of her vantage point.

Conditions were a hundred percent in her favor with the no-moon time of month meaning a less aggressive tide, little more than a murmur. That would change as the front began moving in bringing with it the tide.

Mark wasn't pacing, but he was nervous, glancing at his phone periodically, the screen's light shining blue on his face. Soon Amalia walked up, a tote in her hand, Callie having watched her park two houses down in the other direction. Mark painted on confidence when she reached him, and he hugged her warmly while tucking her beneath the stairs with him.

He didn't go through the tote, still maintaining his stance not to handle the evidence Amalia held on Javier's behalf, instead assuring the grandmother everything would be okay. He followed up with another hug.

They'd barely parted when Orson drove up. He maneuvered the Audi around to combat park, backing the vehicle into the gravel drive beneath the house, a car-length past Mark and Amalia to be as hidden beneath the house as possible while still facing the street for a getaway.

As Mark stated, Orson was citified but far from street smart, and not in ways that would be helpful in the beach town. Edisto wasn't urban but not rural, so he wouldn't be familiar with what was wise and what wasn't. Callie would've chosen one of many silt roads in the middle of the island, but Orson was out of his element anywhere out here. His driving right up to the house showed arrogance, but also that he didn't plan to stay long. He'd been comfortable at the choice of address, he'd told Mark. It was on the main road that quickly led him off the beach.

Not much more than a half mile from the causeway.

He got out, halting long enough to scrutinize the grounds, to include around the house where Callie hid. Finding no need to worry there, he scanned behind the rental where he was, and on around, doing a full three sixty.

Mark waited for him to come to them, as would Callie since he'd chosen the most hidden spot on the property. Orson recognized that and closed the gap, approaching with hand out, as if they were meeting for dinner.

Mark declined the offer, looking past Orson toward the Audi. "Where is Lily?"

"Hello, Amalia," Orson said instead, waving at Mark to present himself for another pat-down. Mark put arms out and let him.

Amalia watched, probably having been told by Mark not to speak, again like Callie would do. Victims tended to beg, plead, and say way too much, with the risk of making the adversary change the plan midstream, whether for a lesser or more violent option. It's why they called it a *plan*, not commandments in stone.

Victim. *Huh*. Amalia was the blackmailer, Orson the kidnapper, and Mark the intermediary and representative for the Harred family in collecting blackmail money. Everyone was some degree of a victim. Everyone was also guilty of a crime.

With Orson satisfied at the body search, Mark took a half step back and waited, attempting to show confidence, if not to settle Amalia but to stand firm with Orson. One didn't need to appear needy when confronting a kidnapper with his whole future on the line.

"Lily's in the car," Orson said, finally, and Amalia flinched, containing herself from running to the vehicle. Callie gave her credit for the restraint.

Callie shifted to her knees on the bench, finding another slit, assuming a better position she could handle for a long spell yet give herself the angle to leap to her feet as needed. She wished she heard them better, but this was as good as it could get without a wire or being there. She wished they'd wired the stairs, dammit. Orson hadn't checked them.

Now was as good as any to dispel any concern about cops. Orson kept glancing up and down Palmetto. Might as well give him a reason to quit worrying.

Callie and Stan had swapped phones, and she texted the simple word, *Now*.

Stan eased out of the driveway down the road, slowly creeping up Palmetto.

With Orson facing Palmetto, and Mark's back to it, Orson caught sight of the cruiser first. "Don't move," he said.

Mark lifted his phone. "I've got this."

Callie watched as the call went through to Stan instead of her, hoping Mark still went through as planned. He would have no other choice.

"Hey, Callie. Just witnessed a wreck in front of the marina." He paused. "No, no injuries I can tell, but it's blocking the road. Nothing you can't handle alone. Hey, babe, I need to run. I'm getting a call from the guy closing the restaurant. Sorry."

He waited, a split second of puzzlement gone in an instant as Stan pulled the cruiser around, flipped on the lights, and hauled tail in the opposite direction down Palmetto, LEDs reflecting off houses as he put distance between the police car and Mark's meet. The three of them watched, speechless, until he was out of sight.

Mark put away his phone. Amalia deflated, hating to see police leave.

Orson settled back into the game. "Give me the proof, and you get twenty thousand and the girl back alive and in good health," he said. He didn't want to be there any longer after the brush of police presence.

"She's okay?" Amalia asked, shake in her words.

He glanced at her but didn't answer, continuing his offer. "Accept that and we have a deal and everyone goes home happy and healthy. If you do not accept, I leave with the girl, lose her, then take the money I have saved to vanish to a country with no extradition. Show me the proof."

And you wanted no wire, Mark. Callie would give just about anything for one right now.

Amalia waited, pleading silently for Mark to handle this. Contrary to what he told Orson, Callie knew Mark hadn't asked Amalia for a figure. He'd hoped Orson would just agree to do something on his own accord and walk. Something reasonable, that didn't break any more laws than were already being broken. Something that both sides could agree to, try to forget, and move on with their lives.

"Show him," Mark said to the grandmother.

Amalia opened the handles of the tote bag. Orson lifted what appeared to be a photo off the top. Probably the soccer-game picture, tossed back into the stack after having been shown to him at the restaurant.

Orson chuckled1. "Spics love their damn soccer, don't they? Excuse me, *football*." He dropped it back in. "Is this all?"

"Yes," Amalia said, still holding out the tote, handles opened.

"Everything is original?" Orson asked, pilfering through paper, lifting a flash drive and putting it in his pocket. "If not. . . ."

"Yes," she said, quickly.

"No copies?"

"N-no."

"If this is fake . . . if this is nothing but to bait me, I'll be coming for you."

The handles shook harder in Amalia's grip.

Orson stood there as if he had a decision to make, basking in the power with Amalia trembling before him.

Mark laid a hand on her shoulder. "She didn't feel comfortable making copies, Orson. She didn't want you doing to them what you had done with Javier."

Was that true? Callie wouldn't have been able to help herself if she were Amalia. She'd have made several copies, secreting them away in strategic places, with instructions on what to do with them if tragedy befell her.

But Amalia wasn't in law enforcement and her only concern was Lily.

"Just business," Orson said. "And Javier must've reneged on his deal to get killed."

Amalia stared at him, her grandmotherly jawline tight with a silent anger.

Mark spoke for her. "Playing games doesn't look good on you, Orson."

Orson reared back some. "The man shot you, Mark. Cost you your own career. Doesn't that bother you in the least?"

"I got over it," Mark replied. "I've moved on with my life."

Shaking his head, Orson said, "We all need to get on with our lives."

A suggestion that wasn't very comforting. Getting on with their lives wasn't a hundred percent in anyone's favor. Any one of them could talk sometime downstream. Any one of them could play the blackmail game again. This could be the start of a long relationship amongst these people, and that reality weighed heavy on Callie's heart.

This agreement should've been simple, and could've been no more than a simple exchange, but Orson had recognized Mark's weakness.

Mark was the only person Amalia could turn to who wouldn't discount her . . . who would believe her. He'd been Javier's friend. Nobody else would've believed the mother of a convicted agent-turned-criminal. Mark, however, remembered Javier in a different light, and had a reputation to uphold with a new life full of promise with El Marko's.

Which was why Callie was there. Orson had no plan to give up any money, assuming he had any on him. Too little time had passed for him to get his hands on that kind of funds.

Orson had ulterior motive. She knew it. And she knew Mark knew it. He protected her by keeping her out of things. She protected him to keep him alive.

"Where's the money?" Mark asked, with Orson standing there with nothing in his hands.

"In the car," he replied.

Bullshit.

Orson scouted around again. "How much does your girlfriend know, and is she a problem down the road?"

Mark shook his head. "Haven't told her about tonight. Plausible deniability. Didn't want to cost her her job. You heard me. It's why I sent her attention to the opposite end of the island, but she's not stupid. When she finds no fender bender, she'll call. Let's get to it."

Cocking his head, Orson glanced out at Palmetto. "Don't want to see police. Not in sight nor in my mirror, is that clear?"

"Clear," Mark said. He seemed to take a breath, to segue into something. "You left those notes with the bullets, to tarnish Lily, before Amalia might have a chance to come to me for help," he said. "You hoped I'd ignore her, maybe get Lily arrested by my girlfriend. Clear that up at least. So I can get my girlfriend off Lily's back."

Silence. Orson wasn't admitting to anything, just digesting what Mark said. Never say anything you wouldn't be happy to hear played back from a wire.

Mark scowled. "You hadn't thought this out much since Lily breaking into El Marko's was impromptu, taking advantage of the storm in a rush of anger. She's a kid. She was mad. But you seized the opportunity and set up the notes and bullets to reflect on her. A little sloppy, maybe even a little slow in practice, but you had ground to make up in learning who lived in my circle of contacts. You started with Callie, a no-brainer, then began with El Marko's and worked your way out from there. Wesley and Sophie worked at the restaurant. You probably caught sight of the officers coming by and paired that with my familiarity with Callie and Edisto PD. Stan, of course, was last since he was solely a friend you'd seen come in one time too many not to use him, too."

"You give me too much credit," Orson said. "These days all you need to dissect a person's life is their social media."

Callie was surprised at his almost, sort of admission.

"I don't do social media," Mark said. "Except El Marko's."

"Sophie Bianchi does."

Oh, how right that was. Sophie posted her entire life on Facebook.

Callie couldn't see Orson grin, but she could read his body language. Yeah, like Mark kept inferring, Orson had an ego.

He wasn't going to stand there and admit to anything. He had enough law enforcement savvy under his belt not to. He'd said nothing that could be construed as an admission, and he'd simply said Lily was in the car, not that he had kidnapped her and held her for ransom. Wires were too easy to hide. Callie just hadn't had time to hide one.

Mark filled in the blanks. This whole meeting was about leverage.

"You went to the funeral to check on Amalia, not in a noble, caregiving way, but to feel out if she was aware of what Javier had threatened you with. When she wouldn't give you the time of day, you put a tail on her, studying her comings and goings. I'd bet El Marko's there's a bug in the house and a tracker on her car. If she hadn't decided to come to Edisto, you'd have broken into her house. Probably did that anyway and knew you'd have to follow her here. Then you followed Amalia that night when she went to collect Lily. You saw the damage done, the anger, and a plan began to form."

"I refuse to confirm or deny," Orson said, half laugh, half sarcasm.

"You probably loved hearing Lily fighting with her grandmother on that bug."

Amalia tensed. "You bastard."

The man only shrugged.

"Why six bullets?" Mark asked.

"Who counts? Now, are we doing this or do I leave?"

Amalia reached out then drew a fist back to her chest. "No, don't go! Please give me my Lily back."

"Bring it and come on," Orson said, turning to walk back to his car. He didn't wait for them, didn't glance back. He was leading them to believe he would exit with Lily or with the proof, and the choice was theirs.

Amalia scurried, Mark touching her arm to control her to keep in step with him.

Orson stood on the driver's side, beside the trunk.

Callie eased off the bench, hand on her weapon, and positioned herself on the least obvious side of the shower, poised to accomplish whatever was needed of her. Stan, she hoped, had driven back around by now, moved in closer, hidden close enough to assist or block Orson in. He couldn't be far. It's what Mark had told Callie to do. It's what Callie had delegated to Stan in order to be on site for Mark.

"Show us Lily," Mark ordered.

Using his key fob, Orson popped the lid.

From reactions, Lily was clearly sequestered in the trunk.

Amalia came forward with the tote, but Mark held a hand on her. "Now the money."

In a fell swoop, Orson snatched the tote, threw it into the trunk, and slammed the lid.

Amalia screamed.

Mark ran around her to get to Orson, but the man reached his door first, locking himself in.

"Open up," Mark yelled. "Give us Lily."

But Orson only shook his head and threw the car into drive.

Mark spun and went for Amalia, yanking her out of the vehicle's path, the Audi hitting his hip as Orson accelerated, tires kicking up gravel in the drive as he gained traction.

Putting himself between Amalia and the gravel flying at them, Mark clinched his eyes, the rocks and crushed oyster shell pinging off him like sleet. A thud told Callie a decent-sized piece nailed him in the head.

"Umph," he exhaled, hand going to the spot, as he dropped to a knee.

Callie bolted to him, a glance up at the Audi veering left in front of the Pavilion to leave the town.

She touched the back of his head, a patch of blood coloring her fingers. "We've got to call—"

But he waved her away, face still contorted in pain. "Just get *him*, Callie. He's still got Lily."

She lifted Stan's phone to call, but the cruiser peeled up, window down. "Get in!" Stan hollered.

He didn't have to say it twice. She ran and jumped in, Stan taking off before she had her door shut.

"He went toward the causeway," she said, yanking the seat belt.

"And Thomas will keep him from getting on it," he yelled back. "Orson will take off down Jungle Road. Damn fool probably thinks there's another exit."

Callie assimilated the new intel. She was supposed to have been the only uniform on duty for what she told her officers should be a quiet night. She hadn't wanted her officers involved in any of this Javier blackmail crap. Apparently Stan hadn't listened to a word she said. *Thank God.*

"I'm on him, Chief," came Thomas's voice over the mic.

"He has a hostage in his trunk, Thomas," she replied. "Be careful." She turned to Stan. "You—"

"—told him," Stan said. "Up there." He indicated up the road.

Thomas's lights were rolling, the narrow road and thicker collection of trees containing their activity brighter. Stan gained ground on them, gaining faster than they would if Orson were mobile.

"He's not moving," she said.

"Maybe Thomas got him." Stan pushed the gas.

"Chief?" Thomas again.

"I'm here, Thomas," she answered.

"The son of a bitch refuses to get out of the car," he said.

"Almost there," she said. "Thanks for stopping him."

"Wasn't me, Chief," he replied. "It was Brice."

Chapter 26

WITH ORSON STOPPED, Thomas had pulled to the side, right behind him. Stan and Callie reached the commotion in seconds. The lights on Thomas's cruiser rebounded off trees, and he yelled at people to go back inside their houses. Two rental houses were empty, but two others held permanent residents. Occupants retreated inside only to watch through their windows.

Brice's brown Olds had somehow cut off Orson's Audi, the long, dirty, dated vehicle parked slanted on Jungle Road, blocking traffic both ways.

Orson suddenly had no escape. His closest left was Thistle, which dead-ended into the lagoon, coincidentally past Thomas. The right ended at the marsh. Even if Orson had managed to drive further, he'd have reached yet another dead-end unless he knew to turn onto Lybrand, but he'd have to get turned around then drive two miles to the causeway again. He'd have been stopped one way or another.

Callie laid a hand on Stan's forearm. "No further." He stopped about four car lengths back, Orson's rear now blocked.

Orson was doubly dangerous now, which also raised the odds of Lily getting hurt.

Brice, however, had tired of waiting for Thomas to do something and finally made his way to Orson's door, mouthing off. "You know how fast you were going, sir?"

"Brice!" Thomas shouted. "Get back in your car."

Thomas turned his spot on Orson's car, blinding him, Brice, and anyone in Thomas's way.

Callie's favorite officer was doing all the right things, positioning himself, a shotgun in his grip. A shotgun that neither Brice nor Orson could see.

Callie and Stan left their vehicle, lights left on, that whole block of Jungle Road lit up like a summer day. Sidearm out, she maneuvered down the side of the road, out of Orson's view. Stan stayed behind his door, his personal firearm at the ready.

Thomas bellowed at Brice again. Brice shouted at Orson. Orson watched Brice, heard Thomas, and probably worried where the rest of Edisto's uniforms were or when they'd arrive. He was trapped. But all he would see was Brice.

"Get the hell out of there, Brice!" Thomas tried again.

"This guy was hauling ass on our street, Officer," Brice said, his volume trying to match Thomas's. "Get out of the car," he told Orson again.

Orson rolled down his window. "Move your car or somebody dies," he told Brice

"Seriously?" Squinting in the spotlight, Brice pointed to the side of the road. "Get the hell out of the vehicle."

Jesus Christ, he was empowered by the presence of cops.

"Get out of my way," Orson yelled.

Callie tried again. "Brice! Back away."

Instead, Brice moved toward the vehicle, emboldened, assured he had police backup. "I said get the hell out! We don't allow—"

Orson fired, the double-tap of basic law-enforcement training putting two nine millimeter slugs into Brice's chest.

Thomas advanced on Orson with his 870 twelve gauge, releasing his load through the open window into the senior SLED agent.

A scream came from one of the houses.

The echoes of the shots seemed to go on forever.

The Audi rolled forward, its dead driver's foot no longer holding the brake, and rested to a stop against the bumper of Brice's Olds.

Thomas advanced on the Audi, ensuring Orson was dead.

A bit deafened from the firefight, the reverberation having been contained by the tunnel of trees and houses, Callie spoke loud and hard. "Turn off the Audi's engine . . . and pop the trunk, Thomas."

No doubt Orson was dead. Thomas would check that first and foremost before following his boss's orders.

In those few seconds, she sorted. Was Lily dead? Was Brice? She tried not to pray that Orson was.

"Stan," she ordered, pointing at the trunk, meaning for him to see to Lily.

Callie, however, ran around the vehicles to Brice. Thomas came up quickly behind her.

The chair of the Edisto Beach Town Council lay spread-eagle on his back in the middle of Jungle Road, his fishing tournament tee shirt splattered dark with blood, the hem hitched up to flash the pudgy belly. He stared wide-eyed up past the roadside's clusters of Palmetto trees into the cloudy night sky.

"Oh, Brice," she whispered, putting fingers against his neck and finding no life.

"Is he?" Thomas asked.

She nodded.

"Son of a bitch," he whispered, giving a moment of respect before telling Callie, "This other guy is gone, too."

"Are you all right?" she asked, halfway squinting, the police car's lights still blinding the road.

"Yeah, I believe so."

"You did fine," she said, giving him enough of a look to show she meant it.

He hesitated but not much. This wasn't the time for Callie to think about being proud of her youngest officer and his instincts, but she would when the dust settled.

"Thanks, Chief," he said.

"Go do your job, Thomas," she said low, returning her attention to Brice. "I'm sorry, you idiot," she whispered, and rose to do her job.

Thomas called his fellow officers as he began cordoning off the area.

Walking back past the Audi, Callie found Lily seated in her patrol car. Stan stood guard at the door. Callie raised her brows queryingly, and he winked that Lily was fine, holding up the cut zip ties he'd removed.

Callie peered inside the open door. "Are you okay, Lily?"

The child's lips trembled, and she seemed unable to trust herself to speak, but she could nod.

Seeing this child safe gave Callie a small spell of relief amidst a scene that wreaked of chaos and stupidity. The fact Lily had made it through this mess unscathed defied the odds. It was about time something happened in this poor girl's favor.

Callie left Stan with Lily and began making the appropriate calls. An ambulance, the coroner, then she dialed the one she hated the most, SLED. This was one of their own, and they'd be all over this. The scrutiny would be intense.

While she was still on the phone, explaining the unexplainable in as few words as possible, wanting investigators to find evidence instead of her handing them this whole package wrapped in a bow, Mark and

Amalia drove up, him parking the grandmother's vehicle in the drive of an empty rental three houses short of the scene.

Amalia rushed to Lily. Mark took in the scene, noted Callie safe, and strode quickly to Stan.

Took Callie a half hour to get off the phone. In that time, Annie and Webb had arrived, Russell pulling up in jeans as Callie hung up, his badge on his belt.

She wanted to rush to Mark, check on his head, see how Amalia was doing, but she had a scene to tend to. Someone had covered Brice, and Annie stood outside the Audi, guarding that scene and Orson's body inside. The trunk lid was still open.

The Audi had the cleanest trunk she'd ever seen. No sign of Lily having been there whatsoever.

No sign of the tote bag either.

AUTHORITIES OF ALL sorts wouldn't leave Edisto until after dawn, so no surprise that a crowd grew as the sun made its presence known. Sophie stood on the side of the road, taking in all the information she could. She had been joined by the mayor, the remaining members of town council, a few business owners, most of the residents of Jungle Road, and half of those on Jungle Shores. Half of them fought tears, the other half donned stoic expressions fighting to stand strong. They talked amongst themselves, but remained amazingly quiet in their whispers, their respect for Brice evident, their appreciation for Callie clear as she methodically handled things.

Callie kept waiting for Brice to stride out of the crowd and accuse her of botching the situation. If not for her, none of this would've happened, he'd say. And there was nobody else left in that sea of personalities who could take his place.

Brice had made one traffic stop too many.

After studying the details, the summation was that Brice had been to the grocery store, replenishing his stock of beer. A receipt in his pocket showed he'd just left the store. He hadn't even followed Orson. Instead, Orson had run up behind him. He'd been in the wrong place at the wrong time. And they'd learn later that Brice had gone by the restaurant to brag he'd stopped another speeder, hoping to catch Mark cleaning up and Callie waiting for him. In his pocket was found a note, a makeshift ticket folded around a hundred dollar bill from some tourist he'd stopped earlier in the evening.

After the last official vehicle left, after the tow trucks rambled away, and the coroner shut doors to the van, Sophie ventured under the tape to Callie.

"I canceled my yoga class in honor of Brice," she said.

Callie hadn't the energy to joke or criticize or make note of the true reality that Sophie wasn't missing this current event for anything. Not with it being only five blocks from her house, and most definitely not with it involving Brice LeGrand. It went without saying that Sophie had more guts than the mayor in coming over with the questions everyone else had delegated her to ask.

All Callie could do was sigh to her friend. This didn't feel real yet. Brice wasn't her favorite person, but his presence served as a weird kind of mainstay on the beach. This would leave a hole in Edisto, and his demise would be talked about for years to come. "He didn't deserve what he got, Soph. He was an idiot, and he had no business pulling people for speeding, but he did it in the name of keeping Edisto safe. He just pulled the wrong damn guy." Then she caught herself. "Don't go running back to everyone spouting I said he was an idiot, please."

Sophie rubbed Callie's sleeve. "No, of course not. Everyone here already learned the lesson of how life goes to hell when you're not on duty. Nobody's about to blame you for any of this."

Bless her, Sophie could have a sweet side, but Callie waited for the other shoe to fall.

"Maya left," Sophie continued.

In slow motion, Callie shook her head. "Don't go there, please. I do not have the patience to cope with her and her voodoo right now."

Sophie leaned in. "I know. I know. But she was right, Callie. Think about it. Six bullets. Six days. Then someone shot with the seventh bullet. She nailed it!"

The fog in Callie's head parted. The shooting had taken place after midnight, in the early hours of the sixth day. The dead man had been Brice.

The stunned woman affected in the background . . . had been herself. Callie could feel it. The drawing wasn't about the case. The vision wasn't about the past. Maya's reading was a forecast about how hers and Brice's lives would intersect yet again, only this time they'd collide, with him dying. No more controversy. No more butting heads. No more groaning as he walked into El Marko's. No more telling her how he could do her job better.

Somehow all that sounded frivolous now.

She sort of wished him back.

"The ideogram was about you," Sophie whispered. "I told you I kept feeling it. I told you I believed in her."

No, she hadn't. Nor had she believed in the predictions in the beginning. Callie stood stunned at how a psychic's dream casting had become reality.

"Where is she again?" Callie asked, expecting Maya to be standing alongside Sophie in the crowd. She scanned the roadside, hunting for Zeus's height and his dark curls.

"I told you." Sophie's carefully sculpted brows raised. "She left this morning. We scared her away, she said."

No, the course of events scared her away. Maya had scared herself with her own remote viewing.

"Guess she's returned to wherever she's from," Sophie said, with ever an eye back on the people watching her, expecting her to report back word for word.

Callie could picture Maya hidden away in her Appalachian mountains, no longer wanting to taste and smell the salt air anymore.

"How's Zeus?" Callie managed to ask.

"On the boat. Alone. Sad."

"Tell him . . . I'm sorry."

Sophie stopped fidgeting and studied her friend. "Hey, are you all right?"

"Not today, but I will be," Callie said. "Listen, just tell people Brice pulled someone and got shot. An accident on his part. Murder on the other guy's part, but we shot him. Now he's dead."

"That's it?" Sophie said.

"Isn't that enough for you?" Frustration tried to bubble up, and Callie pushed it down. None of this was Sophie's fault. "Soph," she said, toning herself down a bit. "That's it."

"He just pulled a guy who decided to shoot him?"

"Yes. A bad guy, Soph. I hate he was on the beach. Fate somehow put him in Brice's path. It's as simple as that."

Sophie wanted more, but there was no more. That's how a lot of death happened, in Callie's opinion. There one day, something crazy happens, then you're dead. Sometimes it makes sense and at other times it doesn't. In her opinion, it rarely did.

More would come out in the press over time, but that's all the town needed to hear at the moment. Every one of them would be expecting to see Brice in some fashion or another, coming through one door or another, complaining to one business or another. His absence would be felt for some time to come.

AMALIA AND LILY were told to stick around a day or two, then authorities allowed them to return to Blythewood, invited to come into SLED for more questioning a couple times more.

The town decided Brice's funeral arrangements would take a while, plus, the autopsy stretched out the time.

The investigation didn't drag as long as expected, not that it ended quickly. Callie entertained agents of assorted sizes and shapes for three weeks.

Callie explained she only knew what Amalia had told her, having met the woman during one of her El Marko visits. Instead of a Boy Scout, Amalia claimed Orson had been just as involved with the cartel as her son, just as entrenched into the skullduggery. Her son had told her so.

Mark was interviewed numerous times, once requiring a trip to Columbia.

The tote might have disappeared, but the flash drive was found tucked in Orson's pocket from the meeting under *The Great Escape*. Since Callie wasn't supposed to even be present at that meet, she feigned ignorance. Mark feigned ignorance as well, his instinct to not touch or see Javier's stash of evidence sound.

Lily was clueless and easily believed since she'd been a child when her father went to jail. Amalia received a little more scrutiny.

The drive held connections to Javier and the cartel, downloaded to the device by Javier, so of course there was nothing on it about his child, his wife, or his mother for no other purpose than their protection. The drive proved the only pure evidence of Orson DeLuca's participation with the cartel, and without Orson around to deny, dilute, or distort the evidence, SLED did its own research, coming to its own conclusions. There were no fingerprints on the drive other than some smudges and a fingerprint of Orson's.

Amalia could honestly say she had no idea what any of the items on the drive meant. She did say that Orson was interested in Javier's belongings, asking, no, demanding that she tell him where her son may have stashed money and evidence of his dealings, to be collected when he got out of jail. She said she assumed Orson wanted money. The bug and the tracker validated her story that he'd stalked them, and she admitted going to Edisto for no other reason than to ask for Mark's financial assistance. Orson had then taken her Lily. Mark had tried to talk Orson into giving up the girl, but when Amalia had no money, he took off with the granddaughter, with Orson still convinced that Amalia had squirreled away ill-gotten gains from Javier. Amalia had no idea how Orson wound up on Jungle Road. She'd been with Mark, the two of them worried Orson would kill Lily.

Callie didn't ask Amalia or Mark about the tote's disappearance, and they didn't offer the information. She didn't want to know.

Thomas had been left out of most of the loop that night, informed by Stan only that there was a criminal element on the beach, and he was to block the causeway that night if said culprit tried to get away. Stan hadn't told him squat other than be the soldier on the wall in case he was needed.

Edisto was a one-way-in-and-one-way-out town, and when something went down, an officer was always perched near Scott's Creek. Stan took it upon himself to inform the only officer who understood why from past experiences. The only officer who'd already saved Callie's life on more than one occasion.

Thomas knew better than to ask a lot of questions. He would assume that one day he'd be told. Might not be in the next few months, might not be for years, but one day Callie would let him in. She protected him, and he got that. He also knew that any man with a girl in his trunk was all the evidence he needed to believe he'd been on the side of angels that night. She'd struggle with her own conscience but felt much the same way Thomas did. Doing the right thing didn't always feel good.

The FBI got involved for a short period. Callie'd touched base with Knox on that. But even with the FBI's oversight, the case was deemed conclusive in a rather expedited manner since nobody was left breathing who could be charged with anything. The bad parties had been dealt with.

SLED and the state quickly quelled the rumors about the rebirth of an investigation with roots in a story that had gone silent five years ago when the only supposed turncoat had been arrested and charged. The only negative was aimed at Mark for not involving SLED earlier, but with him being a decorated retiree, there wasn't much to say other than they wished he'd called sooner.

Callie kept doing her job. She didn't inquire as to the status of the investigation, not wanting to appear too interested. Frankly, she didn't want to think about the ordeal if she didn't have to, and when she realized two weeks later an entire day had passed of nothing but unleashed dogs on the beach, illegal parking, and a group running out on their dining tab, she thanked God for the return of some semblance of normalcy.

She, Stan, and Mark, however, had quit discussing things long ago. And she missed Brice telling her what to do.

Chapter 27

CALLIE AWOKE before Mark. Not unusual with the late hours he kept and the early ones she was committed to at the police station. Since they weren't crime-solving anymore together, she ate half her meals at El Marko's and waited up to welcome him to bed, their Sundays reserved for them. Law enforcement had been their connection before, but they'd voted to make it the last topic of discussion for a while.

She lay under the sheet only, having knocked off the blanket at some unknown hour of the night, and allowed herself to take in just how she felt about this day. Boxes stood stacked around the bedroom, most of them packed. Nothing remained on the walls, and the only piece of furniture in the room was the bed they slept in and an empty dresser. Her new house had been approved for occupancy.

She had mixed feelings about that.

Windswept had become a safe haven. A memory of Seabrook while embracing Mark, the best of both worlds, a bridge from her past to her future. Moving to *Chelsea Morning* with Mark in tow was a good thing. *Chelsea Morning* came with enough memories of its own, and she'd designed the rebuild to relieve her of some of them while preserving others. She did the best she could do, but she couldn't deny that the simple setting of the lot would remind her of Papa Beach who used to live next door before he died, and now Brice who had died a couple blocks down on the very road she'd be living on.

But it was time. She'd graduated to this period in her life, and being the big girl she bragged to be, she'd accept the change. The move into the new house represented the move into a new phase of her life.

It's why she'd taken this Saturday off. That and one other responsibility.

She'd shower, dress, and go into the station, but she didn't intend to stay long, her only purpose being to ensure a sign on the glass-door entrance and to retrieve her gloves. She had no idea why she'd left her dress gloves there.

Edisto Beach was burying Brice LeGrand at noon, and dress

uniform was the order of the day.

Four weeks had passed. For a while Edisto Beach became fodder for the press, the loss of Brice overshadowing that of Orson, mainly because nobody cared who Orson was around this neck of the woods. Brice, however, was fifth-generation Edisto, and a loss akin to royalty. While this funeral wouldn't be quite as large as Seabrook's, the ceremony would attract a sizeable group at Trinity Episcopal Church.

For reasons she couldn't exactly pin down, not that she made herself think hard about them, she thanked fate that Brice would be laid to rest at Trinity while Seabrook was at the Presbyterian Church. Having them both in the same ground, within sight of each other, did something to her. Seabrook would've been fine with the arrangement, but she wasn't so sure she could visit one without feeling pangs and regrets about the other.

Stan had told her to get over herself when she'd tried to discuss it with him one evening while Mark worked and she was feeling particularly melancholy. "Your days should be more about Mark, Chicklet," he'd said, rocking with her on the red swing. "For that very reason it's time you left *Windswept*. Seabrook would tell you the same thing, I bet."

He was right.

Finally she'd showered and beheld herself in the bathroom mirror, measuring, ensuring her formal dress accouterment properly arranged on her chest, her belt correct, her cover straight and bill buffed.

"Mark," she said, loud enough to reach him still in bed. "Time you got up. We have to be there in an hour and a half. If we're on time we're late."

Mark's phone rang from the nightstand. He answered and listened. She couldn't hear his conversation, but he shared a few words then called, "Sunshine," not yet with his full awake voice. "It's for you."

On his phone? She fast-walked in, praying this wasn't something work related. An employee or friend of Mark's who decided to call him first knowing his connection would put them straight through to her.

She took the phone, using it to gesture for him to rise and get ready, and remained standing, not wanting to crease anything more than she had to. "Hello?"

"Callie? Amalia. I heard this is the day of the funeral, and I wanted to give you my best. This day cannot be easy for you. Lily and I escaped by coming home, but you continue to live amidst all that happened. I just needed to tell you that we are thinking of you, and I wanted to thank you again."

"Oh, Amalia." Callie sucked in a breath, not wanting emotion to take over. She had too much day to attend to without starting it with tears. "That means so much to me. How are you? How is Lily?"

"We are good. Lily is better. This incident made her put some things into perspective."

Callie wasn't sure of the details, but she was happy that at least their lives weren't worse. Now maybe they could recover.

The conversation wasn't long but satisfying. "They sound good," she said to Mark, walking into the bathroom where he was just getting out of the shower.

"I guess so," he said, towel drying his hair. "That was pure luck."

Callie reran what she'd said, hunting for what she'd missed. "What?"

"They found a stash Javier had put aside," he said. "Not a fortune, but enough to keep the wolf away from their door until Lily gets straight and in school, or finds a decent job, whichever she decides."

Callie raised the phone in her hand. "She didn't—"

"I told her not to tell a soul. No one at all." He threw the towel over the shower door. "I'm glad she listened to me."

"How much . . .?"

He peered down his nose.

"No, I don't want to know."

"Right answer," he said. "Now let me get some clothes on. You look incredible, by the way."

She smiled. "Meet you in the kitchen in ten minutes. We're expected to be there earlier than most."

CARS FILLED THE parking lot and every piece of ground a vehicle could fit in. Most tourists flocked to the Presbyterian Church, where Seabrook and so many of his ancestors rested behind the sanctuary. The Julia Legare mausoleum attracted most of them. But Trinity's campus held live oaks with their dangling moss and so much flora as to be breath stealing, especially when the azaleas were in bloom like now.

The main church, however, wasn't quite as large as the Presbyterian, but it filled, nonetheless, the overflow moving to the fellowship hall. Callie had driven a patrol car, Mark riding with her, allowing her to move closer to the doors.

Mark at her side, she shook bare hands with her gloved one, speaking about how good it was to see this person and that when it really wasn't. Not at an occasion like this. But that's what you did, what you said.

She'd left Thomas manning the town. He had no business being here forcing himself to relive that night and his actions. A council member had walked by and leaned in to Callie to ask how he was. Did her heart good to see how consoling people were to him, many thanking him for avenging the loss of their friend, but killing a man wasn't something you wore like a badge of honor.

This was Thomas's first and hopefully his last taking of a life. There had been no other way of handling that night, and Callie was ridiculously proud of how he'd handled himself, but he needed to process. She'd spent one long evening speaking with him, listening to him, relating to him even more deeply than the deep relationship they already shared. He'd joined a club, so to speak, she'd explained. And like Alcoholics Anonymous, if he needed to talk to someone at any time, day or night, she was there for him.

The rest of her officers, however, spit-polished and fine, assisted in managing the crowd. This was early May. The flowers bragged, the air clean, the temperature as close to perfection as it could be.

The room fast filled with business owners and natives from beach and island alike. Stan arrived, unable to find a seat beside Callie. Her officers stood against the wall. Edisto's firefighters were decked out as well, doing the same except for the chief who sat on Callie's row. She'd arranged for a law-enforcement honor guard and tried to imagine what smart sassy retort Brice would have to say about that.

The service began.

Callie sat three rows back this time, and this time nobody asked her to deliver a eulogy. Nobody gave her condolences for her loss. For all that, she was extremely grateful.

Her history with Brice had been adversarial from day one, with few truces, to include the time she pulled strings to get him out of jail when he went nuts over his, now, ex-wife. People weren't sure what to say to Callie. At the end, however, broker Janet Wainwright approached her, and Callie steeled herself. Janet never spoke in ways approved by etiquette tomes.

"I imagine you'll miss Brice," she said, casting a quick glance at Mark to suggest he let her have this moment. Mark stepped away but didn't go far.

"Already do," Callie said, smiling at someone who walked by, nodded, and continued. Nobody invaded Janet's space.

Janet smiled, not something she normally did, but the change complimented her. "Callie, we all saw he was an ass, and he tried to be his best ass to you. You, however, cared about Edisto, and he cared about Edisto, and nobody can deny that you both did the best you could on behalf of these people we are seeing here today, even if he made your job harder trying to get his way. I wanted to thank you in case nobody else does. Brice died being his typical dumb-ass self, but your team didn't hesitate taking out the guy who took him down. As a Marine, I recognize the sacrifice . . . on everyone's part."

Callie reached out for a handshake. Janet took the grip. The exchange said as much or more than the words. "Semper fi, Janet," Callie said.

"Semper fi, Chief."

Janet turned on her heel and left. Callie lightly nodded at Mark, and the two of them made just enough of a presence at the gathering afterward, drinking one glass of punch each, before returning to *Windswept*. After all, they had to put the finishing touches to the move. She'd promised Janet she'd have the keys turned in by close of business today.

THE BED REMAINED, bare and benign in the master bedroom of *Windswept*, which had been and was, after all, a rental—furnished, its temporary nature perfect for her in her temporary phase of life. Still, emptied of her things, she felt as if it begged her to stay.

She and Mark made one more sweep through to see that drawers, cabinets, and closets had been emptied.

"Guess that's about it," he said from the kitchen, waiting as Callie gave a final once-over inside the bathroom closet.

She tried to keep walking, not to dawdle, but the history of the house pulled on her like a child on his mother's skirt.

Mark found her standing in the middle of the bedroom. "You okay?"

With a huge sigh from the bottom of her belly, she replied, "Yes, I think so."

Then that was that. With a touch on her elbow, he steered her to the door. Holding the last box of odds and ends, Mark offered to lock up, but she shook her head and did so herself. Then, refusing to look back, she turned and took the stairs, trying hard not to pay attention to the ball of feelings in her chest.

But in reaching *Chelsea Morning*, she had to admit the emotion had dissipated a bit. What wasn't to love about a newly constructed house? Fresh flooring, counters, paint . . . the new smell welcomed her more than expected. Coming through the door knowing this would be their first night there put more life in her step.

She deserved this, she told herself. They dove into setting up home.

The first knock from a visitor was not whom she would've expected. She scurried to answer the door, surprised at how much she was enjoying all the firsts she was experiencing under this new roof.

"Wesley? How are you? Come on in," she said. "Mark? It's Wesley." She assumed the young man had come over to enlighten Mark about something to do with El Marko's.

"I actually came to see you, Chief," Wesley said, his six-foot height doing nothing to toughen up the awkward nervous stance he held. He'd covered his work clothes with a nice windbreaker, zipped up the front.

Callie's radar went up at the sign of a situation that would pull her away from unpacking. "What's wrong?"

"Um."

Mark came up. "Hey, fella. What's up? Want to come in? Not sure where we can sit, but—"

"No, sir. I came to confess."

Callie took a quick peek at Mark who met her glance.

"I mean." Wesley started in again, then stopped to collect himself.

"It's okay," Callie said. She drew him inside and set him on one of the chairs to her kitchen table, sliding one more for herself. Mark grabbed a stool. "What is it?"

"Came to tell you who broke into The Undercurrent," he said.

She hadn't expected that. Frankly, after ruling out Lily, they had no other leads. She'd given Mr. Lassiter her report for his insurance and been done with things, or so she thought. It was still an open case, though.

"One of my cousins was dating this guy who stayed a while at another cousin's house with his mother." He seemed to be dodging names.

"Go on," Callie said, not bringing that to his attention.

"He's the one, the boyfriend, not the cousin he was staying with, who broke into the place. I noted his girl, my cousin, wearing several pieces she hadn't had before and shouldn't have been able to buy herself. Like eleven different pieces."

Eleven. That was a rather exact number.

Wesley unzipped his windbreaker and lifted a plastic grocery bag that hung heavy with contents. He passed it over to Callie. "I remember when someone gave me that Christmas sweater, Chief. Being stolen, it wasn't theirs to give and about got me into hot water. I didn't want my cousin in the same boat."

Inside the bag was a mishmash tangle of jewelry. Nothing overly expensive but enough of the pieces fit the descriptions Mr. Lassiter had given Callie to likely be the stolen loot.

"Where is he?" she asked, setting the bag on the nearby table.

"He took off, Chief. I'm sorry. My cousin got mad, and she told him he was wrong. She remembered what almost happened to me. The next morning that fool was gone."

"Name?"

Wesley gave a name, and Callie would check the boy out. She took down a description and the name of his cousin but doubted she would bother said cousin. Mr. Lassiter wouldn't push her to pursue this either.

"Tell your cousin thank you," she said instead. "And thanks to you for taking care of this for her. You're a good man, Wesley." She started to stand, but Wesley remained solidly in his chair.

"Um, ma'am, I know it's behind us, but I have to apologize again to the both of you for running away like I did. I left Mark with the kitchen short-staffed and wasn't around to aid you, Chief, in finding whoever left that bullet." He hesitated, as if he wanted Callie to validate him only to refocus his attention to Mark for the same. He was working up to something. Finally, he asked, "Was he the man you had to shoot?"

"He was," Callie said. "And you had to think of your and your family's safety. Don't worry about it." She turned to Mark.

"You know I wound up staying closed part of the time anyway," he said. "You're fine, Wesley. Don't want to lose you, though. You're about the best there is around here, and I'm lucky to have you."

To that the boy smiled. "You can't begin to understand how glad I am to hear that."

Yeah, Callie did. Good people always worried more than the bad about doing the right thing.

Wesley left on that note. Mark headed out the back door and Callie to the bedroom. There was a lot to do before their energies gave out.

But barely five minutes later another guest knocked. Callie listened for someone to enter, then realized the fresh door wouldn't have a squeak.

"Hello?" came a voice Callie was glad to hear and hoped to hear on a more regular basis now that she once again lived next door to Sophie.

"Back here," Callie hollered from the bedroom. They'd be exhausted in a few more hours, and not having to make up the bed then would be a blessing. Mark had gone downstairs, setting up the storage room. They'd decided that area was his to maintain however he desired. It had been a while since she'd had to share home responsibilities with anyone.

Sophie peeked in. Bumps and thumps sounded from the front porch.

"What's that?" Callie asked, moving to go around her friend.

Taking Callie's arm, Sophie stopped her. "Wait. I figured out the building on the ideogram."

Callie backed into the bedroom, putting a step between Sophie and a subject she had no inclination to revisit. "Don't want to think about that, Soph. I don't even want to say the word."

Hands on hips, Sophie continued. "But don't you see? The building is your house since it all happened on Jungle—"

"Not interested." Another thud echoed from the porch. "What is that?"

"Probably something Mark is doing. Hey! Listen to me." The yoga queen leaned against the doorway, blocking her, forcing Callie to pay attention. "This brings things around, ending them. This ought to give you some peace. Since the people were you and Brice, the house has to be this one partially constructed. I was thinking—"

More bumps.

"All right, Soph, out of the way," Callie said, slipping her way past. "What are you up to?"

As she entered the entry hallway, people's vague and choppy images moved on her front porch, but she couldn't identify them through the door's etched glass. This door didn't have a sailboat etched into it like *Windswept*; instead her door sported waves and a couple of gulls, and the tinted design distorted the view. Her goal had been to give her some semblance of privacy when people came to call.

She opened the door.

Mark, Stan, and Wesley stood around the red swing from *Windswept*, Mark tugging on the chains anchored to the ceiling. All three froze, staring at her for a reaction.

She'd forgotten. Months back, when she'd asked Mark to move to *Chelsea Morning* with her once the house was completed, she'd mentioned moving the red porch swing. Nothing had been said since.

The perfection of that swing on this porch couldn't touch her any deeper.

"Oh, y'all," she said, moving over, brushing her fingers across the seat.

"Well," Stan said in his boisterous manner. "That's that. Gotta go." He went to take the stairs, and Wesley had the sense to follow him.

When Callie looked back for Sophie, she had disappeared, probably out the rear door.

Mark shined so proud of himself as he maneuvered himself around one end and sat. He bounced a couple times, deemed the weight safe, and patted the space beside him.

Gingerly, Callie eased down, waiting any second to be dropped to the floor.

"It's good," he said. "I watched them take it down from the other house and double-dosed the support on this end." He beamed. "This swing matters a lot to you, Sunshine. I couldn't see leaving it behind. Besides, I believe Seabrook would want you to have it."

God, she loved this man.

Not wanting to dispel the moment, she pushed with a toe to start the swing, then like they'd done at the other place, she tucked herself up and let him keep the sway going.

After a minute or two, Mark spoke. "Didn't want to say this in front of Wesley, but after he confessed to us for the cousin and the boyfriend, I got to thinking. Lily might have gotten the idea to break in from the other guy. He was already there, busted in. She was angry and thought, why not?"

Of course he wouldn't mention Lily in front of anyone. He might be right, but all that didn't matter anymore.

"We'll never know," she said, relaxing against the back of the swing. "And don't care. Let these people move on." She rested her head against the crook of his shoulder. "Let us move on."

They rocked for a good half hour.

No more watching waves across the street, but she didn't need that view. She had all she needed right here, in this house with its memories, good and bad, because they'd defined her. Along with the guy seated beside her. Because he defined her, too.

The End

(Please Continue reading for more information)

Acknowledgment

Regardless however many books get published, regardless how easy people think this endeavor as an author is, there's a sea of people in the background required to keep me going.

On the ground, two particular bookstores keep my books alive. Thanks to Anne Shon and The Coffee Shelf for supplying the South Carolina Midlands with an ample supply of these stories. And thanks so much to Karen Carter and The Edisto Island Bookstore for making these tales a mainstay for tourists and residents alike on the island.

Much appreciation to my past editor and publisher, Debra Dixon for believing in my little worlds and keeping the world supplied with them.

Blessings to Stephen and Tara at Kingfisher Strength for convincing me that my physical health is important to keeping my stories even more fresh and alive . . . maybe for much longer than if I didn't lift weights.

Love to Jack and Duke for keeping me happy and young and for telling all their friends what a famous grandmother they have.

Finally to Sweetie, my very significant other half who rights my world when I think whatever I'm writing is the worst book I've ever written.

About the Author

C. HOPE CLARK has a fascination with the mystery genre and is author of the *Carolina Slade Mystery Series* , the *Craven County Mystery Series*, as well as the *Edisto Island Series*, all set in her home state of South Carolina. In her previous federal life, she performed administrative investigations and married the agent she met on a bribery investigation. She enjoys nothing more than editing her books on the back porch with him, overlooking the lake, with bourbons in hand. She can be found either on the banks of Lake Murray or Edisto Beach with one or two dachshunds in her lap. Hope is also editor of the award-winning FundsforWriters.com

C. Hope Clark

Facebook - facebook.com/chopeclark
Instagram - instagram.com/chopeclark
Author website www.chopeclark.com